Highlander
for the
Holidays

JANET CHAPMAN

JOVE BOOKS, NEW YORK

THE BERKLEY PUBLISHING GROUP
Published by the Penguin Group
Penguin Group (USA) Inc.
375 Hudson Street, New York, New York 10014, USA
Penguin Group (Canada), 90 Eglinton Avenue East, Suite 700, Toronto, Ontario M4P 2Y3, Canada
(a division of Pearson Penguin Canada Inc.)
Penguin Books Ltd., 80 Strand, London WC2R 0RL, England
Penguin Group Ireland, 25 St. Stephen's Green, Dublin 2, Ireland (a division of Penguin Books Ltd.)
Penguin Group (Australia), 250 Camberwell Road, Camberwell, Victoria 3124, Australia
(a division of Pearson Australia Group Pty. Ltd.)
Penguin Books India Pvt. Ltd., 11 Community Centre, Panchsheel Park, New Delhi—110 017, India
Penguin Group (NZ), 67 Apollo Drive, Rosedale, Auckland 0632, New Zealand
(a division of Pearson New Zealand Ltd.)
Penguin Books (South Africa) (Pty.) Ltd., 24 Sturdee Avenue, Rosebank, Johannesburg 2196,
South Africa

Penguin Books Ltd., Registered Offices: 80 Strand, London WC2R 0RL, England

This is a work of fiction. Names, characters, places, and incidents either are the product of the author's imagination or are used fictitiously, and any resemblance to actual persons, living or dead, business establishments, events, or locales is entirely coincidental. The publisher does not have control over and does not have any responsibility for author or third-party websites or their content.

HIGHLANDER FOR THE HOLIDAYS

A Jove Book / published by arrangement with the author

ISBN: 978-1-61793-304-2

JOVE®
Jove Books are published by The Berkley Publishing Group,
a division of Penguin Group (USA) Inc.,
375 Hudson Street, New York, New York 10014.
JOVE® is a registered trademark of Penguin Group (USA) Inc.
The "J" design is a trademark of Penguin Group (USA) Inc.

PRINTED IN THE UNITED STATES OF AMERICA

To Alex and Abby and Max,
Merry Christmas, babies!

Chapter One

"OHMIGOD, JESS," MERISSA WHISPERED, PULLING JESSIE to a halt inside the door of Pete's Bar and Grill. "Not only are we not in Kansas anymore, we were blown clear into another *century*. I haven't seen this much wool and flannel since you took me on your shoot for that hunting lodge commercial."

"Hey, lady," the giant behind the bar growled, "no dogs allowed."

Jessie lifted her hand, which held Toby's leash. "He's a service dog."

The man instantly softened. "Oh, sorry," he said gruffly. He motioned to the waitress at the end of the bar, who had stopped filling bowls with popcorn to stare at them. "Paula, go kick Ray and Lucy out of their booth and give it to these ladies."

Jessie stepped closer to be heard over the music. "That really isn't necessary. We can wait until a table opens up."

"That one just did," the bartender said, his grin making

his beard bristle. "I was one second away from telling them to go get a room anyway." He gestured at the waitress skirting the crowded dance floor. "That booth is the farthest from the jukebox, so it'll be easier on your dog's ears. You want me to send over a big fat bone with your drinks? It'll be on the house."

Jessie gave him a grateful smile and shook her head. "Thank you, but Toby's not allowed to eat on duty."

"Can he drink? *Water*," the bartender rushed on at her surprise. He chuckled, pointing down at Toby. "He looks to be over twenty-one in dog years, but if he can't eat, then I don't suppose he can knock back a beer."

"Thank you again, but he's fine." She nudged Merissa into the throng of people, following with Toby as they headed toward the booth the waitress was unapologetically making available for them, even as Jessie wondered what in the name of God she was doing coming to this lively little bar her first night in town.

Oh yeah, that's right; she was taking her life back.

Several people on the dance floor stopped in surprise, then scrambled out of the way to let them pass. So much for not calling attention to themselves, Jessie thought with a sigh. But then, the hundred-pound rottweiler at the end of her leash didn't exactly make her and Merissa invisible, did he? She gave a smile of thanks to the dancers who'd stopped, but then had to pull Toby to a halt when another man gyrated backward into their path.

Toby immediately stepped between Jessie and the perceived threat. The man's partner tried dragging the guy out of the way but ended up stumbling into him instead when another dancer bumped into her trying to see what was going on. Jessie pulled on Toby's leash, her command to heel getting lost in the song belting from the jukebox.

She might have succeeded in redirecting Toby if the man's windmilling arm hadn't smacked her in the shoulder hard enough to make her stumble. Apparently deciding her attacker hadn't heeded his first warning, Toby gave an ominous growl and this time used his body to shove the man away.

The panicked guy shot into the crowd, pushing his dance partner behind his back as he spun around. "Your dog just tried to bite me!" he shouted, incredulous.

"Oh no, sir, I assure you he didn't," Jessie said, the last of her words sounding overloud when the song ended. She patted Toby's head as he sat quietly beside her. "Service dogs are strictly forbidden to bite anyone."

The man pointed at Toby, completely ignoring the woman tugging on his arm. "He sure as hell growled at me."

"No, I believe he was coughing up a hairball," Jessie said sweetly. She turned and walked to the vacant table, unbuttoning her coat as she slid into the booth. "What's your house special?" she asked the wide-eyed waitress.

"Anything on tap," the woman said, pulling a pad from her apron and a pencil off her ear. She gave them a quick once-over, then shrugged. "We carry a couple of decent wines, if you don't mind waiting for Pete to hunt down a corkscrew."

"I'll have a Tropical Breeze," Merissa said.

The waitress sighed, resting the tip of her pencil on her pad. "Would you happen to know what's *in* a Tropical Breeze?"

"She'll have a Shipyard Pumpkinhead Ale," Jessie interjected. "And I'll have their Prelude Special."

"What in hell am I drinking?" Merissa asked as soon as the waitress left. "You know beer makes me crazy." She waved at the air. "It's all those bubbles; they go straight up my nose to my brain and turn me into a bar slut."

"Not if you *sip* it. I Googled Maine breweries before we left Georgia and found the Shipyard Brewing Company in Portland. Their Pumpkinhead Ale appears to be popular this time of year." Jessie turned in her seat and motioned for Merissa to do the same. "Make room for Toby so he can lie down under the table, out of the way."

Merissa twisted to lean against the wall and arched a delicate brow. "A hairball, Jess? You honestly think that guy believed Toby was coughing up a *hairball*?"

"I couldn't very well admit my dog would have gone for his throat if he smacked me again. We'd have been thrown out of here faster than the man and woman we stole this table from."

Merissa looked out at the crowded bar. "Exactly where *is* here?" Up went her brow again. "Because honestly? I think we overshot New England by several hundred miles and are in Newfoundland or something."

"We're still in the U.S. of A.—although just barely. We're about fifty miles from the Canadian border."

Merissa's other brow arched. "When you came up with this crazy notion of moving to New England, I thought you meant *Boston*." She waved at the throng of people. "Half the men in here have more facial hair than Toby."

"Oh, come on, Mer. Where's your sense of adventure?"

Merissa patted her pockets. "I'm pretty sure I had it when we left Atlanta. No, wait; I distinctly remember watching it fly out the window when you drove past *Boston*." She turned serious. "Okay, I get New England in the fall, as the ride up here was positively Norman Rockwell.

But again, why *Maine*? And not even Portland, but some forgotten little mountain town a hundred miles north of nowhere. For a woman who's determined to get her life back, it sure looks to me like you're hiding from it instead."

Jessie leaned her cane on the edge of the seat near the wall and then shrugged out of her coat. "It's called baby steps, Mer. Pine Creek has a population of less than eight hundred year-round residents, which means I'll finally have a sense of community instead of feeling lost in a sea of strangers." She leaned on the table to continue talking when a soft ballad started on the jukebox. "You have to admit, the TarStone Mountain Ski Resort is everything the brochure promised."

"Including a perfectly nice restaurant and lounge," Merissa shot back. "But did we go there? Oh, no; we dumped our bags in the room, headed into town, and stopped at the first bar we came to."

Jessie adjusted the leafy silk scarf around her neck. "I wanted to get an immediate reaction to Pine Creek so I'd know for certain I've made a good choice. I swear I could feel the knot in my gut loosening the farther north we drove, but . . . but I still don't know if it's far enough."

Merissa blinked in surprise. "Are you saying you're not *sure*? Jessie, every worldly possession you didn't give away is right now on a truck headed for Pine Creek, and you don't even know if this is where you want to live?"

Jessie turned in her seat to look around, taking note of the patrons thoroughly enjoying themselves, eating and drinking and dancing, then turned back to Merissa. "I'm pretty sure." She gestured over her shoulder at the crowd. "They look like a nice bunch of hardworking and fun-loving folks to me, and the atmosphere in here is friendly." She leaned on the table again and lowered her voice. "And

I'll bet they couldn't care less about what happens in Atlanta. This is my best chance for a real do-over, Mer. In Pine Creek I can be plain old Jessie Pringle instead of poor, tragic Mrs. Eric Dixon."

"I hate to ruin your fantasy," Merissa drawled, "but they probably get the national news in this three-car town. You know you can't run from your past any more than you can hide from it."

"Four years and a couple thousand miles is a damn good start." Jessie sucked in a calming breath when Toby sat up and rested his head on her thigh. "I have a chance to be my old self here," she said, rubbing Toby's ear to soothe him. "So it won't matter if someone eventually does put two and two together, because instead of seeing a woman to be pitied, they'll already have decided that I am *not* a victim."

Merissa smiled crookedly. "Actually, it's these poor, unsuspecting shmucks I'm worried about, when they discover there's a backbone of steel hidden inside what only looks like a fragile woman." She shook her head. "The good people of Pine Creek aren't going to know what hit them the first time you get a bee in your bonnet about something. I just wish I was going to be here to see— Ohmigod," she hissed, her eyes widening as she stared past Jessie's shoulder. She grabbed Jessie's arm when she started to turn. "No, don't look! We can't let them think that we're interested."

"Them?" Jessie echoed, grinning. "As in *male* thems?"

Merissa groaned. "Okay, you already know beer isn't my problem. I only need to get a whiff of testosterone to turn into a bar slut," she said, fluffing her short hair with her fingers as she shifted her gaze past Jessie again. "Throw in broad shoulders and a manly swagger and I can be talked out of my clothes faster than a guy can say 'your place or mine?'"

The waitress set a heavy tray on the table. "Prelude Special for you," she said, setting two frosted glasses and two bottles in front of them. "And Pumpkinhead for you."

"No popcorn?" Merissa asked, eyeing the large platter of appetizers on the tray.

The waitress set the platter between them. "I can go get you a bowl if you want."

"We didn't order appetizers," Jessie pointed out.

"Pete sent them, compliments of the house."

Jessie shifted uncomfortably. "Does Pete give free appetizers to all his patrons?"

The waitress tucked the tray under her arm. "It ain't what you're thinking, honey. Pete usually comps the first-timers if he thinks they're from the resort. TarStone has a live band on the weekends that we have to compete with, so he hopes you'll go back and tell the other resort guests that Pete's Bar and Grill is a right friendly place."

Jessie relaxed, feeling bad for thinking the bar owner had been patronizing her. "Oh. Then tell Pete thank you for us, will you?"

"Sure, honey. You need anything else, you just holler for Paula."

"Wait," Merissa said when Paula turned away. "Can you give two single women far from home a little advice as to who's safe and who's not?" She smiled crookedly. "I just spent four days cooped up in a car, and my legs are in serious need of exercise." She waved toward the dance floor. "Are there any lechers out there we should avoid?"

"Well, now," Paula drawled, "that would depend if dancing is the only exercise you're interested in."

Merissa arched a brow. "I guess that would depend on the guy." She leaned to the side to see past Paula. "Like those two," she said, covertly pointing at the end of the bar. "If I were to ask one of them to dance, would I be risking life and limb?"

"Those two?" Paula asked in surprise. "Hell, you don't mess around kissing a bunch of frogs, do you?" She shrugged. "If you don't mind dealing with brawn *and* brain, the MacKeages are good men."

Merissa took a long swig of her ale straight from the bottle, wiped her mouth on her sleeve, and started to slide out of the booth.

"Hey," Jessie yelped, reaching across the table to grab her arm. "You can't just walk over and ask one of them to dance."

"Why not? Paula said they're harmless."

The waitress snorted. "Honey, calling a MacKeage harmless is like calling a tiger a pussycat. I said they're good men; I didn't say anything about them being harmless." She leaned down when the music stopped and lowered her voice. "The only complaint you'll get from any woman brave enough to leave here with a MacKeage is that dawn arrives way too early." She looked at Jessie then back at Merissa and smiled sadly. "I suggest you ladies might want to start a bit lower on the food chain."

Jessie groaned inwardly. Now she'd done it; Paula might as well have just clanged the dinner bell. Nobody loved a challenge—especially one that involved the opposite sex—more than Merissa.

Her friend actually rubbed her hands together. "Oh, I don't know," Merissa said, eyeing the two men at the bar again. "I've always felt kissing frogs was a waste of time." Her eyes suddenly widened. "Ohmigod, they're coming over," she said, grabbing her bottle and taking another sip.

After giving what appeared to be a sympathetic look, Paula disappeared into the crowd. Jessie poured her ale into her frosted glass, only to notice her hands were trembling. It didn't help that Toby had sat up again to rest his chin on her thigh, his big brown eyes filled with concern. "I am so going to kill you," she said as she gave Toby a reassuring pat.

"Hey, you're the one looking for adventure," Merissa countered, sneaking another peek at the approaching men as she raised her bottle to her mouth again.

"Baby steps, Mer," Jessie reminded her. "I'm not sure I'm ready to deal with brawn *and* brain. And by the look in your eyes, I don't think you're ready, either."

"What you're seeing is pure, unadulterated lust," Merissa whispered, leaning on the table. "They're positively gorgeous."

"Then where the hell are they?" Jessie asked, not daring to look. She sighed in relief. "They were heading to some other table, not ours."

"No, somebody stopped them to talk." Merissa finally poured her ale in her frosted glass, only to discover there was barely a sip left. "Damn. I didn't even taste it. Okay, here they come. Put Toby next to the wall so they can sit down."

Not really sure how Toby would react to two strange men invading their space, Jessie nudged him over her legs. Oh God; she had thought she was ready for this, but her racing heart said differently.

"I can't imagine what Pete was thinking when he tucked you two lovely ladies way back here in the corner," a deep-timbred voice said from above her. "He usually likes to show off his prettier patrons."

Jessie looked up, her smile freezing only half-formed when her eyes landed on the tall, green-eyed, broad-shouldered,

clean-shaven man standing next to another equally gorgeous and no less intimidating giant.

Nope; she definitely wasn't ready for this.

"Would you ladies like some company?" the second
man asked.

Merissa immediately scooted toward the wall. "We'd love
some," she said as she motioned for Jessie to do the same.

Toby scrambled right back across Jessie's legs when she
scooted over and planted his solid body between her and
the giant sliding into the booth beside her. She immediately
clamped her hand over Toby's snout when the man reached
down to him. "Just let him sniff your fingers," she instructed.
"He's rather . . . protective."

The guy gave a chuckle. "So I noticed. Is that part of
his job description?" he asked, turning his hand palm up
to tickle Toby's chin as the dog sniffed his thumb.

"He sort of comes by it naturally," she said, releasing
Toby when she felt him relax against her leg.

"I'm Duncan MacKeage," the man beside Merissa said.
He gestured at the man sitting beside Jessie. "And this is
my nephew, Ian MacKeage."

"Nephew?" Merissa repeated, her gaze darting to Ian
then back to Duncan. "But you look the same age."

Amusement twinkled in Duncan's deep green eyes as
he nodded toward Ian. "His mother is my half sister, which
makes *my* mom his grandmother." His smile widened.
"And our fathers are cousins, so I guess that makes us
cousins, too."

Merissa burst out laughing. "Oh, man. If that's your
best pick-up line, no wonder you were sitting at the bar
waiting for new victims." She felt her forehead. "Am I
wearing a sign that says *gullible city girl*?"

Duncan looked wounded. "Scout's honor, lass, it's true."

"You ladies decide the TarStone lounge is too tame for your liking?" Ian asked, apparently deciding to redirect the conversation.

Jessie stiffened. "How do you know we're staying at the resort?"

"I saw the two of you arrive this afternoon." His easy smile kicked up a notch. "I was leaving the parking lot in the side-by-side when you were unloading your luggage."

"Side-by-side?"

"The two-seater ATV. Miss . . . ?" he asked, holding out his hand to her—much the same way he had to Toby.

Well, since Toby hadn't bitten him, she shook Ian's hand. "Jessie Pringle."

"Merissa Blake," Merissa chimed in. "And Jess and I are just *friends*. So, do you guys work at the resort?"

"Ian does," Duncan said. "I'm in construction." He motioned for Paula to come over. "Can we buy you ladies a drink?"

Jessie lifted her glass to show it was still half-full. "I'm good."

"Another one of whatever Merissa is having," Duncan told Paula. "And could you tell Pete to give us *real* Scotch this time, please?"

Paula's eyes widened. "Are you saying he gave you guys the cheap stuff?"

"No," Ian said with a chuckle. "He claimed it was a new brand he was trying, and asked our opinion." He gestured at the appetizers. "Order us up another sampler while you're at it, would you, only ask Mike to leave off the wings and double the ravioli."

Realizing Ian and Duncan were regulars here, Jessie couldn't decide if that was a good thing or not, considering they appeared to be settling in for the evening.

"Where are you ladies from and what brings you to Pine Creek?" Duncan asked, his own easy smile directed at Merissa. "If you're leaf peepers, I'm afraid you missed the fall foliage by over a month."

"Actually, Jessie's moving to Pine Creek," Merissa said. "And I'm just along for moral support. I have to fly back to Atlanta at the end of the week."

Both men looked at Jessie. "You have family here?" Ian asked.

"No," Jessie told them. "Well, my maternal grandmother was born in Maine, but she moved to New York City when she married my grandfather."

"Is she from Pine Creek? What was her maiden name?"

"It's Beal, but she was from a small town down on the coast."

"So are you both from Atlanta?" Duncan asked. "Because neither one of you has much of an accent."

"I'm originally from Chicago," Merissa explained, "and moved to Atlanta six years ago." She nodded at Jessie. "She moved there four years ago from Dallas, although she's really a New York City girl."

"Pine Creek isn't exactly a bustling metropolis," Duncan said, looking at Jessie. "Have you come here for a job? I can't think of any local business other than the resort with the clout to lure a city girl into the wilds of Maine, unless you're an artist or craftsman and plan to open a gallery."

"I'm neither. I was in advertising down in Atlanta, but I'm taking a hiatus from work," Jessie said. She felt her cheeks heat up, realizing her reason for moving here might sound silly to them. "But when I happened across a brochure for TarStone Mountain Ski Resort while researching ad campaigns for northern resorts and spas, I thought Pine Creek looked like a wonderful place to live."

Duncan gave a soft snort. "It is if ye like snow that's measured in feet instead of inches and windchills that reach forty below."

"Or if you don't mind winters that last six or seven months," Ian added. "So, are you planning on buying a place or renting?"

"I hope to buy a small house, maybe on the lake."

"We have a cousin who's a real estate agent," Duncan said, filching a cheese stick off their platter. "We could hook you up with her tomorrow if you'd like. Tell me what room you're in, and I'll have Katy come see you in the morning."

Jessie shifted uncomfortably, suddenly feeling claustrophobic between the wall and Ian's large body.

"Duncan knows better than to ask for your room number," Ian said when she hesitated, shifting slightly away from her. "Katy can have the front desk call your room. That is, assuming you're ready to start house hunting."

"Ah . . . yes, I'd like that," Jessie said before quickly taking a sip of her ale.

Paula showed up with their drinks. "Mike's backed up in the kitchen, so it'll be a few minutes before that platter comes out. I'd say you've got enough time for a dance," she added, shooting Merissa a conspirator's smile when another slow tune started.

Confirming Paula's claim that the MacKeages had brains as well as brawn, Duncan stood up and held out his hand. "Would you care to dance?"

Merissa shot out of the booth before he'd even finished asking.

"How about you, Jessie?" Ian asked, although he didn't move.

Oh God, was she really ready for dancing? She desperately wanted to feel a man's arms around her again—even, or maybe especially, a stranger's—but then, she wasn't in any hurry to embarrass herself, either. Jessie adjusted the scarf on her neck and smoothed it down over her breasts, unable to look at him. "Um . . . I haven't . . . I'm not all that steady on my legs sometimes."

Ian lowered his head level to hers. "I won't let ye stumble, lass."

God help her, the gentle timbre of his faint brogue already had her feeling weak in the knees. Still unable to look at him, Jessie leaned back to glance under the table. "I don't know what to do with Toby."

Ian chuckled and stood up. "I'm afraid he'll have to find his own dance partner."

Jessie took a fortifying breath, scooted across the seat, and stood up. "No, stay," she told Toby when he tried to follow. "You can watch me from right here."

Ian took two steps and stopped well short of the dance floor, then turned. Jessie hesitated only a second before stepping into his arms, which he gently closed around her in a loose embrace. Ian slowly began swaying them to the music, and she lifted her hands to his broad shoulders and closed her eyes on a silent sigh. Oh yeah, she was ready for this; unable to remember the last time she'd been this close to a man who wasn't only interested in poking and prodding her. And suddenly Jessie knew she'd made the right decision to stop physical therapy and simply get on with her life.

Ian was a good head taller than her own five-ten, which meant he had to be well over six feet tall. Large men usually made her uncomfortable—an affliction she hadn't had until four years ago—but Ian had a way about him that seemed to put her at ease. Maybe it was the fact that Toby had accepted him after only one sniff. Then again, maybe it was because she also thought Ian MacKeage smelled nice. Sort of outdoorsy, like fresh air and the woods. And . . . well, male.

He certainly was solid. She might imagine his shoulders were made of granite if they weren't so warm, and his hair—a dark, sun-streaked blond—was tied back in a short tail low on his neck. He was also apparently good for his word about not letting her stumble, and Jessie soon found herself dancing as naturally as if she hadn't nearly lost the ability to walk four years ago. She could stay in his embrace all night, she decided with another sigh, resting her head against the crux of his shoulder. Oh yeah, coming to Pine Creek had to be one of her wiser decisions.

Jessie could have wept when she heard the song wind down, but instead lifted her head with a smile, which froze half-formed when Ian gently eased her back to his shoulder. "There'll be another song," he said softly. Only the next song had a fast beat—not that he seemed to notice, sway-ing her gently. "Unless you're tiring?"

"No, I'm good," Jessie murmured, relaxing into him to let her smile finish forming against his soft flannel shirt. "Can you see Toby?"

"He really is rather protective, isn't he?" Ian said, his voice filled with amusement. "He's sitting just under the table, his eyes trained on you like lasers."

She leaned back to look up. "Toby's one of those males that insist a girl leaves with the one who brought her."

Ian hesitated a heartbeat and said, "Then I would say you have a very wise pet."

Jessie dropped her head back to his shoulder to hide her chagrin, wondering what had possessed her to say something so suggestive. God, she hoped he didn't think she was considering going home with *him*.

Okay, maybe even baby steps were too much of a leap and she should try crawling first—preferably into a crack in the floor before she turned into Merissa.

Chapter Two

Ian couldn't remember the last time he'd been so instantly attracted to a woman; likely because even though Jessie Pringle appeared to be a paradox of fragile beauty and poise, he had quickly recognized her potential for recklessness. She was also one hell of a straight-faced liar, he decided, sipping his Scotch to hide his smile as he remembered her telling the guy who'd nearly knocked her down that Toby had been coughing up a hairball.

Ian had thought he might actually have to fight Duncan for her, as his cousin had also started toward the dance floor when they had seen the small disaster forming—only to both be upstaged by her dog. So they'd sat back on their stools and watched the two women for a few minutes while Ian had remembered out loud that Duncan really wasn't into willowy brunettes. To which Duncan had felt compelled to point out what happened the last time Ian had been stricken with hero syndrome.

But Jessie didn't appear to be the least bit helpless, much less in need of rescuing. Hell, the woman had a hundred pounds of lethal canine running interference for her, which had him wondering if Toby's role wasn't that of protector rather than helper. Because despite Jessie's claim that she was unsteady on her feet, she'd spent the better part of the evening in his arms on the dance floor and hadn't stumbled once.

Damn, he had a thing for intriguing women, especially when they came packaged with large hazel eyes, light brown hair that softly curled down past her shoulders, and a decidedly feminine figure—which also had him wondering if the men in Atlanta weren't idiots for letting her leave. Then again, maybe she was running from one man in particular, and had gone as far north as she could without actually leaving the country.

Oh yeah, he was definitely attracted to Jessie Pringle.

"No, seriously," Merissa said, pointing her bottle at Jessie even though she was talking to Duncan. "When she first told me she was moving to New England, I thought she meant Boston. I mean, really," she said, looking directly at Jessie, "the last decent shopping mall we saw was in Portland. No offense, guys, but would you mind telling me why anyone would *choose* to live hundreds of miles north of nowhere?"

"So they can get away from city girls who can't handle their beer," Jessie drawled before either of them could answer.

Merissa stopped her bottle halfway to her mouth. "I told you beer makes me crazy," she muttered, darting a quick glance at Duncan. "Except I'm beginning to think testosterone is the real culprit."

Jessie groaned, and Duncan stood up with a laugh.

"I believe I have a cure for what ails ye, lass," he said, holding out his hand. "Let's dance."

Ian decided Jessie had probably had enough dancing for one night, as he'd noticed a slight tension creeping into her face that made him worry her legs might be paining her. Then again, it might have something to do with the text message she'd received a few minutes ago that she'd read but hadn't answered. He suspected Toby was also attuned to the subtle vibe she was giving off, as the dog had sat up and was resting his head on her thigh again.

Ian slid an arm on the seat behind her to lean close so she could hear him. "I won't consider it rude if you want to respond to your text," he offered.

She gave him an appreciative smile that didn't quite reach her eyes. "Thanks, but I'd rather not." Her smile turned derisive. "Responding to Brad's constant requests for updates of my 'harebrained notion to move to Maine' sort of defeats the purpose of *leaving* Atlanta, wouldn't you say?"

"Brad?"

She gestured dismissively. "An overly protective brother-in-law."

Okay, then. Apparently her tension was from the text— or, more precisely, from Brad, who as far as Ian was concerned was an overly *interested* brother-in-law. "How long have you had Toby?" he asked, reading her desire to change the subject.

"Almost three years," she said, her smile turning genuine.

"And was he trained professionally?"

She fingered Toby's ear. "He had two years of service dog school, with six months of it concentrated on his specialty." She snorted. "And then his handler spent a couple of months training *me*."

"Training the two of you to do what, exactly?"

She gave a negligent shrug. "Sometimes my legs just . . . get lazy, and Toby helps out by fetching things for me and stuff like that." She gave him another smile, only this one appeared to be forced. "I've tried to teach him to cook, but he insists on tasting everything first."

Knowing damn well she was lying about Toby's full role in her life—this time by omission—Ian nevertheless gave an appropriate chuckle. "I imagine the big man has quite an appetite, yet he hasn't once begged for a handout."

"Probably the hardest part for me was learning not to spoil him rotten by giving him treats. But he's been trained not to be distracted by food. Would you mind very much if we danced again?" she asked when a soft ballad started on the jukebox.

Speaking of distractions, Ian supposed that one worked—although he didn't care that she made it sound like an imposition for him. "Anytime, Jessie," he said, sliding out of the booth and holding out his hand.

She pushed Toby's head off her leg, but the dog shot out from under the table and blocked her from getting up. "No, Toby," she said, nudging him to the side. "You stay right here like before and watch. I'm not going far."

Toby reluctantly sat down, only to give a protesting whine when Jessie stood up. But when he still didn't get the response he wanted, the rottweiler actually turned his large brown eyes on Ian, apparently looking for support.

"It's okay, big man," Ian said, settling Jessie into his embrace without bothering to head toward the dance floor. "I'll take good care of your lady."

Not that he was sure what taking care of her actually involved, since instead of relaxing into him like she had all evening, Jessie seemed to grow even more tense as he gently swayed her to the music. Toby suddenly appeared at their side, but it wasn't until the dog started tugging on Jessie's pant leg that she finally bent down to her pet.

"Now?" she whispered tightly. She gave Ian an uncertain glance as she took hold of Toby's face, but it was long enough for him to see her anxiety. "Are you *sure*?" he heard her ask the dog.

Toby gave an equally anxious whine, and Jessie straightened and stepped over to their table and grabbed her coat. "I'm sorry, but I have to take him out. I'll be back in . . . in about twenty minutes or so." She shot him another forced smile. "Sometimes he takes even longer. I'm sorry."

"I'll go with you."

"No!" She sucked in a deep breath, although he could see it did little to quell her growing urgency as she started backing toward the crowded dance floor. "I mean, thank you, but I don't . . . Toby won't . . . He's shy, okay? We need to be alone."

Her lying straight face was starting to falter. "Do you want me to get Merissa?"

"No! No, please don't tell her I'm gone."

And then she *was* gone, disappearing into the din behind her dog, which was effectively clearing the dancers out of their way. Ian stood staring after them, an uneasy feeling tightening his gut. He turned back to their table with a muttered curse and saw that she'd forgotten her purse and cane.

Having come close to being kicked out of the military on more than one occasion for not following orders, Ian grabbed Jessie's belongings and headed after her. Only he hesitated when he saw Merissa in Duncan's arms, thinking he should tell them what was going on—not that he knew.

"Screw it," he ground out, heading out the door. Because

the only reason he hadn't been kicked out of the military was that he'd usually been guarding someone's back when he'd been disobeying orders. He didn't know what Jessie's problem was, but he sure as hell intended to find out.

Instead of heading straight into the parking lot, Ian stayed in the shadow of the building as he scanned the lot for Jessie's late-model Volvo wagon, only to hear her before he actually spotted her trying to get in her car. He stopped next to a utility van parked two slots away, trying to figure out what had her so upset.

"Dammit, Toby, the keys are in my purse," she cried, a distinct edge in her voice as she uselessly pulled on the handle again and then banged her fist on the roof.

Ian stepped back to peer through the truck's windows when she looked around the parking lot, the streetlight illuminating her growing panic as she suddenly started toward the woods. And though he wouldn't say she was limping, her gait definitely was stilted, he decided as he followed.

"We need to find a safe place," she said frantically. "*Hide*, Toby. *Safe place*," she repeated, practically stumbling by the time they reached the trees. "S-safe place," she stammered, openly sobbing now. "Hurry!"

Becoming rather frantic himself, Ian silently stepped into the woods parallel to them and stopped behind a large tree to let his eyes adjust to the streetlights filtering through the bare branches. He heard Jessie faltering in the dried leaves, and then she and Toby disappeared beneath a low-branched spruce.

Ian crept closer, being mindful to keep silent despite her sobs urging him to rush to her aid. Except he didn't think Toby would allow him anywhere near her, and Ian didn't want to distract the dog from what was obviously his true job. So he stopped about ten paces away, balling his hands into fists when he saw Jessie curled into a fetal position on the ground. Toby was settled at her back with his head tucked in the crux of her neck, his massive body absorbing Jessie's jerking spasms as one of her hands, curled like a claw, lashed out at the empty air.

A seizure? Had Toby sensed one coming on?

Only Jessie's movements didn't appear mindless, but defensive, as if she were fighting off an attacker only she could see. Ian broke into a sweat, the knot in his gut rising into his chest to nearly strangle him as he realized Jessie appeared to be having a flashback of some horrific trauma she had experienced. And Toby, perfectly calm, was doing what he could to help her survive the emotional maelstrom.

Christ, he couldn't just stand there and do nothing. Ian stepped out of the shadows but stopped when Toby immediately rose up and stood straddling Jessie's body, his hackles raised and his lips rolling back on a soft growl.

Jessie wasn't even aware of the two males silently battling over her, so deeply consumed by terror that she continued whimpering and twisting, her hands continuing to ward off her unseen demon. She suddenly made the sound of a mortally wounded animal and curled back into the fetal position, her body wracked with tremors. Toby gave one last snarl at Ian, then nosed her shoulder and carefully settled against her again with his head resting on hers.

Ian retreated only a few yards before he came up against a tree and his legs gave out. He dropped to his knees and sat on his heels, his eyes trained on the woman he'd just spent the evening dancing and laughing with. Holy hell, did she have these episodes often?

Christ, she must if she needed a service dog.

Then why was she moving to Pine Creek, not just alone, but thousands of miles away from family and friends and

whatever support system she must have had in place? Ian
rubbed his hands over his face, trying to come to terms
with what he'd just witnessed. How much courage did it
take for Jessie to get out of bed every morning knowing
what she might face at any given moment? How did she
even *function*, much less find the courage to move someplace the exact opposite of what she was used to?

He froze with his hands on his face. Was that it? Had
Jessie chosen Pine Creek precisely because it wasn't a
crowded city?

"Oh, T-Toby, you're the smartest, bravest dog in the
whole w-world."

Ian dropped his hands to see Jessie pushing herself into
a sitting position.

"I didn't hurt you, did I?" she asked, running her trembling hands over her pet. "Because you know I certainly
didn't mean to."

Ian blinked in disbelief and felt some of the pressure in
his chest give way as he stifled a snort. Was she serious?
He doubted anything short of a baseball bat could hurt
Toby, as the dog was solid muscle.

"You are such a smart boy," she continued, resting her
head on Toby's shoulder. "You gave me enough warning
so I didn't embarrass myself and you picked a good place
for us to hide. I think we're going to be okay here in Pine
Creek, Tobes," she whispered, hugging him fiercely. She
gave a soft snort. "These trees sure are a lot nicer than a
public bathroom stall or janitor's closet, and there certainly
seem to be plenty of them around here."

Oh, Christ; Ian's gut knotted again imagining Jessie
searching for a decent place to hide in the city. Toby suddenly
looked directly at him—as if to let Ian know he was still on
guard—then turned his attention back to his mistress.

"So," Jessie said on a heavy sigh as she brushed leaves and spruce needles off her coat, "what do you think my chances are of keeping this from Merissa? I have her convinced I haven't had an episode in over a month, and we both know if she finds out I had one tonight, I'll never get her to leave on Thursday."

When all she got for an answer was a lick on her cheek, Jessie rolled to her hands and knees and grabbed an overhead branch to awkwardly pull herself to her feet. Ian took advantage of the noise she made and also stood. He picked up her purse and cane, then stepped behind a large tree, peeking back around it in time to see Jessie grab a sapling when she lost her balance. But since Toby obviously expected her to be unsteady, the dog had positioned himself at her side to let her take hold of his collar.

Ian started out of the woods so he could make it appear as if he were just coming out of the bar to find her, but hadn't taken two steps before he heard her gasp.

"Oh no, my boob fell out! We have to find it. Boob, Toby. Find my *boob*."

Ian staggered backward, completely nonplussed as he watched Jessie drop to her knees and Toby put his nose to the ground, and they both began searching the area under the spruce. No, he couldn't possibly have heard right; she couldn't really have said she'd lost her boob, could she? Seriously? Her *boob*?

"Oh, good boy!" she cried, taking something out of the dog's mouth.

Ian ran a hand over the back of his neck as he watched Jessie wipe an object the size of a woman's fist on her sleeve. She pulled herself to her feet, pushed her coat aside, lifted her sweater, then tucked the . . . object inside the left cup of her bra.

"There," she said, facing Toby as she looked down at her chest. She took a deep breath and pulled at the hem of her sweater. "Do they look even?" She suddenly palmed both breasts, gave them a jiggle, then threw back her shoulders and smoothed down her sweater and scarf again—only to suddenly giggle. "I wonder what Mr. Sexy Ian MacKeage would have to say if I walked back into Pete's with one of my boobs half the size of the other. 'Why, lass; I do believe there's something different about you. Why don't ye let me slip my hands under yer blouse and see if I can find out what the problem is,'" she said in an exaggerated brogue. She snorted. "In his dreams," she muttered, grasping the dog's leash and letting him lead her out of the woods.

For the love of Christ, how could the woman joke about losing a boob?

Wait—had she just called him sexy?

Walking a bit taller and with the knot in his chest slowly loosening, Ian stayed just ahead and to the side of them but halted at the edge of the woods when they emerged into the parking lot and Jessie stopped.

"Hey, Tobes," she said, sounding excited. "I just realized I'm not completely wiped out like I usually am. Heck, I'm not even shaking with lingering terror. Oh Toby, it's *working*," she said with a laugh, bending to give her dog a hug. "Everyone thought I was crazy for wanting to move to Maine, but I *knew* this was a powerful place to start my brand-new life." She straightened with another laugh, and then walked between the cars and pickups toward the bar.

Ian ducked down and ran alongside her two rows away. Oh, the lass would be safe here, all right—from everyone but him. Because whether or not Jessie Pringle knew it, her brand-new life was going to include Mr. Sexy.

"Jessie!" Merissa said in surprise as she came around the side of the building, Duncan not two steps behind her. The woman's already flushed face turned an even deeper red. "We were just . . . It's not . . . I was . . ." Merissa sighed, and finished tucking her shirttail into the waist of her pants. But then her eyes suddenly widened when Ian stepped out from behind a nearby pickup. "Ohmigod, *Jessie*?" she squeaked, covering her mouth as she stepped closer. "You came outside with Ian?"

Jessie turned and took a step back when she saw him, her face washing pale in the streetlight. "You *followed* me?"

Ian held up her purse and cane even as he gestured toward the parking lot. "I realized you'd forgotten your cane and was coming to look for you."

Merissa plucked a leaf off Jessie's shoulder. "Jess?" she whispered, pulling another leaf from her hair. "Did you have . . . Were you—"

Jessie laughed. "I fell," she said, brushing at her coat. She darted a suspicious glance at Ian, then waved toward the trees. "I took Toby into the woods to do his business, and I tripped on a root or something."

Merissa's eyes narrowed. "That's all? You just . . . fell?"

Jessie walked over and took her purse and cane out of Ian's hand, then headed toward the entrance. "I don't know about you guys, but I could use a drink."

Merissa pulled her to a stop. "Um, I was just heading back inside to tell you . . ." She looked at Ian, then leaned closer to Jessie. "That I'm going to have Duncan bring me back to the resort . . . later."

Ian couldn't decide if he should wipe that smug look off Duncan's face right here in the parking lot or drag the arrogant bastard into the woods to beat some sense into him. Duncan had read both women just as easily as he had, and the idiot knew leaving with Merissa would put Jessie in an awkward position.

"Oh. Okay. I'll see you back at the room . . . later," Jessie said, giving Ian an uneasy glance as she continued into the bar.

After a pointed glare at Duncan that even an idiot could interpret, Ian followed Jessie inside only to find her and Toby standing on the edge of the dance floor staring at their occupied booth. She jumped in surprise when he took hold of her elbow. "We can have our drink at the bar," he suggested.

She pulled free with a heavy sigh. "No, I think I'll just call it a night." She smiled up at him and patted his arm, letting her hand linger as she said, "But I had a wonderful time this evening, Ian. Thank you." She gave his arm another pat, then turned and headed over to Paula at the bar.

As dismissals went, Ian decided as he followed, that was as good as any—if it had come from a *maiden aunt*.

"Did you say Duncan paid both bills?" he heard Jessie ask Paula, looking up from her open purse in surprise. She started rummaging through it again and pulled out a twenty. "Well then, here, take this for . . . for your good advice."

Paula snorted, shoving the twenty in her apron. "Fat lot of good it did your friend," she said, shaking her head.

Jessie laughed. "Did you ever consider that maybe Duncan and Ian are the ones who should have made sure Merissa and I are harmless? Because all us city girls are taught from the cradle how to turn tigers into pussycats."

Realizing Jessie didn't know that Ian was standing

directly behind her, Paula pulled her down the bar—wrongly thinking she'd moved them out of earshot. "Then you better start thinking like a wilderness girl, honey," Paula said, "at least when it comes to MacKeages, since Merissa told me you're moving here." She leaned closer. "The MacKeages and MacBains and Gregors are like one big Scottish clan, and are a good chunk of our population. And although their wives are real friendly, all the men are so old-fashioned it's scary, even the ones born here. So you might want—"

Ian stepped over and took hold of Jessie's arm before Paula could do any real damage, and started for the door. "Thanks for the service, Paula," he said with a wave over his shoulder. "I believe I'll walk ye to your car, lass, and then follow you to the resort to make sure you arrive okay. It's starting to mist, and it may freeze on the road."

"How much of that did you hear?"

Ian stopped in the parking lot to face her, and folded his arms over his chest. "Enough to wonder how many tigers you've turned into pussycats since you emerged from your cradle."

She strode off, forcing Toby to break into a trot to keep up. "I was talking about *Merissa*," she said when Ian fell in step beside her. She fished her keys out of her purse, pushed the button on the fob, and opened the rear door of her car. "So you don't have to worry; I'm so out of practice, I don't even remember the rules of engagement," she muttered, tossing her cane and purse on the floor in the back.

Ian waited until Toby had hopped in the backseat before he used his hip to close the door even as he pressed his palms to Jessie's face and tilted her head back. "Maybe all you're needing is a little reminder," he murmured, capturing her gasp of surprise in his mouth.

She went perfectly still, not resisting but not participating, either. In fact, it appeared as if she wasn't quite sure what was happening.

She certainly tasted as sweet as she looked, and not ten seconds into the kiss Ian began to worry that his own arrogance might end up ruining his chances of seeing her again. That is, until he felt her hands slide up between them to settle on his chest; not to push him away, apparently, but to grip his shirt as if she were afraid he'd stop.

Not likely, and definitely not any time soon. He slid an arm behind her shoulders and tucked her head in the crook of his elbow, dropping his other hand low on her back to pull her more intimately against him. Her lips parted enough to allow his tongue to go in search of hers, and Ian felt her shiver. And then he felt her soften at about the same time she made a sweet little sound that sent all his blood to his groin—which told him that if he didn't stop now, he might not stop at all.

He lifted his head to find her big hazel eyes staring up at him, unblinking.

"A matronly pat on the arm might be how ye handle this sort of thing in the city," he said, his voice sounding thick even to him, "but in the wilderness, *that's* how we say good night to someone we just spent the better part of an enjoyable evening with."

Her cheeks flushed. But when she still didn't move, Ian decided to kiss her again. Only his heart nearly pounded out of his chest when she pressed a hand to his face and kissed him back—although hesitantly, as if she were worried her boldness might encourage him to ask for more liberties.

But he came by his patience honestly, thanks to his highlander genes. And since Jessie was moving here, Ian was content to let her grow comfortable with him at her own pace—assuming her sweet torture didn't kill him first.

He heard Toby growing restless inside the car, which suggested the dog wasn't used to seeing his mistress wrapped in a man's arms being repeatedly kissed. Then again, maybe the big man was jealous. If that was the case, he'd have to make sure he and the dog came to an understanding. Ian reluctantly lifted his head again, but only enough to kiss first one of Jessie's flushed cheeks and then the other before nudging her upright to stand facing him.

She started to say something but stopped, then tried again—only to drop her gaze to her hand, still clutching his shirt. Her fingers unclenched and she started to give his chest a pat, but stopped in midpat and sighed.

Ian bit back a laugh and opened her door, helped her inside, and handed her the seat belt. "Welcome to Pine Creek, Jessie," he said, softly closing the door.

Chapter Three

JESSIE LAY IN HER HOTEL BED, STARING OUT THE WINDOW at the big fat snowflakes drifting past the parking lot light, and decided that four years was way too long for a girl to go without being kissed. Or be asked to dance. Or *almost* get picked up in a bar.

And three years was way too long to have only a dog to cuddle up to at night. "No offense, Tobes," she whispered to her sleeping pet as she absently stroked his head. "But for as handsome and strong and gallant as you are, you're not exactly the man I had envisioned myself growing old with."

Someone like Ian MacKeage came closer to her vision, though. He was definitely tall and solid and handsome, as well as interesting and attentive and a really good dancer. He was also quite considerate, considering he hadn't tried to pressure her into going home with him even after he'd found out Merissa certainly was game.

Unless he'd thought odd Jessie Pringle was okay for an

evening's entertainment but not for taking home. Except he'd kissed her like he had wanted more. And by God, she'd kissed him back once she'd gotten over the surprise of feeling his mouth on hers.

Would she ever make love again? Was there a man out there smart enough to see past her physical and emotional scars, and strong enough to want her anyway?

Lord, she hoped so. But she wasn't about to hold her breath waiting for him to show up. And if someday she did meet such a shining example of brain and brawn, Jessie hoped that *she* would be brave enough to let him past the defenses she'd spent the last four years erecting.

She couldn't explain to anyone—not even herself—why she'd chosen Pine Creek as the place of her reincarnation, other than the fact that she'd nearly worn the ink off that TarStone Mountain Ski Resort brochure. Its pictures had captured her immediately, making her wonder what it would feel like to live in such a rugged, powerful place— which is exactly why she'd thrown it in the trash the first time she'd caught herself believing all that power could be hers for the taking. She'd tossed it away several times, actually, only to find it sitting under a bunch of papers on her desk the next day, or in her briefcase a week later, and one morning she'd even found it on her nightstand.

She couldn't escape that damn brochure any more than she could deny the spark it had ignited inside her, despite all the resistance she'd run into when she'd started talking about moving. Just visit Maine, her parents had suggested, or move back home to New York if she wanted a change. It's too far from needed services, her physical therapists and doctors had argued, certain she'd regress if she walked away now. "Are you out of your friggin' mind?" Merissa had shouted when she'd told her.

But every time Jessie had picked up that brochure . . . well, just holding it seemed to give her the courage to do and feel and *be* more than a scar-riddled, hollow shell of her former self. Until finally it had empowered her to turn in her resignation, put her house—that she hadn't lived in for four years, anyway—on the market, give away most of her belongings, and ask Merissa to make the trek north with her to see for herself that this was a sound plan.

So here she was not four months after first coming across that brochure, and already she had danced, been kissed, and almost picked up in a bar by a sexy stranger.

Not bad for her first day in town.

Jessie heard the electronic lock on the door trip and glanced at the clock as she put a steadying hand on Toby when he lifted his head. She smiled, undecided if Merissa was tiptoeing into the room really late or really very early.

"I'm awake," Jessie said.

Her friend fell back on the other bed with a loud groan. "In what civilized world does anyone go to work at *five* A.M.?" Merissa muttered. "The only living things crazy enough to be up at this hour are owls, a family of raccoons, and one suicidal moose the size of a Clydesdale trotting down the center of Main Street." There was enough light coming through the window for Jessie to see Merissa's smile. "Duncan said it's the tail end of moose rutting season, and that the old boy was too busy chasing a lady-love to be concerned about the rules of the road." She snorted. "I told him he should know, since he seemed to be of the same mind."

"You didn't!" Jessie sputtered on a laugh.

"Hey, the guy is a *machine*. I swear to God that I got maybe twenty minutes of sleep all night." Merissa rolled onto her stomach, propping a pillow under her chin. "Not that I'm complaining. Paula was right: MacKeages are *not* harmless." She closed her eyes on a sigh. "I think Duncan just ruined me for other men."

"Yeah, I know what you mean," Jessie said, remembering Ian's kiss.

Merissa's eyes snapped open and her head popped up. "Ohmigod, I am such a scumbag. I didn't even ask how you made out after I left. Was Ian very disappointed that Duncan scored and he didn't?"

Jessie arched a brow. "What makes you so certain that Ian didn't score?"

"Jessie, you didn't!"

"No," she said with a laugh. "But I did get thoroughly kissed."

Only instead of smiling like Jessie expected, Merissa sat up, suddenly wide awake and utterly serious. "Oh, Jessie, what are you doing?" she whispered. "You just got here; you can't kiss the first guy you meet."

"You did."

"Only because I'm out of here in six days, so it doesn't matter what Duncan thinks of me. But you're *moving here*, Jess, and you'll probably run into Ian all the time. What are you going to do if he asks you out on a real date?"

"Maybe I'll say yes."

"And by date number three," Merissa growled, "when he decides good-night kisses just aren't working for him anymore? Then what are you going to do?"

Jessie threw back the covers, got out of bed, and headed to her suitcase. "I don't know what I'm going to do," she muttered, yanking out her bathrobe and putting it on. "I only know that I have to do *something*, or I might as well have let that guy finish hacking me to pieces four years ago." She grabbed her slippers and waved them in the air.

"Even totally humiliating myself has to be better than doing *nothing*."

"Oh, Jess!" Merissa cried, rushing to her. "I'm an idiot. Please don't be mad."

Jessie took a calming breath, giving Merissa a sheepish smile. "I'm not mad. I'm just frustrated, because . . . well, because *this* is the entire extent of my reincarnation plan," she said, gesturing at the room. She nodded when Merissa's eyes widened. "I was so focused on just getting to Pine Creek that I never actually worked out what to do once I got here." She walked over and sat on the bed to put on her slippers. "And I sure as hell didn't think ahead to dating, much less when—or rather, *if*—I ever reached the getting naked part."

Merissa plopped down on the bed beside her. "If the guy can't get past a few measly scars, then I say you don't want him, anyway."

"I'm missing half my left breast, Mer. That's not exactly something a man's going to be able to overlook."

Merissa nudged her shoulder with her own. "My two boobs together don't fill a C cup. So if your one really impressive breast isn't enough for him, then I say you kick the greedy bastard out on his ass in the snow." She flopped back on the bed. "Promise me that if Ian does ask you out, you'll run in the opposite direction. Because if he's anything like his *uncle* Duncan, he'll have you practically naked before you even make it through his front door."

Jessie patted Merissa's leg and stood up. "I promise I'll think about it," was all she was willing to concede, going to her suitcase again.

"I'm serious, Jess. Paula wasn't kidding when she said we should start lower on the food chain. I think I would have been safer with that moose." Merissa snorted. "I know she said any woman who goes home with a MacKeage complains that dawn arrives way too early, but I thought she meant it was because they're such great lovers. I didn't even consider that he'd roust me out of a nice warm bed at four-friggin'-A.M., dress me almost as fast as he undressed me, stuff me in his truck, and drive me back here through an obstacle course of wild critters." She lifted her head to arch a brow. "Do you know he actually gave me a pat on the ass as I headed for the lobby door wondering where in hell I was?"

Jessie stopped rummaging through her suitcase. "Are you having morning-after regrets, Mer?"

"Good God, no!"

Jessie set her hands on her hips. "So did Duncan live up to Paula's bragging or not? Because I can't tell if you're happy or mad or still drunk."

Merissa dropped her head back on the bed with a moan. "Neither can I. Maybe I'm all three. Last night I actually caught *myself* thinking about moving here right around the time Duncan was . . . when he was . . ." She rolled onto her stomach with a groan. "I am such a slut," she muttered into the pillow.

"You really need to start working on your opinion of yourself," Jessie said, pulling Toby's sweater out of the suitcase. She walked back between the beds. "Or one of these days you're going to start believing it."

"A rose by any other name is still a rose."

Jessie pulled a blanket up over her. "Bar sluts go home with anyone, whereas *you* are discerning. And there is absolutely nothing wrong with appreciating men."

"I'm thirty," Merissa mumbled. "It's time I got serious about *keeping* one of those men, don't you think?" She rolled over, pulling the blanket with her then propping her head on the pillow. "Did you appreciate a parade of men before you married Eric?"

"I kissed my share of frogs." Jessie clutched Toby's sweater to her chest and sat down on her bed with a sigh. "Only I can't say I would have gone home with Ian last night even five years ago. All through high school and college I kept looking for the . . . for . . ." She shrugged. "For fireworks, I guess; one defining, magical moment that would tell me he was the one."

"And did you find it with Eric?" Merissa whispered.

Jessie stood up with a snort. "I told you, I was so drunk the first time we made love that a nuclear bomb could have gone off and I wouldn't have known it. About the only thing I do know is that we didn't use any protection and I got pregnant. We got married in Las Vegas not twenty-four hours after I told him, and three months after that . . . well, you know the rest, because that was the day you walked into my hospital room and saved my life," she finished thickly. She touched Merissa's short curls. "So the next time I hear you calling yourself a slut, I swear I'm going to have Toby sit on you while I wash out your mouth with soap. Duncan MacKeage is the luckiest man on the planet, because he got to spend last night with an angel disguised as Merissa Blake."

Merissa pulled the blanket up over her face and made a snoring sound. "Go take Toby out to pee before anyone wakes up so they won't see him wearing that prissy sweater," she muttered. "I need my beauty sleep, because I'm afraid I agreed to see Duncan again tonight."

Jessie stood staring down at her friend, remembering how Merissa had dragged her kicking and screaming—and more often than not, crying uncontrollably—out of her hospital bed, refusing to let her hide in that dark place in her mind. It had taken Jessie several months to realize their relationship had gone from nurse-patient to friends, and every day she thanked God for sending her such an angel.

Well, an angel who appreciated men far more than they appreciated her.

"Come on, Toby," Jessie said, taking her room card out of her purse and slipping it in her robe pocket. She patted her leg when the dog just blinked at her from the bed. "Come on, Tobes. Don't you want to see your very first snow?"

"Not if he has to wear that prissy sweater, he doesn't," Merissa said from under the blanket. "It's bad enough some sadistic lout turned him into an *it*; you don't have to finish emasculating the poor thing by dressing him in pink."

"Go to sleep, Mer. I don't think Duncan's going to appreciate having you nod off in your beer this evening."

"I'm not drinking around that man anymore," Merissa grumbled from under the covers. "Because I'm afraid I also agreed to go for a moonlight horseback ride with him when I come back to visit you next spring." She shot up with a gasp. "Ohmigod, can two people actually *do it* on a horse?"

"Probably not and live to tell about it," Jessie said with a laugh, opening the door and stepping into the hallway. "Come on, Tobes, or I'm gonna go play in the snow without you," she threatened.

"Tobias Pringle," Merissa snapped in her nurse's voice, pointing her finger at him. "Don't make me come over there and drag you out of bed. Jessie, will you hide that damn sweater? He remembers it from when you made him try it on in the store."

Jessie slipped the sweater inside her bathrobe and patted her leg again. "Come on, Toby," she said excitedly, showing him her empty hands. "Let's go for a walk."

Merissa flopped back when Toby finally jumped down and trotted into the hall. "Don't forget your cane."

"I don't need it. I'm just going to stand by the door and send him into the woods," Jessie said softly in deference to the other hotel guests as she closed the door.

She took the elevator down to the floor below the lobby, assuming it was the service area, and then peeked in both directions when the doors opened. She stepped out, waving Toby to follow, and headed toward the door at the end of the hallway.

"I know it felt funny when you tried it on," she said, pulling the doggy sweater out of her bathrobe. "But if you'll just give yourself a chance to get used to wearing it, I promise you're going to thank me this winter. And nobody's going to laugh at—" Jessie stopped when she realized she was talking to herself, and turned to see Toby sitting halfway down the dimly lit hall. She pointed at the floor at her feet. "Stop acting like a petulant child and get over here, you big lug. It's *snowing* out, and you haven't grown a winter coat of your own yet."

Hanging his head until his nose was nearly touching the floor, Toby slowly walked to her. Jessie immediately straddled his body and slipped the sweater over his head. "You don't listen to Merissa; this is not pink, it's *salmon,*" she explained, pushing first one paw and then the other through the leg holes. "And salmon is this year's fashion statement for handsome, debonair men." She kissed the top of his head and opened the door, then stepped out into the dusting of snow and glanced around to make sure the coast was clear. "Okay, this looks like the employee parking lot, and there's the woods," she said, pointing to the back of the lot. "Just do your business and come right back," she said, holding the door with her hip as she hugged herself against the cold.

She finally had to give him a shove to get him going, as Toby wasn't all that sure he wanted to actually *step* in the snow. He did start eating it, though. "Hey, cut that out," she scolded, nudging his head. "Dr. Pace said it would give you diarrhea. Now go on, go pee."

Acting as if he were walking on eggshells, Toby slowly made his way into the parking lot. Jessie gathered her robe at her neck with a laugh, wishing she'd brought her camera. "Damn, I forgot my cell phone," she muttered, pushing the door open wider to keep Toby in sight. She looked at the outside knob to make sure it had a card lock and noticed the sign over the lock that said only employee cards would work.

Maybe she'd ask the front desk for an employee card so she wouldn't have to traipse through the lobby just to let Toby out first thing in the morning. She'd only been able to book a room for two weeks when she'd called for reservations, because the entire resort was closed for a special event the middle week of December. When Jessie had told them she wanted to stay longer, the person she'd spoken with had explained there were several nice inns in town.

That is, unless the impossible happened and she bought a house by then. Maybe it was just good luck that Ian and Duncan had a cousin who was a real estate broker. Katy, they'd said her name was. Well, if for some reason Katy didn't show up this morning, she'd ask at the front desk how to reach the woman.

"Toby?" she called, noticing he'd wandered out of sight. "Where are you?"

That's when Jessie heard what sounded like heavy

machinery rumbling down the mountain toward the back of the hotel. They couldn't be grooming trails yet, could they? There were only two, maybe three inches of snow. She stretched out arm's length from the door and saw headlights flickering through the trees. "Toby!" she shouted, realizing the woods were maybe fifty feet wide and that there must be a ski trail on the other side of them. "Toby! Get back here! Now!"

Jessie stepped back into the hall to look for something to prop open the door, but apparently the resort managers were neat freaks. She started undoing her belt to wedge it in the door when she heard Toby give a loud, excited bark. "Toby, no!" she shouted, turning toward the woods, only to spin back to see the door click shut. "Dammit," she growled, heading into the parking lot at a run when Toby barked again. But she hadn't taken three steps when her smooth-soled slippers went skidding in opposite directions and she fell, landing with a thud that sent up a cloud of fluffy snow.

Realizing Toby was headed toward the ski trail when she heard him give a series of excited barks, Jessie scrambled to her feet and started running, this time being more careful of her footing. She slipped again just as she reached the woods, and grabbed a tree. "Toby, come here!" she commanded, not knowing if he could hear her over the revving engine that was so close now, she could feel the ground shaking. So she started praying instead as she made her way toward the trail. "Please see him. Please see him," she petitioned the driver, suddenly glad she'd bought Toby a brightly colored sweater. She slumped against a tree in relief when she saw the large, brightly lit, bulldozer-tracked machine suddenly halt and heard the engine slow to an idle.

A door opened and a man got out. "Toby?" the guy said,

his hand outstretched as he walked toward the middle of the trail. The guy looked around. "What are you doing out here all by yourself, big man?"

He knew her dog's name?

"Ian!" Jessie cried, pushing off the tree to go to him, only to fall flat on her face in the snow—which on this side of the woods was a hell of a lot deeper than two inches!

Chapter Four

"JESSIE!" IAN SHOUTED, RUNNING OVER AND DROPPING to his knees beside her. "Aw, lass, what are ye doing out here?" he asked, carefully rolling her over and lifting her onto his thighs. "Hell, you're not even *dressed*."

Toby rushed up and immediately started lapping her face, and Ian pushed the dog away. When Jessie attempted to stand up, he tightened his hold on her even as he tried to imagine what she was doing out here in only her bath-robe and slippers. "What in hell are you doing out here?" he repeated.

"I'm walking my dog," she snapped, scrunching the lapels of her robe to her neck and then elbowing him in the ribs as she tucked her arms against her sides. She took a calming breath. "I didn't know there was a trail back here, and I certainly never expected machinery to be running at this hour."

That said, she tried standing again, but Ian merely slid his hand under her knees and stood up with her in his arms.

"Wait. No! What are you doing?" she cried, wiggling and squirming so frantically that he slipped and nearly fell when she threw him off balance.

And then he nearly stumbled again when he finally realized *why* she kept trying to reposition her unconfined breasts: She was afraid he'd feel her mismatched boobs. He started walking toward the hotel, giving her a threatening squeeze when her head clipped his chin in her struggles. "You will *cease*."

She went perfectly still. "Did you just growl at me?"

The poor woman appeared so indignant that it was all Ian could do not to laugh. "Aye, and I'm about to toss you over my shoulder like a sack of grain if you don't quit squirming." As he'd hoped, the hollow threat certainly got her mind off her missing anatomy. He arched a brow at her glare. "What? City men don't growl at their women?"

"Put me down. I can walk now that I'm in the woods," she growled right back at him. "I'm not an invalid."

Lord, she was beautiful when she was too angry to be self-conscious. "No, you're merely an idiot for coming outside in your bathrobe and slippers."

"Oh, I see what you are, Ian MacKeage; you're one of those men who justifies using brute force whenever he thinks he's doing it for a woman's own good."

He stopped. "Have you had experience with some of *those men*, Jessie?"

"As a matter of fact, I was married to one—for exactly *three months*."

One more piece of Jessie Pringle's puzzle fell into place. She'd been married—only not very happily or for very long, apparently. When she went back to furtively trying to reposition her breasts, Ian turned and started walking toward the snowcat, which nicely redirected her worry from herself to him again.

"Where are you going?" she squeaked, looking over his shoulder at the hotel, and then down at the ground—he assumed to get Toby to rescue her. "I told you I can make it from here."

"You're shivering." He sat her on the rubber track on the passenger side of the snowcat to open the door. "And you weigh more than I thought."

He clearly heard her gasp over the rumble of the idling engine. "I do not."

She swatted his hand away when he tried to pick her up and set her inside, then turned and awkwardly scrambled in on her own. He gallantly helped by cupping her lovely backside, remembering how his dad liked to call his mom *gràineag* whenever the old man wanted to get a rise out of her, and Ian decided he also found prickly little hedgehogs to be quite beautiful when they were riled.

Jessie immediately sat down and gathered her robe closed at her neck, pulled the length of it over her pajama legs, and held her arms over her breasts—all while shooting him a beautifully riled glare hot enough to toast bread.

Toby placed his front paws on the track, looked up at Ian, and whined.

"What in hell are you wearing, big man?" he asked, staring down at the dog.

"It's his sweater."

"That's a terrible thing to do to a noble beast," Ian muttered, grabbing the sweater by the hem and pulling it up over Toby's head.

"Hey, he needs that," Jessie said as the dog reared back and pulled his legs out of the sleeve holes. "He's from *Georgia*, and he hasn't grown a winter coat yet."

Ian tossed the sweater on her lap. "And he won't grow one if he keeps wearing that blasted thing. Lean forward," he said, picking Toby up and setting him in the cubbyhole behind the seats. He stepped back and gestured at the sweater. "You can't ever put that on him, Jessie, if he's running loose in the woods. It could easily snag on a branch and fetch him up, and he could strangle to death trying to get free. He shouldn't even wear a collar or a work harness if you have one for him, if he's loose. I've come across more than one cat or dog when I was hunting that had hanged itself on its collar."

She clutched the sweater to her chest, looking so stricken that Ian was sorry for being so blunt. But she needed to understand the danger she'd put Toby in. "And why in God's name would you dress him in *pink*?" he asked, hoping to get her riled again.

"It . . . it's salmon," she whispered, looking down at the sweater, which sure as hell appeared pink to him in the glow of the interior light.

He took hold of her chin to make her look at him. "I'm sorry for being blunt, Jessie, but I need you to understand how dangerous that sweater is. And you needn't worry; Mother Nature will give Toby a winter coat soon enough."

She pulled her chin free, saying nothing, and Ian softly closed the door and walked around the snowcat and got in. But he stopped from reaching for the throttle when he saw Jessie holding Toby's snout facing her as she frowned at the dog.

"What?" he asked.

"I just realized Toby didn't even react when you picked me up. But he should have, because part of his job is to protect me."

Ian arched a brow. "I guess he's one of *those males*, and understands when something's being done for a woman's own good."

That certainly made her stricken look disappear.

Ian pushed on the throttle when she opened her mouth to protest, and then hit the lever to lift the hydraulic drag on the back of the groomer. "Animals react to the smell of fear," he continued over the rev of the engine as he headed the snowcat up the mountain. "And because Toby sensed anger coming from you but not fear, I believe he decided to let me save you this time." He answered her thunderous glare with a grin. "Then again, maybe he was just paying you back for dressing him in pink."

"It's *salmon*." Her chin lifted. "And *real* men can wear any color. Hey, the hotel is that way," she said, pointing past his shoulder.

"But the only way for us to get there is to go up, then over, then down. Are ye thawing out?" he asked, adjusting the heater vent on her side to blow down on her feet.

"Yes. Thank you."

Ian dropped the grooming drag again, figuring he might as well make one last pass before he called it quits. He saw Jessie finally start to relax, and smiled when she started looking around the interior of the snowcat at all the knobs and dials.

"Have you been grooming trails all night?" she asked, craning to look out the back window—though he noticed she made sure to hold her robe closed at her neck.

Ian turned off the interior lights. "That'll help you see outside better. And to answer your question, I've been working with the rest of our crew making snow, and we only started grooming an hour ago." He pointed at the lights to their right, farther up the mountain. "Everyone else is working on the tube run, but I wanted to make a couple of passes over the beginners' trail before the sun comes out and packs down the snow." He sighed tiredly. "We could use more help from Mother Nature, though, as we only have two weeks to build up a good base before the campers arrive."

"What's a tube run?" she asked, wiping the fog off her side window to see out.

"Are you saying you've never snow-tubed? Aw, lass," he said when she shook her head, "ye haven't lived until you've shot down a mountain on an inner tube. It's way more exciting than a roller coaster, as the speed and trajectory and bumps are different on every trip."

She smiled. "I've sledded down small hills in Central Park when I was a kid, but are you saying you actually have a trail dedicated to just sliding?"

He nodded, finding her smile as beautiful as her anger, even or maybe especially because she looked as if she'd just gotten out of bed. "If you'd like, I'll take you up the mountain later today, and you can help us test out the tube run."

"I, um, I don't know if I should be doing that sort of thing," she said, glancing back at her dog before suddenly giving Ian a cocky grin. "Toby would probably smell my *fear* and chase after me and bite the tube."

Oh, but he liked her sassiness. "Then we'll bring him on the tube with us." He chuckled at her surprise. "There's a less steep section for toddlers and chickens, Jessie. And if you don't have the physical strength to hold on, I'll do the holding on so you can enjoy the ride." He shrugged when the dial lights showed her blush. "That's what we do with a good many of the campers."

"You mentioned campers before and that you only have two weeks to get the trails ready. Is that why TarStone is closed for the middle week of December? You rent out the entire resort to some sort of camp?"

Ian lifted the hydraulic drag to turn onto the cutting that ran between trails and nodded. "In the summer my parents run a camp on the other side of the mountain for disabled and disfigured children, and every year they invite the kids and their families to TarStone for a snow vacation. They've had the camp going for nearly thirty years now, but only started the December session . . . oh, about fifteen years ago, I believe."

"Dis-disfigured . . . how?" she asked, having gone perfectly still.

He shrugged again. "They have physical impairments or disabling diseases, mostly; some have lost a limb, others are badly scarred." He smiled over at her. "But all that disappears for a week, because they're so busy having fun that they forget to be self-conscious." He leaned closer and lowered his voice. "Don't tell anyone, but each year a bunch of us sneak the more daring boys down to the pool to go skinny-dipping. And the next night our female cousins do the same with the girls."

"You take them skinny-dipping? Of all the things to—Why?"

He turned the snowcat down the lift path. "For the simple pleasure of swimming in their birthday suits, little miss Goody Two-shoes," he said, laughing at her scandalized expression. But then he sobered. "Those children spend every day of their young lives hiding their scars and imperfections from the world, Jessie. But when they're here, none of it matters, because every one of them has learned that it's what's *inside* a person that counts." He leaned closer again. "And there's nothing as liberating as splashing around naked in a pool with your friends."

"But are you telling me you're doing this without the parents knowing?"

"No, they know."

"And they don't care?" she asked, incredulous. "It doesn't worry them that not only are their children sneaking behind their backs, but that they're skinny-dipping? With adults?"

"Of course they care, Jessie. That's why the parents then sneak down to watch their children being *children*." He blew out a sigh. "Skinny-dipping in a moonlit solarium or lake with a bunch of your friends isn't a crime, lass; it's a childhood memory in the making—which, I might add, nicely sums up Camp Come-As-You-Are's mission statement."

The radio on the dash suddenly beeped, followed by static. "Hey, out there, especially anyone near the hotel," a female voice said over the speaker. "Keep an eye out for a woman guest and her dog. They left the hotel half an hour ago, and according to the roommate, the woman wasn't dressed for outside. Um . . . the dog was, though."

Jessie buried her face in her hands with a groan, and Ian picked up the mike. "I've got her, Rachel. I found Miss Pringle trying to get a jump start on the season on the beginners' slope, and I'm bringing her in now. Tell Merissa that she can meet Jessie in the lobby in five minutes."

"No!" Jessie yelped, grabbing his arm. "Not the lobby. Just drop me off at one of the side doors. I have my key card," she said, reaching in her pocket, only to reach in the other pocket and come up empty-handed. She grabbed his arm again. "Then at least take me to the employee entrance and let me in that door."

Ian clipped the mike back on the dash. "Sorry, city girl,"

he said with a shake of his head, "but the best way I know for someone not to repeat a foolish mistake is to live with the consequences. And this morning that means going through the lobby in your pajamas." Ignoring her glare, he idled through the parking lot, stopped under the portico, and shut off the snowcat, then grinned at her. "Now, Jessie, you know I'm only doing this for your own good."

She started groping at the door looking for the handle, and Ian reached down and snatched her slippers off her feet.

"Hey!" she yelped, trying to grab them back as he straightened and quickly climbed out of his side.

He strode around the front of the snowcat and opened her door. "What, you want to get me fired for negligence if you slip and fall? You can have your slippers back once I get you inside," he offered, shoving them in the bib of his ski pants.

"I'm too heavy, remember?" she snapped, swatting at him as she leaned away, which actually made it easier to slide his hands behind her back and under her knees.

"I've gotten my second wind and feel much stronger now," he said, picking her up. "But thank you for caring." And then he suffered through her wiggling and squirming all over again as she tried to keep her decidedly full right breast from bumping his chest while holding her bathrobe closed at her neck. "Come on, Toby," he said over his shoulder. "You need to face the consequences, too, as you're likely the reason Jessie got into this mess in the first place," he continued when Toby jumped out and trotted to catch up. "You don't run into the woods to hide just because you think someone might see you in a silly sweater."

"Now you're scolding *my dog*?"

"Jessie!" Merissa cried, pushing through the outside set

of lobby doors. "What happened? Are you hurt? Why aren't you walking? Is she hurt?" she asked Ian, grabbing his arm to stop him as her eyes roamed over Jessie.

"She's okay, Merissa," Ian said, stepping past her to go inside.

Merissa shot around him to open the inner door and grabbed his arm to stop him again. "Then put her down," she said, darting a quick glance around the empty lobby.

"I intend to, in her room."

"No. You will put her down right here, *right now*," Merissa said with such lethal authority that Ian stopped in midstep. "Now," she quietly repeated.

He took two strides and set Jessie down in one of the lobby chairs, then turned and silently walked toward the front desk.

"Is there a reason Toby didn't rip out his throat?" he heard Merissa say in a heated whisper. "Or better yet, why you didn't?"

"Apparently Toby only reacts to my fear, not my anger. And . . . and I must have been too numb with cold to freak out this time."

Watching the mirror on the wall beside the front desk, Ian saw Merissa smooth down Jessie's hair. "He didn't know better, Jess, and was only trying to help. You're okay now, I've got you," she said, helping Jessie stand and then guiding her toward the elevator. "What happened? Did you get locked out? I heard Ian say over the radio that he found you on one of the ski slopes. Did you have a flashback?"

"No. Honestly, I didn't. Toby ran into the woods, and when I heard equipment running, I went chasing after him."

Feeling about two inches tall to learn that Jessie apparently had a problem with being carried, Ian pulled her slippers out of his bib. "Toby, come here, boy," he said, patting his leg. "Take these to your lady," he instructed, placing the slippers in the dog's mouth. He immediately turned to the front desk when he saw Jessie stop. "Rachel, you wouldn't have any doughnuts hidden out back, would you?" he asked, sensing Jessie walking up to him.

Jessie touched his arm. "Thank you for rescuing me," she said softly. "And for explaining how dangerous Toby's sweater is."

Ian looked into her sincere eyes and smiled. "You're welcome, Jessie."

"And . . . and I think I'd like to try speeding down a mountain on an inner tube. That is, if you really do need someone to test the trail before the campers arrive."

"Just leave a message here at the desk," he said, nodding toward Rachel, "saying when you'd like to go, and someone will get ahold of me."

She started to pat his arm, then suddenly thought better of it. "I'll do that. Thanks again," she said, turning back to Merissa—who was still wearing the clothes she'd had on last night, Ian noticed—her hands fisted on her hips as she glared at Jessie.

"What's this about speeding down a mountain on an inner tube?" she hissed in a whisper, taking Jessie by the arm again. "Are you friggin' nuts? You can't—"

Jessie shrugged free. "I can't believe you panicked and came looking for me. They broadcast it over the radio to everyone."

Ian heard Merissa blow out a heavy sigh just as they stepped into the elevator. "I'm sorry. You know I panic easily when I'm sleep-deprived."

"I forgive you, but only if you teach me how to make that nurse's voice when you want someone to do something, because I swear I—"

Ian lost the rest of their conversation when the elevator door closed, the last thing he saw being Toby still holding Jessie's slippers in his mouth.

"It's a good thing you were grooming the beginners' slope," Rachel said, sliding a box of doughnuts across the counter toward him. "Miss Pringle could have gotten hypothermia or even frostbite."

"Oh, I don't know, Rachel. I believe hedgehogs are a lot tougher than they look," he said, grabbing three of the doughnuts and heading for the door. He waved over his shoulder. "Tell Dad I said hi when he comes in later." He stopped and looked back. "Oh, and have another key card sent to Jessie's room, would you, along with an employee card that will work on the parking lot door. A good part of this morning's mess could have been avoided if we'd thought to make accommodations for her to take her dog out. You might want to have Dad look into making that a policy for guests with service dogs."

Rachel lifted one of her matronly brows. "Any reason why *you* can't tell him?"

"Now you know I don't want to encourage him to think I might be interested in what goes on inside this resort. I've just spent the better part of this last year convincing him I'm barely interested in what happens outside."

Rachel made a *tsk* sound as she snatched up a key card and used it to wave him away. "You have him convinced about as well as you've got any of us believing that you don't care about TarStone."

"I care about the *outside*," he said, taking a bite of doughnut as he pushed through the door. Ian climbed in the snowcat and set his two remaining doughnuts on the dash, but stopped from starting the engine when he spotted Toby's sweater. He plucked it off the floor to toss it onto the passenger seat, but held it up to his nose when he caught a whiff of something familiar. And sure enough, instead of smelling like dog, the sweater smelled feminine and flowery—exactly like Jessie.

"Okay, Miss Prickly Pringle," he said with a smile, stuffing the sweater inside the bib of his ski pants. "Game on."

Chapter Five

THE FARTHER DOWN THE NARROW DIRT ROAD KATY MacBain drove, the more Jessie was tempted to pinch herself to be sure that she wasn't dreaming. It had stopped snowing around sunrise, and the clouds had given way to a crystalline blue sky, the weak November sun causing the melting snow to glitter like diamonds. Pine Lake on their right was a stunningly dark cobalt blue with the gusty north wind pushing its massive waves into crests of brilliant white froth.

Oh yeah, if that unexplainably persistent brochure had captured her imagination, actually being here was fanning the spark it had ignited inside her into a bonfire. And if she hadn't been completely sure about moving here, she definitely was now, as Jessie couldn't remember ever feeling so alive.

Honest to God, the power was palpable.

"You two must have made quite an impression on Ian

and Duncan last night," Katy said, darting a smile at Jessie and then at Merissa in the backseat. "Because when Ian called me this morning not ten minutes before Duncan did, and I told them our cousin Megan and her husband Jack just asked me to sell their house out here on Frog Point, both men told me *not* to put it on the market until I showed it to you first. Actually," she said, smiling at Jessie, "Ian threatened that if I didn't sell you this house, he was going to write my phone number on the wall of the men's bathroom at Pete's."

"Nice cousin," Merissa drawled from the backseat.

Katy laughed. "I told him he was too late, because I snuck in not a month after Pete's opened and wrote it next to the mirror myself."

"How's that been working for you?" Merissa asked.

Katy shrugged. "I probably would have gotten more calls if I'd left off my last name. Apparently there's not a man living within fifty miles of Pine Creek who's brave enough to ask me out."

Merissa took hold of Jessie's seat to lean forward. "Why?"

"Because they're all afraid of my father and brothers and male cousins."

Merissa flopped back with a snort. "You can't get a date because everyone's afraid of the *men* in your family? You're funning us, right?"

Katy sighed, glancing over her shoulder at Merissa. "I wish I were. Tell me: Last night you didn't find Duncan to be a tad . . . oh, let's go with *overwhelming*, shall we?"

"Overwhelming is an understatement," Merissa said with a laugh.

"So are you saying you don't mind being hustled home at four thirty in the morning, wondering what just happened?"

"He *told* you we spent the night together?"

"Oh, none of my dear sweet cousins would ever kiss and tell. I saw you headed to the resort in Duncan's truck this morning."

"You're a real estate broker. What were *you* doing up at four-friggin'-A.M.?"

"I was going to my family's Christmas tree farm to help with this year's cutting. What, do you ladies think Douglas fir pitch is my perfume of *choice*?" Katy asked with a laugh. She darted a quick glance at Merissa again. "And although I could see you were smiling, you also looked like a deer caught in oncoming headlights. So, back to your question as to why I can't get a date in this town. After spending time with my cousins," she said, glancing at Jessie to include her, "what do you think the odds are that some guy is going to take an interest in me knowing they'll be watching his every move? And you, Jessie, didn't you find Ian to be old-fashioned and rather . . . proprietary? He certainly didn't have any qualms about telling me where you should live."

Jessie remembered he hadn't had any qualms about telling her how foolish she'd been to go outside in her bathrobe and slippers, either. Or scolding her for putting a sweater on Toby. Or saying that she weighed too much—although she knew he'd been using that as an excuse for nearly dropping her because she'd been struggling. But she would have just died if he'd seen the scar on her collarbone or realized she had a malformed breast. She liked Ian, dammit, and didn't want to scare him off before . . . well, at least not before he kissed her again. "He is rather bossy, I suppose."

"They both are," Merissa agreed from the backseat. "But then, I sort of have a thing for large alpha males."

"And yet you usually dump them after only two dates,"

Jessie drawled. "Right about the time the testosterone hangover hits you between the eyes."

"Exactly," Katy said with a laugh. "The very thing that draws us to manly men—namely their strength and confidence—also drives us crazy."

Merissa gave a heartfelt groan. "The deadly combination of brawn and brain. Maybe we'd be better off going after only the brawn."

"Nope," Katy said, braking to a stop. "Trust me, that doesn't work, either. And neither does going after only brains." She shut off the engine. "Which has me seriously considering joining a convent. Here we are, Jessie," she said, leaning forward to gesture out the side window. "There's your new home."

Jessie's heart started thumping so hard it hurt as she stared at the tan-colored, Cape-style house sitting not a hundred feet from the lake, nestled beneath towering trees. There was a porch running across the entire front, the steps lined with pumpkins leading up to a bright red door decorated with a wreath of woven vines. Several mounds of leaves littered the lawn, some of the piles looking as if they'd been jumped in by the owner of the small wagon abandoned on the moss-covered brick walkway.

"It's perfect," Jessie whispered, getting out—only to grab the door when a sharp pain shot through her lower back, making her legs nearly buckle. But still, she couldn't take her eyes off the vision of perfection in front of her.

Oh yeah, in this house on this lake, surrounded by these mountains, was *exactly* where she needed to be.

"Jessie?" Merissa asked, scrambling out of the truck. "What's wrong?"

"I'm okay," she murmured. "Look at it, Mer. It's perfect.

Why are they selling it?" she asked when Katy came around the front of the SUV.

"They built a new home farther up the lake," Katy explained, "and got moved in not a moment too soon. Megan gave birth to a little girl a couple of months ago, and she and Jack just finished getting this place ready to sell."

The front door opened, and a woman wearing an infant carrier on her chest stepped onto the porch just as a toddler bolted past her. "Auntie Katy!" the boy shouted, scrambling down the steps. "You come to buy my house!"

"No, Walker," Katy said, scooping him up in her arms with a laugh. "I've come to *sell* your house to this lady." She gave him a noisy kiss on his cheek. "So I hope your bedroom is spanking clean."

"It's *empity*, Auntie." His gaze moved to Jessie. "You got a little boy? He can have my room, 'cause I got a new one now."

"Nope, no little boy," Jessie said, shaking her head. "But I have a dog that might like your room." She signaled for Toby to jump out of the backseat. "His name is Toby."

Walker's eyes widened and his grip on Katy's neck tightened. "He's awful big," he whispered. "Does he like little boys?"

"He does," Jessie assured him, carefully bending to take hold of Toby's leash and slowly straightening. "In fact, he'll even shake hands with you."

Walker immediately started wiggling to get down. "I want to shake his hand."

"Sit, Toby," Jessie said, positioning Walker in front of the dog. "Hold out your hand and say hello," she instructed as the boy's mother rushed toward them. "Don't worry," she assured the obviously concerned woman. "I know he looks big and scary, but he's a cupcake around children."

"Hello, Toby," Walker said, holding out his hand.

Toby dutifully lifted a paw and set it in his tiny hand, and Walker giggled when the dog licked his fingers.

Merissa handed Jessie her cane, her eyes focused intently on her. "You're in pain," she whispered tightly.

Using the cane for support, Jessie unclipped Toby's leash and signaled that he was free. "Why don't you show Toby around your beautiful yard," she told Walker.

"We can look at the house tomorrow or the day after," Merissa said, still eyeing Jessie as Toby and Walker headed for the nearest pile of snow-covered leaves.

Jessie held out her hand to the homeowner. "Jessie Pringle. And don't worry, I'm not leaving here without a signed purchase agreement."

The woman gave a warm laugh. "Megan Stone. And I have to say, you just one-upped me. At least I got *inside* before I offered to buy it from the previous owners."

"Jessie," Merissa growled softly, looking directly into her eyes again. "Are you high on pain pills or something? You can't just buy the first house you see."

Jessie barely caught herself from reminding Merissa that they had both kissed the first men they saw last night. "No, I haven't taken any meds yet. But I think I better take something now. Could you bring in my purse?"

"If you're not feeling well," Megan said, falling in step beside Jessie when she started up the brick walkway, "there's no reason we can't reschedule." She smiled over at her. "I promise not to sell the house out from under you."

Jessie took hold of the railing and slowly made her way onto the porch, having absolutely no intention of leaving until she owned this house. "I'm just a bit stiff," she assured

Megan. "I fell chasing after Toby this morning, and according to Ian, I now have to live with the consequences of going outside in my slippers."

Megan stopped in the act of opening the door. "He called and said that if I didn't sell you this house, he was going to tell my husband how I shamelessly used to bribe the boys to go out with me in high school."

Jessie blinked at her and then at Katy coming up the steps. "Ian's been threatening both of you into selling me this house? But why?"

"Because he's Ian," Megan said. "And when a Mac-Keage male decides he wants something, he's not above using any means at his disposal to make it happen." She chuckled. "And apparently Ian wants you living here."

"But *why*?" Jessie repeated.

"Because he knows it's a good house."

"And also because he lives just down the cove," Katy added, pointing past the end of the porch. "Well, his *stuff* lives there," she said with a snort. "I think Ian sleeps on the mountain more than he does in his bed."

Megan walked inside. "In fact, you can see his house from here, now that the leaves have fallen off." She turned once everyone got inside and held open the door. "Walker, bring Toby inside and show him your old bedroom."

Walker scrambled up the steps and bolted past them without even looking up. "Come on, Toby. I'll show you where you're going to sleep."

Only instead of following, Toby stopped beside Jessie and pushed his nose into her free hand. She gave him a pat. "It's okay, Tobes. Go play with Walker."

Megan walked toward the wall of windows facing the lake. "Come sit down, Jessie. You can see most of the downstairs and the yard from here."

"Could I get a glass of water?" Merissa asked, heading to the kitchen that was separated from the living area by a counter peninsula.

"Oh, sure," Megan said, changing directions as she waved Jessie toward the large leather chair—which was the only piece of furniture in sight—nestled between the windows and a green enameled woodstove.

"No offense," Merissa said, digging through Jessie's purse, "but don't you ladies think it's a little creepy that a guy Jessie met only last night is so gung ho about her living just down the street from him?" She pulled out Jessie's cosmetic bag, slung the purse over her shoulder, and started rummaging through the bag for Jessie's pillbox. "Where we come from, that sounds an awful lot like stalking." Merissa looked up when her only answer was silence and found Katy and Megan grinning at her. She grinned back, albeit sheepishly. "I know he's your cousin and all, but from our perspective, you've got to admit it's kind of scary."

"Any scarier than leaving a bar with a guy you just met?" Jessie asked, glaring across the room at Merissa.

"Hey, Paula assured us the men were harm—" Merissa's cheeks turned red and she winced. "Touché. But we're not talking about me; we're talking about *you* living in a strange town with only a dog for protection." She looked at Megan. "How many of the homes on this road are year-round residences? This place appears kind of isolated."

Jessie carefully lowered herself into the chair, giving a snort to cover her pained groan. "I am perfectly capable of taking care of myself, Mother Merissa," she said before Megan could answer. "And I'm pretty sure Ian has better things to do than stalk some woman he just met. He probably has half a dozen girlfriends and likely isn't interested in juggling one more."

"Actually, he doesn't," Megan said, walking over with a paper cup she'd filled with water. "In fact, you're the first woman we've seen Ian take any real interest in since he came home from Afghanistan a little under a year ago."

"But that in no way means he's stalking you," Katy rushed to say, sitting down on the stone hearth. "Ian's just . . ." She shrugged, looking at Megan.

"He's just being Ian," Megan finished for her, patting her baby's bottom when the infant stirred on her chest. "You tell him you're not interested, and I swear that'll be the end of it," she said, giving Merissa a reassuring nod.

"Because more than being old-fashioned, all our men are noble to a fault," Katy added. "And if one of them did happen to go astray, there's an entire clan of men *and* women to put them back on the straight and narrow."

"Especially the older generation," Megan continued, "with Ian's father probably being the worst of the lot. Uncle Morgan is the living definition of an atavist." She shot Merissa a smile. "So you really don't have to worry about your friend, because we all look out for one another here."

Jessie was beginning to wonder if they really had blown into another century.

"That'll teach you to be careful what you wish for," Merissa said deadpan, handing Jessie a pill. "You just traded a sea of strangers for an entire *clan* of bossy men." She looked at Katy and Megan. "Only problem is, I can tell you from personal experience that when Jessie gets a bee in her bonnet about something, she tends to forget she's not ten feet tall and bulletproof. I actually spent over half an hour talking a physical therapist out of the janitor's closet once after the guy foolishly told Jessie she was trying too hard."

"The idiot was supposed to be helping me *walk* again,"

Jessie defended, giving Merissa another heated glare, "instead of just getting myself in and out of a wheelchair."

Ignoring her, Merissa shot the two women a smug smile. "So you ladies might want to warn all the noble men in your family—especially Ian—that Jessie Pringle is more dangerous than her dog."

Finally realizing Merissa was so worried about leaving her here alone that she was trying to head off any potential threats, Jessie burst out laughing. "They said Ian was in Afghanistan, Mer. You think he's going to be scared off by a woman with a cane and a dog?" She looked at Katy. "Ian's a veteran?"

The real estate broker nodded. "And so is Duncan. All of our men serve at least one stint in the military."

"Which branch?" Merissa asked.

"Whichever one appeals to them," Megan interjected. She unzipped the pack on her chest and pulled out the squirming infant. "Duncan flew Black Hawks in Iraq, and near as we know, Ian served three tours in the Afghan mountains as part of some secret elite team." She gave her baby's plump cheek a kiss. "It's about time you woke up, sleepyhead. I am *so* ready for you to eat," she said as she turned around, looking for a place to sit down.

"Oh, here," Jessie said, attempting to lever herself out of the chair. "Now I know why you kept this big comfy chair here."

"No, don't get up," Megan rushed to say, sitting down on the floor to lean against the wall. She laid the infant on her lap and took off the chest pack, but stopped in the act of pulling her blouse out of her waistband. "You ladies don't mind, do you?"

"Good heavens, no," Jessie said. "What's her name?"

"Sarah Dreamwalker Stone, after Jack's mother,"

Megan said, tucking her daughter to her breast under her blouse with a sigh. "But I call her his little coyote." She nodded at the doorway her son and Toby had disappeared through. "And Walker is his little shadow. Katy, could you go check on them? It's awful quiet in there."

Katy jumped up from the hearth and headed into what looked like a short hallway just off the living area, only to suddenly stop and pull something out of her pocket. A flash went off, and then Katy walked back into the main room. "The little imp fell asleep, and Toby is cuddled up beside him," she said, holding her cell phone down to Megan. She then walked over and showed Jessie. "That's quite a pooch you've got there."

Jessie smiled at the picture of Walker sleeping with one arm wrapped around Toby's neck, her dog resting his head on Walker's torso. "Oh yeah, Toby is fascinated by children. I think they bring out his protective streak."

"And I think it's because their cute little faces are just the right height to lick," Merissa said, standing beside Katy to see the picture. She looked around the large living room and kitchen before leveling her gaze on Jessie, then sighed. "Nothing I say is going to stop you from buying this house today, is it?"

Jessie merely shook her head.

Merissa handed Jessie her purse before heading to the opposite end of the living room. "Then come on, Katy. Let's go check out the upstairs while these two settle on a price so I can see where I'll be staying when I come visit."

"It's a solid, comfortable house and everything works," Megan said once the women had disappeared up the stairs. "There are one large and one small bedroom and a bathroom on this floor," she added, nodding toward the hallway, "with two large bedrooms and a bath upstairs.

And we're leaving the four cord of firewood stacked in the shed, as well as the walk-behind snowblower. Um . . . except you might prefer to hire someone to plow you out. We've been trying to decide whether or not to leave the hot tub," she quickly rushed on, her cheeks turning pink as her gaze slid away from Jessie's cane. "The garage is only a year old. It's not connected to the house, but it sure beats brushing a foot of snow off your vehicle." She gave Jessie a curious look. "When Katy called this morning, she said Ian mentioned that you're from Georgia. You do know we measure snow in feet up here, don't you?"

"I'm actually looking forward to it." Jessie fussed with her silk scarf, feeling her own cheeks heat up. "Do you suppose I could hire Duncan's crew to build a wheelchair ramp for . . . for in case I need it? Or maybe you could point me toward some other local carpenter?"

Megan looked down at her daughter, patting the infant's bottom. "I'm sure Duncan would be happy to put his crew to work. This is the time of year his business starts slowing down, since he's mostly into earthwork."

"Have you and your husband settled on a price yet?"

Megan nodded even as she gave Jessie a sheepish smile. "The housing downturn hasn't really affected lakefront property all that much in Maine." She then took a deep breath and named a figure that started Jessie's heart pounding.

"Seriously?" Jessie squeaked despite her best effort to hide her shock. But then she laughed. "Good Lord, you can't buy a small condo in Atlanta for that." She nodded. "Okay, then. You leave the hot tub, and I won't even try to haggle you down."

"Just like that?" Megan asked in surprise.

Jessie opened her purse and dug around inside it. "My

father's an architect, and he's always told me that you can fix anything on a house except its location," she said with a laugh. She pulled out her checkbook then dug around for a pen. "But he'd have a heart attack if he knew I was paying asking price and writing you a check on the spot, so let's keep this our little secret when he shows up in . . ." She smiled. "I give him and Mom two days to be standing on my doorstep from when I tell them I am the proud owner of a beautiful house on a lake in Maine, which is why I'm going to wait until *after* I've moved in." She opened her checkbook, but stopped with the pen poised to write. "Are you and your husband sure about this?"

"Oh yeah, we're sure," Megan said thickly, holding her daughter against her shoulder to close her bra and smooth down her blouse. "We've been worried that we'd have to heat two houses this winter." She stood up and walked to the counter and started digging through her own purse. "I know we'll both have paperwork to fill out and the lawyers will need to do their thing, but as far as I'm concerned, the house is yours."

"So do I make the check out to you or to Katy's real estate company?"

"Make it out to Jack and Megan Stone," she said, walking back to Jessie. "We haven't actually listed it yet, so I guess this is a private sale. But don't worry, Katy and I will work out the commission."

Jessie wrote the check and held it out to Megan.

Megan swapped it for the ring of keys she was holding. "You might as well take these now so you can come back and look around when you're feeling better," she said, tucking the check in her pocket. "You're going to love it here, Jessie, because whether or not you realize it yet, you just bought a magical little piece of heaven."

Chapter Six

THE FIRST THING IAN NOTICED WHEN HE WALKED INTO the resort's massive swimming pool solarium was his father sitting on the footrest of a lounge chair, talking to someone reclining in another lounge facing the panoramic view of Pine Lake. The second thing he noticed was Toby lying on the floor between them, wearing a rugged harness with a thick leather handle protruding from it. But it wasn't until he saw the sleek, low-backed wheelchair that he truly grew alarmed.

Toby lifted his head, his tail nub wagging his whole rump in greeting.

"Maybe my son will have better luck persuading ye," Morgan said when he spotted him.

"Jessie?" Ian asked as he rounded the chairs to stand in front of her, making sure to hide his concern behind his smile. Christ, she was as pale as new snow but for the hint of red in her cheeks. "Have your legs gotten lazy on you this afternoon?"

"No, actually," she said, her chin lifting as her unusually bright eyes locked on his. "I aggravated an old injury when I fell chasing after Toby this morning."

"Which is why I was just telling Miss Pringle that one of our people can take Toby out for her in the mornings," Morgan said, his voice unusually soft.

Ian could see how well that suggestion had been received, if the look in his old man's eyes was any indication. He dropped his swim bag on the floor and pulled over one of the wrought-iron end tables in order to sit at the foot of Jessie's lounge chair.

"And I was just thanking your father," she said with equally evident frustration, "and assuring him that Merissa and I have it covered."

Apparently deciding to ignore the edge in Jessie's voice, Ian's father folded his arms over his chest. "I was also telling the lass that we have a fine doctor here in Pine Creek, and that it wouldn't be any bother for Libby Mac-Bain to come take a look at her."

"To which I explained," Jessie said through her forced smile, "that I swore off doctors two months ago."

Ian dropped his gaze to hide his consternation, tempted to walk away and let the two of them duke it out; because truth be told, he wasn't exactly sure which one of them needed his support. Where Morgan MacKeage was legendary for his antiquated view that women needed looking after, Ian suspected Jessie Pringle could give the old highlander lessons in stubbornness.

Toby came to the rescue by standing up and trotting to the sliding door leading outside, where he stopped and looked back at Jessie and gave a soft whine—which Jessie answered with an equally soft groan. She gathered the catalogs and notepad off her lap and set them on the table beside her, then awkwardly started to get up.

Morgan touched her arm to stop her. "If your pet is needing to go outside, Ian can take him," his father magnanimously offered. "Seeing how ye just spent the better part of ten minutes getting settled in that chair."

"I'm sure your son has more exciting things to do than walk my dog," she said, attempting to get up again—even as his father once again stopped her.

Uncertain if the fine sheen on her forehead was a sign that Jessie was in pain or merely the result of trying to keep her frustration in check, Ian stood up and went to the exit. "I believe Toby is capable of taking himself for a walk."

"Wait," Jessie said. "He's wearing his harness."

Ian opened the door and waved Toby outside. "He won't wander far. Not while he knows he's on duty."

Ignoring the startled birds flapping away from the feeder that had been put up to entertain guests, Toby padded across the patio and down to the nearest tree, relieved himself, then immediately trotted back through the door Ian was holding open. The two of them returned to the row of lounge chairs, Toby flopping down on the floor with a doggy sigh, and Ian sitting on the table at her feet again.

Morgan stood up. "Well, for as much as I've enjoyed our visit, I'm afraid I need to be getting back to work. Ian, I'd like you to stop by my office after your swim." He smiled at Jessie. "And since I can't talk ye into seeing Doc Libby, maybe all you're needing is a toddy of hot cocoa and fine Scotch to cure what ails ye. I'll send one over, along with some snacks," he said, giving her a bow before heading toward the lobby.

Ian touched Jessie's foot when she started to protest. "Just say thank you, lass."

"Thank you," she called after his father even as she shot Ian a frown.

He chuckled, giving her shoe a squeeze. "Dad doesn't realize you're on pain medication, Jessie. And he'll go to his grave believing a healthy dose of Scotch cures *everything*. Trust me; sometimes it's simply easier to agree with him."

"What makes you think I'm on pain meds?"

"Oh, maybe those overbright eyes of yours," he drawled, "or are ye just that excited to see me?" He sobered when she snorted, and touched her foot to get her to look at him when she picked up her catalogs and notepad. "I don't understand, Jessie. Ye seemed able to walk just fine this morning when you left the lobby with Merissa."

Two flags of color darkened her cheeks as her gaze dropped to her lap. "I was fine. But over the course of the day my lower back muscles inflamed and now they're putting pressure on my . . . on an old injury. I'll be back to normal in a day or two." Her chin lifted. "It's not like I'm an invalid or anything."

"Yes, I believe you mentioned that this morning." He nodded at the catalogs. "So is shopping your true medicine of choice, then?" he asked, kicking his smile up a notch when her eyes narrowed. "Because I feel I should warn you that even on a good day, delivery trucks have a hard time negotiating the Frog Point Road."

Those expressive eyes of hers went from defensive to surprised. "You already know I bought your cousin's house?"

He laughed and stood up. "Welcome to small-town life, lass. Anyone within fifty miles of Pine Creek who *doesn't* know you bought Megan and Jack's house is either gone on vacation or dead." He picked up his swim bag and walked up beside her to blatantly read her list, where she'd written *long johns*, *turtleneck*, *fleece scarf*, *wood rack*, and *bird feeder*. "If you're shopping for winter gear, then I suggest you also order a pair of ice creepers that fasten over your boots. Smooth down your quills, little *gràineag*," he said with a chuckle when her chin lifted again. "You won't be the only person in town wearing creepers this winter."

"What's a *gra-neeg*?"

He pointed at her lap. "And you can cross that bird feeder off your list, because I intend to get you one as a housewarming present."

"But I don't—"

He bent at the waist to bring his face level with hers. "Say thank you, Jessie."

"Thank you," she muttered, only to suddenly blow out a heavy sigh. "Look, I'm sorry for acting so grumpy today, okay?" she said, giving him a derisive smile. "But at least now I know you come by your bossiness honestly. When your father walked by and caught me trying to get out of my wheelchair and onto the lounge chair, he strode in here like a house on fire and picked me up before I could stop him."

Ian squatted on his heels beside her. "I'm sorry, Jessie. I'll have a talk with him."

She set her hand on his arm. "Please don't. I know he was only trying to help, and I'd hate to hurt his feelings. It's just that . . . well, it's important that I do things for myself." She nodded toward her legs, her grip on his arm tightening. "I've spent the last four years working my tail off to go from being totally helpless to finally being independent again."

"Is that why you've come to Pine Creek? You believe moving so far away from everyone will prove you don't need their help? Or are ye trying to prove it to yourself?"

She started to pat his arm, only to stop in midpat and softly snort instead. "I *believe* I've done that already. Now it's just a matter of making everyone else believe it. Go on, go for your swim," she said, waving him away as she picked up her pen and notepad, "while I finish medicating myself with shopping." She pointed at the patio when Ian straightened back to his feet. "But just so you know, I want a bird feeder just as big as that one and a large bag of whatever birdseed the resort uses."

"Would you like me to have a little talk with all the birds as well, and tell them to head down to Frog Point?"

"Oh yes, I'd like that," she said, her smile so sassy that it took all of his willpower not to kiss her—that is, until she pointed out the window again and scowled. "But when you do, you tell the blue jays and those big gray and black birds that they are *not* invited to the Pringle feeder. There, did you see that?" she hissed, pointing the pen like a sword. "Those big bullies keep driving off the little chickadees and finches. And then they scatter the seed while stuffing their mouths so full, it's a wonder they can even fly."

"What?" he said in mock horror, not even trying to hide his amusement. "Ye think because the jays are big and bold that they don't deserve to eat?"

"They're being gluttons."

"Nay, Jessie. They're being jays. And see," he said, pointing at the patio under the feeder. "The mourning doves wouldn't get any seed if not for them, because doves are ground feeders."

"That doesn't mean they have to go around using their size to bully the others," she muttered, shooting the jays an evil eye—which had Ian wondering if Jessie hadn't been on the receiving end of a bully herself.

"I'll have a talk with them, then," he said with a chuckle,

leaning down to give Toby a pat on the head—just barely restraining himself from giving Jessie a pat, too, before he headed toward the men's changing room.

"Hey, wait," she said, making him stop and turn. "You didn't tell me what *gra-neeg* means. You said 'smooth down my quills.'" She pointed the pen at *him*. "You better not have just called me a porcupine."

He started walking backward. "My bossiness isn't the only thing I come by honestly, but I believe I'll let my mom tell you what a *gràineag* is."

"When will I meet her?" she asked, raising her voice to carry the length of the pool as he neared the changing room door.

"I'm surprised ye haven't already. I expected Mom to show up here within an hour of my telling her there's a big-time advertising exec staying at the resort."

"You *what*?" Jessie yelped. "Why would you tell her that?"

"Mom wants to start marketing the children's camp overseas, so I suggested she talk to you."

"But I don't know anything about promoting a children's camp!"

Ian decided he'd been wise to wait until he was on the other side of the solarium to tell her. "It's not rocket science, Jess. The only requirements needed are that you like kids and know advertising."

"But I told you, I'm on hiatus from work."

Oh, he was a wise man, all right, because he'd likely be a dead one if he were still within kissing distance of that upturned nose. "I give you until mid-January when the snow's halfway up your windows before you become bored to tears." He pushed open the door with his back and shot her a smile. "And don't worry, you'll learn what you need to know about the camp when ye help my cousins take the young girls skinny-dipping," he finished as he wisely disappeared into the men's room.

WELL, SHE MIGHT HAVE A HANDFUL OF UGLY SCARS AND be missing a small piece of anatomy, and her legs didn't always want to cooperate, but at least Jessie knew there wasn't anything wrong with her libido. She took advantage of the fact that the four men in the pool were all underwater at the same time and fanned herself with her notepad.

Was there some sort of magical elixir in the drinking water around here, like a naturally occurring growth hormone or something? Because honest to God, every male she'd met so far was well over six feet tall. Heck, she had estimated Robbie MacBain to be over six foot six before he'd dropped to his haunches beside her and introduced himself as Katy's oldest brother. The gray-eyed, soft-spoken man had then welcomed Jessie to Pine Creek, told her she was smart for buying Megan and Jack's house, and offered to send for his mum if she was needing a doctor—to which Jessie had sweetly thanked him but politely declined.

Then, not five minutes after Robbie disappeared into the changing room, Duncan had walked into the solarium accompanied by another giant appearing to be in his late twenties, who had longish dark blond hair and eerily familiar eyes. And after only a moment's hesitation upon noticing her wheelchair, Duncan had introduced her to Ian's baby brother, Alec.

Oh yeah, there had to be something in the drinking water if all that gorgeous brawn and old-fashioned brain splashing around in the pool was any indication. No wonder Katy couldn't get a date; it would take either a very brave man or a suicidal idiot to mess with any female belonging to one of these . . . clans.

From what Jessie gathered, these particular clansmen were having a meeting, as she caught snippets of their conversation between bouts of a water game only they knew the rules to. It seemed the men were going over last-minute details of a week-long hunting trip that was to begin tomorrow morning at the ungodly hour of three A.M., with everyone meeting at Robbie MacBain's house because it appeared they were riding horses into the mountains.

Good Lord, she and Merissa had been blown clear into the *nineteenth* century.

Speaking of which, it appeared her friend's little vacation affair was going to be yet another one-night stand, as Merissa would be back in Atlanta by the time the men returned from their trip. She only hoped Duncan broke the news to her gently, because she had a feeling Merissa really liked him.

Jessie wished Mer would stop looking so hard and just *pick* one. The woman had dated no less than five perfectly nice men this past year alone, but for some reason, whenever they started getting serious, Merissa suddenly got too busy to see them again. Jessie sighed and took her cell phone off the table to check the time, and saw she should probably take another med—or else start sipping the now-cooled toddy that had been tickling her nose ever since it had been delivered. She opted for the drink, figuring it couldn't make her any more dopey than the pain pills did.

Only she flinched and ended up taking a large gulp when a deep voice just beyond her feet said, "Ye put that right back on the table. You know better than to mix meds with alcohol."

Jessie sat up with a sputtering cough to glare at Ian

resting his arms on the side of the pool, glaring back at her. "For your information," she said in a strangled whisper, trying to catch her breath. Holy hell, there had to be more Scotch than cocoa in that mug! "I'm trying your father's cure *for what ails me* instead of taking another pill."

Three more heads rose out of the water, and three sets of muscular arms rested on the side of the pool, so that now there were four men glaring at her. That is, until Alec suddenly chuckled and pointed. "You've got a chocolate mustache."

Jessie wiped her mouth with the back of her hand, then very deliberately took another drink—and immediately started gasping for breath again. Okay, maybe she should find some other way to make her point, since all she'd proven was that she could make the four of them smile.

"Ye need to *sip* fine Scotch," Duncan said, giving a pained expression as he looked at Ian. "Did I hear her say your father sent over that toddy?" He looked back at Jessie. "Have a care, then, if Morgan had anything to do with it, as there's probably enough Scotch in there to make a horse drunk."

Jessie decided it was time to call in reinforcements, seeing how she was woefully outnumbered. And she was including Toby on their side, as he'd gotten up and padded over to the men to solicit a few scratches behind his ear and a couple of pats.

"Hmmm?" Jessie murmured when Ian said something as she typed, HELP! I'M DROWNING IN TESTOSTERONE! and sent the text message speeding off to Merissa. She looked past her feet to find him scowling at her. "What did you say?"

"Can Toby come for a swim?"

"In the *pool*?" She glanced around the solarium then

leaned forward. "Are you trying to get me kicked out of the resort?"

"We won't tell if you don't," Duncan interjected, lifting out of the water enough to reach Toby's harness buckle. "And being between seasons, this place is all but empty."

"Wait. I . . . I'm not even certain he knows how to swim."

"Then don't you think you should find out?" Ian asked, taking off Toby's collar, "considering ye just bought a house on the lake?"

Toby moved out of the men's reach the moment he was free of his harness and collar and turned his big brown eyes on Jessie. "Go on," she said, giving him the signal he was free. "Go play with your new buddies."

Ian pushed off and started swimming toward the shallow end of the pool. "Then come on, big man," he called out. "Come get in the water this way."

Jessie nervously took a sip of her drink, hoping she hadn't made a mistake. She wasn't afraid the dog would actually drown, since there were four obviously capable men to rescue him, but she didn't want Toby to be traumatized if he sank to the bottom.

Then again, Ian was right; she really should find out if the big lug could swim.

"How about you, Jessie?" Alec asked, starting to lift out of the water. "You want to come for a swim, too?"

Jessie squeaked in surprise and pressed into the lounge chair, uncertain if he was joking or not. But she was saved from finding out when Duncan pulled Alec back in the pool and effectively stifled his shout of surprise by shoving him underwater.

"Where's Merissa?" he asked—even while still holding Alec down.

God help her, Jessie had no idea how her friend had survived last night, as Duncan's naked chest and bulging muscles were making *her* light-headed. "She's . . . um . . . napping. Let him up before he drowns, Duncan."

Alec came up swinging but had no target, as Duncan was already swimming toward Ian and Robbie at the other end of the pool, where both men were trying to coax Toby down the shallow stairs. Jessie sucked in a worried breath as she watched her pet paw at the water, his whole body quivering with nervous energy.

Good Lord, Toby really couldn't swim?

"Oh. My. God."

Jessie turned to see Merissa standing with her hands covering her mouth and her eyes widened in awe. "Kinda makes you understand Katy's problem of finding a date with these guys for chaperones, doesn't it? Come sit down, Mer, before all the testosterone in here knocks you over."

"Who are they all?" Merissa whispered, bumping into a nearby chair because she couldn't stop gawking. She eventually collapsed into the lounge chair beside Jessie with a sigh. "I've changed my mind; I *am* moving here. Or am I still upstairs in bed, dreaming?" She looked at the pool again and sat up. "Hey, what's Toby doing? He's supposed to be glued to your side today."

"He's on break. But . . . oh, Mer, I'm not certain he can swim."

Merissa snorted and stood up. "Of course he can swim; he's a *dog*. Tobias Pringle!" she shouted, pointing her finger as she marched down the side of the pool. "You jump in that water right now, you big wuss, before I throw you in."

Only she came to an abrupt halt when Duncan vaulted out of the pool in front of her. "You'll be the one getting thrown in if ye so much as try."

"Are you *threatening* me?" Merissa asked, taking a step back.

Duncan folded his arms over his massive wet chest and shrugged. "Call it what you want, so long as it gets my point across. Ye don't bully a reluctant animal into doing something it's not ready to do."

Jessie had to use both hands to hold her mug steady as she took another sip, because honest to God, dripping wet and nearly naked, Duncan MacKeage made all the warriors in the movie *Braveheart* look like wimps. Forget the nineteenth century; she'd just bought a house in *medieval Scotland.*

"Go sit down, Merissa," Duncan said quietly, "and leave Toby to Ian. The man has a way with animals."

Clearly nonplussed, Merissa turned without saying a word, walked back to Jessie, and sat down beside her. Jessie handed her the toddy, then had to lift it up to her mouth to get her to take a sip—which turned into a long guzzle.

"I've changed my mind again," Merissa said on a winded gasp, wiping her mouth with her sleeve. "I'm not moving here." She looked at Jessie. "And I'm dragging you back to Atlanta with me." She pointed at Duncan, who was now sitting on the edge of the pool with his feet dangling in the water, watching Ian quietly talking to Toby. "Did you see what just happened? The man actually threatened me."

Jessie gave a nervous laugh, her attention divided between Toby and Merissa. "Now you know what it's like being on the receiving end of your nurse's voice. Oh, come on, Mer," she said when Merissa glared at her. "If you can dish it out, then at least be woman enough to take it. You like alpha males, remember?"

"I like *civilized* alphas."

"I'm pretty sure that's an oxymoron," Jessie muttered.

Unable to stand it any longer, she carefully slid her feet to the floor, grabbed the closest arm of her wheelchair, and pulled it up beside the lounge chair. She didn't care if *all* the men threatened her; she couldn't just sit here and do nothing. Toby was always there for her when she needed him, and dammit, she could do the same for him.

"Hey, what are you doing?" Merissa asked in surprise, jumping out of her chair.

"I have to go help Ian with Toby," Jessie said, gritting her teeth against the pain as she pulled herself to her feet.

"Just call it off," Merissa snapped, helping Jessie turn to sit in the chair. "Tell Toby to come back to you."

Jessie started wheeling toward the end of the pool. "Toby's no more of a quitter than I am. He . . . he's just scared," she whispered, seeing the dog nervously creep down one more step, his dark eyes uncertain as he stood trembling in water up to his chest. "I want to help," she said, causing the three men in the pool to turn to her and for Duncan to stand up as she rolled past.

Ian hesitated half a pounding heartbeat before he gestured at Robbie to stay with Toby, then waded to the side of the pool and silently held up his hands to her.

"No," Merissa hissed, grabbing Jessie's shoulder when she bent over and slid off her shoes. "You can't swim. She can't swim," she repeated more firmly to Ian, only to turn to Duncan. "Make this stop," she growled.

"Ian has Jessie now," Duncan said quietly, wrapping his arms around Merissa and pulling her away. "Ye need to let her go, lass."

Despite sensing far more than just a fully-clothed dip in the pool was happening, Jessie gave her friend an apologetic smile and slipped out of the wheelchair and into Ian's strong arms.

"I've got you," he said when she gasped at the feel of the water soaking through her clothes. "Ye truly can't swim? Because of your injury or because ye never learned?"

"I-I've tried to learn," she said, clutching his shoulders in a death grip as he waded toward the center of the pool. "But I sink like a lead balloon."

Oh God, she really hadn't thought this through. What if her prosthesis popped out of her bra and the damn thing floated to the surface? Or worse, what if Ian felt the ugly, puckered scar on her lower back?

He suddenly stopped when she twisted to pull down the hem of her fleece, and sighed. "Are we going to go through this again, Jessie? Because Toby *is* going to react to your struggling this time, and I prefer this be about him right now, not you."

Nope, she hadn't thought this through at all. Jessie turned away from his steady gaze to focus on Toby instead of her own predicament. "What do you want me to do?"

"I'm going to have you stand here in the middle," he said, wading away from Toby instead of toward him. "The water will support your weight," he quickly added when she tightened her grip. He nodded to Alec, who came over and stood beside them as Ian dropped his arm from under her knees, holding her until she found her footing in the chest-deep water. "Alec will be right here to steady you. Then you call Toby to you, and I'll stay with him the whole way."

"You promise not to let him sink?"

"He can swim, Jessie, he just doesn't know it or has forgotten. But he's liable to splash at first, so don't panic, okay?" He stepped away when she nodded, hesitating until she released him to clutch Alec's arm instead, and gave her a reassuring smile. "Toby's not a lead balloon, lass."

"I'm calling his trainer first thing tomorrow," she

growled, deciding anger would serve her better right now, "and asking why in hell nobody taught him to swim."

"You don't know that he wasn't," Ian said, reaching Toby. "But it's possible he had a bad experience involving water at some point before you got him, and he's just taking his good old time getting over it."

Oh God, what if that was true? "Then we should stop, because it's better if he *doesn't* remember something horrible," she said, unable to keep her growing horror out of her voice. "The fear could *immobilize* him and he could drown."

Jessie heard a loud gasp followed by a muffled yelp and nearly lost her footing when she spun to see Duncan striding out of the solarium with Merissa in his arms. "Hey!" she shouted, only to have Alec stop her from trying to go after them.

"Jessie," Ian said firmly, drawing her attention again. "Do you want Toby to spend the rest of his life being afraid of water? Because it appears to me that he's determined to do this."

"But we could make it worse," she said as she tried to go to Toby, only to have Alec stop her again. "He could start having nightmares," she rushed on. "Or a flashback or something, and be traumatized all over again. Please, Ian," she whispered, hugging herself as she dropped her gaze from his silent scrutiny.

"Do you trust me, Jessie?"

She snapped her head up. "I don't even know you."

His eyes turned unreadable, and he gave a barely perceptible nod. "That's true. Then do you at least know Toby well enough to trust him?"

"With my life." She dropped her hands below the water to ball them into fists. "The same way *he* trusts *me* to protect him."

"Can't you see he's wanting to do this, Jessie? He wouldn't have left your side if he didn't, or allowed us to take off his gear. But animals loathe feeling helpless, and to stop Toby from conquering this particular demon will only give it more power over him." He gestured at the trembling dog. "He's just spent the last ten minutes slowly winning the battle; don't make him leave in defeat."

Jessie rubbed her palms up and down her thighs, torn between wanting to throw a hissy fit to make this stop and trusting that Ian was right. She finally sucked in a shuddering breath. "O-okay," she said, watching Ian turn away before she could read his expression. Jessie took another deep breath and held out her trembling hands. "C-come on, Tobes. Swim to me, brave boy."

Toby pawed at the water, yipping frantically as he worked himself into a terrible frenzy, until he suddenly gave a sharp bark and lunged off the step toward her. Jessie in turn lunged toward him as he immediately sank beneath the surface, and she would have gone under herself if Alec hadn't caught her.

"Give it a second, lass," he said next to her ear. "Ian's got him."

Toby resurfaced, although she couldn't tell if it was under his own power or because Ian's hand under his chest was lifting him up. Toby thrashed violently, wheezing and hacking as he eventually started moving forward, his big brown eyes locked on Jessie the entire time.

And so began their water dance, with Alec continuing to move her just out of Toby's reach and Toby slowly doing more swimming than thrashing, until Alec led Jessie to the steps when Ian nodded and she sat down. Finally able to reach his prize, Toby scrambled onto the step beside her, his chest heaving with ragged pants as he licked her chin.

Jessie threw her arms around his trembling body and buried her face in his wet fur. "Oh, Toby, you're so brave. You swam!" She gave him a fierce squeeze. "I'm sorry you had to go through that," she whispered. "But you know I—"

"Ye need to let him breathe," Ian said with a laugh, pulling her arms away as he sat down on the step beside her. "And look, the poor beast is blushing to have ye coddling him like a baby in front of us. Why don't you let him practice his new sport?"

Jessie threw herself at Ian. "I was so scared!"

"Hey now, don't cry," he crooned, lifting her onto his lap. He brushed his thumb across her cheek and turned so she could watch Toby paddling toward Robbie, who was swimming backward while softly calling to him. "See? The big man just needed a good reason to remember he can swim." Ian tapped the tip of her nose with his finger. "And you gave him one."

"But I wouldn't have." She dropped her blurry gaze to her hand clutching his arm. "If you hadn't pushed me, I would have taken him upstairs and kept him from ever going near water again." She looked up, blinking away her tears. "H-he's all I've got. Toby means *everything* to me."

Ian pressed her head to his shoulder. "And you mean everything to him," he said, his lips brushing her hair. "Which is why he was so determined to do this for you."

"I am such a coward."

"Nay, Jessie. You're the bravest woman I know."

Suddenly aware that she was sitting on the lap of a nearly naked man—the same one who had kissed her quite thoroughly last night—Jessie felt her cheeks flush with heat. "I have to go save Merissa," she said, trying to get up.

Ian folded his arms around her with a chuckle. "Are you sure it's not Duncan who needs saving?" He sobered.

"She's having a hard time letting you go, Jessie, which makes me wonder if *Merissa* isn't the one you need to prove your independence to."

Jessie blew out a sigh. "It's going to take an act of Congress to get her on the plane Thursday." She tilted her head back to look at him. "We've been like sisters ever since she barged into my hospital room and turned her nurse's voice on me four years ago." She looked out at the pool, watching Toby paddling after Alec and Robbie, and sighed again. "I feel like I'm abandoning her."

"Seeing the two of you together, I'm surprised she's not moving here with you."

Jessie wiped the last of her tears off her cheeks. "Merissa is expecting me to come to my senses any day now." She snorted. "So are my parents and brother-in-law and my old boss. And to be honest, I think I'm more surprised than any of them that I'm actually here." She gestured at the wall of windows facing Pine Lake. "I still can't explain it, but from the moment I found that TarStone Mountain brochure four months ago, all I could think about was living in such a magical, powerful place."

Jessie felt Ian go utterly still—as if he momentarily stopped breathing—before he softly chuckled. "You'll definitely feel its power the first time a blizzard dumps two feet of snow in your driveway. Can Duncan and I take you and Merissa to dinner tonight? We can dine right here at the hotel," he quietly added. "I'm afraid it'll be a quick evening, though, as we're headed out quite early tomorrow morning and will be gone all week."

"I gather you're all spending the week running through the woods with guns?"

He arched a brow. "Are you a vegetarian, Miss Pringle?"

Jessie turned to face the pool to hide her smile. "I'm not opposed to eating the Easter Bunny."

"How about Bambi?" he whispered, giving her a gentle squeeze. "If I bring you a nice venison roast, would you invite me to your new home for dinner?"

"Only if you do the cooking."

"Ye don't cook?" he asked—although Jessie couldn't tell from his tone if he was surprised or horrified.

She laughed. "I'm afraid if you were so hell-bent on my buying your cousin's house because you thought I was going to coo—um, Ian," she said, trying to slide off his lap. But when he only tightened his grip, she nodded toward the lobby door. "Your father and two other men just walked in, and they don't look all that happy to see a dog and a fully dressed woman in the pool."

He chuckled. "You're about to meet the founding fathers of TarStone Mountain Ski Resort. The one on the left of Dad is his older brother, Greylen—Megan's father. And on his right is their cousin Callum, who is Duncan's father. Smile, lass; it'll confound them."

Oh yeah, there definitely was something in the drinking water, making Jessie wonder if she wouldn't be an inch taller herself by this time next year. She plastered a bright smile on her face as the three older men stopped at the edge of the pool and Morgan MacKeage folded his arms over his chest and frowned—although she could see he was frowning at Ian, not her.

"Was there an accident?" he asked, glancing at Robbie and Alec as they swam toward the steps, Toby paddling after them in hot pursuit.

Could dogs smile? Because she'd swear she'd never before seen a look of such joy on Toby's face. "Actually,"

Jessie said, drawing Morgan's frown to *her*, although it did soften slightly, "I felt so good after drinking your wonderful toddy that I got out of the lounge chair *all by myself* to go shoo those greedy jays away from the feeder. But I guess I wasn't as steady as I thought and I fell in the pool, and Toby jumped in to save me," she said, ignoring Morgan's eyes narrowing. "But it seems Toby had forgotten how to swim, and I *can't* swim because I sink like a lead balloon. Merissa was so distraught, Duncan had to carry her out of the solarium while Alec and Robbie and your son saved me and Toby from drowning." She gave the now-incredulous man her best confounding smile. "I will say this for you, though: Scotch is definitely good for what ails me."

And there it was: the barest hint of a grin.

Ian slid a hand under her knees and stood up, then stepped out of the pool before she even finished gasping. "Call your pet, Jessie," he said, his voice sounding gruff as he headed for the lobby. "Alec, gather Jessie's things and bring them to her room."

Oh God, she couldn't tell if he was appalled that she'd just lied to his father or trying to hold in his laughter. "What are you doing?" she hissed. "You can't go traipsing through the hotel half-naked. And we're both dripping water all over the place."

He suddenly switched directions, only instead of heading for her wheelchair, the infuriating man strode right up to the three elder MacKeages. "Grey, Callum," he said with a nod. "I'd like you to meet Jessie Pringle, formerly of Atlanta but now of Pine Creek. She bought Megan and Jack's house this morning."

"Miss Pringle," Grey said, his sharp green eyes shining with amusement as he gave a polite nod. "Ye do realize that we measure snow in feet up here, don't you?"

"Yes, I've been told that. You have a very lovely resort, Mr. MacKeage, and whoever designed your brochure certainly knew what he or she was doing."

"That would be my youngest daughter, Winter," Grey said, his smile turning proud. "She's the artist in the family."

"Ye might want to stop by her gallery in town when you begin to decorate your new home," Callum said, his older but equally sharp green eyes crinkling with his smile. He also gave her a nod. "If there's anything we can do to make your stay with us more pleasant, please let us know. Besides Scotch toddies, that is, as we'd hate to have to keep fishing you out of the pool."

Wow, brain and brawn and *charm.*

"Yes, thank you. I will definitely stay away from toddies. Well," she said, pushing on Ian's shoulder to get down, "if you gentlemen will excuse me, I think it's time I went upstairs and changed." She looked at Ian when he still refused to cooperate. "You can set me in my wheelchair now." She patted his shoulder, smiling apologetically. "As I'd hate to see you throw out your back because I'm so heavy."

Alec, who had just set her purse and catalogs and Toby's gear in the wheelchair, suddenly turned away in a fit of coughing—which seemed to be contagious, as Grey and Callum also started clearing their throats behind their hands. Morgan MacKeage, however, just looked incredulous again.

And Ian? Well, he sighed hard enough to move her hair, and headed toward the lobby with her still in his arms. "Careful, *gràineag,* as I'd hate to see ye get pricked on one of your own quills."

Chapter Seven

"I COULD HAVE KISSED MEGAN AT LUNCH YESTERDAY when she suggested I rent the house from her and Jack until we sign the papers," Jessie said, wrestling a large piece of firewood down through the top of the woodstove. She closed the lid and adjusted the back damper like Megan had shown her, then brushed bits of bark off her pants. "Now you can help me start decorating before you have to leave."

"Lucky me," Merissa said, rolling her eyes as she slipped on her jacket. "Do you remember which store we bought that orange ribbon from? I'll stop and tie a piece of it to a tree limb on my way to Greenville, so the movers will know where to turn this afternoon. Assuming this two-car town even shows up on their GPS," she muttered, searching through one of the bags on the counter. "I hope you know I nearly choked on my salad when Grace Mac-Keage told us the nearest real grocery store is almost twenty miles away. And then she said you have to drive *eighty* miles to find an actual shopping mall." Merissa stopped hunting and looked up. "Remind me again why you want to live here? Or didn't you hear Grace also tell me the closest Starbucks is in *Bangor*?"

"We saw a nice bakery right here in town this morning," Jessie said through a tight smile, getting tired of Merissa's criticism. "And driving twenty miles in the wilderness isn't the same as it is in Atlanta because there's hardly any traffic. My moving here is working out perfectly, including my finding a nice house on the lake." Jessie flapped her arms like a bird as she strode over to her frowning friend. "And look how quickly my inflammation went down. I swear my back hasn't felt this good in years. This is a healing place for me, Mer," she said softly, touching Merissa's arm. "Can't you see how happy I've been since we got here?"

"What I see is a woman who kissed the first guy she met, and suddenly she's thinking with her ovaries instead of her brain."

"This isn't about Ian." Jessie pointed at the windows. "It's about Pine Creek, and the lake and mountains and *all* the people who live here. It's about Katy and Megan and the moms. When do you remember ever being in the company of such genuine women?" Jessie took hold of Merissa's shoulders when she started to protest. "Don't you dare tell me you didn't enjoy having lunch with them yesterday. It might have taken you a while to warm up to everyone, but by dessert *you* looked genuinely happy, too."

Merissa shrugged free and buried her face in the bag from Dolan's Outfitter Store. "The only reason they invited us to join them was to recruit you to help with their camp program next week." She lifted narrowed eyes at Jessie. "And what in hell went on between you and *Doc* Libby out in the lobby? Don't think I didn't see your expression when she shook your hand. You turned pale and then your face got bright red."

"I can't say what happened, but I swear I thought I was having one of my mother's hot flashes," Jessie said with a laugh. She sobered, touching Merissa's arm again. "But when we all walked into the restaurant afterward, I realized my back wasn't killing me anymore. And you know what? It hasn't hurt since."

Merissa actually stepped away. "Are you saying you think Libby MacBain *healed* your back?"

"No, I know that's impossible. I'm only saying the inflammation is gone."

"Well, of course it is," Merissa snapped. "Along with pain meds, you've been taking a powerful anti-inflammatory for the last three days. Where in hell's that ribbon?" she growled, snatching the feed store bag off the counter.

Jessie snatched it away from her. "Never mind the ribbon. Toby and I will go tie it on the branch. I feel like some exercise, anyway."

"It's almost a mile to the main road."

"Which I intend to walk every day to get my mail. In fact, I'll probably walk the entire two miles to town when the weather's permitting." She smiled at Merissa's glower. "That way, instead of just physical therapy, I'll be getting emotional therapy as well." Jessie nudged Merissa toward the door. "Now go find that grocery store they told us about, and don't come back until you have enough food to fill all my new cupboards. You remember the PIN for my debit card?"

Merissa stopped at the door to glower at her again. "If I get arrested for using a card that's not mine, you'd better come bail me out. Greenville might be bigger than Pine

Creek, but they probably still put thieves in stocks in the town square." Her glower suddenly turned sinister. "I hope you have plenty of money in your checking, because I intend to buy one of everything." She turned with a snort and headed onto the porch. "What am I saying? That probably won't even fill one cart."

Jessie went to the door to watch her friend get in her car and back out of the driveway. Waiting until the Volvo disappeared down the camp road, she dumped the contents of the bag on the counter with a heavy sigh, afraid her decision to slip into Ian's arms in the pool two days ago not only had hurt Merissa's feelings, but irrevocably changed their friendship.

Could Ian have been right when he'd walked her to her room after dinner that evening—while Merissa and Duncan had gone for a walk in the moonlight—when he'd once again suggested that Mer was having a hard time letting her go? How had he put it—that nobody wants to get off a comfortable couch? And from what he and Duncan could see, Jessie was Merissa's couch. Both men, apparently, believed Mer found it easier to focus on Jessie's life instead of on her own, because . . . well, only Merissa knew what she was hiding from.

Jessie suspected it had everything to do with the guy in Chicago who'd broken Merissa's heart six years ago, which had sent her running to Atlanta to lick her wounds. "What a mess," she muttered, pushing aside the cakes of suet she'd bought for the birds and picking up the roll of orange tape. She then grabbed her new house keys and cell phone and walked to the row of pegs by the door to shove everything in her coat pocket. It was easy for Ian to say it was time to kick Merissa off her comfortable couch, but had *he* ever had his heart broken?

Jessie went to the woodstove and stared through the glass doors at the flames. "Still, six years is a long time to lick your wounds, Mer. Four years was about all I could take before I got tired of feeling like a victim."

So, was she a terrible friend for abandoning Merissa or actually doing her a favor? Jessie sighed again, deciding only time would tell. "Okay, the big damper is closed," she said, checking its position before eyeing the small knob on the opposite side. "And the little one is . . ." She pushed the small damper toward the back and stepped away, watching until the flames settled down. Wonderful, she thought as she headed to the pegs and grabbed her long wool coat. Despite Megan's assuring her that the stove was designed to function unattended, Jessie was afraid she was going to burn down her new home before she officially owned it.

"Come on, Tobes. Let's go explore our new neighborhood."

Toby jumped up from his bed beside the hearth and trotted over to her. Jessie clipped on his leash and gave him a kiss on his big head. "I guess I'm not the only one benefiting from moving here, am I? Don't think I haven't noticed your manly swagger ever since your swim in the pool," she said as she pulled on her gloves. "You're not only feeling proud of yourself for conquering your demon, as Ian put it, but I can see how much you like having some male buddies." She opened the door with a laugh. "Poor Tobes. Are you tired of dealing with nothing but estrogen for the last three years?"

Jessie gave one last glance at the woodstove to make sure it was behaving properly—not that she was certain what a properly behaving woodstove should look like—then grabbed her cane and stepped outside. She stopped on the porch and took a deep breath. "Take a whiff, Tobes.

That's what real air is supposed to smell like, with just a hint of wood smoke and the aroma of pine."

She walked down the steps and out the brick pathway—a little sad to notice Walker's wagon was gone—and started up the road. "What do you think, Tobias? Would you like for us to have a little boy of our own?" she asked, placing a hand over her belly. "The doctors said it's not impossible for me to get pregnant again, just highly unlikely." She dropped her hand with a snort. "But considering all the testosterone running loose around here, there's a good chance I could get pregnant without even taking off my clothes." Jessie winced and picked up her pace. Maybe Merissa was right and Ian's kisses had started her thinking with her ovaries. Because the sad truth was, even though he'd only been gone two days, she already missed him.

She smiled, remembering his second kiss two nights ago after dinner. "Poor Ian," she said with a laugh. "Did you see the look on his face, Tobes, when he realized he'd have to get down on his knees if he wanted to kiss me good night? And then his shirt got caught on the brake of my wheelchair and he popped a button."

Meeting his mother yesterday certainly explained Ian's matter-of-fact attitude toward people with . . . imperfections. Probably because other than having parents who ran a camp for disabled children, the man had grown up seeing imperfection up close and personal. When Sadie MacKeage had introduced herself to Jessie yesterday, the hand she'd extended had been badly scarred, as if from a fire. And if Jessie wasn't mistaken, the tall, blue-eyed blonde had been wearing some sort of body sock under her jersey, as she'd caught a glimpse of it when Sadie had bent over to pat Toby.

No wonder Ian acted so casual about her condition;

his mom was just as scarred as she was, possibly even more. And that gave Jessie hope that if Sadie MacKeage had found thirty-odd years of happily-ever-after in the arms of a handsome man, then there wasn't any reason she couldn't, too.

Oh yeah, she was going to help market the children's camp all right, if only to spend more time with Ian's mom on the chance the woman's quiet confidence and strong sense of purpose was contagious. She was not, however, helping Megan and Katy take the young girls skinny-dipping, no matter how fun they'd made it sound at lunch yesterday. But she had volunteered to help with the less risqué activities.

"We've been in town four days," she told Toby, "and I've danced, been kissed twice, and become an honorary member of a clan of amazing women. And you, you big lug, conquered your fear of water and found some new buddies." She laughed softly. "And everyone thought I was crazy for wanting to move here."

Jessie continued down the narrow peninsula, breathing in the crisp December air as she marveled at the beauty around her. She passed several seasonal camps tucked in amongst the towering trees on her left, with Pine Lake on her right, which, according to the map the Stones had thoughtfully left hanging in the downstairs hallway, stretched nearly forty miles north toward Canada. Toby suddenly stopped when they rounded a curve just as Jessie also spotted the man sitting on a stool by the side of the road, in front of what looked like one of TarStone Mountain's giant trail groomers.

The man saw her and Toby and stood up. "Morn'n," he called out, giving a wave as he strode toward them. "You out enjoying this fine day by walking to town?"

Jessie shortened her hold on Toby's leash, although the dog seemed more curious than defensive. "We're only going to the main road," she said, finding the man's smile endearing. At least, she thought he was smiling behind that scruffy white beard.

He stopped two paces away and wiggled his fur-lined hat back and forth on his head, which only served to further mess up the tangle of wild white hair all but hiding his sparkling green eyes. "Well, you keep on your toes then, missy. A car just went screaming out of here a short while ago, kicking up a terrible dust that covered all my wares," he said with a scowl as he dropped into a squat. "What's the big fella's name?" he asked, extending his hand.

"It's Toby," Jessie said, loosening her hold on the leash.

"Hey there, Toby," he murmured, waggling his fingers. "Come on and give me a taste, then, so you can decide for yourself that I'm harmless."

Toby stepped toward him and did indeed lick the man's fingers, and was quickly rewarded with a scratch under the chin.

The man stood up and extended the same hand to Jessie. "Name's Roger, but I'll answer to most anything said with respect." His beard spread into a smile again as his large, calloused fingers wrapped around hers. "You be the lady who bought missy Megan's house?" But then he scowled before she could answer. "I don't know what that girl was think'n marrying that pagan Canadian Jack Stone." He finally let go of her hand to resettle his hat again. "I swear that quiet bastard is gonna be the death of me. What's your name, anyway?"

Good Lord, who was this colorful character? "Jessie Pringle."

His bushy eyebrows rose into his hat. "What in tarnation

kind of name is *Pringle*? You from one of them foreign countries?"

Jessie bit back a smile. "No, I'm originally from New York City, but most recently from Atlanta. *Georgia*," she clarified when he frowned. "And my great-great-grandfather chose the name Pringle when he immigrated to America so no one would know where he was from." Jessie leaned forward and lowered her voice. "But rumor has it, he was from Russia."

Up went those brows into his hat again. "You consider fun'n an old man to be entertaining, missy?"

Jessie glanced right and left and then behind her before looking back at him. "What old man? I don't see anyone here but you and me and Toby."

Roger blinked at her, then suddenly gave a bark of laughter. "I've decided I like you, Jessie Pringle. So come on, then," he said, pivoting on his heel and starting off down the road. "I do believe I got some stuff you need."

"What kind of stuff?" she asked, following as Toby fell into step beside him.

Roger stopped again, his vaguely familiar eyes locking on hers as he motioned at her hand. "How come you got that cane? I swear ye don't look a day over forty."

"I'm *twenty-eight*," she blurted out, uncertain if he was teasing or not. "And I carry a cane because my legs are . . . they get weak sometimes."

He snorted and started walking again. "I still say it makes ye look old." He rubbed his beard, eyeing her spec-ulatively. "Now, if'n you were to carry a proper stick instead of that old-lady cane, nobody around here would pay it no mind." His beard parted with his smile, and he nodded. "Lucky for you, I got just the walking stick you be needing." He went back to eyeing her again. "And what's up with your scarf, anyway? Is that what all them ladies is wearing down in *Georgia*? 'Cause I gotta tell ye, that flimsy thing ain't gonna keep you warm once the weather finally turns." He stopped beside his folding canvas stool and faced her. "What you're needing is a fine tartan scarf." He looked down at Toby. "And maybe a matching scarf for the big fella, too, if'n he's also most recently from Georgia."

"Thank you, but I'm good. And Ian said Toby will grow a winter coat soon."

Roger whipped his head around to look up the road, and then turned his narrowed eyes on Jessie. "You talking about Ian MacKeage?" He scowled when she nodded. "You belong to that big bastard, do you?"

"No, I don't *belong* to him," Jessie said with a laugh. "I just met him four days ago. You . . . um . . . you don't like Ian?"

Roger apparently had to think about that as he gave his hat another wiggle, which ended with his eyebrows scrunched into a frown. "Well now, I can't say I outright *dislike* the guy," he said slowly, as if picking his words. "But he ain't exactly one of my favorite people, either." He pointed a short distance up the road, at what appeared to be a narrow driveway hidden in a stand of young evergreens. "It was right nice around here before that big bastard came back from his war and bought himself that rickety old camp. Now I can't hock my wares here no more." He walked to the groomer. "Only reason I dared set up here today is because he's hunting up on the mountain with his brother and cousins."

Jessie finally noticed all the . . . wares displayed on top of the groomer's rubber track: a dented old teakettle, a large cast-iron pot, several neatly folded plaid scarves, a stack of positively ancient books, an overflowing basket of mittens, at least a dozen pie tins, and several tall sticks. She also noticed the faded emblem on the door that said the machine was indeed from the TarStone Mountain Ski Resort—except that its paint looked more orange than red under a good deal of dust, one of the lamps on the roof was dangling by a wire, and there was a small crack in the windshield.

She looked at Roger. "Why isn't Ian one of your favorite people?" she asked, although she suspected the old goat placed most everyone in that category.

"No particular reason," he said with a shrug. "Other than all them MacKeages are sneaky bastards, just like them MacBains and Gregors and that pagan Jack Stone." He suddenly grinned. "But I suppose being sneaky is a fine quality to have, if'n a fella was needing one of them to guard his back." He turned to face the groomer again, folding his arms on his chest to rest his chin on a fist, and began studying the walking sticks. "You ever find yourself in trouble," he said somewhat absently, "you send yourself running straight to one of them highlanders. What exactly is the problem with your legs, anyway?" He looked over his shoulder when she didn't immediately answer, and frowned. "You born that way or did you have an accident? It's important you tell me," he said when she still didn't answer, "so I can decide which one of these fine sticks I'm needing to give you."

"I'm sorry, Roger, but I didn't bring my wallet with me."

"I'm willing to barter." He turned to fully face her. "In fact, I'll trade you one of my magical sticks for that puny cane of yours, and . . ." He eyed her up and down, then pointed at her neck. "And that flimsy scarf, I suppose. I ought to be able to find some crippled old lady willing to bake me a pie in exchange for them. So, were you born carrying that cane or not? I need to know to match you up proper."

Uncertain how to turn him down without hurting his feelings, Jessie stepped up beside Roger to also study the sticks leaning against the groomer, only to discover they were really quite lovely. Actually, they were works of art. Varying slightly in length but all nearly as tall as she was, they'd been peeled clean of their bark and sanded smooth to a natural patina. They each had unique characteristics; one was quite stout and riddled with burls that made it appear almost grotesque, several had only a few smaller burls, and two had dark vertical indents that looked like elongated, sunken eyes.

Jessie hadn't given much thought to the cane she'd been using ever since her new physical therapist had handed it to her, asking Jessie if she intended to ride her butt around in a wheelchair for the rest of her life or if she wanted to start using the legs God had given her instead. "I . . . My back was injured four years ago," she finally admitted when she noticed Roger glaring at her again.

"Well then, which one of these catches your fancy?" he asked, plucking two of the more delicate sticks away from the track and holding them up in front of her.

"I think I prefer one of those," she said, pointing to the sunken-eyed sticks. "I like how they're not perfectly straight and the dark brown eyes show off the rich yellow of the wood."

"Forget those," he muttered, moving to block her view. "Diamond willow ain't near potent enough." He thrust the two sticks he was holding toward her again as he nodded over his shoulder. "And don't even think about asking for that big gnarly one; its magic is way too powerful for a woman to handle."

Jessie had started to reach for one of the sticks he was holding but pulled her hand back and arched a brow. "Too powerful for a *woman*?"

He dropped his arms to rest the ends of the sticks on the ground and sighed. "It be common knowledge that women are physically weaker, missy *gràineag*, so don't you go raising your quills at me none."

Jessie caught her breath at the realization that she'd completely forgotten to ask Ian's mother what that meant yesterday. "What's a *gra-neeg*?"

Roger went back to frowning at her. "Everyone knows it be Gaelic for *hedgehog*. And it's spelled *g-r-à-i-n-e-a-g*, and ye got to *spit* the *g* at the end to sound like a true highlander." His beard parted with his smile when she glowered at him. "Prickly little hedgehogs are cute little beasties, you know. And if'n ye treat them right, they get all cuddly on ye."

Ian had called her a *hedgehog*?

Roger held up the sticks again. "Ye gonna choose before the sun sets, missy, or you gonna make me risk my neck coming back here?"

"What do you mean about the sticks having different . . . magical powers?"

He rested the tips of them on the ground again, this time sighing so hard, it was a wonder his chest didn't implode. "It be common knowledge that trees gather the energy of the sun and moon and stars, and hold on to it until it be needed," he explained impatiently. "And some woods are better than others at transferring that energy to us."

"Then I want that one," she said, pointing past his shoulder. "The big gnarly one that you said has the most energy."

"Well, ye ain't getting it," he snapped. "I'll not be responsible for you blowing yourself and anyone nearby to kingdom come." He thrust the stick in his left hand at her. "You take this one. And when you get used to its magic, maybe then I'll consider giving you a more powerful one." He arched one of his bushy brows. "Or ain't you ever heard of something called baby steps?"

Okay, this conversation was getting weird. How could Roger possibly know her personal litany of taking baby steps? And of all things to call her, why *gràineag*? And magical walking sticks? Really?

Jessie wondered if there wasn't a retirement home nearby that he'd wandered away from, or maybe even a mental hospital. "Do you live around here, Roger?" she asked as she finally took the stick from him—only to gasp in surprise when a spark of static electricity shot through her glove and up her arm. "What was that?" she whispered, carefully closing her fist around it again only to feel a gentle hum.

"That was the magic aligning itself with you; energy that's traveled clear across the universe to take up residence in the wood." He tapped the stick while staring directly into her eyes, his own deep green gaze appearing old and wise and as solid as the mountains surrounding them. "Powerful, ageless energy destined for you alone, Jessie, that's patiently been waiting for you to come here and finally claim it."

Clutching the still-humming stick to her chest, Jessie looked down to see Toby sitting at her feet with his nose pressed up against the smooth wood, and she wondered if this wasn't the same powerful magic she'd felt looking at that brochure.

"Okay, that's done," Roger said, setting the other stick on the track before turning back to her. He thrust out his empty hand and waggled his fingers. "Our deal was your old-lady cane and that scarf in trade, so give them up, missy," he said, the soft-spoken man disappearing and the colorful, bartering character effectively snapping Jessie out of her fanciful daze.

Still holding her new walking stick to her chest, Jessie dropped Toby's leash to unknot her scarf and slipped it off, then handed both it and her cane to Roger.

"Okay, then," he said, turning to set them on the groomer's track. "So tell me, how much are you liking that MacKeage fella, anyway?" he asked, rummaging through the pile of scarves. He looked over his shoulder when she didn't answer, and frowned. "I'm only asking so I'll know which one of these I'm needing to give you."

"Thank you, but I'm good," she said, bending to grab Toby's leash. She slowly started backing away, deciding she'd better leave before Roger finished unloading all of his wares on her. "I just ordered a fleece scarf from the L.L.Bean catalog. It should be delivered in a few days."

Roger turned to her, his hands on his hips and a scarf dangling from one of his fists. "What color is it?"

"White. And I also ordered a pair of matching mittens. Really, the walking stick is more than enough." She gave him a lopsided smile. "And besides, all I've got left to barter are my house keys, a roll of orange tape, and my cell phone."

That perked him up. "Ye got one of them newfangled phones that'll let a person go on the Internet from almost anywhere? One with a screen that works off the heat of your finger, that ain't got no buttons?"

Good Lord, the man appeared positively eager. "I'm not trading you my phone," she said with a laugh. She started backing up again, wondering if she should continue to the main road or just go home so he couldn't ambush her again on her way back. "But I'll bring my wallet with me next time and *buy* a scarf from you."

"I don't got no need for money. But I sure could use me a cell phone."

She stopped retreating. "But you do need money to buy service for the phone."

He smiled. "Not if a fella knows how to harness what can't be seen, he don't." He waved at the sky. "The air's full of all sorts of energy, so I can just borrow some of it from any one of them blasted towers they've put up all over the place."

"But that's stealing. You have to *pay* for the energy coming from those towers."

He folded his arms over his chest and rested his weight back on his hips. "My my, ain't we little miss Goody Two-shoes all of a sudden."

Okay, now this crazy conversation was deteriorating to name-calling. Jessie wasn't actually afraid of Roger, considering Toby was lying at her feet calmly nosing her new walking stick, but really, little miss Goody Two-shoes? "Do you live around here?" she asked again.

"More or less," he said with a nod. "Why?"

"Well, I was just wondering why you didn't set up your wares on the main road where there's actual traffic?"

"Because then that sneaky bastard Jack Stone might catch me."

Jessie tugged on Toby's leash to get him to stand up, and started walking backward again when Roger started toward her—only to stop when she saw a look of desperation wash over his face.

"If'n you don't want any of my scarves," he said softly, using the one he was holding to weakly gesture behind him, "then maybe I could interest you in a sturdy pot. It's perfectly seasoned, and has cooked up many a fine venison roast and rabbit stew."

Oh God, the poor man was lonely. "How about if I come back tomorrow, and I'll bring something to barter with for the pot? And I'll also bring my friend, and we'll check out all of your wares and see what else I might need. Are you going to be set up here all week, Roger?" She smiled warmly. "I'm certain Merissa would like one of your scarves, and she's really into antique books."

His shoulders slumped, and he shook his head. "It's gonna be storm'n something fierce tomorrow," he muttered, walking back to the groomer. But then he suddenly changed direction and strode directly up to her and held out the scarf. "I don't want you catching your death 'cause I took your old scarf before your new one gets delivered, so you take this one for now and we'll settle up later."

Jessie sighed in defeat and took it from him, then trans-ferred Toby's leash to her hand holding her stick so she could drape the scarf around her neck. "It really is beauti-ful. In fact, I like it a lot more than the one I ordered."

His smile returned and he nodded. "That's because them red and green and lavender stripes on that field of gray speaks to your woman's heart." His eyes took on a twinkle. "Those particular colors carry a mighty powerful promise, Jessie. Now," he suddenly barked out, rubbing his hands together. "About that seasoned pot."

Jessie stifled a groan. "Really, Roger," she said through a forced smile—that he didn't even see because he was already heading back to the groomer. Jessie followed, determined to get her point across. "There's no way I can carry that large pot home today, but I promise I'll come back tomorrow in my car."

"No need," he said, opening the door on the groomer.

He reached inside and began wrestling something out from behind the seat. "I got just the thing for you," he continued with a strained grunt.

Jessie had to scramble out of the way when Roger staggered backward under the weight of a wooden wagon nearly twice as large as Walker's. "Roger, be careful!" she yelped, grabbing his arm to steady him.

He set the wagon on the ground between them and straightened with a scowl. "I might be old, but until the day I'm push'n up posies, I don't need coddling by no weak-kneed woman." He grabbed the cast-iron pot and plopped it in the wagon. "There, now you can take it home, no problem."

Jessie started backing up again, only she didn't get two steps away because Toby seemed more interested in sniffing the pot than following her. "Toby, come," she said, giving his leash a tug.

"See?" Roger said. "The big fella also wants you to have the pot."

How in hell had she gotten herself into this predicament? And more importantly, how was she going to get herself out of it? "But I told you, I have nothing left to barter."

"Ye still got one of them cell phones, don't you?"

Jessie slapped a hand over her pocket. "I'm not giving you my phone!"

"Why in tarnation not?" He folded his arms over his barrel chest again. "If'n you did, it would stop all those pesky calls you keep getting from everyone asking if you've come to your senses yet."

Jessie went perfectly still. "How would you know people have been calling and asking me that?"

"Well now, maybe 'cause you're a single woman

hell-bent on moving here all by yourself? What else they gonna ask you?"

"You don't know that I moved here by myself," she said, growing truly alarmed.

"I told you I ain't push'n up posies yet, but now you're thinking my ears don't work, either? Everyone within fifty miles of here knows that a big-time advertising executive named Jessie Pringle, recently of *Georgia*, just bought Megan and Jack Stone's house."

Jessie released her breath, finally realizing why Roger had set up his little display on her road. The cunning old goat had even risked being caught by Jack Stone, Pine Creek's chief of police, in order to barter his wares to the new girl in town. She gave him a warm smile, nodding in acquiescence. "Guilty as charged. So tell me, what's the word going around town as to *why* I've moved here?"

Roger folded his arms again and rubbed his beard, his answering smile somewhat smug. "Well now, I do believe something powerfully strong was pushing ye out of Georgia." He arched a brow. "Or should I say something even stronger was *pulling* you north."

Jessie went back to being alarmed.

"It's not going to work, you know," he continued quietly, dropping his arms to his sides. "Not as long as you persist in believing this is something you can do alone. It's not enough to move here merely hoping all this powerful energy will help you remember what happened that night, Jessie; any more than hiding up on his mountain is helping Ian forget. Healing one's self is nearly impossible—and far less rewarding—compared to the magic that's created when two souls combine their strengths and heal together."

Jessie stood perfectly still, utterly speechless. There was no way this crazy old man could know what she'd hoped to accomplish by coming here, much less that she'd spent the last four years trying to remember what had happened that night. And what did he mean that Ian was hiding, trying to forget? Forget what?

"You answered your heart's call to rejoin the stream of life, Jessie," Roger continued softly. "But for you to fully reincarnate, I'm afraid you're going to have to allow yourself to be vulnerable again." His eyes shone with tender warmth. "Ye have my word, lass, that if you find the courage to grasp the hand being offered, you'll not only heal yourself, but also the one extending that hand—which you will then have the privilege to still be holding long into old age."

Fighting the fear threatening to immobilize her, Jessie somehow managed to respond to Toby's sudden insistence that she move and allowed him to lead her down the road toward home.

"I would also warn you to be mindful whose hand it is that you grasp, Jessie," Roger quietly continued behind her, "and that you carefully weigh what both men are offering, because neither of them is quite what he seems."

Jessie silently walked toward the curve in the road, not daring to look back.

"I'm sorry to have scared you, lass," Roger called after her. "Because my honest intention today was only to warn you of the danger you're still facing, and of the decision you must make as to where you place your trust."

Jessie tried throwing the walking stick in the ditch the moment she rounded the curve, but her fingers were frozen so tight she couldn't let go. So she picked up her pace now that she was out of Roger's sight, and concentrated only on setting one foot in front of the other on the frozen dirt road.

"You'll be okay if you keep listening to your heart,

Jessie," he continued, his voice growing distant, "and you have the courage to embrace the magic."

Jessie didn't know who was more surprised, she or Toby, when she suddenly broke into a run. And almost as if her feet had sprouted wings, they covered the distance home in what seemed like only a heartbeat. She dropped Toby's leash and pulled off her glove to fish her keys out of her pocket as she rushed onto her porch. It took her several tries to fit the key in the lock because she was shaking so badly, and after a frantic glance up the road, Jessie finally stepped into the house behind Toby, slammed the door shut, and threw the dead bolt.

She slowly backed to the center of the room, her chest heaving painfully as she unbuttoned her coat, only to clip herself in the chin with the walking stick. Taking a calming breath, she forced her fingers to relax enough to drop it and then flinched when the stick clattered to the hardwood floor, the sound echoing through the empty house like gunshots.

She shed her remaining glove and coat and the scarf Roger had given her as she continued backing toward the woodstove. "Toby, come," she whispered, collapsing onto his bed beside the hearth. Sitting with her back pressed against the wall, Jessie held out trembling hands to Toby, who was standing in the center of the room straddling the walking stick, staring at her quizzically. "C-come, Toby. Safe place."

He picked up the stick in his mouth, then padded over and dropped it in her lap, causing Jessie to suck in her breath at the feel of its weight on her thighs. "No, I don't want it," she said, pushing it away. She held her hands out again. "Toby, come. I need you to keep me safe."

The dog placed his front paws on his bed and lazily

stretched backward, then lay down and rested his head on her legs with a heavy sigh.

She lifted his snout to make him look at her. "Are you trying to tell me that I'm *not* going to have a flashback?"

Toby licked her fingers and pulled free, gave a huge yawn, then rolled onto his side with another heavy sigh and rested his head on her thigh again.

Jessie took a shuddering breath, fighting back tears. "But I could feel it," she whispered, running a trembling hand over his shoulder. "I saw the dark curtain descending when Roger started talking about that night as if . . . as if he *knew*. But he couldn't; nobody around here knows what happened in Atlanta."

She stared at the stick lying half on the bed and half on the floor, and realized that Toby had also felt its vibration. But it was wood, not metal; a branch off a tree or even a young sapling that Roger had cut and peeled and sanded smooth. So how could it have given her a shock, and why had she felt a gentle hum when she'd held it?

Unless . . . well, rubbing a balloon on wool created static electricity, and balloons certainly weren't made of metal. And her coat was wool, as was the scarf Roger had given her. And the air had been quite dry lately, she'd noticed, making her hair fill with static whenever she brushed it.

Jessie finally started to relax, and she even smiled when she touched the walking stick with the toe of her boot and didn't feel anything. It was just an ordinary piece of wood, not some magical conductor of energy that had traveled clear across the universe and had patiently been waiting for her to come here and claim it.

Releasing another deep breath that left her feeling totally drained and utterly boneless, Jessie started to lie down on the doggy bed next to Toby. But she suddenly bolted upright again, realizing that she still hadn't explained how Roger knew there even *was* something she was trying to remember. And why had he said that two men were extending a hand for her to grasp? Which two? Was Ian one of them, maybe? But who was the other one?

And what had Roger meant when he said neither man was quite what he seemed?

Chapter Eight

"HAS THE MOUNTAIN AIR AFFECTED YOUR BRAIN?" Merissa asked, slamming through the door laden down with grocery bags. "You were supposed to tie one piece of ribbon on one branch of *one* tree, not use the entire roll to decorate half the forest at the end of the road." She set the bags on the counter and turned to Jessie, her eyes dancing with laughter. "I hope nobody drove by and saw you, or word's going to spread that an insane woman just moved to town. What in hell possessed you to drape all that ribbon on all those trees? I swear some of those branches are over thirty feet in the air."

Jessie stood in the doorway of the downstairs hallway, blinking in surprise and no small amount of confusion. "But I didn't . . . . I never got . . ." Not sure how to explain that she'd been ambushed by a crazy old man and never even made it to the main road, Jessie simply shrugged. "I guess I didn't want the movers to miss the turn."

Merissa snorted. "Subtlety never was one of your strong suits." She waved at the bags on the counter while heading to the door she'd left open. "You'd better start putting stuff away to make room for what's still in the car. I heard them saying in the grocery store that a huge storm is coming tonight, so I bought enough food to last us at least a month on the off chance we get snowed in."

Jessie rushed over to the pegs the moment Merissa disappeared outside, and drove her hands into her coat pockets looking for the roll of ribbon. But all she found was her cell phone.

Then where in hell was the ribbon? Jessie slowly backed away, certain she'd put it in her pocket before she'd left. But then she sighed in relief, realizing the ribbon must have fallen out—probably when she'd steadied Roger as he'd struggled with the wagon. And Roger must have found it, and he had . . . decorated all the trees.

Except she couldn't remember mentioning why she'd been walking to the main road, so how would he have known?

"Come on, Jess," Merissa said, striding in with another armful of bags. "I saw a van with the name of your moving company on it parked at a diner in Greenville. We have to put the groceries away before they get here." She set the bags on the counter, then turned with her hands on her hips. "Hello? Earth to Jessie. Is anyone *home*?"

Jessie snapped out of her stupor. "I guess that would depend on whether or not you saved me some of whatever's smeared all over your chin."

Merissa used her sleeve to wipe the chin in question, her cheeks turning pink around her smile. "It's icing off three of the best damned éclairs I've ever had. Don't worry; I bought enough of them to last us through the blizzard. And

I bought hot cocoa and some baby marshmallows, and a pound of big fat hot dogs." She gave Jessie a salute. "I'll play Girl Scout and go cut us each a stick before it starts snowing, and we can open the doors on the woodstove and cook them over the flames."

Jessie walked to the counter and started pulling items out of the bags. "Jeesh, if I'd known it was sugar withdrawal making you so cranky this morning, I would have taken you to the Pine Lake Bakery and Bistro."

"I have not been cranky."

Jessie looked over her shoulder with a laugh. "*Toby* was running for cover this morning, Mer." She sobered. "Are you missing Duncan?"

"I wish someone would tell me what's so all-fired exciting about running around the woods with a bunch of men and shooting innocent deer. I only got one night with Duncan, and I'll be gone before he gets back. The guy friggin' lives here and can go hunting anytime he wants."

"Ian told me they always spend the week after regular hunting season to black-powder hunt together." Jessie shrugged at Merissa's frown. "I didn't know what that meant, either, but he explained there's a special season to hunt with muskets like Davy Crockett and Daniel Boone used, where you pour gunpowder down the barrel and then cram a lead ball behind it." She laughed when Merissa's frown turned ugly, and held up her hand. "Don't say it. I know these guys can't seem to decide what century they're living in, but Ian explained that having only one shot is more sporting."

"And during his little lesson, did he happen to explain why Duncan couldn't spend the week with me instead?"

Jessie snorted. "Only women are willing to cancel plans they've made with their girlfriends to be with the opposite sex, Mer. And Ian said their trip this year was special, since it's the first time he's been home in over four years. As it is, he and Robbie each have brothers missing out because they're in Afghanistan."

Merissa's shoulders slumped and she headed back outside, muttering something about hoping the jerks got snowbound in the mountains until spring.

Jessie walked around, opening every cupboard door except the two over the dishwasher, then started taking items out of the bags and placing them on the shelves. Half an hour later, wondering if there was any money left in her checking account, she had just finished when Merissa walked in carrying two skinny sticks and announced the moving van was coming down the road.

It was nearly seven o'clock before the three-man crew finally left, their pockets lined with all the cash Jessie had in her wallet as thanks for being so careful with her belongings—that they'd patiently moved several times throughout the house until Merissa was satisfied everything was exactly where *she* wanted it.

"Did you see how that one guy kept making a wide circle around Toby?" Merissa asked from the cushion she'd stolen off the couch and plopped down in front of the woodstove. She pulled her flaming hot dog out of the fire and blew on it. "And you, you dastardly dog," she said, pointing the blackened hot dog at Toby. "I saw you watching his every move as if you expected him to steal your kibble."

Jessie walked over with two mugs of cocoa laced with tiny marshmallows and sat one on the hearth in front of Merissa. "Toby probably remembers him from when they packed up my condo in Atlanta," she said, pulling her tapestry footstool in front of the stove to sit on. "Apparently someone packed his squeaky toy, and that guy started shouting when he walked in and caught Toby tearing apart one of the boxes."

Merissa's eyes widened. "He actually had the balls to scold Toby? I mean, you and I both know the big lug's only dangerous if someone is threatening *you*, but the guy couldn't know that. What sane person yells at a hundred-pound rottweiler?"

Jessie set her own mug of cocoa on the hearth and picked up the stick Merissa had cut her. "I wish you could have seen his expression when Toby backed out of the shredded box with his squeaky toy in his mouth. That's when the guy decided he probably shouldn't be yelling at a dog with fangs the size of his little finger." She skewered a hot dog over the forked end of her own stick. "Did you happen to hear how much snow we're supposed to get?" she asked, glancing out the window at the snowflakes blowing past the deck floodlight.

"Duncan and Ian weren't kidding when they said it's not measured in inches up here," Merissa said, wiping her fingers on her pants. "I heard two feet is predicted, and that the storm will probably last into Wednesday." She pushed another hot dog down over the charred end of her stick. "There's a good chance I'll be your houseguest for a little longer than we'd planned."

Merissa started to hold her hot dog over the flame, but stopped to look at Jessie. "On the drive to Greenville I thought about what you said before I left, and . . . well, I decided you're right. I've never seen you happier, Jess," she said quietly. "Only it's not just since we got to Maine; I swear you turned into a brand-new woman the moment we left Atlanta's city limits. Even when we stopped in New York to have Thanksgiving with your parents, and they spent the entire two days trying to talk you out of coming here, you just kept smiling and nodding." She shrugged. "I've seen you depressed and angry and frightened over the last four years, but I've never seen you so . . . well, so peaceful."

Merissa turned back to stare at the fire, smiling sadly. "Duncan told me that if I truly love you, then I need to let you go. So I guess it's time I rejoin the living, too, even if that means risking having my heart tromped on by some no-good rotten jerk again."

"Maine needs good nurses, Mer. And I don't think Duncan is the kind of man who would tromp on a woman's heart."

Merissa snapped her head around, her expression horrified. "Are you nuts? I could never get serious about Duncan. The guy's a . . . He's too . . . I couldn't . . ." She burst out laughing. "Ohmigod, Jess; having an affair with an alpha male is one thing, but I couldn't ever live with one." She sobered and looked down at the stick in her hand. "No, I need someone who's a little less . . . well, someone like Andy."

"Andy the computer geek?" Jessie asked in surprise. "The same Andy you said had the sexual prowess of a two-year-old?"

Merissa's cheeks turned as red as the fire. "Hey, just because he thought I was talking about computers when I mentioned that I like hard drives doesn't mean he's not trainable. But you know what really makes Andy perfect for me? Whenever we went out, he never even *realized* there were other women in the bar, so I sure as hell didn't have to worry about him asking for their phone numbers when I went to the bathroom so he could have sex with them in *my* bed while I was at work."

"Oh, Mer," Jessie whispered. "Greg was a world-class idiot."

"And even though I haven't spoken to Andy in almost three months," Merissa continued through her scowl, "this morning while I was standing in front of the milk case trying to remember if you prefer 1 percent or skim, he suddenly texted me out of the blue. So I texted him back and told him I was in Maine, but that I was flying home Thursday. Then I mentioned that my plane was landing at one in the morning on Friday, and that I really hate taking taxis in the middle of the night." Merissa's eyes started sparkling with amusement—or maybe that was lust. "And the big sappy geek immediately texted me back saying he would love—and he capitalized *love*—to pick me up and take me home."

Stifling her own smile, Jessie arched a brow. "To your home or his?"

"I don't care which one," Merissa growled, shoving her hot dog into the flames. "Just as long as he doesn't roust me out of bed at four-friggin'-A.M."

IDLING THROUGH THE SURPRISINGLY BUSY STREETS OF Greenville late Thursday afternoon, Jessie marveled at how a three-inch snowstorm practically shut down Georgia but a two-foot blizzard appeared to be nothing more than a nuisance to Mainers. Thus Merissa's plane had departed on schedule, and more than once during the eerily silent drive back from Bangor, Jessie had found herself experiencing pangs of doubt over what she honestly expected to accomplish by moving here.

It didn't help that she kept thinking about her encounter with Roger and all the cryptic things he'd said. She'd explained finding him selling his wares on the side of the road when Merissa had asked where she'd gotten the beautiful walking stick and scarf, but Jessie hadn't mentioned their crazy conversation. Nor had she asked Mer if she hadn't seen Roger when she'd covered all his wares with dust on her way by, a little afraid Merissa's answer might have been no—which is why Jessie had hidden the stick and scarf in her bedroom closet before her friend had arrived home with the groceries.

But she'd been forced to dig them back out the next day because it had been 'storm'n something fierce' just like Roger had predicted, and eager to try the snowblower, she and Merissa had gone outside when it stopped snowing Wednesday evening. Toby, however, had been content to watch from the safety of the porch as they'd wheeled the scary-looking machine out of the garage.

They'd been trying to figure out how to start the blower when Jack Stone had arrived not five minutes after the town plow had created a snowbank at the end of the driveway higher than her car. Jack had made short work of it with the plow on his pickup, though, telling Jessie that Ian would likely be the one digging her out next time. He'd also suggested that even though her station wagon had four-wheel drive, she might want to get studded tires put on it the first chance she got—which she had done today, right after watching Merissa's plane lift off the runway.

Jessie had also intended to find a pharmacy in Bangor and replace the simple aluminum cane she'd given Roger; because honestly, she really couldn't see herself going around town with a five-foot-tall walking stick. But it had taken so long to get the studded tires put on that she hadn't bothered, wanting to get home before dark—which at this time of year and this far north happened around four P.M., apparently.

"Home," Jessie whispered into the silence broken only

by the soft canine snores coming from the backseat, feeling the word resonate deep in her chest. Fifteen miles to go and she'd be *home*. She'd been on her own since college, but her apartments had always felt transient, with someone else's paint colors and draperies and hand-me-down furniture her parents and aunts had donated. Even when she'd married Eric, it had been *his* home she'd moved into.

But not two weeks after Eric Dixon had placed a diamond-encrusted gold band on her finger in an over-the-top chapel in Las Vegas, Jessie had decided that a woman suffering from pregnancy hormone overload probably shouldn't be making life-altering decisions. With the clarity of twenty-twenty hindsight, she'd realized the honeymoon had ended on the flight back from Vegas, with her turbulent marriage ending three short months later—just about twenty minutes before the intruder had murdered Eric and then come after her with the same bloodied knife.

At least, that's what the police detectives decided had happened, since the last thing Jessie remembered about that night was Eric pulling things out of her suitcase as fast as she'd been throwing them in it. When coaxing her to stay hadn't worked, he'd started threatening to spend every last dime of his substantial wealth to get sole custody of their child the moment it was born. The same wealth, the detectives had said, which had likely been the motive for the home invasion that had left her widowed and crippled and childless, and suffering from trauma-induced memory loss.

Jessie knew she'd been leaving Eric, yet bizarrely, she couldn't remember exactly why. Although she'd known for weeks that she wanted a divorce, to this day she still sensed—quite strongly—that something major had triggered her decision to end their marriage that particular evening instead of leaving on her planned business trip. And no amount of counseling or even hypnosis could make her remember what had happened between running into the bathroom when Eric had suddenly slapped her and waking up in the hospital three days later, when her distraught parents had tearfully explained that she was widowed, childless, and likely would never walk again.

She'd remained insensate for over a week, preferring the dark, emotionless cavity her attacker had carved out of her soul instead of facing reality, and refused her father and mother's desperate petitions that she let them transfer her to a hospital in New York. She wasn't being stubborn or heartless; Jessie simply hadn't wanted anyone she loved—or who loved her—to witness her struggling to regain control of her life. But not two days after her parents' teary good-byes, an angel had walked into her hospital room and introduced herself as Merissa. She'd then proceeded to drag Jessie kicking and screaming out of bed and into a wheelchair, and pushed her out into the sunshine.

Slowing down to turn onto Frog Point Road, Jessie smiled sadly at the memory of Mer wading through the snow to retrieve the yards of ribbon hanging off no less than six trees. The wind had been blowing, causing the ribbon to repeatedly flutter out of reach, and Merissa had expended more energy cursing Jessie than capturing it.

"Lord, Toby, I miss her already," Jessie said, glancing in her rearview mirror to see Toby had sat up and was looking out the window. "But don't worry, Mer said she'll come visit us this summer. And who knows, maybe she'll bring Andy."

Jessie suddenly brought the car to a halt when she saw what looked like groomer tracks coming out of the woods in the spot where Roger had been set up four days ago. "Oh

God, he's back," she said, seeing the tracks had turned down the snow-covered road toward her house. She craned her head to look out the rear window, trying to see Ian's driveway. "Unless Ian came back from his hunting trip early because of the snowstorm and he's using one of Tar-Stone's groomers to get around."

Which wasn't that odd a notion, actually, since she'd seen snowmobiles zipping through the streets of Greenville like cars.

Jessie shifted into reverse and backed up until she reached Ian's driveway, and her heart sank when she saw it hadn't been plowed and that there weren't any tracks or even footprints. She put the car back in gear, but just sat staring out the windshield at the road ahead. "What if Roger's sitting on my steps waiting for us?" she whispered, glancing at Toby in her rearview mirror. "I know he's harmless, but I really don't want to deal with the crazy man right now."

When Toby merely yawned, Jessie took her foot off the brake and started toward home again, wracking her brain for a believable lie to get Roger to leave. But at the next curve in the road, she saw where the wide rubber tracks had climbed over the snowbank and back into the woods.

She blew out a relieved sigh. "He's been here and gone already, so I guess I won't be going to hell for lying to a lonely old man." She laughed softly. "Well, at least not today." When she pulled into the driveway, Jessie could see where the machine had been parked long enough for the snow to melt from the warmth of its engine.

Remembering the forecaster had said the sky would remain cloudless tonight, allowing the temperature to drop below freezing thanks to the new snowpack, Jessie didn't bother getting out of the car to open the garage door. She shut off the engine, wondering for the tenth time why the Stones hadn't installed an automatic garage door opener, but silently thanked them for the motion-activated flood-lights that were now lighting up the entire front yard.

"Well, we almost made it home before dark," she told Toby, getting out and opening his door. She looked around, her gaze stopping at the darkened windows of the house at the end of the peninsula, then moving on to the camp just beyond her garage with its windows boarded up. She looked to the right, barely able to make out another vacant camp through the trees. "Wow," she said as Toby padded over to a snowbank and lifted his leg. "I guess Merissa was right and this place really is isolated. Our closest winter neighbor is halfway between here and Ian's driveway."

She'd met Ava and Richard Randall this morning when she and Merissa had walked along the camp road to see if she had any mail as well as retrieve the ribbon, and they'd come across the couple stringing Christmas lights on their garage. Ava had welcomed Jessie to the neighborhood, and said that if she needed anything to just give them a holler. Richard had asked Jessie if she intended to let Toby run loose, and warned her that once a dog got a taste for chasing deer, it was a hard habit to break.

Jessie had assured him Toby was a service dog, and that he stuck pretty close to her side. The man had instantly warmed up, and suggested she keep an eye on the road just before dawn and right after dusk if she wanted to see the only other winter Frog Point residents, which consisted of two mama deer each with twin fawns and a couple of last year's offspring. He'd also told her to watch the lake once it froze—which should happen tonight, he'd said, since calm winds and single-digit temperatures were predicted—as the deer would be using the lake to get around once it had a good snowpack.

Jessie had asked if she could buy feed to put out for the deer, and with eyes twinkling and tongue in cheek, Richard had told her it was illegal—although he did recall seeing bags at the feed store with pictures of deer and turkeys and other wildlife on them. Sort of like that one, he'd said, pointing just inside his open garage door at the large bag of wild game feed standing in the corner.

Watching her breath puffing into the crisp night air, Jessie walked around her car to get her purse and walking stick out of the front passenger seat. She then headed up her neatly shoveled walkway, wondering if there were any young local boys she could pay to shovel her out this winter. She should also ask in town if she could hire someone to plow, not wanting to presume Ian would come running every time it snowed. She snorted softly, figuring that offering to pay him would probably go over about as well as it had with Jack Stone, as she remembered the man had still been chuckling and shaking his head as he'd driven away.

Jessie suddenly stopped at the foot of the stairs when she spotted the huge wooden wagon parked on the porch in front of her door. Her shoulders slumping in defeat, she continued up the steps just as Toby bounded past her.

"What do you suppose this is going to cost me?" she muttered, standing over the wagon as Toby sniffed the large cast-iron pot sitting inside it on a bed of fir boughs. She stepped around the wagon as she fished her keys out of her purse and unlocked the door. "If that old goat thinks he's found a new chump to pawn off his junk on, he's in for a surprise." She smiled as she stepped inside, leaned her cane against the counter, set down her purse, then hung her coat on one of the pegs. "Maybe 'what I be needing' are his boots and fur hat. What do you think; should I insist on bartering the clothes off *his* back? Toby?" she called, opening the door when she realized he hadn't followed her inside. "Get in here."

Instead of obeying, Toby sat down next to the wagon and gave a soft woof.

"No. Bringing that pot in the house will only encourage Roger to drop more stuff off on my porch, and the next thing you know he'll want to trade my car for that beat-up old trail groomer. Now get in here, you big lug."

Toby stood up and nosed the pot until its lid fell off, exposing an envelope inside. Jessie stepped onto the porch and snatched it out of the pot, then followed Toby into the house. He trotted over to his bed and plopped down, and Jessie went to her chair and tossed the envelope on the side table. "I'll read it after I build the fire back up," she said when Toby lifted his head, his gaze going to the envelope. "What is it with you, anyway?" she asked, grabbing the poker and kneeling down to open the front doors of the woodstove. "Do you think Roger's going to pay you a commission?" She poked at the ashes, looking for embers that might still be glowing. "Or are you taking his side because you think you've found another new male buddy?"

Toby rested his snout on the hearth and silently watched.

Jessie continued their one-sided conversation, mostly to ward off the absolute silence of the house. "Do you suppose Roger bartered one of the MacKeages for that old groomer, Tobes? Or maybe they put it for sale by the side of the road like all the snowmobiles and ATVs we saw on the drive back, and he bought it." She placed several pieces of the kindling on the exposed embers, then sat back on her heels to see if they were going to catch fire. "No, Roger said he had no use for money, so he must have traded—oh, damn!"

Jessie lunged forward to shove open the large lever when smoke started billowing out the stove doors, then pulled the small lever on the right side toward her. "I forgot to open the dampers," she explained when Toby lifted his head and sneezed.

Seeing the kindling burst into flames, Jessie immediately closed the doors, stood up, and grabbed a split log from the washtub Merissa had lugged in from the garage and then filled with wood. She opened the top lid and set the log into the flames, then added two more pieces before closing the lid and brushing her hands on her pants.

"Okay, now I'll read Roger's letter," she said over the snaps and crackles coming from the burning kindling. She settled into the perfectly sized recliner she'd moved from the condo her parents had rented and furnished for her in Atlanta before her release from the rehab facility, lifting up the footrest. Jessie then slid her finger under the flap of the envelope with a sigh, both wondering and dreading what cryptic warning Roger had for her this time.

She gasped in surprise when she pulled out a Christmas card of a beautiful angel floating in a small clearing in the woods, surrounded by fir trees dusted with snow. Jessie studied it for several seconds, noticing the crow sitting on a branch overlooking the clearing, as well as what looked like . . . She squinted at the card. Were those groomer tracks disappearing into the woods behind the angel?

She opened the card with a frown and, ignoring the folded piece of paper that fell into her lap, read the handwritten inscription out loud.

Yuletide greetings to you, Jess, along with my wish that all your dreams come true in this enchanted place throughout this magical season. Welcome home, lass.

Roger AuClair de Keage

PS: Don't worry, Tobias; there'll be something under the tree for you.

Jessie held the card for Toby to see. "Look, Roger sent it to both of us. And apparently he wants you to believe he's Santa Claus."

But then she looked at it again and frowned. De Keage. Was Roger related to the MacKeages? Maybe that was how he'd gotten hold of one of their groomers.

She frowned again when she realized he'd called Toby *Tobias*. But how could he know that she often called the big lug Tobias? She snorted, standing the card on the table beside her and picking up the folded piece of paper, only to discover there were two pages. "Everyone knows Toby is short for Tobias, and Roger was obviously trying to sound formal."

But then why had he called her *Jess* instead of Jessie or even Jessica?

She scanned the top paper and snorted again, waving it at Toby before sliding it behind the second page. "The old goat included detailed instructions on how to cook a venison roast. Ohmigod, listen to this: *It's a sin against humanity for a woman not to teach her daughter to cook,*" Jessie read aloud. "*And don't think I won't be telling your mama exactly that when she comes for Christmas. Doesn't she know the way to a man's heart is directly through his belly? At least you inherited your papa's acumen for business, Jess, and he'll be right proud of you for purchasing such a fine home."*

Feeling the fine hairs on her neck stir, Jessie stopped reading. "Toby," she whispered. "How would Roger know I even have a mama and papa, much less that they're planning to come spend Christmas with us?"

When Toby merely blinked at her, Jessie took a steadying breath and started reading aloud again. *"The house will serve you well, lass, until you start filling it up with bairns the way Megan did. But don't you worry; you'll have another fine home by the time your third child is conceived—that is, assuming you're not only careful whose hand you grasp, but that you also have the courage to accept all that comes with the man extending it."*

Jessie let the pages flutter to the floor, glancing toward the window at the blackness outside before staring wide-eyed at Toby. "Is Roger crazy, or am I? How can he possibly know all this . . . this stuff? Everything he's said, from calling me a *gràineag* to my trying to remember what happened that night to even knowing I don't cook—they can't *all* be coincidences. And . . . and what did he mean, when I conceive my third child?" she whispered, placing a hand on her belly.

Toby got up from his bed and picked up one of the fallen papers in his mouth. He dropped it on her lap, then gave a soft whine and nosed her arm. But when Jessie only stared at him, her heart threatening to pound out of her chest, Toby licked her hand and gave a soft woof.

She slowly picked up the paper and started softly reading aloud again. *"Forgive me for scaring you, lass, but I'm afraid I don't have the luxury of time to gently ease you into the magic, seeing how you took so long to get here because you kept throwing away that brochure I sent you."*

Jessie lowered the letter when her trembling made it

impossible to read any more. "Roger sent me that brochure?" she asked, her mind's eye seeing it on her desk and in her briefcase and on her nightstand. She looked down at Toby resting his head on her reclined leg. "But I e-mailed Tar-Stone Mountain Ski Resort and asked them to send me their brochure, although . . . although that still doesn't explain why it kept reappearing after I kept throwing it away."

She looked down at the letter. *It was the magic, Jess,* she continued reading, this time silently. *The same powerful energy you'll need to master if you intend to have that houseful of bairns you're wanting so badly. So listen up, lass, because by the winter solstice, you'd best be holding the correct man's hand when the tragedy that's been haunting you for the last four years finally plays itself out.*

"Dammit, Roger! If you know so much about my life, then why not just tell me whose hands I'm supposed to grasp?"

Toby lifted his head at her outburst.

"And why are you so insistent that I continue reading his letter?" she asked more softly, giving Toby a pat as he scooted closer to rest his chin on her thigh. "I know you're unusually perceptive, Tobes, but . . ." She sighed when he softly whined. "Okay, I'll read it out loud so you can hear for yourself how crazy Roger is."

Ignoring her own craziness for talking to a dog as if he were human, Jessie scanned down the page until she found where she'd left off. "*I can't be . . .*" She took a steadying breath at the realization that Roger was actually answering her question. "*I can't be outright telling you which man you should trust, Jess, because it's really not my place to interfere.*" She looked at Toby with a snort, then back at the letter. "*But I can give you a couple of nudges in the right direction, and I do believe if you think back, you'll realize that I've already given you several hints. If you missed them, well, I'll see what I can do to jog your memory when the time comes."*

Oh God, she could practically hear Roger cackling with laughter. Jessie turned over the page with a scowl, sighing in relief to see the letter was winding down.

"But until we meet again, I suggest you keep your new walking stick as close as you keep Tobias, because I'm afraid you're going to need both to get you through the next few weeks. Which is why I also suggest that you trust them when they're telling you not to believe what you're seeing or hearing."

Jessie lowered the paper again to smile at Toby. "I always trust you, you big lug." She looked at the walking stick leaning against the counter. "As for that stick . . . well, after giving me a shock the first time I touched it, it's only been an ordinary stick."

She sighed and looked back at the letter. *"One last thing, Jess,"* she continued aloud, *"concerning what I said about allowing yourself to be vulnerable again. What if I were to tell you that a woman's greatest strength lies not in her beauty but in what is wrongly perceived as her weakness? Because it's true, you know; the courage it takes for a woman to open her heart and body to a man actually makes her the stronger of the two. Realize your own strength, Jess, and bring the right man to his knees simply by giving him your trust as well."*

Her eyes suddenly so blurry she couldn't see the words anymore, Jessie swiped at the tears running down her cheeks and then wiped her sniffling nose on her sleeve. "Oh God, Toby, Roger makes it sound so . . . like I can just undress in front of a guy and he'll be so overwhelmed by my courage that he won't even notice my ugly scars and missing breast."

She started to crumple the page, but stopped when Toby lifted his head with a soft growl. She blinked at him, and then wiped her nose on her sleeve again. "Okay," she muttered, uncrumpling the paper to continue reading. *"This is the season of miracles, Jess, and the one you're about to receive—as well as give—has been waiting four long years for you to crawl out of your deep dark hole and come here and claim it.*

"So if I can be of service over the coming weeks, or if you're needing the perfect Christmas gift to give a certain fella—say, a big gnarly walking stick that would nicely complement your own—all you need do is walk your road with the intention of seeing me, and I'll be waiting for you.

"Sincerely, your greatest ally and humble servant, Roger de Keage

"PS: You have exactly two weeks and four days to practice cooking a proper venison roast, as I'm not wanting to be poisoned when you thoughtfully invite me to Christmas dinner with you and your family. Oh, and I'll bring the Scotch, and we'll see if it might be good for what ails your overheating mama."

Okay, it was official, Jessie decided as she folded the wrinkled letter and set it on the table next to the card; if Roger was crazy, then she was crazy, too. Because instead of being freaked out by what she'd just read—out loud to a dog, no less—Jessie felt her last pang of doubt evaporate at the notion she'd been drawn here to create a miracle.

No, two miracles; one for her and one for the man whose hand she intended to still be holding well into old age. "Come on, Tobes," she said, closing her recliner and standing up. "We need to get that pot inside before Roger changes his mind and takes it back because he didn't get something in trade. So first thing tomorrow," she continued as she headed for the door, "we'll look through my catalogs and order him something nice in exchange for the pot and wagon."

She stepped onto the porch, set the lid on the pot and picked it up—surprised by how heavy it was—and carried it inside to the counter. "And then we'll drive to Greenville and buy a huge beef roast to practice on, and I'll use Ian as a guinea pig when he comes back from his hunting trip." She turned and smiled at Toby, who sat in the middle of the kitchen, and she'd swear he was smiling, too. "Ian will think I'm trying to learn to cook to impress him, and he'll be so grateful, he might even take us dancing at Pete's again this Saturday. Oh, damn, he can't. The campers begin arriving Saturday, and I promised Sadie I'd man the registration table and hand out packets."

And that would keep her and Ian busy all week, Jessie thought with a sigh as she started opening cupboard doors looking for something to fix for supper. Then Ian would be busy getting ready for the resort to open to skiers once camp was over, and she'd be busy . . . Damn, she didn't have a job to go to anymore, did she? No, that wasn't true; she could start working up an international marketing campaign for Sadie's camp.

Jessie grabbed one of the boxes of cereal and a can of dog food, then opened another cupboard and took down two bowls. She popped the top on the dog food and started spooning it into one of the bowls. "Once I start cooking regular meals, I can mix gravy and vegetables in with your dry food," she told Toby, walking over and setting his dish on the floor next to his water bowl. "And you know what?" she said, straightening with a smile as he sniffed the food then looked up at her. "I do believe I *will* invite Roger to Christmas dinner, if only to watch him go nose to nose with my *mama*."

Chapter Nine

BLINDED BY TEARS SHE COULD NO LONGER HOLD BACK, Jessie groped her way down the hallway, concerned only with reaching the women's restroom before anyone saw her. Honest to God, despite being in rehab beside scarred and disabled people, she'd been completely caught off guard when the first child had rushed up to the registration table ahead of her parents and older brother. The young girl—who couldn't be over seven years old—had thrust out her prosthetic hook to Jessie and introduced herself as Courtney, in the same breath asking if her friend Peyton had arrived yet. Jessie had apparently hesitated just long enough that Sadie MacKeage had rushed around the table to sweep Courtney up into a laughing hug.

Utterly ashamed of herself, Jessie had plastered a smile on her face and spent the rest of the morning in a numbed daze as child after disabled and disfigured child arrived with their families, until the lobby was a study in chaos of campers and staff boisterously reconnecting. Her only saving grace was Toby, who became an instant celebrity as well as a perfect distraction. But it was the young boy with the biggest eyes Jessie had ever seen and curly blond hair that belonged on an angel—instead of the heathen Sadie called him—that had been Jessie's tipping point. Asking for directions to the restroom then politely excusing herself, the image of that boy—whose name was Mark, she'd learned when his mother had shouted for him to slow down—propelled Jessie through the sea of wheelchairs and crutches and laughing adults and children.

Jessie stumbled into the restroom far less gracefully than Mark had burst into the lobby on high-tensile, curved steel springs instead of legs, remembering how he'd caught the tip of one of the springs on something and skidded on his belly across the lobby, only to pick himself up before anyone else could and start running again.

Jessie collapsed into a heap on the floor and burst into tears, burying her face in Toby's fur. "Oh, Toby, have you ever seen anything that sad?" she sobbed as Toby tucked his head over her shoulder against her neck in a doggy hug. "You were so brave, I wouldn't have survived without you. I . . . I don't think I can do this all week, Tobes. Not with— Hey, the bathroom's occupied," she said, trying to reach the door with her foot when it opened.

"Jess?" Ian asked, peeking inside. "Are you okay?"

"Yes, I'm fine." She hid her face against Toby again, hugging him tighter when he tried to pull back. "Please go away."

She sensed Ian step into the restroom and squat down in front of her. "Ye don't look fine," he said quietly.

"Please go away. I want to be alone."

"Well, since Toby isn't growling at me, I can only assume he wants me to stay," he said as Jessie heard him sit down beside her with a sigh. "I'm only guessing here, lass, but I'm sorry no one took the time to prepare you for what you'd be seeing today."

Her face still hidden in Toby's fur, Jessie tried to give a negligent shrug but released a betraying sob instead, only to gasp when she was suddenly lifted off the floor. She turned and hid against Ian's chest when he settled her across his thighs and wrapped her up in a hug.

"You don't look at their broken and scarred bodies, Jess, you look at *them*," he said thickly. "Did ye not notice the barely contained excitement in their eyes?"

"B-but they're just *children*. What did they ever do to deserve such . . . such terrible disabilities?" She gathered his shirt in her fist. "Why is life so *unfair*?"

Ian's thumb gently brushed her cheek. "Easy, now," he said into her hair. "Life isn't fair or unfair; it simply is. Sometimes bad things happen to good people no matter how hard we try to prevent them. All we can do is deal with what comes at us, Jess, which is exactly what those children are doing. They don't live in the what-ifs; they live each day in the moment." He tilted her head back and smiled at her, brushing a lock of hair off her cheek. "And today they're beginning a week-long winter adventure, their only concern being whether or not *this* is the year they finally work up the nerve to sneak away from their parents to swim naked with their friends."

Trying to stifle her sniffling, Jessie hid her face against Ian's chest again.

"Hey, did you just wipe your nose on my shirt?" he muttered, using his shoulder to nudge her upright.

Oh God, had she? "No. No, I'm pretty sure that was my hand you felt," she said, wiping his shirt under the pretense of smoothing it down. She gave another sniffle and stared at her hand. "I'm sorry for running off like that," she whispered, "but I felt . . . I got so overwhelmed. I don't know if I can come back here, Ian." She made a valiant attempt at a smile. "Because the last thing those kids need is to be around a grown woman who can't even swim, much less have the courage to take them skinny-dipping."

"No, we certainly wouldn't want the little heathens to have to rescue a naked drowning lady," he said, setting her off his lap and standing up, then lifting Jessie to her feet. "So wash your face," he instructed, nudging her toward the sink, "so ye don't alarm anyone on your way out. I'll pick you up under the portico in ten minutes." He held out his hand and grinned. "But it'll have to be in your car, since the passenger-side door on my truck won't open at the moment."

"I can drive myself home."

"You could *if* you were going home. But I'm taking you someplace that's guaranteed to cure what's ailing you at the moment."

Jessie eyed him suspiciously. "Does it involve Scotch?"

He chuckled, waggling the fingers on his outstretched hand. "No, it involves a trek through the snow followed by hot cocoa and doughnuts in front of a roaring fire." He arched a brow. "You can make hot cocoa, can't you?"

Jessie wiped her cheeks and then her nose with her sleeve. "I've been known to scald a batch or two. Um, where are we getting the doughnuts?"

"From the same place we're trekking through the snow."

"And that would be?"

"A surprise," he said, waggling his fingers again.

Jessie wondered if Ian wasn't the best cure for what ailed her. "My keys are in my purse under the reception table."

He dropped his hand with a snort and headed for the door. "There's not much that scares me, but I'd rather cross a minefield than rummage through a woman's purse. I'll meet you in the lobby in ten minutes."

"Wait," she said, managing a small laugh even as she gave her nose another swipe. "The keys are in the side pocket, so you don't have to go anywhere near the minefield inside."

He opened the door and looked back, specifically at her feet. "Are those the sturdiest boots you own?"

She looked down. "Why? Are we trekking to Siberia?"

It seemed he had to think about that. "Never mind, I've just come up with a better idea. Ten minutes," he said, disappearing into the hall.

Jessie blinked at the closing door as she pulled in a steadying breath and looked at Toby, and shrugged. "I guess I'm game if you are." She walked to the sink, only to gasp when she looked in the mirror. "Oh, Tobes, I'm afraid it's going to take a lot more than hot cocoa and doughnuts to cure me," she said, turning on the faucet to splash water on her face. She pulled several paper towels out of the holder and scrubbed her face dry, then undid the clip at the back of her head and ran her fingers through her hair to pull it over her tear-blotched cheeks. Then with one more fortifying breath, Jessie plastered a smile on her face that she wasn't feeling and headed back into the chaos.

It took her only two minutes to get her coat and purse and thank Sadie for letting her help out today, but it took another fifteen minutes for Jessie to work her way to the lobby doors—although that was Toby's fault for attracting children like a hundred-pound, fur-covered magnet.

Feeling much better now that she focused only on the excitement in their eyes instead of their disabilities, Jessie's smile disappeared when she stepped outside to find Ian leaning against an ATV that had rubber tracks where the wheels should be. She actually took a step back when she noticed Toby's blanket and pillow from her car in the back cargo area, and she shook her head. "We're not riding around town in that thing."

He straightened without saying a word and patted his leg at Toby, who trotted over and reared up to set his front paws on one of the tracks. Ian lifted him into the cargo box, then turned to Jessie. "You want us to bring you back a doughnut?"

"You can't just steal my dog."

He folded his arms over his chest. "It's not stealing if they come willingly."

Seeing the TarStone shuttle bus arriving from the Bangor airport with more campers, Jessie walked to the ATV, set her purse in the back next to Toby—giving him a good glare as she did—then glared down at the passenger door that was nothing more than a webbed harness as she tried to figure out how to get in.

Ian reached past her and unclipped one side of the webbing and held it out of the way. "It's just like getting in a car."

She lifted her left leg and tried to slide onto the seat, but Ian ended up having to cup her backside to keep her from falling and gallantly pushed her into place. "Oh, and look," she said brightly, hoping he'd mistake her blush for excitement. "It's even got a windshield just like a car." She looked up. "And it's a convertible, which everyone wants to ride around in when it's nearly freezing outside."

After silently clipping the webbing, Ian strode around and got in the driver side. But instead of starting the machine, he grasped her chin and kissed her right on her startled lips. "Did ye miss me this past week?" he asked, his eyes crinkling with his smile.

Jessie pulled free and settled the flaps of her long coat over her legs. "I've been pretty busy, what with getting moved into my new home and shoveling my way out of a blizzard and taking Merissa to Bangor." She looked out the corner of her eye at him. "Were you gone all week?"

He leaned closer, his deep green gaze taking on a sparkle. "You know, you get the faintest little twitch at the corner of your mouth when you're telling one of your straight-faced lies." He sat up and reached for the key. "So ye might want to do a bit more practicing in the mirror before you—"

The rest of what he said was lost in the rev of the starting engine, and Jessie grabbed the roll bar with one hand and Ian's arm with the other when the machine started shaking and rattling. "Wait. Aren't we supposed to wear helmets?"

He looked over and shrugged. "I don't have one that fits Toby, so it wouldn't be very fair of us to wear them if he can't. Don't worry, Jess; I'll take it slow and easy with you," he said, giving her a reassuring smile. At least, she thought it was reassuring and not salacious. He glanced briefly over his shoulder at Toby, then adjusted some sort of shifting lever, and with a wave at his mother and father coming out the lobby doors to greet their arriving guests, Ian headed into the parking lot.

"Um, I think your father wanted to speak with you," Jessie said, relaxing her grip on the roll bar when the machine smoothed out and she realized she probably wasn't going to die today.

"Whatever he wants will keep until tomorrow."

"Shouldn't you be helping your parents with the campers

instead of taking me trekking through the snow in search of doughnuts?"

"There's an entire army of staff and volunteers to look after them," he said, stopping at the main road to check for traffic before turning toward town. "They'll survive without me until we open up the tube run tomorrow. Are ye warm enough?"

"I'm good. Do you have to register this thing like a car?"

"No, it's illegal to run ATVs or snowmobiles on town roads." He glanced over at her and grinned. "So if Chief Stone happens to catch us, you beam him your best smile, okay? And maybe bat those pretty eyelashes at him."

"You expect me to use my feminine wiles to get you out of a ticket?"

He arched a brow. "Isn't that what they're for?"

Oh yeah, Ian definitely was good for what ailed her. "Jack's my *landlord*," she said with a laugh, feeling the last vestige of sadness slip away. "I don't want him to think I'm that kind of girl." She batted her eyelashes at *him*. "And besides, I have to save my ammunition for when I need to get myself out of a ticket."

Toby stuck his head between them, his tongue lolling out the side of his smiling mouth as he lifted his snout to the breeze, and Ian gave him a scratch under the chin. "Feminine wiles are an unlimited currency, lass, and if they work once on a man, they'll work every time. I looked for your cane in your car but couldn't find it." He glanced over at her. "Is the Maine air making it obsolete?"

"I guess so," she said, looking down to adjust her coat again so he wouldn't see the corner of her mouth twitch, "since I seem to keep forgetting to bring it with me."

When in actuality Jessie had left her walking stick at home on purpose, not wanting anyone to ask her where she'd gotten it. She'd left the scarf home, too, because she suspected Roger had given her that particular one because it was the MacKeage tartan, which she'd confirmed today when she'd noticed both Sadie and Grace MacKeage wearing scarves of the same plaid. Roger wasn't giving her little nudges; he was all but hitting her over the head. It would be nice, though, if he'd give her a hint who the other guy was.

"Wait, wasn't that the bakery?" Jessie asked, pointing behind them.

"Aye, Marge Wimple makes good doughnuts, too, but you're going to have to earn the ones you're getting by trekking through the snow first."

They continued through the tiny town, and Jessie got excited when Ian turned up another road. "Is that where we're going?" she asked, pointing at the Bigelow Christmas Tree Farm sign. "But I thought Katy's parents own a Christmas tree farm. Why aren't we going there?"

"We are. Michael MacBain bought it from the Bigelows over thirty years ago, but he kept the name out of respect for them and still didn't have the heart to change it after John Bigelow died." He shot her a grin. "You did intend to put up a tree, didn't you?"

"Do they sell stands? And decorations for it?"

His grin disappeared as he took his foot off the gas, stopping the machine right in the middle of the road. "Ye don't own any Christmas decorations?"

Jessie started fussing with her coat flaps. "I . . . No, not at the moment." She looked at him. "But I'd like to get some this year."

His smile returned and he started down the road again. "Libby and her mom, whom everyone calls Gram Katie, have a shop full of locally handmade decorations," he assured her.

Jessie touched his arm. "Thank you for bringing me here, Ian."

"Remember that thought, okay, when you find yourself kneeling in two feet of snow to chop down your own tree."

WITH TOBY'S HEAD RESTING ON HIS BELLY AS THEY BOTH lay sprawled in front of the woodstove watching Jessie making hot cocoa in the kitchen, Ian started to worry that he could get used to spending his evenings in a house that wasn't sparsely furnished and drafty and empty. Hell, he didn't even care if she scorched the cocoa, because it sure beat the heck out of making his own. Ian gave Toby's ear a rub as he let his gaze travel around the living room filled with knickknacks and flowery furniture and wondered why he wasn't feeling out of place, considering he hadn't felt comfortable even in his own skin, much less indoors, since he'd joined the service five years ago.

He looked toward the stairway at the bullwhip of a tree he'd placed in the stand and smiled. He'd assumed he'd be putting up a tree the MacBains had actually cultivated, but oh, no; Jessie had spotted the "poor lonely fir" growing on the other side of the fence behind Michael's field of carefully shaped trees, insisting *it* was the perfect tree for her first Christmas in her new home.

Though he'd told her cutting it would in essence be stealing, since it wasn't growing on MacBain land—*not* telling her it was growing on MacKeage land just to see how daring she really was—Jessie had snatched the saw out of his hand, saying nobody was going to miss one little tree in a gazillion million others. She'd then taken a quick look around to make sure there weren't any witnesses, then tromped through the knee-deep snow and cut the poor lonely thing off at the stump. She'd tromped back dragging it behind her, slapped the saw against his stomach, and told him to cut a cultivated tree, then proceeded to wrestle her prize up onto the roll cage of the ATV—all the while telling the poor lonely thing it was beautiful.

But when Ian hadn't moved quickly enough, she'd frantically shoved him toward a perfectly shaped tree as she continued scanning the field for witnesses, saying they needed the one they'd already paid for in order to disguise the one she'd stolen. And if they got caught . . . well, she'd batted her pretty lashes at him and asked if he'd come bail her out of jail if her feminine wiles didn't work on a happily married chief of police.

They sure as hell had worked on him, because that's when Ian had felt a powerful blow to his chest that nearly brought him to his knees, and damn if he hadn't taken a proper breath since.

Oh yeah; Jessie Pringle stole his breath away when she was being sassy and daring, and now she was making a run at his heart just by making him cocoa while he grew way too comfortable in her warm, intrinsically feminine home.

Dislodging Toby, which sent him ambling to his bed with a doggy sigh, Ian sat up when Jessie walked over with two mugs and handed him one. He looked down to see an army of tiny marshmallows and frowned. "Are there any doughnuts left?" he asked, pushing the marshmallows to the side to find the cocoa. He licked his finger as he looked at her. "I'm pretty sure we bought half a dozen and only each ate one on the way home."

"I ate one and you inhaled three, so I ate the last two

while you were filling the wood box." She disguised her sassy smile by lifting her mug to her mouth and blowing on it. "Thank you for doing that."

Ian patted a spot beside him on the thick wool rug. "Come sit down and enjoy the fruits of my labor with me."

She set her mug on the hearth then used his shoulder to steady herself as she carefully knelt and slowly sat down beside him. But instead of tucking her legs underneath her or crossing them, she stretched them out in front of her, only to laugh when she realized she couldn't reach her cocoa.

"We could sit on the couch if you prefer," he said, handing it to her. "Or you could sit between my legs and lean back against me."

"Thanks, but I'm good," she murmured, this time lifting her mug to hide her blush behind its steam. "Do you have activities this week for the kids who aren't disabled? And the parents; is anything special planned for them?"

He wiped his upper lip after taking a sip, then wiped his sticky hand on his shirt and nodded. "We have a live band in the lounge two of the nights for the parents, and we run a shuttle bus the other nights so they can go down to Pete's and really cut loose. And Thursday, Alec and I and some of our regular ski patrol staffers will take a group of the older siblings up the mountain to backcountry ski, thanks to Mother Nature's cooperation this year. But a lot of the activities are designed for everyone to do together. There's a treasure hunt that's ongoing all week, pitting families against each other as they follow clues that lead them all over the resort and even into town. Each treasure is a prize in itself, but the family that finds the most wins a trophy, an all-expenses-paid vacation at TarStone, and bragging rights."

"Wow. I don't want to volunteer; I want to *attend* Camp Come-As-You-Are."

"Sorry, we don't allow thieves to enroll," he said, nodding toward her Christmas tree. "If ye want, I could come by tomorrow evening and hang the garland and lights you bought on your porch." He nudged her shoulder with his own. "Say . . . in exchange for you cooking me supper?"

"Sorry," she said, drawing out her *R*s to mimic his burr, "but only if you like something out of a can, since the crows ate the beef roast I bought to practice on."

Ian leaned away in surprise. "How can anyone ruin a roast? Ye put it in the oven and it cooks itself."

"Yes, it's so easy, it cooks itself into a big black brick," she muttered, quickly taking a sip of her cocoa—only to suck in half her tiny marshmallows as well.

Ian grabbed her mug and set it on the hearth with his, then rubbed her back as she chewed and swallowed and finally grinned at him, sporting a white mustache. So of course he had to pull her face toward him and kiss the confection off her lips.

Oh yeah; his chest still hurt from the blow she'd given him earlier, and was now throbbing quite painfully with wanting her. Keeping her lips occupied while being mindful she wasn't very limber, Ian maneuvered Jessie onto his lap and tucked her head in the crook of his arm to get serious about loving her mouth.

Her response was more than he'd hoped for and somewhat surprising as she daringly darted her tongue between his lips. His want turned into a sharp stab of need when she then maneuvered herself around until she was straddling his thighs, pressing herself intimately against his groin.

But when Ian cupped her backside to urge her even closer, his thumbs naturally slipping under the back of her jersey at her waist, Jessie reared away with a gasp, pushing off his chest so quickly that she tumbled to the floor despite his trying to catch her. Her startled cry brought Toby off his bed with a snarl, and the dog was standing over her and giving him the evil eye before she'd even finished falling.

"Sweet Christ, Jess, calm down," Ian said quietly, going perfectly still.

"I'm calm," she said, taking gulping breaths as she lay on her back holding down the hem of her jersey. "It's just that I got . . . I forgot and I . . . I'm calm." She pushed Toby off her and then used him to awkwardly pull herself into a sitting position. "I'm okay, Tobes," she crooned, rubbing him soothingly. "Ian wasn't hurting me."

Ian snorted, though he did so without moving a muscle.

Her face as hot as the flames licking the glass on the woodstove, Jessie nudged Toby back to his bed, then crawled over to sit down beside Ian again and touched his arm—which is also where she aimed her gaze. "I'm sorry. I didn't mean to lead you on like that, and then . . ." She finally looked up, and the sadness in her eyes started his chest hurting again. "Where are we going with this, Ian?" She gestured weakly toward the hallway that he knew led to her bedroom. "I think you've realized by now that I'm not like Mer—that I'm not a casual . . . Dammit, I have scars."

Ah, yes, her scars. And he didn't want to forget her missing boob, now did he? *Finally* she was going to openly acknowledge them. With a furtive glance at Toby, only to find the dog watching him like a hawk, Ian gave Jessie a sinister grin. "Would these scars happen to be in any interesting places?" he asked, arching a brow. Seeing her surprise— or maybe that was horror—he immediately pulled his shirttail out of his pants. "Let's play show-and-tell; I'll show you one of mine and you show me one of yours."

"Ian, no," she said, grabbing his arm to stop him.

Yup, that was definitely horror. "See there?" he said, leaning back on his elbow and touching his side just above his belt. "That one's compliments of Duncan, when I was six and he was seven and the little snot convinced me I could fly just before he pushed me off the barn roof."

Her horror turned to concern, and she squinted and leaned closer to touch the skin beside his finger, only to straighten and glare at him. "That's barely a scratch." But then her cheeks reddened again and she turned away. "I . . . I have big ugly scars."

"Scars aren't big or small or pretty or ugly, Jess," he quietly told her, straightening back up. "They're just skin that's done a damn fine job of healing itself. And I don't know about you, but that impresses the hell out of me." He nudged her shoulder with his own. "Show me one of your scars, lass, and I'll show you a miracle."

Her head still bent so her hair hid most of her face, Ian saw more than heard her sigh and guessed he was pushing a little too much too soon. But before he could tell her it was probably time he went home, she pulled the right sleeve of her jersey up to her elbow, and still without looking at him thrust her arm in front of his chest.

With one more glance at Toby, Ian gently took hold of Jessie's wrist and turned her arm to the light coming from the lamp beside the chair, and immediately recognized the defensive wounds as well as the weapon that had made them.

Being careful not to let her see how badly the idea of someone going after her with a knife angered him, Ian brushed his free hand down the length of her forearm. "Well, I suppose they might be more impressive than mine," he said, tightening his grip on her wrist when she tried to pull away. He traced one of the three-inch scars with the tip of his finger. "But look at what a wonderful job this one did of healing itself, leaving only a thin white line of baby-soft skin." Not wanting to push his luck—and wanting her to start breathing again—Ian let her go and turned to face the fire. "Did you see my mum's right hand, Jess?" he asked quietly.

"I saw it. She . . . It looked to me as if she'd been in a fire."

"Aye, when she was seventeen. She had a sister who died when their house caught fire, and her dad died five years later from having his lungs damaged when he ran back inside to search for her after getting my mother out." He looked over at Jess. "For a long time Mom thought her scars were ugly, only not because of how they looked but because they were reminders that the candle she'd left burning in their den had killed her sister. It didn't, Jess," he rushed on at her soft gasp. "An intruder had caused the fire." He smiled sadly. "For years Mom wore a soft leather glove on her right hand, claiming she didn't wish to make people uncomfortable. But she threw her stash of them away the summer she and Dad opened the camp, and only wears one now if they're attending a function out of town."

"I thought I noticed she also wears a body sock," Jessie said thickly. "Does she . . . does your mom go skinny-dipping with the others?"

"She doesn't, though not from lack of wanting to. But it's more fun for the campers if they believe they're pulling the wool over her eyes as well as their parents'. If you come back to TarStone this week and stay alert, you'll hear a lot of whispering going on as the children make their plans." He shrugged. "The midnight skinny-dips started out innocently enough about ten years ago, when a bunch of us men stripped off and jumped in the pool after a long day of giving tube rides. We'd forgotten our suits, and when we heard a couple of boys giggling, Robbie dared them to join us. And boys being boys, the little hellions jumped in and then spent the rest of the week bragging about it to their friends. That started the tradition, and now skinny-dipping is more popular than any of the regular activities."

"Sort of like a rite of passage?"

"Exactly." He gave a chuckle. "Mom made a huge production of catching us once about seven years ago, and I wish you could have seen the boys' faces when she flipped on all the lights and started yelling and carrying on as if she'd just caught them robbing a bank. I swear they thought she was going to pack them up and send them home the next day."

"Sadie?" Jessie said in surprise. "But I can't imagine she would yell at the children, especially knowing you guys had instigated it."

"Mom gave them hell *precisely* because people are reluctant to scold a child who's disabled. But they don't want to be coddled or pitied or let off the hook, Jess; they want to experience the consequences of being bad just like every other kid." He chuckled again. "Alec didn't know Mom and the parents had plotted to catch us, and he nearly drowned the boy he'd been helping by hiding the little heathen behind his back. But the campers who'd been caught were instantly elevated to heroes, and they strutted around the rest of the week feeling quite proud of themselves," he said, undecided if Jessie was appalled or trying to contain her laughter behind her hands.

"We're not really targeting the younger kids," he explained, "but rather the older children and the teenagers, as they seem to be the most self-conscious about how they look. So Mom figures that by strictly forbidding the swims she's not only giving them a safe way to rebel, but also encouraging them to interact with their normal-looking siblings as well as us adults. And the parents have told her it's working, because they've seen a difference in how the kids interact with their peers at school."

"Your mother is one of the most amazing women I've ever met," she whispered, lowering her hands to expose her smile. "I've decided that if I can be half as brave as she is, and now half as wise, I'll die a happy woman."

"You're already there, *gràineag*," he murmured, leaning forward to kiss her.

She reared away. "I am *not* a hedgehog," she growled— though she was still smiling. "And if you think you can treat me with care so I'll get all warm and cuddly on you, you've got another think coming, buster."

Ian arched a brow. "Mom actually told you what *gràineag* means?" He sighed. "I didn't think she would, but I guess women sticking together trumps ratting out a son."

"Hey, you men have an even tighter brotherhood." Her gaze suddenly dropped to his chest. "Except your mother isn't the one who told me *gràineag* is Gaelic for *hedgehog*. Um, do you know someone named Roger AuClair de Keage?"

"How do you know de Keage?" he asked softly.

But when Ian saw Jessie suddenly pale, he realized she'd heard the alarm in his voice. "I . . . I met him the day before the storm. He was selling his wares on the camp road just down from your driveway. And he had an old TarStone trail groomer; I know it was one of yours because there was a faded resort emblem on the door."

Ian stood up so she wouldn't see how badly her news disconcerted him. What in hell was de Keage doing here, and more importantly, why was he messing with Jessie? "So the old bastard's still running around with our snowcat, is he?"

"Did he steal it?"

"Yes and no." Ian rubbed the back of his neck, wondering what to tell her. "Roger bartered it off Camry, Megan's sister, in exchange for a wedding two years ago." He waved toward the window. "She and her not-yet husband were up on Springy Mountain looking for a satellite that had crashed up there the summer before." He sat on the stone hearth and, resting his arms on his knees to clasp his hands, decided telling Jessie a half-truth might be wiser than pretending he didn't know Roger. "Camry and Luke, both physicists, had been having a heated e-mail exchange for over a year but had only met in person a couple of weeks earlier. In fact, none of us thought they even liked each other." He snorted. "Well, they obviously did, because when Camry discovered the old hermit they'd stumbled upon happened to be a justice of the peace, she asked him to marry them. And Roger said he would in exchange for the snowcat Camry had *borrowed* from the resort to go look for the satellite."

He snorted again. "But nobody thought the old bastard would actually keep it. He left Luke and Cam stranded on the mountain in a snowstorm, and they had to walk thirty miles with only one pair of snowshoes and an old sled Roger had made out of what remained of the satellite. So, what did de Keage have to say, Jess? Did he happen to mention why he was in town?"

It took her a bit of a struggle to get to her feet, but Ian decided not to help her. "He didn't mention why he was here," she murmured, her lying straight face paling again. "But he did persuade me to trade my cane for one of his walking sticks." She gave a forced laugh. "He also wanted me to give him my cell phone in exchange for a heavy cast-iron pot and wagon, but—"

Ian straightened. "You gave Roger your cell phone for that wagon on the porch?"

"No! I told him the phone wouldn't do him any good without a service plan, but when I arrived home from taking Merissa to the airport, I found the wagon and pot sitting in front of my door. And inside the pot was a card," she said, going to the chair beside him and picking something up from the table. "It's a Christmas card," she said, handing it to him then sitting on the edge of the chair to clasp her hands on her knees.

Ian stared at the angel on the card, remembering something about Grace and Greylen getting a similar one when Camry had been missing two years ago, and his gut tightened. If Roger had given one just like it to Jessie . . . well, this couldn't be good. He opened the card and read the inscription.

Yuletide greetings to you, Jess, along with my wish that all your dreams come true in this enchanted place throughout this magical season. Welcome home, lass.

Roger AuClair de Keage

PS: Don't worry, Tobias; there'll be something under the tree for you.

Wonderful; the old bastard had mentioned the magic even while managing to make it sound harmless. "That's it?" he asked, turning to Jessie. "Just the card?"

He saw her hands tighten with her soft laugh. "There

were detailed instructions on cooking a venison roast." She sobered. "And also a letter."

"What did it say?"

"I don't . . . It was personal," she murmured, looking down at her hands. She suddenly stood up. "Do you want to see the walking stick? Roger said it won't draw attention in town nearly as much as my cane did."

Ian also stood up and set the card on the table beside her chair. "Yeah, I believe I would like to see it."

She disappeared into the downstairs hallway, and he walked over to the window and stood staring out into the black, moonless night. Dammit, what was de Keage doing here and what did he want with Jessie? And what in hell had he said in that letter?

Ian turned when she came into the room carrying a walking stick about five feet tall, and made sure not to show his alarm when he saw the thick burls on the top third of the stick, which—sweet Christ, Roger had given Jessie a *staff.*

The damn thing was a conductor of energy.

Jessie started to hand it to him but hesitated, her large hazel eyes filled with what appeared to be trepidation. "It gave me a shock the first time I touched it."

Ian reached out but waited for her to place the stick in his hand, and quietly released the breath he'd been holding when he didn't feel anything but the insubstantial weight of its warm, smooth wood. He ran a thumb over one of the unsanded burls. "Roger didn't have a more feminine-looking stick you could have chosen? Or any with animals carved in them? Hand-carved sticks are popular."

She took it back and clutched it to her chest protectively. "He wanted me to have this one. Who is he, Ian?" she whispered. "Who is Roger AuClair de Keage?"

Not exactly sure how to answer her, Ian pulled Jessie into his embrace—walking stick and all. "He's an old hermit who lives up on the other side of the lake and usually prefers his own company to others."

"Have you ever actually met him?"

Shrugging to disguise his shudder, Ian leaned back just enough to smile at her. "Once, not long after I returned from my last tour in Afghanistan. I was hiking the back side of TarStone, and this wild-haired old man ambled into my campsite one evening and made himself at home. He told me a tall tale while he ate the entire rack of trout I'd cooked, and then he broke out a bottle of the best Scotch I've ever had the privilege to taste. And when I woke up the next morning, he was gone."

"Did . . . did you wonder if you might have only imagined him?" she asked, her eyes searching his.

"Actually, I did," he said with a chuckle. "But between my belly rumbling from missing supper and the roaring hangover I had, I figured he must have been real. He's not anyone you need fear, Jessie. Tell me, what was Toby's reaction to him?"

Her gaze went to her pet lying on his bed beside the hearth, then returned to him with a lopsided smile. "Toby thinks Roger is Santa Claus."

Ian kissed the tip of her nose then leaned back again. "Don't hide your stick in your bedroom, Jess; carry it when you go out just like you did your cane. Roger's right; everyone around here is used to seeing people with walking sticks, as the Appalachian Trail is nearby and hikers come through town year-round. And many residents use them as well, especially in the winter."

With that he kissed her again, this time on the lips, and silently sighed in relief when she relaxed against him. She

opened her mouth, but when her tongue did a bit of delicious exploring, Ian knew he was in trouble because he
didn't want to go home.

He broke the kiss and rested his forehead against hers.
"I need to leave."

"Yes, you do."

"Are you okay about Roger?"

"Yeah, I'm good."

"And will you come to the resort tomorrow afternoon?
You can help out on the tube run," he added when she took
a little too long to answer.

"I . . . I'll be there."

He kissed her forehead then rested his own against it
again. "Bring your walking stick, but put it in your car
before you come in, okay? We don't need any of the little
heathens getting hold of it, thinking it would make a wonderful sword."

"Why do you call them little heathens? Your mom
does, too."

"Any child who hasn't reached puberty is a little heathen," he said with a chuckle. "And when they do, they
become hellions. Or didn't you witness the chaos in the
lobby today?" He finally straightened away, but seemed
unable to take his arms from around her. "I believe Aunt
Grace is the one who started using the term *little heathen*
about the time she had her fourth of seven daughters."

Jessie's eyes widened. "Megan has *six* sisters?"

He finally managed to let her go. "Push me out the door,
Jess."

She suddenly gave him a sassy smile as she grabbed his
arm and started dragging him across the room. "Just so
you know, I'm only doing this for your own good," she
said, letting him go to grab his jacket off the peg and

shoving it at him. She leaned on her stick to bend down and get his boots, and then shoved them into his arms as well. "I promise, you'll thank me in the morning," she added with a perfectly straight face as she opened the door and pushed him outside. "Ian," she said when he started toward the steps to put on his boots. "Thank you for this afternoon and evening; for the ATV ride, for taking me to get a Christmas tree and doughnuts, and . . . and for rescuing me from myself."

"It was my pleasure, Jess. Good night."

He sat down to the sound of the softly closing door and slid on his boots, and without bothering to lace them headed out the neatly shoveled pathway. But he stopped when he reached the road and stood staring back at the house, wishing he could have been uncivilized just long enough to ask Jessie how she'd gotten those scars. But, he thought with a sigh as he started down the road, he really didn't want to continue spending his evenings in a sparsely furnished, drafty, empty old cabin.

Ian rubbed his chest where it felt a little bruised from the blow he'd taken earlier at the Christmas tree farm, guessing he'd have to find some other way to learn what had happened in Atlanta four years ago, since for the first time in almost a year he also didn't want to continue spending his nights on the mountain.

Chapter Ten

JESSIE SAT ON THE TOP STEP OF HER PORCH WRESTLING with the tangled string of Christmas lights, one second away from throwing the damn thing in the snow. She'd bought two fifty-bulb sets at the tree farm yesterday along with a thick pine garland, and had come outside this morning determined to put them up. She wanted the lights running so that after helping out at the resort this afternoon she could arrive home to a brightly decorated house. But so far all she'd managed to do was nearly give Toby a heart attack when she'd lost her balance while standing on the railing trying to nail up the pine garland, and then fallen off with a yelp of surprise. Toby had scrambled down the steps with an equally startled yelp, whining frantically as he plowed through the snow that was deeper than he was tall, and then licked her face as Jessie had lain there laughing.

It had taken ten minutes for them to help each other wade back to the pathway, and another ten minutes for

Jessie to drag Toby's bed and a blanket out onto the porch, get him to lie down so she could cover him up, and kiss his shivering head with the promise that she would be more careful. Then she'd been extra careful taking the lights out of their package, but instead of unwinding nicely, the damn things had turned into an unbelievably intricate knot. Getting more frustrated by the minute because she really wanted to impress Ian by putting up the lights herself, Jessie unbuttoned her coat, reached under her fleece, and adjusted the silicone blob that passed as her boob when it started making her itch.

She caught the tangle of lights slipping off her lap, and with a heavy sigh sat staring through the trees across the street at the frozen lake. She really wished now that she'd had reconstructive surgery on her left breast. Merissa had been the first to suggest it three years ago, but had quickly dropped the subject when Jessie had explained that she couldn't get past the horror of having another knife pierce her body, not even a scalpel trying to make her whole again. And even though her brother-in-law, Brad, had gently been urging her to have the surgery over the last two years, finally persuading her to go see a reconstructive surgeon—even going to hold her hand when she'd finally given in—she still hadn't been able to do it. But now she couldn't help but wonder whether, if she had had the surgery, it would be easier for her to consider getting naked with Ian.

He was right; scars were really nothing short of little miracles, and she could probably find the courage to make love to him if a few scars were all she had to worry about. But missing half a breast touched on the very core of her femininity. Just the thought of seeing horror or disappointment—or worse, pity—in Ian's beautiful green eyes when he saw the puckered remains of what used to be a really impressive boob was even more terrifying than going under a scalpel.

Maybe she could order a sexy teddy or something equally naughty to wear—and keep on—in bed. Because Merissa was right: A few heated kisses certainly weren't going to keep the man interested for very long.

Jessie felt her side vibrate with a jaunty tune that signaled she had a text, and reached in her coat pocket for her cell phone. Seeing it was from Merissa, she opened the text with a smile—only to have the smile disappear as she read the message.

Brad cornered me work said wants send xmas card so gave him yur address

Jessie sighed even as she smiled at Merissa's shorthand texting, and started to slide the phone in her pocket when it suddenly started vibrating again.

Hey sorry he caught me busy & didnt think ;-(got idea he might visit u sorry call u soon ;-)

Jessie blew out another sigh and texted her back—using capitals and punctuation—telling Mer she still loved her. She slid the phone in her pocket with a snort and stood up, guessing that would teach her not to answer Brad's calls or texts, since it was apparent the poor man was having a harder time dealing with her leaving Atlanta than Merissa was.

Maybe she *should* give Roger her cell phone and let the old goat deal with Brad.

Jessie set the tangled lights inside the bag with the other box then grabbed her walking stick, which was leaning against the house. "Have you warmed up enough to go see if we have any mail, Tobes?" she asked, looking at her watch and then at her empty driveway. Her car was still in the TarStone parking lot because Ian had brought her directly home in the ATV, saying he didn't want to get caught with a stolen Christmas tree while the thief innocently drove herself home. "Damn, we only have an hour before Ian picks us up. Wait, I know," she said, heading inside the house, grabbing her purse, and shoving Toby's leash into it. "We'll start walking and catch him on his way in."

She locked the door, then used her stick to push the Christmas lights out of sight behind the railing, but hesitated. "Hey, you want to see just how magical this stick is? Watch this, Tobes. Abracadabra!" she said, pointing it at the lights in the bag. "I hereby command you to unravel." She moved the tip of the stick in an arc across the front of her porch. "And nail yourself up!"

Toby shot out from under his blanket and nearly fell down the steps, he was in such a hurry to get away, and Jessie burst out laughing. "You big lug," she chuckled, heading after him. "It's a plain old ordinary walking stick, not a magic wand."

Jessie gave Toby the signal to heel and hiked her tote-sized purse up on her shoulder as they started toward the main road. "Have you noticed how steady my legs have been all week, Tobes?" she asked, picking up her pace. "And I haven't had a flashback since the night we arrived. But I figure a bad case of nerves at finally getting here is what triggered that one. And I probably overdid it by going to Pete's and dancing with a stranger and—"

Jessie reached in her pocket when her phone gave a loud ring that told her this was a call instead of a text. She read the caller ID and stopped walking. "Damn," she muttered even as she answered. "Hey, Brad, what's up?"

"Where in hell have you been? I've been calling and texting you all week."

"Yeah, sorry about that, but reception is spotty up here

in the mountains. The only reason you got me now is because I'm in Greenville. So, how are you doing?"

"I've been going out of my mind with worry, Jess," he said, his tone turning plaintive. "And the question is, how are *you* doing? Merissa told me you purchased a house, so it sounds like you really do intend to stay there."

"Merissa mentioned you stopped by the hospital," Jessie said as she started walking again. "And yeah, I'm staying. I love it here, Brad; this place is beautiful."

A heavy sigh came over the phone. "I miss you, Jess, and I really don't like you living so far away," he said gently. "Who's going to help me get through the holidays?"

"I told you to go to Bermuda or St. Barts or take a cruise over Christmas. Just don't stay in that big empty house and mope."

There was a short pause, then, "Or I could spend Christmas in Maine with you."

Jessie stopped walking again. "Um . . . my parents are coming for Christmas."

"Great," Brad said, suddenly cheery. "I'd love to see your dad again. How is Jacob? I've been meaning to contact him about building an addition on my gallery. And Maureen," he quickly added. "How's your mom doing?"

Jessie gave a silent sigh and started walking again. "They're both doing well, and like you, they're still waiting for me to come to my senses."

"That's because, like me, they love you. Look, I'll be in Boston on Thursday, and there's no reason I can't just rent a car and drive up to Maine. It can't be over . . . what, a two-hour drive?"

"Try six," she said with a laugh.

There was another pause, and then, "I'd really like to see your new house and the area you're living in, Jess. It would make me feel better about your being so far away all by yourself. I can head on up there Friday, or maybe even Thursday if my meeting ends early. I can stay at that resort in your brochure," he rushed on before she could answer. "And maybe I'll even try skiing again. I miss you, Jess."

"The resort's closed all this week." Jessie felt her shoulders slump. "But there are some nice bed-and-breakfast inns in town."

"Thank you," he said with obvious relief. "When Tracy died so shortly after Eric did, I felt . . . well, you were all that kept me going, Jess." He chuckled sadly. "Hell of a bond, huh. Two people clinging to each other after losing their spouses. But this past year I found myself thinking that you and I might . . . well, I thought . . ." She heard him sigh again. "I'll be there Thursday afternoon or Friday. Bye, sweets."

"Good-bye, Brad. I'll see you in a few days."

"Jessie," he called out just as she was about to hit the END button, making her lift the phone back to her ear. "I was wondering if you still . . . well, has moving to Maine stopped your flashbacks like you hoped? Or maybe jogged your memory?"

Jessie stopped walking and pulled in a shuddering breath. "Yes, I think the flashbacks are gone, or at least lessened in frequency, but no, I still can't remember."

"Well, you know my feelings about that. I say knowing the details would be even more traumatic for you. Hell," he said gruffly, "I still wake up in the middle of the night drowning in sweat. I know that's nothing compared to your flashbacks, Jessie, but . . . well, I'm glad you can't remember."

"Yeah, I guess the devil probably is in the details," she

said. "Okay, Brad; I'll see you soon," she added in an upbeat tone and hit the END button. Now she was sorry she'd confided to Brad why she'd wanted to move here, because honestly, she'd also left Atlanta because she'd sensed he was beginning to want them to be more than just friends. And although she cared deeply for him as a brother-in-law—as well as someone who'd lost his wife as suddenly and tragically as she'd lost Eric—she really wasn't romantically interested in Brad.

Brad and Eric were as far apart as brothers could be when it came to their personalities. Where Eric had been a bit rough at the edges and rather intense, Brad was sophisticated and quite enjoyable to be around. Both men, however, were equally sharp when it came to business, and had turned the gallery they'd opened together in Atlanta seven years ago into a world-renowned fine arts import-export company.

Jessie stopped walking again. "Ohmigod, Tobes. Do you think *Brad* is the other man extending his hand to me?" She headed off again with a snort. "I mean, really, it's not that I don't care for him; in fact, we've pulled each other through some pretty tough times. And he's actually seen the scars on my back and hip, and he didn't appear at all put off. Well, there definitely was pity in his eyes the first time he saw them, but since then he's acted so matter-of-fact that I even felt comfortable enough to do my exercises in the shallow end of his pool when he was home."

Jessie fell silent, since Toby didn't appear all that interested in her opinion of Brad Dixon, and she shoved her free hand in her pocket to use her elbow to keep her purse from battering her side. She rhythmically swung her walking stick like a ski pole to match her stride, quite surprised to find it was easier to use than her old cane. The few burls on it were perfectly spaced to make a handgrip at just the right height, and the bark-covered burl at the top was so gnarly that it was actually quite pretty. It reminded her of TarStone Mountain, she realized, glancing up to see the mountain rising out of the forest like a rugged, looming protector. Sort of like the family who owned it.

And so *unlike* her dead husband. She still couldn't believe she'd married Eric, much less that she'd gotten drunk enough to leave the wrap-up party at the week-long art conference he'd been attending in Dallas—that she'd been the coordinator of—and gone back to his hotel with him and hopped into bed. Eric had been so enamored with her that he'd extended his stay another whole week, keeping Jessie in a whirlwind daze of dinners and dancing and charmed attention. But then he'd reluctantly returned to Atlanta with the promise they could make a long-distance relationship work, which they more or less had for five weeks with him flying to Dallas two of the weekends.

But figuring a man had the right to know he was going to be a father, Jessie had found herself placing the call every woman dreaded making. Eric was standing on her doorstep the very next morning, and after a day and night of cajoling and reasoning and pie-in-the-sky promises, he'd whisked her off to Las Vegas in search of an over-the-top wedding chapel.

And as far as Jessie was concerned now, the day Eric Dixon had slid that diamond-encrusted wedding band on her finger was the day her dream of happily-ever-after had turned into a nightmare. He'd then whisked her directly back to Atlanta, saying he couldn't wait to introduce her to his brother and friends, persuading her to hire a company to pack up her apartment in Dallas and even to hold off calling her parents until after he'd carried her over the threshold of his over-the-top home.

Oh yeah; pregnant women—especially those suffering from debilitating morning sickness—should never make life-altering decisions.

Her only defense, Jessie had since decided, was that any normal twenty-four-year-old girl would be so captured by the charms of a rich, handsome, attentive suitor determined to seduce her that she wouldn't even see the predator lurking behind such a carefully crafted mask of civility.

Jessie suddenly stopped walking. "Oh, Tobes," she whispered, clutching her walking stick to her chest. "That's it— Eric was a *predator*. I think the reason I was leaving him was because I found out he'd been watching me through the entire conference, *plotting* to seduce me. And that evening when I told him I wanted a divorce, he got so angry he admitted he'd planned the whole thing, right down to his lie that he'd had the mumps as a kid and was sterile when I freaked out that first morning because we hadn't used protection."

Jessie started walking again, so inwardly focused that she continued clutching her stick to her chest instead of using it. "Eric had been *trying* to get me pregnant the week we spent together. And when I called and told him I was, he flew to Dallas and didn't let up until I agreed to marry him. But why? How did I find out he'd hoped I'd get pregnant, and why was he so determined to marry me?"

Could she have discovered something in the house when she'd come home early to pack for her business trip? Because honestly, what man in this day and age seduced a woman *hoping* she got pregnant and then insist they get married? Divorce was too easy if the woman ever found out she was nothing more than another addition to the art collection he was amassing.

"That's it!" she cried, stumbling to a halt. She'd somehow discovered she was just another piece of the fairy tale Eric had been building to showcase his world-renowned success. Because the one thing she did remember with full-blown clarity was him shouting through the bathroom door that if she made him look like a fool, he was going to make sure the entire world knew she was a tramp and an unfit mother. And that's why he'd hoped she'd get pregnant: to use the baby as leverage to make her stay by threatening to fight for sole custody.

"Toby, no," she said, pushing him away when he started tugging on the flap of her coat. "This is important; I'm *remembering*."

Toby grabbed her coat again, giving a rumbling growl that made her stop trying to tug free. "Now?" she whispered tightly, staring into his determined eyes. "Are you sure you're not mistaking my being upset for a flashback coming on? Th-they might smell the same, you know."

Toby tugged harder, using more of his weight until Jessie stumbled forward a couple of steps. "Okay. Okay," she said, patting his head even as she looked down the road toward home. She glanced in the direction of the main road, then at the boarded-up, vacant camp nearby, and then at the woods. "D-do we have time to make it home?" she asked. Still gripping her coat in his teeth, Toby started pulling her to the forested side of the road, whining frantically now.

"Okay. Okay," she said, realizing he was leading her toward the tracks where Roger had come out of the woods. She glanced over her shoulder at the vacant camp again just as Toby suddenly let go of her coat and trotted over to the snowbank, where he turned to her and gave a soft bark. Trusting his instincts even more than his training, Jessie walked over and grabbed Toby's collar in a death grip, then allowed him to pull her up the snowbank in a stumbling crawl.

Following the tracks, Toby continued leading Jessie deep into the woods as the familiar descending curtain darkened the forest into contorting, colorless bodies, their long stretching fingers clawing at her. "S-safe place, Toby," she sobbed as the immobilizing terror started to consume her. "I-I can't go any—there he is! He's coming after me!" she cried, dropping to her knees and scrunching into a ball just as the malevolent force lunged toward her and Jessie once again began fighting for her life.

Chapter Eleven

JESSIE SLOWLY OPENED HER EYES WITH A PAINED MOAN, trying to figure out why she was so cold, only to realize she was lying in the snow and Toby was—instead of being cuddled up to her as usual, she could feel the underside of his belly pressing into her side. Jessie very slowly turned her head to see him standing over her, and went perfectly still when she noticed his hackles were raised and his lips rolled back just enough to expose his teeth, his attention trained on a spot behind her.

"You can call off your dog, missy, 'cause I ain't the one who attacked you."

Jessie rolled over with a scream and scrambled backward at the sight of Roger sitting on a stump only a few yards away. Toby moved right along with her, his gaze remaining trained on the old hermit, until Jessie came up against a tree and Toby positioned himself over her legs.

"That's one contrary pet you got there, missy. The big

fella wouldn't let me get anywhere near you, even though I tried to assure him I only wanted to help." Roger looked around the woods, then back at her. "I didn't see who or what done attacked you, but it was long gone when I got here. I'm figuring it was a man, though, 'cause of the things you were muttering. Except you didn't even realize the bastard was gone, and just kept fighting him off someth'n fierce." He nodded. "You're safe now. You wanting me to go get my machine and take you to Chief Stone to report this crime?"

Oh God; he'd witnessed her having a flashback? Jessie pressed her hands to her chest in a vain attempt to slow her racing heart. "Th-there was no attacker—at least not today. I was having a . . . a flashback of when I was attacked before."

"Then we still gotta go report it to Stone, in case the bastard comes back."

Jessie placed an unsteady hand on Toby when he tensed at her slightly hysterical laugh. "He's not coming back because I shot the bastard to death."

The old hermit straightened in surprise and arched one bushy brow. "Well, if'n he's dead, then why you still fighting him?"

Jessie gave a snort, wiggling through the snow to lean against the tree she'd run into. "Drop the act, Roger; we both know you're not some lonely old hermit."

"I most certainly am," he said, his sharp green eyes crinkling at the corners. "Well, okay, I might not be all that lonely, but I am a hermit."

"Exactly who are you, Roger AuClair de Keage? Or should I ask *what* are you?"

He nodded toward Toby. "Have your pet stand down,

lass, and in return I promise to give you another hint as to who and what I really am."

Jessie urged Toby over beside her, then wrapped her arm around him when he leaned into her side and nuzzled her cheek in concern. "Okay, let's start with the *who*, and I want more than a hint."

Roger squared his shoulders and smoothed down the front of his shirt. "I'm Roger de Keage, first laird of the clan MacKeage. Or, more precisely, Ian's ancestor," he clarified when she snorted. He nodded, his eyes glittering in silent laughter. "As for the what, I said in the card that I'm your greatest ally and humble servant." He held his hand up when she tried to speak. "And to answer your next question, I'm here to make sure justice is served and that two miracles happen."

"But—"

Roger pushed himself to his feet with a loud grunt followed by a long-winded sigh. "I'm afraid I need to be going now. But first, could you tell me why you're not carrying your staff? I thought I made it clear in my letter that you need to be keeping it near to hand." He suddenly grinned. "It's doing a fine job helping you remember, is it not?" He nodded when Jessie gasped in surprise. "You keep asking your questions, Jess, and it'll keep giving you answers. Because contrary to what some people might think, it *is* important you remember the details of that night." But then he shot her a scowl that made Jessie go perfectly still as he pointed at her. "And don't you be messing with that stick's energy, you hear? It's not a toy, you know; it's a powerful staff designed for working serious magic."

Jessie straightened with a gasp when she heard someone calling her name out at the road. "Oh, that's Ian," she said, looking back at Roger only to see him heading into the woods. "Wait, you have to help me. I can't let him find me like this."

Roger stopped and turned to her. "You need to tell him everything, Jess, because it's damn difficult for a man to fight an enemy he doesn't know or can't see."

"Jessie!" Ian shouted again, his voice moving closer.

"And Jess," Roger said, drawing her attention again. "Don't go ordering anything out of your catalogs for him for Christmas. I told ye in my letter that I have the perfect thing he be needing," he said, the bartering hermit suddenly returning with a cackling laugh, even as he pointed a threatening finger at her again. "But you keep it hidden in your closet, missy, and don't you be touching it until the time comes," he added cryptically, "or you'll be wishing you'd *burned* that brochure."

"Jess, where are you?" Ian shouted again. "Answer me!"

Jessie looked back at Roger, but he had disappeared. She cupped her hands to her mouth in the direction of the road. "I'm here, Ian!" she shouted. She tried to stand up but fell back with a gasp when a sharp pain shot through her lower back, and she grabbed Toby's snout to stop him from licking her cheek. "I'm okay. We're okay now, Toby. Ian's coming to save us. Again," she added with a snort.

Toby suddenly pulled away, but instead of going to intercept Ian, the dog started pushing his nose through the snow just beyond her feet, then lifted his head with something in his mouth and came back to her. "Ohmigod," Jessie said with a gasp as she snatched her prosthesis out of his mouth. "How did that escape? Ian's almost here!" she cried softly when she heard branches breaking nearby. She shoved the blob in her coat pocket and looked down, taking a calming breath. He wouldn't notice she was uneven because of her coat, and besides, she had a turtleneck and heavy fleece on underneath it. So how had the damn thing escaped? She'd never had this problem in warm, humid weather. Was she going to have to start *taping* it to her bra?

She wrapped her arm around Toby again just as Ian came striding into sight.

"Aw, Jess," he murmured, dropping to his knees beside her. He tossed down her purse and walking stick, then reached out to give Toby a quick pat before moving the dog out of his way. He took hold of her coat by both shoulders, his eyes roaming over her face and body. "Are you hurt? What happened? Did you . . ." He darted a quick glance at Toby then focused back on her. "Did you have another episode?" he asked quietly, tightening his grip when she reared away in surprise.

"H-how do you know I have flashbacks?"

His gaze roaming over her again, apparently more concerned with her physical appearance than her emotional condition at the moment, Jessie saw Ian's face darken. "I witnessed the one you had your first night here when I followed you out of Pete's to see what had you so upset." He nodded toward Toby, now standing at her feet. "Toby saw me, but he didn't seem to mind my being there as long as I didn't go near you."

"You lied! You said you were just coming out of the bar to look for me."

"Aye, I did." He finally let her go and sat beside her in the snow. "I can be a real bastard like that sometimes." He grinned over at her, although it didn't quite reach his eyes. "But I prefer to see our mutual lying as something we have in common."

Jessie looked down at her hands, feeling her own cheeks heat up at the thought that he'd witnessed one of her flashbacks. "Okay, I guess I'm nobody to be calling the kettle black. How did you know to come looking in the woods for me just now?"

He gestured toward her legs. "I saw your purse on the road, and the stick was standing in the snowbank in the middle of the snowcat tracks."

Jessie glanced at the woods where Roger had disappeared, then back at Ian. "I . . . There's something I need . . . I want to tell you that . . ." Her shoulders slumped in defeat and she hugged herself.

"Whatever it is can wait until I can get you someplace warm," he said, pushing to his feet. "Do you know how long you've been lying here in the snow, Jess? Ten minutes? Half an hour? How long?"

"I really don't know. But I've been told my flashbacks can run anywhere from three or four minutes to . . . to half an hour." She shook her head when he reached a hand down to her. "I tried to get up when I heard you calling, but I must have twisted wrong during my . . . I can't get up. I hurt my back again. Roger was here," she said, causing Ian to rear up just as he was bending to her. "He was sitting on that stump when I woke up," she said, pointing across the old groomer tracks. "And Toby was standing guard over me, not letting him come any closer."

Ian glanced only briefly at where she was pointing, then bent over again and slid one arm under her knees and the other around her back. "You tell me if it hurts when I lift you," he said, his muscles tensing in preparation.

"Wait. You can't carry me out of here," she said, trying to push him away. "The snow's too deep and I'm too heavy."

He carefully lifted her up and settled her against his chest with a chuckle. "When I'm pushing up posies, *then* you might be too heavy," he said, heading down the track.

"Wait—my purse and stick."

He stopped, and sighed, and turned around. "Toby, bring me the purse," he said, nodding at it lying in the snow.

"Oh, I can't believe he understood that," she said when Toby grabbed the bag's handle and dragged it over to them.

"Heft it up here, big man," Ian said, bending slightly. He snagged the handle with his fingers and straightened, and Jessie immediately took it from him and set it on her lap before grabbing his neck again. "Now the stick, Toby," Ian said, again nodding his head to point. "But you can carry it."

Jessie looked over Ian's shoulder when he started walking again and saw Toby following with the stick clamped in his teeth. "How did you get him to do that? One, he won't take orders from anyone but me, and two, even when I try to get him to fetch something it can take forever to get my point across."

He shrugged, shrugging her with him. "It seems I've a knack for getting animals to cooperate."

"That's right, that day in the solarium Duncan told Merissa you have a way with animals." She eyed him suspiciously. "You were joking when you offered to send all the birds to my new feeder, right? Right?"

"Yes, I was kidding."

She squinted at him. "Did the corner of your mouth just twitch?"

It twitched into a full-blown grin, and he hefted her higher on his chest to adjust his grip. "You know, I do believe you have gotten heavier."

"Ian?"

"Yes, Jess?"

"Do you want to make love to me?"

He nearly dropped her when he staggered to a halt. "Excuse me?"

Oh God, had her flashback addled her brain? Or had the fact that she was starting to believe Roger wasn't crazy finally turned *her* crazy?

"Jessie."

She tucked her head against his shoulder with a sigh. "I'm sorry. My flashbacks leave me feeling a little drunk sometimes."

He started walking again.

"But do you?"

He stopped. "Now?" he growled.

"No!" She rested against his shoulder with another sigh and tapped his back to get him moving again. "But maybe we could soon?"

Instead of stopping, he picked up his pace.

"Like maybe tonight. Or tomorrow. Or anytime before Thursday."

That managed to stop him, and Jessie leaned away from his expression. "What happens Thursday?" he asked ever so softly.

She studied the missing button on his shirt peeking out of his ski bib. "Brad is coming Thursday afternoon or Friday. And I . . . um . . . I want to be able to tell him I have a boyfriend, and if we've made love, then it won't be a lie."

"Brad your brother-in-law?"

She nodded, still keeping her gaze aimed at that missing button.

"Is he married to your sister?"

She shook her head. "No, he's my dead husband's brother."

"Is *Brad* married?"

She shook her head again. "His wife died in a boating accident down in Nassau a couple of months after Eric was killed. Um . . . Eric was my husband."

"Your dead husband," he said, hiking her higher in his arms and starting down the tracks again. "So why is it so important that Brad believes you have a boyfriend?" he asked, apparently more worried about the alive Dixon than the murdered one.

"So he'll stop hoping I'll see him in a romantic way." She dropped her head to his shoulder again. "Brad's a really nice guy who's rich and handsome and civilized and everything, but I don't . . . I can't put my finger on it, but there's something not quite . . ." She lifted her head. "You know how sometimes a person can seem *too* perfect?"

"What does Toby think of Brad?" Ian asked, stopping on top of the snowbank when they reached the road.

Jessie laughed softly. "Brad's always complaining that Toby doesn't like him, but I think Tobes just scares the bejesus out of him."

"And *does* Toby not like him?"

She shrugged the shoulder that wasn't plastered up against his chest. "I think Toby only tolerates Brad because he knows I like him."

"Aye, you like him so much that you don't want to lie to him." Ian carefully made his way down the snowbank and headed up the road instead of setting her in the—good Lord, he'd come to pick her up on a *snowmobile*?

"Don't you own a normal vehicle?" she snapped, only to realize he was walking in the wrong direction. "Hey, my home's that way," she said, pointing behind him.

"I find I'm feeling a bit weak in the knees and my house is closer."

"Maybe I can walk home now that we're on the plowed road. I have my stick."

"But my condoms are at my place."

Chapter Twelve

WHEN ROGER HAD REFERRED TO IAN'S HOME AS A RICK-ety old camp, Jessie could see he hadn't been being derisive, just merely stating a fact. There was a tired-looking old woodstove sitting in the middle of the one-room cabin that had only two pieces of furniture but enough camping and hunting equipment cluttering the floor and walls to put Dolan's Outfitter Store out of business. The obviously expensive chair she was sitting in, an oversize recliner made of soft Italian leather that had molded itself perfectly to Ian's body, was definitely out of place, although she certainly could picture Ian sitting in it while facing the huge flat-screen television hanging at eye level on the opposite wall. The second piece of furniture—the guy didn't even own a table and chairs—was the bed, which sat in a nook created by the bathroom jutting out from the back wall. The wooden four-poster—which she'd need a ladder to reach—would definitely accommodate the man who owned it—as well as two or more . . . guests.

Feeling a little like Goldilocks in Papa Bear's house, Jessie settled deeper into the chair with a sigh, remembering how the rest of their walk here—well, Ian's walk and her ride—had been ominously silent, Ian's last comment closing her throat so tightly that she couldn't even ask if he'd been joking.

"Ye have a choice between chicken soup and beef stew," he said from what Jessie supposed passed as a kitchen area.

She pulled the blanket he'd tossed over her up to her chin as she stared down at the size-twelve wool socks he'd slipped on her feet after pulling off her boots and socks— and a good deal of encrusted snow—which he'd set under the snapping and crackling woodstove Toby was all but hugging. She hadn't really asked Ian if he wanted to make love to her, had she? By Thursday? Really, she'd given him a deadline?

"Chicken or beef?" he repeated, making Jessie flinch to find him standing beside her. He squatted down to eye level, his hand covering hers on the arm of the chair. "I was joking, Jess," he said quietly, not a crinkled eye corner in sight. "My condoms are in my truck back at the resort."

"I knew you were joking," she said, pulling the blanket up over her head so he wouldn't see her mouth twitch. "I'm just utterly embarrassed," she muttered from under the blanket, which started lowering despite her efforts to stop it.

"You can be happy or angry or utterly frustrated with me, but you can't ever be embarrassed." His eyes finally crinkled with warmth. "And you can always be utterly truthful. There's nothing you can do or say that will send me running."

Jessie had to look away in order to work up the courage to test his claim. "What if I were to tell you that I killed a man?"

He took hold of her chin to make her look at him. "Then I would say you saved me the trouble of having to kill the bastard myself." He went from squatting to kneeling beside the chair and clasped her hand in his. "Last night after I left your house, I went to my father's office to get on the Internet. I searched online for *Jessica Pringle*, which led me to Jessica Dixon, which led to enough articles on what took place in Atlanta four years ago to wallpaper every house in Pine Creek."

His grip on her hand tightened when she tried to pull away. "You would have done the same thing in my shoes, Jess. I waited for you to tell me, but you were taking too long, considering I've known since the night you arrived that I want to make love to you." His thumb caressed the pulse on her wrist and his eyes took on a twinkle. "I thought I was going to have to fight Duncan for you and then your canine protector."

Jessie slouched deeper into the chair to lean away. "P-please don't make it sound like you were plotting to get me."

"Hey. Hey," he said, pressing her hand against his chest. "I'm not a stalker. Ye just caught my eye and . . . it wasn't . . . it *isn't* like that, Jess." He suddenly straightened to his full kneeling height. "This isn't about me; it's about your dead husband. Eric Dixon was a bully. Did you try to leave him and he threatened you?"

"I was leaving him. That night, actually." Suddenly feeling stiflingly hot, Jessie pushed the blanket down to her waist, twisting her hand inside of his to grasp his shirt. "I only just remembered that part today when I was walking out the road to meet you. I was supposed to be leaving on a business trip that evening, but I discovered something— only I can't remember what—and Eric and I were fighting as I was packing my stuff to move out, when . . . when . . ." She pulled her hand away. "The last thing I remember is running into the bathroom when he slapped me. But according to the police detectives, that's when some guy entered the house and stabbed Eric to death, then broke down the bathroom door and came after me."

She pulled in a shuddering breath and folded her hands on her lap. "But what they never quite figured out was, considering the severity of my wounds, how I managed to get ahold of the gun Eric kept in his nightstand and put three bullets in the guy."

"Nobody else was in the house?" Ian asked quietly.

Jessie shook her head. "As far as I know, there was only Eric and me. But Brad is the one who found us and called 9-1-1. He told the police he was coming to talk to Eric about business, and when he heard gunshots he ran upstairs and . . . well, Brad thought the robber moaned or some- thing, and he told the detectives that without even thinking he grabbed the gun out of my hand and shot the man three more times in the head."

Toby walked over and rested his chin on Jessie's reclined legs with a concerned whine, and Ian set his elbows on the arm of the chair, rubbing his face. "Christ, no wonder ye have the flashbacks," he said behind his hands.

Jessie took another deep breath, figuring since Ian already knew a good deal about her past that she might as well tell him what his Internet search hadn't. She touched his arm. "I had married Eric three months earlier because I was pregnant with his child. We . . . we'd had a week-long affair when he came to a conference in Dallas that I was coordinating, and we kept a long-distance relationship going until the day I called and told him I was five weeks pregnant."

Ian finally dropped his hands, the anguish in his eyes having turned them a dark, glistening green. "So you were four months pregnant at the time of the attack?"

Jessie nodded. "It was only today I remembered I was leaving him that evening because I'd found out Eric had lied about being sterile in hopes I *would* get pregnant so I'd have to marry him, because . . ." She waved at nothing. "Because apparently I fulfilled some fairy-tale image Eric had of a beautiful home filled with a trophy wife and child. I lost the baby in the attack, and the doctors said I might not be able to conceive again because the knife . . . One of the wounds is . . ." She sucked in another breath and released it slowly. "There's a lot of scar tissue. And the guy stabbed me in the back when I was trying to get away, and the doctors really didn't think I would walk again."

Ian took hold of her hand and pressed it over his pounding heart. "I'm sorry for what you went through, Jess." He reached down with his free hand and rubbed Toby's head. "And I'm glad you have this big man to keep you safe now. From what I've seen, he's been doing one hell of a job."

Jessie ran a finger over Toby's nose. "I think I would have gone insane without him. Actually, I nearly did the year before he came into my life because I lived in constant fear I'd have a flashback in public. I can't feel them coming on, but apparently Toby can smell a chemical change in my body or something. And besides buying me time to find a place to hide, he seems to realize how vulnerable I am and stands guard. Because of him, I was able to go back to work instead of locking myself in my condo."

"Aye, animals have remarkable abilities," Ian said, gently

smoothing down Toby's concerned brow. "Given a choice, I could spend the rest of my life working with them."

"You mean like being a veterinarian?" she asked in surprise.

Jessie saw a different kind of anguish enter his eyes despite his grin. "Can you really see me spending four more years in college at my age, just so I can spend my days taking cats' temperatures and trying to persuade little old ladies that Fido will survive without his daily pound of treats?"

She gave him an equally serious smile. "Well, honestly, no. But I can see you—even at your advanced age—going back to school so you could spend your days taking horses' temperatures and pulling baling twine out of goats' mouths. No, no," she said, shaking her head and broadening her smile at his glare, "I see you more as a wildlife biologist crawling inside some hibernating bear's den in the middle of the winter. What was your major in college?"

"Business," he snapped. "Or didn't you notice I'm in line to take over running TarStone when the elder Mac-Keages no longer can?"

She grabbed the front of his shirt when he started to stand. "Isn't it a *long* line?" She waved at the air with her free hand. "Aren't there enough young men and women in your clan to keep the resort running without you?"

"Ye don't understand," he said, carefully peeling her hand away and rising to his feet. "From the time we were born, it's been expected that Duncan and I would take over running TarStone."

"Then why isn't Duncan working at the resort?"

He turned away and headed back to the kitchen area. "Because he prefers moving dirt to moving people up a mountain on a chairlift." He looked back at her. "Duncan will take his place at TarStone when the time comes. Meanwhile, he's learning to run a business by running his own construction company. Now, do ye want chicken or beef?" He gave her a tight grin. "Both out of a can."

Jessie covered her snort by stretching her arms over her head and yawning loudly. "What I want is for you to ride that big ugly snowmobile back to TarStone and take the kids down the tube run while my pain med finishes putting me to sleep and the anti-inflammatory does its job." She yawned again. "I'm more tired than hungry, Ian."

"Do you want me to go get your car and take you home?"

"No, I'm good," she said, settling deeper into the chair and closing her eyes. "Do me a favor, though? Could you turn off my cell phone that's in my coat pocket and set it on this . . . crate beside the chair? Oh, and bring over my walking stick, too?"

"Anything else?" he asked quietly—maybe too quietly.

"Yeah, a glass of water would be nice."

"I couldn't find your phone," he said from right beside her, making Jessie open her eyes to see him holding something in his fist. "All I found was this," he said, opening his fingers.

"Ohmigod!" she yelped, trying to snatch her prosthesis out of his hand.

Only she missed, and the bottom half of her left boob plopped onto the floor. Toby immediately jumped up and had it in his mouth before Ian could reach it. The dog then walked around the chair, reared up on the arm, and dropped it onto her lap.

Jessie scooped it up and then pulled the blanket up over her head again.

"And here I thought tennis balls were the fetch toys of choice," Ian drawled.

"Go away."

She heard him walking away but she also heard him chuckling under his breath.

She gasped again, dropping the blanket. "What if *Roger* has my phone?"

Ian came back carrying another cell phone, and Jessie shoved the prosthesis down between her and the arm of the chair before reaching for it.

"You can use mine until we find yours or get you a new one," he said, handing it to her. "Anyone you might need is programmed in, including the resort. If there's an emergency or you want to reach me this afternoon, call Alec or Duncan, as we'll all be together up at the tube run. Do ye want me to help you get settled in my bed instead? It would be more comfortable."

"No, I'm good," she said, snuggling down into the chair and closing her eyes again—mostly so she'd stop seeing the laughter in his.

How in hell had she forgotten the prosthesis was in her coat?

Jessie heard him set something on the crate beside her and felt him lay her walking stick on the blanket, then heard him putting on his outdoor gear over by the door. Which is why she gave a startled squeak when he touched her arm and she opened her eyes to find him standing beside her again, dressed in his ski bib and jacket. "You walk like a cat," she muttered.

"Don't try to stoke the stove when the fire dies down," he said through his smile. "The furnace will take over. Are ye sure you wouldn't prefer the bed?"

"No, your chair is really quite comfy and easier to get out of it I have to use the bathroom," she said, eyeing the tall bed. She reached over and took the remote control off the crate, pointing it at the opposite wall. "And I might feel like watching some television." She grinned. "You get any porn channels?"

He snatched the remote away and shoved it in his pocket as he strode toward the door, but not before she saw his cheeks darken. "You need anything, call Alec," he growled as he opened the door, then stopped. He turned to her, his expression making Jessie go perfectly still. "And don't worry; I'll be stopping by my truck before I drive your car home."

Jessie blinked—several times, actually—because she couldn't imagine why he thought she needed to know that. But then she suddenly gasped at the closing door and pulled the blanket up over her head again even though he was gone.

The condoms were in his truck!

IAN UNLOCKED JESSIE'S CAR AND SLID IN BEHIND THE wheel, unable to believe he'd been kicked out of Camp Come-As-You-Are; first by Alec when Ian had sent three of the tubes down the mountain with no one on them, then by Duncan—who actually took a swing at him—when Ian had accidentally sent his cousin careening toward a tree while they'd been skiing over to the beginners' slope. Then, before he even made it inside the lodge, his mother had also sent him packing when she'd asked where Jessie was and he'd explained she'd hurt her back again and was recuperating in his recliner.

But instead of starting the car and heading home to wait hand and foot on Jessie per his mother's heated instructions, Ian sat staring out the windshield. What in hell had made Jess ask him if he wanted to make love to her? Had she really forgotten the rules of engagement and truly couldn't tell how much he wanted her, or was he the one who was out of practice when it came to engaging the opposite sex?

He glanced over at his dented old pickup sitting at the far end of the parking lot, the plow making its front end sag. He really did have a box of condoms in the glove box, unopened from when he'd optimistically tossed them in there about a week after he'd come home from Afghanistan. He then glanced up at TarStone, its looming weight palpable as it cast its long shadow over the resort. He'd literally grown up on that mountain, and in all likelihood would probably die on it an old man—assuming Jessie didn't kill him first.

Ian finally started the car with a snort, remembering her saying she saw him as a wildlife biologist. Megan was the biologist in the family, as none of Greylen's daughters were expected to take over running TarStone. Grey and Morgan and Callum and Michael MacBain might have been living in this century for over forty years, but they still held on to their eleventh-century identities as highland warriors with the tenacity of a . . . well, of a rottweiler determined to protect his mistress.

First-generation MacKeage and MacBain men were expected to serve at least one stint in the military, and if they didn't make a career of it, they were then expected to come back and serve the clan. The women, however, were only asked to choose their husbands carefully while pursuing any career they chose—and having a little heathen or two was an added bonus for everyone.

Ian didn't feel there was anything intrinsically wrong with holding to tradition, as it grounded everyone in a loving and secure environment. But he didn't like that the men were held to a different standard than the women— although the price the girls had to pay was butting heads with their overprotective male family members.

Ian gave a humorless chuckle and started out of the parking lot. His mom, his grandmother Charlotte (who was Callum's wife and Duncan's mom), his aunt Grace, and Libby MacBain had spent the last thirty-odd years walking a fine line trying to turn stubborn eleventh-century warriors into twenty-first-century businessmen while somehow managing to love them despite their antiquated beliefs. As a result, the elders' personal ethics, strong sense of justice, as well as their code of male conduct were at once both comforting and restricting to the younger Scots.

Ian turned down the Frog Point Road with a sigh, guessing it would take several generations before the MacKeages and MacBains and Gregors learned to successfully straddle both worlds. That the combined clans were rife with members who could manipulate the magic—some being actual *drùidh*s—was on the one hand a plus, but also the very reason they had to stay so tightly bound to the old ways. Magic and modern society were not conducive to each other, and probably the largest hurdle the clansmen of any generation had was finding twenty-first-century mates who could wrap their minds around something that couldn't be seen, much less explained.

Which brought Ian back to Jessie, and whether he could in good conscience make love to her without revealing his own little secret, considering his feelings for her were anything but casual. Hell, he really didn't even know the full extent of his powers, as he'd learned quite young to suppress his ability to get animals to cooperate. And when the magic did rear its ugly head every so often . . . well, it only made him even more determined to ignore it. But now there was the pressing matter of why Roger de Keage had traveled over a dozen centuries through time to come here again, as well as the question of why he was messing with Jessie.

Ian idled down his winding driveway, stopped in front of his ramshackle camp, and shut off the engine. But instead of going inside, he sat staring at the large snowdrift sagging the tired old roof, and decided the only way to protect Jessie from whatever had brought her here—and no doubt brought Roger as well—was to keep as close to her as he could. He snorted and got out of the car. That is, keeping close without looking as if he were stalking her like her bastard of a dead husband had.

Ian cautiously opened the cabin door, not knowing which worried him more: that Toby might think he was an intruder or that he might find Jessie curled up in his bed looking warm and inviting. But when Toby only lifted his head and wagged his tail stub in greeting and Ian saw Jessie sound asleep in the chair, he quietly walked inside, his heart giving a powerful thump not to be walking into an empty house.

Ian put a finger to his lips to signal Toby to keep quiet as the dog got up from beside the woodstove and padded over to the door. He let Toby out, leaving the door ajar, and walked over to open a can of beef stew. He dumped it in a pot and carried it over to the woodstove, but when he turned to go check if he had any bread that was still edible, Jessie let out a soft sigh that made him stop and feast his eyes.

She really was quite beautiful, and he could see why both Dixon brothers had set their sights on her. But where Eric had become so obsessed that he'd only taken five weeks to marry Jessie, Brad Dixon had apparently been trying to slowly entrench himself in her life over the last four years.

Ian finally headed back to the kitchen, willing to bet his snowmobile that dear old Brad hadn't been too keen on Jessie moving to Maine. Hell, she'd been gone from

Atlanta only three weeks, and already the bastard was coming to visit—putting Jessie into such a panic that she'd outright asked Ian if he wanted to make love to her.

He stopped in midstride and turned to look back at her lying in his chair, the blanket having fallen to her waist and her fleece noticeably puckered over her left breast. This didn't have anything to do with Dixon, he realized, but with Jessie's reluctance to let him see her naked. She hadn't given *him* the Thursday deadline; she'd given it to *herself*, wanting the worrisome deed done before she lost her nerve.

Ian staggered backward at the feel of taking another blow to his chest. For some unfathomable reason, Jessie had moved here—to his mountain—with the mindset of starting a brand-new life for herself, and she wanted *him* to be part of it.

He silently snorted. Or else she only wanted a man she didn't know well enough to care too deeply for yet, whom she could test her courage on.

Ian looked at the equipment he used to fill up his time away from the resort, then moved his gaze to his few pieces of essential furniture, then on to the shelves sparsely filled with canned goods. And then he looked back at Jessie and smiled, wondering if he shouldn't find out just how courageous she really was.

He quietly walked over and grabbed an empty satchel and the half-full backpack he used for hiking the mountain and carried them over to the bed. He brought the stew back to the kitchen, and after closing the door now that Toby had come inside to sidle up to the woodstove again, Ian leaned against the counter to eat right out of the pot, feeling the need to fortify himself for the upcoming battle. He then spent the next twenty minutes quietly filling the satchel and reconfiguring his supplies in the backpack, stopping every so often to give Toby a pat or smile down at his snoring houseguest.

He was just coming out of the bathroom carrying his ditty bag when he finally saw Jessie stretch her arms over her head with a loud yawn just as her stomach gave an unladylike growl. He silently ducked back into the bathroom and softly closed the door so he didn't scare the daylights out of her, and loudly cleared his throat.

"Ian, is that you?" she asked on a gasp.

He opened the door but didn't immediately step out when he noticed she'd pulled the blanket back up to her chin and could see her hands frantically moving beneath it. "Would Toby have let anyone else in?" he asked, walking around the back side of the woodstove carrying his ditty bag. He set it in his satchel on the bed and took his time zipping it closed, then stayed busy checking over his backpack.

"I can't believe I slept that long. My pain meds don't usually put me out like that."

"I've only been gone two or three hours," he said, continuing to check his backpack until he heard the footrest on the recliner close.

"Are you going on a trip?" she asked, planting her walking stick on the floor to lever herself out of the chair, only to just sit there eyeing the bed instead. "It looks like you're packed to leave." She frowned at him. "But what about Camp Come-As-You-Are? Don't you have to hang around and help out? I thought you were taking the older kids backcountry skiing on Thursday."

Ian leaned against the mattress and folded his arms. "I'm not going far."

She got to her feet relatively easily, a look of surprise on her face. "Hey, my back feels perfectly normal," she said, leaning one way and the other and then shrugging. "So if you're not going anywhere, what are the backpack and bag for?"

Yes, her back was healed, all right, and Ian noticed the bottom burl on her staff was missing. "I only packed what I might need for the next few days, figuring I can come back and get more stuff later," he said, using his head to gesture behind him. "But I wasn't sure if I'd be sleeping in a bed or a tent, so I packed for either possibility."

She stilled. "What do you mean?"

"Well, I thought about your request that we make love before Dixon gets here, and I realized there was a major flaw in your plan."

"And that would be?"

"Merely calling a man your boyfriend, even if you've slept with him, wouldn't deter me if I'd just spent several years courting you." He shook his head. "The only way you're going to persuade Dixon that he's not even in the running is if I *look* like your boyfriend. How long is he planning to stay?"

"Um . . . through Christmas."

Ian reached behind him and pulled the satchel to the edge of the mattress. "Or maybe not, once he sees I'm spending every night in your bed."

"Excuse me?" she whispered, taking a step back as her gaze darted to the bag then returned to him. "You . . . you want to move in with me?"

He straightened and slid the backpack beside the satchel. "If that's a little more than you're prepared to deal with, then I'm afraid I have to decline your generous invitation, Jessie." Ian rubbed what still felt like a bruise on his chest and shook his head. "Because I'm not that kind of guy any more than you're that kind of girl."

"W-what's the backpack for?"

"If I'm not sleeping in your bed while Dixon's here, then I'm not sticking around to watch him pursue you. I'll be spending my nights on the mountain until he's gone back to Atlanta . . . and maybe taking you with him."

Her cheeks got as red as the fleece she was wearing and she thumped her stick so hard on the floor that Toby scrambled behind the woodstove. "That's not fair! You can't just give me the ultimatum of either moving in with me or running away."

"I told ye life isn't fair or unfair, Jess; it simply is. And you can call it what you want, so long as ye understand there's a good chance I won't be moving out once Dixon leaves."

"But I . . . you can't . . . dammit, I've known you a sum total of a week!"

Ian grabbed the backpack off the bed and strode to the door.

Jessie caught his arm on his way past. "Please, can't we just pretend I never asked? You're right, it was a stupid idea. But running away isn't the answer any more than hiding on your mountain this last year has helped you forget."

Ian stiffened. "Forget what?"

"I don't know what!" she snapped, using her stick to gesture wildly. "A long-lost love, the horrors of war, an old dog that died, not working with animals—I don't know what's haunting you. But I sure as hell know you can't escape ghosts by running away from them." She actually tried to crowd him backward. "Tell me what you're trying to forget and I'll wave my magic wand and fix it," she growled, waving her—sweet Christ, she *knew* it was a staff?

"I'm not running away trying to forget anything," he said, grabbing her hand before she could point it at him. "I merely prefer being outdoors."

She snorted and pulled away, then walked to his bed and grabbed his satchel. "One, I'm not going to be responsible for you getting frostbite just because you're afraid of a little male competition; and two, Roger is *your* ancestor, so that means you're not leaving me alone to deal with him." She walked back and shoved the satchel against his chest. "So I guess we're going to be roommates."

Holy hell, de Keage had told Jess he was his ancestor? "Bedmates," he clarified, striding out the door before she decided to *hit* him with the stick.

"Yeah, well, you're going to have to fight Toby for that privilege," she called after him, just before she slammed the heavy cabin door—making Ian have to jump out of the way when almost a ton of snow cascaded off the roof and nearly flattened him.

The door opened and he saw Jessie holding a hand over her mouth as she looked down at the small mountain of snow in horror, realized she hadn't buried him alive when she saw him glaring at her, and slammed the door shut again, only to have it bounce back and nearly knock her over.

"Don't you dare laugh!" she shouted, rubbing her hip. "A woman asks you for one simple favor—that any *normal* man would love to grant, I might point out—and you turn it into a major production."

"Are you through?" he asked, dropping his satchel and walking up to the mound of snow. "Toby, come," he said, even as he captured Jessie's wrist when she obviously turned to tell Toby to stay.

"He's only supposed to take orders from me," she snapped as Toby scaled the bank of snow and trotted over to sit down beside the satchel. "You must be feeding him treats behind my back."

Ian pulled her just enough off balance that she had to

grab his arm to steady herself, and then he lifted her over the mound of snow, not letting her go even when her stick clipped his jaw. "Ah, Jess, ye can snap and growl and even try to kill me in an avalanche, but ye really have to watch where you're pointing this accursed staff," he said, pulling it out of her hand and driving it into the snowbank out of her reach.

She went perfectly still. "S-staff?"

"Did Roger happen to mention *the magic* or use the word *magical* when he was referring to your walking stick?"

She wiggled one arm free and gestured toward the sky. "He said it was full of energy that had traveled all the way from the sun and moon and stars. And that it's been waiting for me to come here and claim it."

"What else did Roger say?" he asked, hiding his smile when she slid her arm back inside his embrace and relaxed against him with a sigh. "Did he happen to mention *why* you needed to come here and claim it?"

"He said I'm supposed to get a miracle and . . ." She suddenly seemed very interested in his ski bib. "And give one."

"Give a miracle to whom?"

She rested her forehead on his chest. "I don't know. Roger's very cryptic about everything, only giving me hints and nudges." She snorted. "Or hell about something." She leaned back to look up at him, her large hazel eyes filled with worry. "Magic's not real, Ian," she whispered. "Is it?"

He kissed the tip of her nose then cupped her head to his chest. "Ye need only remember three things about the magic Roger is talking about, Jess. One is you don't try to explain it, you just accept it. Two, if you refuse to believe it exists, it will keep knocking you on your butt until ye do. And three, anything is possible if you have the courage to believe."

"Do you believe?"

"Aye, lass, I was born believing anything is possible." He kissed the top of her head and reluctantly let her go, then pulled her staff from the snowbank and handed it to her, nudging her toward the car. "Go on. I'll get your things from inside." He shot her a smile. "It's time we went home so I can unpack and settle in."

He thought to get a rise out of her, but instead she clutched the stick to her bosom. "Um . . . just so you know, I talk to Toby like he's a person."

"Then ye won't mind that I talk to myself the same way."

"And I like to spend my mornings in my pajamas doing the crossword puzzle."

Ian folded his arms, realizing she needed to set some ground rules. "Okay," he said with a nod. "Just so long as ye know I don't wear pajamas."

She didn't even bat an eyelash, but in fact seemed to relax slightly. "I take really long baths, I don't watch any television shows that are violent, and I can be a little grouchy before I get my morning coffee."

"I've been told I have the personality of a bear when I'm hungry."

"Toby doesn't like loud music, and I need—ohmigod! My *parents* are coming for Christmas! How am I supposed to explain that you're living with me?"

"It'll be okay, Jess," Ian said with a chuckle, turning to scale the mound of snow. "I will be a good houseguest and I'll move out when your parents come." He stopped in the doorway and turned to her, rubbing his chest. "And when they leave and Dixon is gone, you can decide then if you want me to move back in."

"You . . . you do realize you don't have to move in *tonight*. Brad won't be here for another four days."

Ian shook his head. "I'm worried we're going to need a few days of practice if you hope to persuade him that we're lovers. It'll be okay, Jess," he repeated. "Nothing's going to happen between us until you're ready for it to happen."

She stared at him, still clutching her stick in a death grip, then finally nodded and silently walked to her car. She let Toby in the backseat, then opened the passenger door and slid the tip of her stick on the floor to lean it against the console.

"Jess," Ian said quietly.

She turned, still not saying anything.

"Just so long as you know that it *is* going to happen."

She took another moment to study him, then nodded again and got in the car. Ian walked into the cabin with a sigh, wondering what Jessie had been doing with her staff—likely unwittingly—as well as how long it might take her to notice its burls were slowly disappearing.

He checked to make sure the fire in the stove was nothing but embers before looking around to see if he needed to bring anything else. He walked over and took down his rifle hanging out of reach of anyone under six foot three and slung it over his shoulder, then grabbed Jessie's coat and purse and climbed back up the mound, turned to kick some of the snow out of the way, and pulled the door shut. He headed to the rear of her car, snatching up his satchel on the way by, put everything in the back of the station wagon, got in behind the steering wheel, and backed out of the driveway.

The short ride down the Frog Point peninsula was made in silence, until Ian suddenly braked to a stop in the middle of the road and sat staring at the blinking lights strung up the length of Jessie's porch, using every ounce of willpower he possessed not to roar. "What in hell were you doing climbing on a ladder to put up that garland and those lights?" he asked very softly.

Not that she would have heard the edge in his voice, since she was excitedly clapping her hands together. "Oh, Ian, that was so sweet of you. And look," she said, pointing at the porch, "you even bought more lights and decorated the cultured tree." She looked over with a lopsided smile and touched his arm. "I tried to hang them this morning, but they tangled into a mess. It must have taken you an hour just to get that knot out. Did you see the snow angel I made when I fell off the porch?" she asked with a laugh, pointing toward the front lawn. "I nearly gave Toby a heart attack and then frostbite when he waded through the snow to see if I'd broken my neck." She pressed her hands to her chest. "Oh, Ian, thank you. My home is beautiful."

"I didn't hang the lights, Jess."

She snapped her gaze to his. "You didn't?" She looked back at the house. "Then who . . . when . . . Please tell me Roger did this," she whispered, looking back at him. "Or Alec or Duncan or . . . or . . ." She dropped her gaze to the stick tucked between her and the console, and slowly leaned away until she was plastered up against the car door. "Ohmigod," she whispered.

Ian leaned closer. "Do ye feel like you've just been knocked on your butt, lass?"

Chapter Thirteen

JESSIE STOOD IN HER STEAM-FILLED BATHROOM, STARING at the definitely male can of shaving cream, a five-bladed razor, and Ian's damp toothbrush all sitting on the shelf over her sink and wondered what sort of mess she'd gotten herself into. Because she still couldn't believe she was about to crawl into bed with a man she was afraid already had the power to break her heart.

"Jess?" Ian called from the other side of the wall. "Could you come in here and settle a little matter, please?"

Giving a quick glance in the mirror to make sure her boobs were even, Jessie tightened the belt on her robe, took a really, really deep breath, and opened the door. "What's the problem?" she asked as she boldly walked into her bedroom on rubbery legs, only to find Toby lying in the middle of her bed glaring at Ian, who was standing at the foot glaring back at him.

"It would appear Toby doesn't understand that a double

bed is barely designed for two warm bodies, much less three," he said, gesturing at the dog.

Oh God, she'd completely forgotten about Toby. Thankful to see that even if Ian wasn't going to wear pajamas he at least was willing to wear boxers, Jessie tried not to notice how the soft light emphasized his muscles when he folded his arms over his utterly glorious naked chest. She smiled to see if she couldn't lighten the mood. "I think Toby thinks sleeping with me is part of his job description."

"Then I guess you're going to have to explain to him that I'm taking over the night watch." Ian gestured at the living room wall. "So tell him he can guard the house from beside the stove."

"I can't just kick Toby out of bed; it would hurt his feelings."

"Well, all three of us won't fit in that bed, which means *one* of us is going to have to sleep on the floor."

Dammit, when she'd hoped and dreamed of making love again, she hadn't even considered she might have to evict one male to make room for the other. Oh God, what if Toby heard them and thought Ian was hurting her? Jessie turned and sat down on the bed and hid her face in her hands. "I . . . I don't know what to do."

Her hands were gently pulled away to reveal Ian kneeling in front of her. "How about if we bring Toby's bed in here and set it on the floor beside you, and you try to persuade him to spend the night there?"

"But what if he hears us or he sees you on top of . . . What if he thinks you're hurting me?" She dropped her head to his wonderful-smelling chest. "This isn't going to work, Ian. I never even thought about the logistics of us making love."

He cupped her face to look at him, his smile making

his eyes glitter with warmth. "We'll figure this out. I'll go get Toby's bed and set it on the floor beside you, and you see if you can't coax him down."

She nodded inside his hands, and Ian pulled her forward and gave her a kiss on her forehead, then stood up and disappeared into the hall. Jessie turned to recline next to Toby, who now had his glare trained on the bedroom door.

"Tobias Pringle," she whispered, holding his snout to make him look at her. "Don't you mess this up for me because it's really important. I've finally found someone I trust as much as I trust you, and if I don't make love to Ian tonight, I might lose my nerve. This is a big part of why we came here, Tobes; so I can get back *all* of my life. Please cooperate and let Ian have your side of the bed." She kissed the soft fur on his cheek. "Please?"

Ian came in with Toby's ratty old bed—because the big lug wouldn't have anything to do with the nice L.L.Bean bed she'd bought him on their way up—and placed it on the thick wool area rug at Jessie's feet. He then pulled Toby's squeaky toy from under his arm, gave it a squeak as he bobbed his eyebrows, and tossed it down on the dog's bed.

Jessie sighed when Toby went back to glaring at him. She stood up and patted—a tad forcefully—Ian's gloriously naked chest. "You're the one who has a way with animals; *you* persuade him to sleep on the floor." That said, she slipped off her robe, tossed it on the chair beside her bureau, shut off the lamp, pulled back the blankets, and climbed into bed.

Toby immediately cuddled up against her back with a loud doggy sigh.

Jessie felt the blankets lift away and was picked up and lowered down to Toby's bed, and before she could even finish gasping, Ian was cuddled up to her back.

"Are you serious?" she said, trying to hold in her laughter. "You expect us to make love on the floor?"

"No, I expect us to *sleep* on the floor, but only for tonight. I'll figure out our sleeping arrangements tomorrow. I thought Dixon was my competition," he muttered, "not some fur-covered, woman-hoarding, overgrown baby with sensitive feelings."

"We . . . we're not going to make love?"

"I forgot to stop by my truck."

"Um . . . I have condoms."

She felt Ian stiffen. "Why?"

Jessie gave a laugh as she turned inside his embrace. "Merissa bought them for me when she got groceries, only she hid them in the linen closet and didn't tell me until she shouted it out in the airport as she was walking to her boarding gate."

"Nice friend," he said, spooning her back up against him. "Go to sleep, Jess." She felt the bed moving above her and Toby's head lowered over the side with a pathetic whine. She started to reach up to pat him, but Ian captured her hand and tucked it back inside his embrace. "Don't reward him for making you sleep on the floor."

"*You're* making me sleep on the floor."

"Consider yourself lucky I didn't drag you up the mountain to sleep in a tent until Dixon gets the hint and leaves."

"Are you forgetting I have a bad back?"

He gave her a squeeze. "What I'm *not* forgetting is that you have a magical wand you seem to think can fix anything."

Jessie stared into the dark cavity under her bed. "Are . . . are we really not going to make love tonight?"

"Yes," he said on a sigh. "We're really not."

Dammit, what was his problem? "Then *when*?" she snapped.

"When ye no longer feel the need to wear your bra to bed, Jess," he said quietly, adjusting his position to tuck her head under his chin. "Or your pajamas. Now go to sleep," he growled, giving her another squeeze. "I've had a really trying day rescuing a woman who finds having three males vying for her affections to be entertaining."

Why, of all the ner—

"And Jess?"

"What?" she snapped again.

"Don't go sneaking around in the dark trying to get up in bed with Toby. I'm still a bit quick to react when I'm startled awake, thanks to my tours in Afghanistan."

Jessie went very still. "Are you serious?" she whispered.

He shrugged, shrugging her with him. "It's only a worry that hasn't actually been tested, as I haven't had any sleepovers since returning." He sighed heavily again. "I do hope ye don't snore too loudly, though."

Lovely. Not only did she still have getting naked hanging over her head, but now she had to worry about *Ian* having a flashback.

JESSIE PATTED HER FACE DRY IN THE SKI LODGE'S LARGE public bathroom, then grabbed another fistful of paper towels as she smiled at the four-year-old girl sitting on the counter trying to talk to Toby while her mother washed her sweet cherub face. After patting it dry, the mom lifted the precious little heathen off the counter and sat her in the child-sized wheelchair with a sigh. "I'm really sorry about that, Jessie," the woman said with a sheepish grin as she glanced at Toby and shook her head.

Jessie ruffled the cherub's soft blond curls with a laugh. "I guess that's why it's called Camp Come-As-You-Are.

Don't worry, Jane, Toby and I have survived worse disasters. But when you go back to the crafts area, could you tell Megan that I had to take Toby home and give him a bath?"

"Sure, Jess." Jane reached down and tentatively patted Toby, then had to grab her daughter when the girl nearly fell out of her chair attempting to give him a good-bye hug. "Come on, hot wheels, let's go finish painting Daddy's Christmas present before he gets back from skiing," she said, pushing the girl out through the door while making the sound of a revving engine and squealing tires.

Jessie dampened the fistful of towels she was holding then led Toby out of the restroom, keeping the huge, two-story-tall granite hearth between them and the chaos, and quickly slipped out through the lodge door leading onto the massive deck.

Four nights, she thought as she sucked in the snow-cooled air. She'd spent four nights sleeping curled up in Ian's arms, and Jessie couldn't decide if she felt like a frustrated virgin or an idiot for not knowing what to do about it. Not only had they not made love yet, but last night Ian had walked in the bedroom from his shower minus his boxers, climbed into bed, and pulled her against his gloriously naked body—the evidence pressing against her backside that if he wasn't willing he certainly was *able* to make love to her.

He'd solved their little sleeping arrangement problem quickly enough if rather diabolically. The next day when they'd arrived home from TarStone after both working at Camp Come-As-You-Are, Jessie had walked in her bedroom to find Ian's giant four-poster bed sitting where hers used to be. And the mattress was so far off the floor that Toby couldn't jump up on it because the monstrous thing took up so much space that he couldn't get a running start.

Jessie didn't mind that Ian had brought over his bed,

considering hers was only a double and barely large enough for him alone. But she sure as hell minded that he'd obviously had Alec and Duncan help him move it, which meant that they—and likely now everyone else—knew Ian was living with her.

That was probably why Ian's mom had been spontaneously hugging Jessie over the course of the last three days, and Morgan had been . . . well, one minute Ian's dad was eyeing her speculatively and the next he was soliciting her advice on ramping up their European marketing campaign for the ski resort.

Jessie had learned some very interesting things about Ian since they'd started living together. For one thing, the man wasn't just grouchy when he was hungry; he also got testy whenever the subject of Brad's impending visit came up—specifically how she intended to spend her time entertaining her brother-in-law—as well as any mention of Roger. Ian also got a tad grouchy whenever Jessie was handling her walking stick, and he and Toby were no longer best buddies, it seemed, since the big lug had realized Ian was poaching his territory.

But they'd fallen into an amazingly comfortable routine, quite similar, Jessie was afraid, to that of an old married couple. They would ride home together from TarStone every evening, eat something she dug out of a can or the freezer, then watch a little television, go to bed—Ian boosting her onto the mattress while smiling smugly down at Toby—and get up the next morning and do it all over again.

Tonight, however, the boy campers were having their midnight swim, so Ian would be returning to TarStone around the time she would be entertaining her brother-in-law, as Brad had called her this morning to say he was just leaving Boston. He'd had to call Ian's cell phone—she'd given him the number, since Roger did indeed have hers. He'd actually texted her—though she had no idea how he knew to send it to Ian's number—to tell her how thrilled he was that she'd decided to give him her fancy, newfangled phone in exchange for the pot and wagon. Oh, and had she learned to cook up a fine, juicy roast yet?

Jessie had fixed the old goat by canceling her service plan, only to have to call her provider in Atlanta a second time and cancel it again when Roger sent all her phone's pictures to Ian's number, saying he thought she might like to have them. As soon as camp was over, she was driving to Greenville to get herself a new phone and giving Ian's back, since he was using one that belonged to the hotel.

Jessie hadn't yet broken the news to Ian that Brad was arriving this afternoon, because he and Alec and Duncan were up on the mountain with the older children and some of the fathers backcountry skiing. Apparently just about everyone in the clans took vacations from their regular jobs to volunteer with the winter session of Camp Come-As-You-Are, and the camp's summer staff who could make it also showed up. The session was so popular with the families that the entire three-story, ninety-room hotel was full to bursting, with the visiting staff staying in the secluded rental cabins scattered across the bottom of the mountain. Most of the daytime activities such as arts and crafts took place in the massive ski lodge at the base of the trails, and weather permitting—which it had been so far this week—the campers and parents rode the gondola up and back to the summit house for lunch.

Jessie straightened from soothing her somewhat traumatized dog when she saw Duncan and Alec swoosh to a stop beside the deck and start taking off their skis.

"What in hell happened to you two?" Alec asked as

Jessie walked over to them, having to all but drag Toby along with her.

"Somebody knocked over a plastic quart jar of paint," she said, wiping her cheek with her dampened paper towel, "and when it hit the floor, it more or less exploded." She laughed, bending to wipe the paint off Toby's snout only to find it was already starting to dry. "And as you can see, Toby was in the direct line of fire. So I'm bringing him outside to roll around in the snow, hoping to make him less . . . green."

Alex shot her a grin. "One of the hazards of arts and crafts and the main reason we work outdoors," he said, nodding to include Duncan—who was *not* smiling.

In fact, the scowl Duncan had aimed at Jessie was heated enough to stop her in midlaugh. "What?" she asked, glancing down at herself and then behind her. "Is there a problem?"

"Well," Duncan said, crossing his arms on his chest, "if I had to guess, I would say *you're* the problem."

"Excuse me?" She looked toward the ski slope. "Um . . . where's Ian?"

"Up the mountain," Duncan said, "*walking* down."

"Why?"

Alec snorted. "Because that's the only way to get down without skis."

"Did he fall and break one of them?" she asked, only to take a step back when Duncan started toward her.

"No, I broke the both of them," he said quietly. "And he's damn lucky I used a tree to do it instead of his back." Duncan stopped his advance when Toby stepped between them, but that didn't stop him from continuing to scowl at her. "When we helped Ian move *his* bed into *your* bedroom Monday, we figured he'd at least become tolerable again, but it seems the problem has only gotten worse."

"W-what problem?"

"You, Jessie," Duncan growled. "You're the problem. Before he moved in with you, the man was merely a menace, but for the last three days Ian's been a ticking bomb." He smiled, and not very nicely. "So I finally detonated him today, and I must say I've never enjoyed myself more."

"Jessie," Alec said a bit more civilly as he walked up beside Duncan. "We don't . . . It's not that we think . . ." Two dark flags appeared on his wind-chapped cheeks and he sighed, looking at Duncan.

"Are you or are you not sleeping with Ian?" Duncan growled.

"I really don't think that's any of your business."

"Oh, but it is our business," Duncan softly countered, "because a sexually frustrated man is a danger to anyone within striking distance. So when ye go home this afternoon *alone*, I suggest you spend your evening figuring out how to fix the problem."

"I'm not the problem; he is," Jessie whispered, feeling her own cheeks turn as red as their ski parkas. She glanced up the mountain, then back at them. "And why am I going home alone?"

"Because it takes quite a while to walk down from the North Slope without snowshoes," Alec explained.

"But he'll be back in time for the midnight swim, won't he?"

"You better hope he isn't," Duncan said, shaking his head. "Or we're likely to gang up and drown him." He then sidestepped around her—or more specifically, around Toby—and headed toward the lodge. "Fix this, Jessie," he said over his shoulder.

"You really do need to fix this, lass," Alec softly repeated, also sidestepping, but then hesitating. He smiled, and it was a much nicer smile than Duncan's. "I can't tell you how glad Duncan and I were when Ian asked us to sneak off and help him move his bed on Monday. I swear, this is the first time since he enlisted that I've seen my brother acting so . . . well, you're good for him, Jessie. No one else would admit this to you, but we've all noticed Ian's been in a downward spiral this last year. But since you arrived and caught his eye, he's been acting more like the man I grew up with." He grinned. "Well, except maybe a wee more intense."

Jessie reached out to stop him when he started up onto the deck. "Are you also in line to take over running Tar-Stone, Alec?"

"Aye, all us boys are," he said with a nod.

"And do you *want* to run the resort?"

His gaze traveled up the ski trails, then to the hotel, and then the lodge before returning to her. "TarStone is in our blood, Jessie, and will be until the day we die. We leave to attend college and then go fight whatever war needs fighting at the time, and some of us even try to move on, but the mountain eventually calls us home. So to answer your question, yes, I will step up when the time comes, just as Ian and Duncan and the others will."

"But what if you didn't want to? *Could* you do something else?"

He shook his head. "There is nothing else; TarStone's hold on us is just too powerful."

Toby gave a frantic whine and nudged Jessie's leg, and she looked down to see him shivering. "Ian said Toby will grow a winter coat," she muttered, backing toward the parking lot, "but it's not happening very fast. Thanks, Alec, for telling me about Ian. I . . . I'll see what I can do to fix the problem," she finished, quickly turning away before he could see her blush.

But she suddenly stopped and turned back, having learned over the last few days exactly how this clan thing worked. "Alec," she called just as he was about to enter the lodge. She gestured toward the mountain. "It's too bad Ian's going to be back so late, because I know he's been looking forward to meeting my brother-in-law." She glanced at her watch. "And Brad should be arriving any minute now." Jessie shrugged and started walking backward again. "I guess I'll just have to take him to Pete's for drinks by myself." She turned away to hide her smile, and waved over her shoulder. "Have fun swimming with the heathens and hellions tonight."

Chapter Fourteen

JESSIE TOOK HER TIME BUILDING THE FIRE IN HER WOOD-stove, stopping occasionally to smile at Toby lying on his bed and glaring at the kitchen, then looking over her shoulder to smile at Brad cooking supper. But those smiles were nothing compared to the little heart thumps she got every time she remembered the scene in TarStone's parking lot about an hour ago.

She'd just been wrapping Toby's car blanket around him when Brad had driven into the resort, spotted her, and stopped right in the middle of the lane to get out and hug her so tightly that he'd lifted her off her feet. But he'd set her down just as quickly when Toby had growled at him from beneath his blanket. Oh yeah; green had been quite the appropriate paint for Toby to be covered in, as apparently the big lug was tired of all the males trying to poach her away from him.

But what really tickled Jessie was that she had seen

Duncan and Alec standing on the deck watching Brad hugging her, then Alec running toward the resort's machine garage only to see a snowmobile go racing up the chairlift path toward the summit not two minutes later.

Jessie figured Ian should be making his appearance any moment now. She hadn't told Brad about him yet, but she hadn't run into the bathroom and hidden all the obviously male paraphernalia when they'd arrived home, either. Still, she probably should break the news to him before Ian showed up, or she was liable to find herself having to deal with three angry males.

"You know, Brad, my life has changed quite dramatically since I've moved here," she began, turning to sit on the hearth to face the kitchen.

"I can see that," he said, shooting a smile over his shoulder before turning back to chop the asparagus he'd brought all the way from Boston. "You've purchased a beautiful house on a lake in Maine, traded your cane for a hiking stick—that you don't seem to need anymore—and you . . ." He stopped chopping and turned to her. "And though I didn't think it was possible, you've grown even more beautiful," he said gruffly.

Oh God; she could see this wasn't going to be easy. Jessie nodded demurely. "Thank you. But I also . . . um, there's something I need . . ." She stood up and rubbed her hands on her thighs. "I've also met a man," she said softly, hugging herself when she saw Brad stiffen. "A really nice man. He and his family run the ski resort, and we've grown rather close. Ian and I are . . . we're—"

"You've been here less than three weeks, Jessica," Brad interrupted. He smiled, waving the knife in the air. "You're just infatuated with him. He's a novelty; some rugged-looking ski bum," he said, gesturing dismissively again.

"You only think you're attracted to him because he's so different from the men you're used to." He laughed. "You might be able to take the woman out of the city, but you can't take the city out of the woman." He turned back to the counter and cut open the bag of fingerling purple potatoes. "This part of the country might be beautiful to look at and visit, but I give you until spring before you start missing the buzz of the city. And work," he said over his shoulder. "What exactly are you planning to do with all your time up here, Jessie?"

"I've already been offered a couple of local marketing jobs."

"For what?" he asked with a derisive laugh, turning toward her. "Are you going to design newspaper ads for the bakery? Or that outfitter store we saw in town?"

"The ski resort wants to ramp up their European advertising, and there's a wonderful children's camp here that the owners want to market overseas. In fact, the reason you couldn't stay at TarStone is that the camp's going on right now; they take over the entire resort the middle week of December every year." She gestured toward Toby, then down at herself. "I was volunteering there today, which is how we both got covered in green paint."

"That's very noble of you to volunteer, Jessica, but how exciting can it be to do arts and crafts with a bunch of kids? And then it's only for a week, you said."

"No, you don't understand. It's not a regular camp; it's especially designed for scarred and disabled children. Oh, Brad," she said, hugging herself again. "Some of those kids are missing arms or legs and some are so badly scarred that I . . . I ran into the bathroom the first day and burst into tears."

He rushed over and pulled her into his arms, pressing

her head to his shoulder. "You shouldn't have put yourself through that, Jessica," he softly scolded even as he rubbed his hand soothingly along her back. "It was difficult enough for you to go to physical therapy and see people like that, but *children*? Oh, Jess, why would you do that to yourself?" He set her away to clasp her shoulders. "Aren't you afraid being around them will trigger one of your flashbacks? That's why I persuaded you to get a private therapist two years ago, so you wouldn't be repeatedly traumatized."

He pulled her back into his arms, threading his fingers through her hair to hold her against him. "And it helped, didn't it?" he asked, his tone slightly scolding again. He leaned away just enough to look at her. "Have you had any flashbacks since you got here?" He gave her a squeeze. "Truthfully, have you?"

"Just two." She wiggled her hand up between them to tuck a strand of hair behind her ear. "But they've been really mild, and I didn't feel drained and didn't walk around in a stupor afterward as usual." She patted his chest and then stepped away. "And it's a lot easier to find places to hide here," she said, waving toward the window, "what with all the trees."

A look of horror crossed his face. "You're hiding in the woods like a wild animal?"

"Hey," she said with a laugh, "it beats the hell out of a public restroom."

One side of his mouth slowly lifted. "Yes, I suppose it does." He looked her up and down, and his eyes widened as he looked down at himself and held out his arms. "Good Lord, now I'm green," he said, snagging her hand as he headed into the hallway. "Come on, I need to clean myself up in order to finish cooking dinner while you take a shower. I am not feeding my gourmet masterpiece to a Dr. Seuss character."

Jessie pulled him to a stop, but not quickly enough. Brad's hold on her hand tightened at the same time she saw him stiffen. His gaze moved from the shelf over her bathroom sink to her, and his expression darkened. "The bastard has spent the night here?" he hissed. "You've *slept* with him?"

She twisted free and turned to head back to the living room.

"Jessica!" Brad snapped, pulling her back around. "Didn't you learn your lesson with Eric?" His fingers dug into her shoulders. "You haven't even been here three weeks and you've crawled into bed with some *ski bum*?"

"No, she crawled into bed with me."

Shrieking in surprise, Jessie jerked away so quickly that she bumped into the sink and knocked several items off the shelf trying to catch herself as Brad spun toward the bathroom door with an equally surprised yelp.

"Ian MacKeage," Ian said with a rather feral-looking grin, extending his hand to Brad. "Jessie's boyfriend."

It took some doing, but Brad pulled himself together, and after smoothing down the front of his sweater, he shook Ian's hand. "Brad Dixon, Jessica's . . . brother-in-law."

It took even more doing for Jessie to gather her wits, especially when Ian turned that grin on her. "Is there a reason you didn't wait to come home with me?" he asked.

"Last I heard, you were walking down the mountain because both of your skis had somehow gotten broken."

Brad cleared his throat. "Yes, well, if you'll excuse me," he said, attempting to leave but then apparently deciding not to crowd past Ian. "I'm right in the middle of cooking

Jessie dinner." He smiled—quite civilly, actually—and Jessie suddenly realized what had always bugged her about Brad. "My biggest fear about Jessie moving here was that she'd starve to death without having me to cook for her." He chuckled. "She's not exactly Julia Child in the kitchen."

Jessie plopped down on the edge of the tub, vaguely aware of Ian stepping to the side so Brad could escape. Her mind's eye played images of Brad's cultured face over the last four years, and she just now realized that Brad Dixon wore a far more elaborate mask than Eric had.

She couldn't believe she'd missed it, because she thought she *had* learned her lesson with Eric. So how in hell had she not even noticed that Brad had methodically been making himself an integral part of her life? The man had set himself up to be her rock after the attack; coming to visit her every day, finding the perfect rehab center to move her to, sneaking in gourmet food to her—all of which is probably why his wife had gone on vacation to Nassau without him. And when Tracy had suddenly died in a freak boating accident, Brad's daily visits had turned into mutual healing sessions that had grown into . . . into . . .

"Ye look like you're seeing a ghost, lass," Ian said, squatting in front of her.

Jessie snapped out of her daze, blinking around the otherwise empty bathroom, only to hear Brad in the kitchen handling pots rather aggressively. She reached up and touched the faint bruise on Ian's jaw, and blew out a heavy breath as she darted a quick glance toward the hallway. "I think Brad and Eric are more alike than I realized," she whispered, "only Brad's far more subtle than his brother, apparently."

"Did he never make an advance toward you, Jess?"

"Once, about two years ago." She smiled sadly. "But I

flew into such a panic when . . . when he . . . well, he apologized profusely, saying he didn't know what had come over him, and he's been a perfect gentleman ever since."

"Yes, maybe too perfect," Ian said, using her own words from the other day. He stood up and smiled down at her. "You want me to give you a bath first, or Toby?"

She snorted and also stood up. "I'll take a shower down here, and you can give Toby his bath upstairs," she said, figuring it might be wise to keep them both away from Brad while she was in the shower. She started to pat Ian's chest but quickly changed her mind and touched his jaw again. "How come I didn't see any bruises on Duncan?"

"Because I had it coming," he said with a sigh, touching her shoulder. "Did Dixon hurt you just now?"

She dropped her gaze to his shirt. "Not nearly as much as I just hurt him." She looked up. "I can't believe I misread his intentions that badly. He had *four years* to tell me how he felt; why did he take so long?"

Ian shrugged. "He probably was waiting for you to make the first move. Only instead of moving into his arms, ye moved a couple thousand miles away." He looked toward the kitchen then back at her. "And it's my guess that he has—or had—every intention of taking you back to Atlanta with him, since you didn't seem to be coming to your senses. That's why just telling him I was your boyfriend wouldn't have worked."

She walked over to the linen closet, took out several towels and Toby's shampoo, and handed them to Ian. "Thank you for not . . . well, thank you for being civil just now. And thanks for offering to give Toby his bath, because—"

"Jessie, do you have a colander?" Brad asked, his voice moving toward them.

She pushed Ian out into the hallway ahead of her. "Yeah, I think Merissa put it in one of the bottom cupboards."

"Jess," Ian said, making her stop. "Does Toby enjoy baths?"

She stepped into her bedroom. "Not particularly," she said, closing the door and turning to lean against it, covering her face and sighing.

If Roger had been right about two men extending their hands to her, then she had to assume he was also right about neither one of them being exactly what he seemed. So if Brad Dixon was more like Eric than she'd realized, what secret was Ian hiding from her?

JESSIE STROLLED OUT THE FROG POINT ROAD BESIDE Brad, marveling at how well he was taking his . . . disappointment, although it wasn't stopping him from giving one more valiant effort to talk some sense into her before he left. But maybe more amazing was the fact that Ian was actually giving Brad the chance to try, since she'd been sure his highlander heritage would have reared its atavistic head and he'd have dragged her off to TarStone with him this morning. But he'd kissed her good-bye and climbed on the snowmobile he'd driven home last night, even giving a wave to Brad just pulling in the driveway, and zoomed off toward his mountain as if he didn't have a care in the world. And that had Jessie wondering if Megan and Katy hadn't been exaggerating about the men of their clans being unreasonably overprotective.

Brad had spent the first twenty minutes of their walk reminding Jessie of all he had to offer her; not material things, since she was basically set for money because Eric had kept at least one of his pie-in-the-sky promises and changed his will and insurance benefits within a week of slipping that diamond-encrusted band on her finger, leaving her everything he owned except his share of the gallery. No, Brad was speaking mostly to Jessie's emotions, gently reminding her of the tragic histories they shared, their mutual interest in the arts, gourmet dining, and crossword puzzles. Oh, and long walks, he'd added with a tender smile.

Although she did notice he hadn't mentioned offering her his love.

But then, neither had Ian.

Brad had tried to hold her hand that wasn't holding her walking stick, but Toby had inserted himself between them, causing Brad to shove his hands in his pockets as he continued his persuasions—only now instead of trying to compete with Ian, he'd started comparing Atlanta with Pine Creek.

"I'm sorry, Jessica, but I still can't see how you feel moving here is going to help you remember anything except why you were living in Dallas when Eric met you." He arched a brow. "Or did you also forget how much you dislike snow? Didn't you tell me that's why you chose the job in Dallas over the one in Chicago when you graduated?" He pulled a hand out of his pocket to wave at the lake on their right. "Trees and snow and ice for as far as you can see." He then gestured to their left, at the Randall house. "And the isolation, Jessie; your nearest neighbor is over a quarter mile away." He touched her arm to stop her and turned to face her. "How is any of this going to help you remember anything?" he growled softly. "Or isn't that why you came here?"

"It's only *part* of why I came here," she said, clutching her walking stick to her and rubbing a thumb over one of the burls. "But I also had to get away from Atlanta to stop feeling like a victim. Everything about that city reminded me of how foolish I'd been to let Eric deceive me like that." She reached out and touched his arm when he started to say something. "And I am remembering. Several days ago I remembered that I was moving out that night because I'd discovered Eric had lied about the mumps making him sterile, and I realized I was just another piece of the fairy-tale image he wanted the world to see. And that's not all," she continued before Brad could say anything. "I've just recently remembered that Eric was having an affair," she said, thumping her stick on the ground. "The entire three months we were married and I was carrying his child, and during our long-distance courtship, and the week we spent together in Dallas; he was involved with another woman the entire time." She shook her head. "Why didn't he just marry her, whoever the hell she was?"

Brad took a step back, his face having gone deathly pale. "You'd learned just that day that Eric was seeing someone?"

Jessie stepped up to him. "Did you know?"

He held up his hands. "No. I mean, I suspected Eric was seeing a woman even after the Dallas conference, but I had hoped he would stop once he married you."

"Who was she?"

Brad took another step back and held his hands up again. "I don't know, Jess. Eric never brought a woman around." He snorted. "But I suspected that was because she was married." He stepped closer and took hold of her shoulders. "You're right. Eric had this grand image of himself as a world player, and it didn't take me long to see that you were just window dressing." He shook his head. "My God, that damn museum of a house he built and kept filling with art nearly bankrupted the business, and then he walked in without any warning and introduced you to

Tracy and me as his wife, and I . . ." Brad let Jessie go and paced away, then spun around and shoved his hands in his pockets again. "Eric told me once during an argument we were having over the cost of that house that he wanted to bury his pedestrian roots so far under a ton of fine art that kings and sheikhs would have him on speed dial."

He walked up and cupped her shoulders, his anger suddenly dissipating into a tender smile. "You were what, Jessie . . . twenty-three, twenty-four when Eric saw you at the conference in Dallas? When you walked in on his arm, I swear my house filled with fresh air. You were so vibrant, so beautiful, so . . ." He shook his head. "So damn naive." He laughed softly. "You were also as green as you were yesterday, and right in the middle of the introductions you ran into the powder room and threw up." He just as suddenly sobered. "I'm sorry, Jessica, for not protecting you from my brother. And I'm sorry for not getting to the house in time that night to stop that guy from reaching you."

She gently pulled out of his grasp and turned and started slowly walking toward home as Toby placed himself between them again. "You got there in time to stop him from killing me," she said, absently rubbing her thumb over the burl above her hand.

Brad reached across Toby and pulled her to a halt. "No, Jessica; you had already stopped him with the revolver Eric always kept in his nightstand. I told you myself how it happened once I felt you could handle it. I just showed up—almost too late—and without even thinking, I merely finished what you had already started."

She began walking again. "I'm not so sure about that, Brad," she whispered. "I've been getting images of that night, but they . . . they're jumbled," she said, glancing over and shaking her head. "I can't seem to put them in order, but I do remember he . . . I could . . . I heard him killing Eric," she whispered. "And I was so scared, and trapped, and I didn't know what to do. Then the guy started kicking the bathroom door, and I remember breaking the window over the tub with the vanity stool, because . . . because I figured jumping two stories to the ground was better than letting him reach me." She drew in a shuddering breath. "But he broke down the door just as I was trying to pull myself onto the sash, and that's when I felt the knife plunge into my lower back." She started walking faster, the images rushing through her with the force of a train as she lifted a hand to her throat. "And I fell back and saw . . . I didn't even see his face, just that knife coming at my throat and my arm rising to push it away."

"Jessica, *stop this*," Brad growled, reaching over and pulling her to a halt again. "You need to stop remembering. Stop *reliving* it."

She stared at his chest, ignoring Toby's whine as he tried to wedge between them. "I remember suddenly hearing gunshots, then I'm sure I remember struggling against being carried into the bedroom, and then more gunshots."

"Jessica!" Brad snapped, reaching for her shoulders only to stumble back when Toby jumped against him. "Jessie, listen to me," he petitioned more calmly, his arms stretched toward her. "The detectives ran forensic tests, including looking for traces of gunpowder on each of us. They found it on both of your hands, and figured you needed both hands to hold the gun because it was such a large caliber. But they found gunpowder on only one of mine because I was holding pressure on the wound on your back because . . ." He looked down at his hands as if they were covered in blood. "Because that one seemed the most severe." He lifted his gaze to her, his glistening eyes reflecting the horror as if it were happening right now. "But you were in the *bedroom* when I ran upstairs. And the guy was lying in the bathroom doorway, and Eric was . . . he was . . ." Brad gestured weakly. "The nightstand drawer was on the floor next to him beside the bed. He must have been going after his gun."

"Could . . . could Eric have shot the robber before he died?"

He shook his head. "According to the detectives, they didn't find any residue on his hands, just yours and mine." Brad started walking again, giving her a concerned glance as he shoved his fists in his jacket pockets. "I know you've refused to read the police report, but since you seem to be remembering, maybe reading it now would put things in perspective."

She drew in another shuddering breath, having to lean on her walking stick because she was shaking so badly. "Maybe you're right," she admitted.

"Do you remember how you found out Eric was having an affair? Or how you found out he'd lied about being sterile?"

She shook her head. "I still can't remember that part, but I do keep hearing a woman's voice, only I can't tell if she was on the phone or in person or even what she was say—" Jessie's coat pocket suddenly belted out an unfamiliar tune that was so loud, she stumbled several steps in surprise.

She reached in her pocket, pulled out Ian's phone, and flipped it open, then squinted against the sunshine to read the message: **Stop talking, missy.** That was all it said, just for her to stop talking. And then she saw it was from her old phone number. Jessie pulled in a calming breath and snapped the phone shut, shoved it back in her pocket, and resumed walking.

"Who was it?" Brad took a calming breath of his own. "Or should I even ask?"

"It was Mom wanting to know if they need to buy a four-wheel-drive truck in order to reach Pine Creek," she said, giving him the best smile she could muster. She turned into her driveway and stopped at the back of his rental car. "I'm beginning to think you're right, Brad; remembering the details of that night isn't going to accomplish anything. So maybe I should just burn my copy of the police report. Yeah," she said with a nod when he seemed to relax. "I'll have a large bonfire down by the lake on the next full moon, and put that horrible night behind me once and for all." She scrunched her shoulders and gave him a crooked grin. "And who knows, maybe sending those memories up to the moon and stars will stop the flashbacks, and I'll finally quit fighting an attacker who's been dead for four years."

Brad opened his arms, and Jessie leaned her walking stick against the trunk of the car, stepped around Toby, and walked into his embrace. He held her fiercely for the longest time, then let her go with a sigh. But instead of getting in the car, he started moving toward the house, holding up his hand when she frowned. "I think I'd better use your facilities before I head out. I'll just be a minute," he said, turning to jog up the pathway and scaling the steps to disappear inside.

Jessie grabbed her stick then walked over and opened her garage door, intending to get a few pieces of firewood so she'd have an excuse not to go through another drawn-out hugging session with Brad, but stopped when she saw something unfamiliar peeking out past the end of the woodpile.

She glanced toward the house, then walked down the length of the pile and pulled back the edge of an old blanket she didn't recognize—only to gasp when she saw the giant bird feeder and a large bag of birdfeed sitting beside it.

"Jessie?" Brad called out.

"I'm coming," she said, quickly lowering the blanket over the feeder and giving it a tug to make sure the bag was also hidden. She rushed out of the garage to find Brad standing by his car again, a sheepish smile on his face.

"Sorry for taking so long, but I had to stop and take a couple of pictures of your Christmas tree. Whatever possessed you to put that one inside instead of the cultured tree on your porch?"

She shrugged. "What can I say? I got sucked in by its beauty."

He snorted, and after checking to make sure Toby wasn't going to attack him, Brad pulled her into his arms again and hugged her tightly. "Do I have even a small chance of getting you to come home with me, Jess?"

Wrapping her arms around his waist, Jessie hugged him just as fiercely. "I'm sorry, Brad, but I already am home," she whispered thickly, her throat aching with remorse. She gave his back a brisk series of pats and pulled away. "Promise me you'll get on with your life, too. Find yourself a nice city girl, preferably one who'll give you a run for your money in the kitchen." She smiled crookedly. "Only try to be a little quicker and a lot less subtle about showing her how you feel, okay?"

He smoothed down the front of his jacket, two flags of red darkening his cheeks. "I . . . er . . . I've never been much of an extrovert, so I'm not exactly sure how to go about finding *another* nice city girl." He grinned derisively. "Any suggestions?"

Jessie slipped an arm through his and started toward the driver side of his car. "Yes, as a matter of fact, I do. For some crazy reason I've caught myself looking through various college catalogs on the Internet lately, and I happened to notice that a lot of them offer cooking classes. Sign up for one or two, and make sure to partner with a gal who likes to cook gourmet more than she likes eating it."

Brad turned from opening the car door, his expression somewhat surprised. "Cooking classes?" He looked off into the distance. "I never would have thought of doing something like that," he murmured, looking back at her. "Are . . . are you *sure*, Jessica?" he asked softly.

"Yeah, I'm sure." She clasped his face and stretched up to kiss his cheek. "We'll keep in touch, Brad, I promise."

"Yeah, we'll keep in touch," he said, turning to slide in behind the wheel. He started to close the door but hesitated. "That ski bum gives you any trouble, you call me, okay?" he said gruffly. "I'll be on your doorstep in less than a day."

"Thank you for that, Brad. And you, too; your cooking partner gives you any back talk in the kitchen, you call me and . . ." She shot him a broad grin. "And I'll call Merissa and send her over to save you."

He gave a loud snort, rolling his eyes as he shut the door. Jessie followed Toby over to the pathway, then stood and watched Brad back out of the driveway and start down the road, waving when he gave a soft honk of the horn.

She ruffled the fur on Toby's head. "Okay, you big lug, are you happy now? I would say by your count, that's one down and one more to go." She headed up onto the porch, stopping to adjust the lights on the cultured Christmas tree before stepping inside. "Just don't think you're going to scare Ian off quite that easily," she cautioned, walking to the center of the room. Jessie slowly looked around her home, her gaze stopping on her beautiful little fir tree with its branches sagging under the weight of the decorations she'd bought, and she broke into a smile just as her pocket started blaring out a . . . good Lord, was that "Hark! the Herald Angels Sing"?

She pulled out the cell phone and flipped it open. **It's not your body Ian is wanting to make love to, Jess, but you. Don't you think it's time you got naked?**

"Now you're giving me advice on my *love life*, you old goat?" She snapped the phone shut on the perfectly punctuated text and started to shove it in her pocket when "Silent Night" started playing.

I've learned that in this century it's quite acceptable for a woman to do the seducing, so when ye finally do get around to it, don't be discounting the power of a warm, inviting home filled with the scent of a fine roast in the oven. Jessie had to push the button to scroll down, wondering how on earth Roger was able to send such a long text. **And doors are designed to close, you know, if you're worried about a certain big fella being traumatized by seeing his mistress carrying on with another big fella. I'm afraid you're down to only thirty-eight hours and forty-five minutes, though, Jess, for you to be holding Ian's hand, so I suggest you get cracking. But if you're hesitating because ye still might be worrying about what secret he's keeping, understand that he's not hiding it from you near as much as he's denying it even exists. So I guess that means you're simply going to have to take a leap of faith, lass, and love him anyway.**

It's time, Jess, to create your miracles.

She softly closed the phone and stood staring at it, utterly speechless as ripples of heat and then cold raced through her. Okay, she got it; Ian was her miracle. But what miracle could she possibly give him in return? Jessie blew out a sigh and unbuttoned her coat when the phone started . . . good Lord, it was playing "Grandma Got Run Over by a Reindeer."

She opened it and started reading again. **I hope you've figured out by now that if creating miracles was easy, there wouldn't be any reason for a crazy old goat like me to have to come along and give you a nudge, now would there? And just so ye know, I'm still waiting for my Christmas dinner invitation, missy. Should I assume it's gotten itself lost in the mail? 'Cause getting to know you as I have, I'm really looking forward to meeting the folks who raised such a smart and courageous lass—although I'm still gonna ask your mama why she neglected to teach ye to cook. And don't ye go worrying none, 'cause I'll still be bringing the Scotch.**

Jessie slowly closed the phone, and after a glance at the wall clock, buttoned her coat back up as she mentally counted how many hours until Ian got home, and decided she had enough time to drive to Greenville and buy another roast.

"Come on, Tobes," she said, patting her leg as she grabbed her purse and walking stick and headed back outside. "If I'm going to stage a seduction, then I guess I probably better get cracking."

Chapter Fifteen

Ian sat sideways on his snowmobile parked in the woods across the road from Jessie's house, his feet crossed at the ankles and his arms folded over his chest, waiting until it was time for him to go home. He stared past the wildly blinking lights strung the length of the porch to the open kitchen window covered in steam, wondering if he'd ever stop feeling like he was constantly being strangled. Hell, he hadn't taken a normal breath since he'd *met* Jessie.

His father had warned him it could happen like this, setting eyes on a woman for the first time and getting sucker punched. Ian had been fifteen when his old man had taken him hiking in the back mountain valleys for their father-son talk about women, after he'd innocently asked how to handle a girl at school who'd set her sights on him. The next thing he knew, he'd been rousted out of bed at three in the morning—on a school day, no less—hustled out of the house before his mom could catch them, and all but tossed up on a horse loaded with enough supplies to last a week.

It had been the first time—and the last, actually—that Ian had ever known Morgan MacKeage to be so . . . demonstrative. His father had really opened up about how he'd first laid eyes on Sadie Quill right there at the same lake they were camped beside. Apparently his father had swum across the lake—naked, of course—and pulled himself up onto that rock right over there to sun himself, he'd said, pointing. That is, until he'd gotten the feeling he was being watched. And that's when this beautiful, long-legged, blue-eyed blonde, realizing he'd heard the shutter on her camera, had stood up in a panic and started running.

Morgan had gone on to explain their unusual courtship— which had taken place out there in the valley more than in town—where his biggest hurdle had been getting the overly self-conscious woman to realize he really didn't see her scarred body because he was too busy looking at *her*.

Ian uncrossed his ankles to kick the snow at his feet, wondering if he shouldn't just ask his mom how to approach Jessie. Because honestly, he didn't think he could take many more nights sleeping with Jessie and not make love to her. The woman knew he already knew she was missing part of her breast, so why in hell wouldn't she give him a chance to prove how much he didn't care that she wasn't perfect? It wasn't her body that had sucker punched him; it was her smiling eyes and lying straight face, her bluntness and courage, and her willingness to get back up every time a flashback knocked her down.

Ian gave a start when the inside pocket of his jacket started vibrating and pulled out his cell phone to look at the caller ID, giving a sigh as he flipped it open. **Tell her**, the text read. **Tell the lass how she's brought a powerful warrior to his** knees with nothing more than her smile. Hell, boy, even your papa eventually got it right, and he was a bigger stubborn ass than you are. Or do ye want to spend the rest of your life walking your mountain alone? Jessie made her choice; ye saw yourself that Dixon drove off without her this morning. So quit acting like some snotty-nosed little heathen, and walk in there like the true highlander ye are and tell her. And Ian, you'd best be telling her everything.

He shut the phone and started to slip it back in his pocket when it rang. "God dammit," he growled in way of answering, "if I ever get my hands on you, de Keage, I swear I'm burying you in that snowcat so far under a mound of posies, it'll take you over a century to see the light of day again."

"Now is that any way to talk to your favorite long-lost ancestor?" Roger asked quietly, although Ian could hear the amusement in his voice. "So, do ye want my sage advice or not, you hardheaded bastard?"

"Not."

Roger snorted. "You do know that if she finds out ye spent the day spying on her—all the way to Greenville, I might add—she'll have you sleeping out by the hearth and Toby will be in that bed of yours. After, that is, she takes her staff to you."

"Then I guess she'd better not find out, had she?"

"Our lass is doing a fine job of accepting the magic, wouldn't you say?" Roger said, his voice deepened with self-importance. Ian heard him suddenly sigh. "Although I'm afraid she's not taking it as seriously as she needs to. Not if ye hope to get her through the coming maelstrom."

Ian jumped to his feet. "What maelstrom?" he growled. "What's happening?"

"The past is what's happening. Tomorrow night Jessie's

past is going to catch up with her, and you and the dog are all that's standing between her and certain death this time. But where Tobias is quite capable of fighting an enemy he can actually sink his teeth into, you're the only one who can save Jessie from this particular demon. And you know why, MacKeage?" Roger asked roughly. "Because deny it or not, you have a gift."

"No, I don't."

"Sorry, big fella," the old hermit growled, "but I really don't have the time to knock any more sense into you. And ye can blame that on Jessie, since it took her so damn long to get herself here. So ye only have until tomorrow night to decide if you want to take on Jessie's demon."

"What's happening, de Keage?"

"What's it matter to you, if you're not willing to accept your calling?"

"You know damn well it matters."

"Do ye recall any of the tale I told you last summer?"

"I remember ye rambling on about some fairy-tale maiden trapped in a gilded cage," Ian said impatiently, "and two masked monsters battling each other for her affect—" He stiffened. "Jessie referred to herself as a fairy-tale wife. Dammit, de Keage, why didn't you just tell me you were speaking about a real person *last summer*?"

A heavy sigh came over the phone. "Because even then I was already interfering more than I was supposed to. I can't force ye to accept your destiny, Ian, any more than I could have forced Jessie to choose you. It's this accursed free will thing that's tying my hands. But I can," he growled when Ian started to interrupt, "give ye fair warning. Ye have all day tomorrow to prepare, so I suggest you skip the birthday party for Greylen's daughters tomorrow night and decide if denying your gift means more to you than Jessie does. And Ian?"

"What?"

"It's an all-or-nothing thing; once you own the power there's no going back. And just so ye know, it never did have anything to do with animals. Ye chose to believe—and let your family believe—in something innocuous rather than face the truth."

"And that would be?"

There was a pause, then a snort. "Ye spent four years in college and five in the military trying to outrun your destiny, yet when you finally did come home ye spent damn near every night on the very seat of your power. You *are* TarStone, Ian; you and the mountain share the same heartbeat. And God willing, tomorrow night you will finally learn what that means. So I bid you Godspeed, you big bastard."

Ian mutely lowered the phone and started to close it.

"Wait, there's one more thing," Roger called out.

"God dammit, *what*?"

A chuckle came over the phone. "Ye might find a sense of humor will go a lot further tonight than compassion will." He sighed. "Although I'm thinking ye might also need a healthy dose of patience."

"Is there anything else—Christ! She's set the house on fire!" Ian shouted, slamming the phone shut on Roger's laughter as he bolted across the road and up the driveway, keeping his eyes trained on the smoke billowing out the kitchen window. He scaled the steps three at a time and burst through the door, causing Jessie to drop the smoking pan in the sink with a shriek as she spun toward him. Ian pulled the towel out of her hand and picked up the pan and headed for the door.

"No!" she yelped, grabbing his arm. "They're not ruined."

He looked down, trying to see through the smoke at what was still sizzling in the pan. "What in hell is it?"

Jessie turned him toward the range. "I'm caramelizing onions," she muttered, pushing on his arm to make him set the pan on the burner. "And they're not ruined, only a little . . . scorched. I can still salvage them," she ended in a shout when the smoke detector in the hallway suddenly started blaring. She began pushing him toward the hall. "Please stop that noise and then go take your shower," she continued loudly as she kept pushing him. "You're early, and dinner isn't ready yet."

But she grabbed his arm again the moment he yanked the detector off the ceiling and pulled out the battery, and Ian saw her cheeks flush with color. "I . . . There's something for you on the bed that I . . ." She pushed him toward the bedroom. "I decided to give you my Christmas present early, so you can put it on after your shower."

Ian stared at the box sitting on the bed, wrapped in deep green foil paper and a large golden bow. "What's in it?" he asked, only to turn and discover he was alone. Toby walked into the bedroom, reared up to set his front paws on the mattress, and grabbed the box. Ian snatched it away. "That's mine," he growled.

But then he set the gift on the bed and squatted down to take hold of Toby's cheeks. "Hey, we're on the same side here. Jessie's got enough heart for us both, big man, so what say we call a truce? Because there's a maelstrom coming here tomorrow, and it's going to take the both of us to keep her safe." Ian gave a chuckle, rubbing Toby's ears between his thumbs and fingers. "I saw ye put Dixon in his place this morning, and you were instrumental in sending the bastard scurrying back to Atlanta alone. Thanks for pretending you didn't see me." He gave the dog's ears one last rub, then let go and held out his hand. "So we're good? You'll share your lady with me?"

Toby stared at him in silence, his big dark eyes searching Ian's, then lifted his paw with a grumbling snarl. Ian closed his fingers around the massive paw with a chuckle. "I know, buddy; she makes my chest hurt, too."

He gave Toby another pat and stood up, then slowly pulled loose the bow on the box. He carefully peeled back the wrapping, lifted the lid, and stared down at . . . sweet Lord, was that a bathrobe? Ian lifted the material and shook it out, and then shook his head. A bathrobe. And matching pajama pants, he noticed, glancing in the bottom of the box even as he rubbed the smooth material between his fingers. He looked back at the bathrobe, which he suspected was silk; the color the deep green of winter spruce with thin gold piping along the collar and down the lapels and on the belt.

He'd never owned a bathrobe, not even as a kid, as they were a bit too civilized for highland warriors according to his father. Ian recalled his dad also telling him on that long-ago trip—or rather, warning him—that women had a tendency to want to smooth out a man's rougher edges, even if that roughness was the very thing that had attracted them in the first place.

Jessie expected him to spend this evening wearing pajamas and a bathrobe?

"Do you like it?"

He turned to find her standing in the doorway, her cheeks the same soft pink as her sweater, her eyes searching his. "Aye, Jess," he heard himself say thickly. "I've always wanted a robe."

"I . . . It reminded me of the color your eyes get when . . . whenever . . ." Her blushed kicked up several notches. "Whenever you kiss me," she whispered. She gestured toward the box. "And you don't have to sleep in the bottoms.

They're just if you want to lounge around on Sunday mornings with me doing crossword puzzles or . . . or something." She took a deep breath, gave him a brilliant smile, and spun on her heel. "Go take your shower. The roast is coming out of the oven in a few minutes," she said over her shoulder as she disappeared into the living room again.

Okay. It would appear lounging around the coffeepot first thing in the morning in his boxers might be one of those rough edges. Toby ambled out of the bedroom in the direction of the living room, and Ian would swear the dog snickered on his way by.

He tossed the robe on the bed and sat down in the chair and took off his boots, stood up and stripped off—making sure he placed his clothes in the hamper—and went into the bathroom and turned on the shower. But instead of enjoying the fact that Jessie hadn't kicked him out on his ass now that Dixon was gone, Ian started getting a tight feeling in his gut as he recalled Roger's warning that he had to make his decision by tomorrow night—which happened to be the winter solstice. It was actually thirty minutes after midnight this year, if he remembered correctly. And knowing a little more than he cared to know about the magic, instead of attending the MacKeage girls' birthday party, he would have to be on top of TarStone finally coming face-to-face with his destiny—or risk taking on Jessie's demon without it. And Ian didn't know which scared him more, embracing the magic or revealing it to her—because if he was standing on the mountain tomorrow night, then by God, Jessie would be standing right beside him.

IAN STRAIGHTENED FROM CLOSING THE DAMPER ON THE stove to see Jessie turn away from the sink and cover her mouth with a loud yawn. "Boy, I seem to be really tired tonight. I'm gonna leave the rest for the morning," she said, walking toward him as she stretched her arms out with another yawn. "I think I'll just go to bed." She stopped beside him and smiled—although he could see it didn't quite outshine the hint of terror in her eyes. "I know you said everything was delicious, but you could at least have disguised your surprise."

"I was surprised that ye tried, not that ye succeeded."

"Yeah, well, cooking's not exactly rocket science," she said with a shrug as she headed into the hallway. "And caramelized onions can make even overcooked beef taste like filet mignon." She stopped to wave dismissively. "No hurry if you're not tired. Stay up and watch television awhile or use the hot tub if you want. I had a soak this afternoon just as it started snowing. It was so quiet and beautiful." She shot him a smile—again one that contained more anxiety than humor. "And I slid a stool under my side of the bed so you don't have to come in and boost me up. Good night."

"Night, Jess," he said as he heard the bedroom door close softly—and then lock. With Toby on the wrong side of it, apparently, as the dog padded back into the living room with his head hanging and plopped down on his bed with a heavy groan. "Sorry, big man, but at least she's not dressing you in silk," Ian muttered, looking down at himself. Who in hell ever heard of eating dinner in a bathrobe and pajama bottoms?

He collapsed onto the couch and stared out the window at the snowflakes drifting through the beam of the floodlight Jessie had turned on just before dinner. Why had she locked the door? When he'd told Toby they were on the same side, he sure as hell hadn't meant the wrong side of the bedroom door. Ian looked right and left, eyeing the couch to see if it would fit him, then stared out at the tracks in the snow on the deck Jessie had made getting in the hot tub, and wondered if she'd worn a swimsuit.

What in hell had her so uptight tonight, anyway? Other than the onions being a bit scorched, dinner couldn't have been tastier; the potatoes had been roasted to perfection, the beef had been tender and juicy, the corn had been . . . well, it's hard to mess up a bag of frozen corn. And he'd recognized the pie as being from the Pine Lake Bakery and Bistro. All of which meant Jessie could cook if she set her mind to it, so what was the big deal tonight? Why had she finally made the effort and then just run off to bed without basking in her success with him, looking scared to death?

Ian sprang to his feet with a muttered curse, making Toby lift his head in alarm, and turned toward the dining table tucked in the corner beside the Christmas tree. She'd put tall, tapered candles in sterling holders on the table, served some pretty expensive wine in some pretty fancy crystal, and set out cloth napkins and fine china. Hell, there was even a bouquet of flowers sitting between the candles.

Ian dropped his chin to his robe-clad chest, not knowing if he wanted to laugh or roar. Jessie's hair swept up in a twist with escaping tendrils framing her delicate face, the baby-soft pink sweater molding her curves, the hint of expensive perfume that still lingered in the air, her hand shaking slightly when she'd poured his wine; Jessica Pringle had spent the day orchestrating a seduction—with *him* being her target.

Then why in hell had she locked the bedroom door?

Ian stilled when he heard the soft but distinct sound of the door unlocking, followed almost immediately by the sound of his bed squeaking as she climbed up on it. And then he smiled, willing to bet his snowmobile that she was right now as naked as the day she'd been born. But then his heart started pounding so hard, he had to reach inside his robe to rub his chest. This was it; he was going to go in there and finally make Jessie his—or completely blow it by saying or doing something wrong.

That's what had caused the terror in her eyes; Jessie still didn't know him quite well enough to gauge whether or not he was going to pity her or be disgusted or turned off. Hell, even a hint that he was disappointed would probably kill her.

Ian scrubbed his hands over his face, wanting to roar. Jessie Pringle had more courage in her one and a half boobs than he had in his entire body. Forget getting up every time she got knocked down; she'd spent the day preparing to take a blow that had the potential to be more devastating than her flashbacks.

He walked over and shut off the deck floodlights but stopped in midstride on his way to check the front door when Jessie suddenly came running out of the bedroom tying her bathrobe at her waist. "I forgot that I bought Toby a special treat," she said, opening the fridge and then wrestling something off the bottom shelf. She set it on the counter and unwrapped the butcher paper, then using the paper like a platter, carried what appeared to be a monstrous cow bone over to Toby and set it paper and all on the floor in front of him. She gave him a quick pat on the head as Toby wiggled forward to give it a sniff. "Enjoy yourself, you big lug," she murmured, getting up and heading back into the hall. She suddenly stopped and looked at the blank television screen, then at the darkened deck, and then at Ian. "I know it's early yet, so . . . um . . . no hurry," she said, disappearing back into the bedroom.

Only this time she forgot to close the door, much less lock it, and Ian smiled when he heard his bed squeak as she vaulted up onto the mattress. Oh yeah, Jessie had planned a very serious seduction if the size of Toby's bone was any indication. Ian continued on to the front door and made sure it was locked, then came back and squatted in front of Toby—wise enough not to reach out to him. "I hope you know the difference between screams of ecstasy and terror, big man," he whispered softly as he picked up the paper and quietly crumpled it into a ball as the dog wrestled the bone— that had to weigh at least ten pounds—into position to gnaw on the smooth joint at the end. "Just don't think you're going to get a bone every night for the next seventy years."

Ian straightened, opened the back damper on the stove, and tossed in the butcher's paper, then went in the bath-room and washed and dried his hands. He stared at himself in the mirror and grinned like the village idiot when he realized his bathrobe certainly matched his eyes right now. He slipped it off and hung it on the back of the door, then reached his thumbs in the waist of his pajama bottoms and started to push them off only to suddenly pull them back up, deciding not to give Jessie an actual target to go after. She might not know him all that well yet, but he sure as hell knew she'd take any opportunity to distract him from exploring every square inch of her body. So he unzipped his ditty bag and took out a string of condoms, snapped off the bathroom light, and headed into the bedroom, fig-uring to use Jessie's own tactics against her.

Leaving the hall light on hoping just enough would shine under the crack at the bottom of the door to allow his night vision to see what he was doing—assuming he finally got to do something tonight—Ian softly closed the bedroom door on the off chance Toby decided saving his lady took precedence over his bone. He then pulled back the covers and slipped into his side of the bed—an argument hard-won once he'd actually had a bed to slip into, as apparently this was Jessie's side. But when explaining he needed to sleep next to the door in case a boogeyman came calling in the middle of the night hadn't worked, he'd simply picked her up and tossed her over on the other side, climbed in, and hauled her back against him.

Only tonight, instead of rolling over and pulling her into his arms, Ian settled on his hip facing the door, tucked the condoms under the pillow, and waited. It took two full minutes for Jessie to grow restless, another minute before he heard her sigh, then not ten seconds after that before she lost her patience altogether.

"What's the Gaelic word for *clueless*?" she asked sweetly. "Or *idiot*? *Moron*? Or even *jackass*?"

"Is there a problem?"

"Better yet, give me the Gaelic term for *denser than dirt*," she growled, yanking his shoulder to roll him onto his back, only to squeak in alarm when he continued rolling on top of her definitely naked body.

"I believe the word you're looking for is *gràdhadair*," he whispered, threading his fingers through her hair, "as that's what a woman calls her lover."

He kissed her then, sweeping his tongue inside her mouth as he positioned himself between her legs. He felt her trying to wedge her hands up between them to cover her breasts, and he kept kissing her until he felt her start to relax, sensing her focus change from herself to him when her hands slid up over his ribs to his back.

He traced a path across her cheek with his lips and felt her shiver. "The moment ye ask me to stop, I will, Jess," he said against her ear, "but I hope ye don't. Let me take ye to a magical place where there's nothing but overwhelming pleasure. Can ye trust me enough to go there with me, lass?"

"Yes," she said on an indrawn breath when he kissed a path down to her throat, stopping to sip at her pulse. Her fingers dug into his back, her legs moving restlessly against his. "You . . . you're wearing your pajamas."

"Not for long," he promised softly. The bed creaked as her restlessness turned to struggles—not to stop him but to urge him on. So Ian untangled his hands from her hair where he'd been restraining himself from touching her and traced a lone finger down the moist path his mouth had made, stopping to slide it across her lips and dip inside. Only she closed her mouth around it and sucked, the sensation making him shudder and instinctively press his hips forward.

Jessie began her own exploration of his body, and Ian was more than willing to let her keep herself occupied, fighting to keep his own focus when her fingers slipped under the elastic at his waist to cup his buttocks. He dropped his hand to the outside of her right breast and palmed its weight, groaning against the pulse in her neck when she shivered in response and strained into his touch when he brushed his thumb over her nipple, her soft gasp of pleasure going straight to his groin.

"Oh," she gasped again when he pulled her nipple into his mouth and sucked. Ian continued his gentle assault, every endearing sound she made urging him on as he moved his mouth lower still, her skin contracting in quivering shudders as he kissed a path to her navel.

But as he'd risen to adjust his position, Jessie's hands had slid around to his front and didn't have any problem finding a target. Ian hissed on an indrawn breath when her fingers wrapped intimately around him right through the silk material.

"Ohmigod," he heard her mutter as she reared up and pushed at his shoulder with one hand while refusing to let go of her prize with the other. She then started tugging on the drawstring. "Will you help me get these damn things off?"

"Not until I'm ready to put on a condom," he growled right back at her, pushing her down to settle over her again.

She stilled. "Oh, they're still in the closet," she cried, pushing at him.

Ian rested his forehead on hers with a pained chuckle. "Ye had all day to plan this and you forgot the most important thing?" He captured her response in his mouth. Once he was certain she'd forgotten what they'd been talking about, he started his journey down her neck, only to stop when he felt her go still again. "What?" he asked before continuing on toward her right breast.

He never did hear her answer, as she started making sweet little noises when he ran his tongue around her beaded nipple before pulling it into his mouth. She was so amazingly responsive, her soft skin dewed with arousal and her hands moving over him with growing urgency. Ian settled onto his hip beside her and slid his hand up the inside of her thigh, and gently pressed into her slickness. Her soft, keening moan music to his ears, he then touched her sensitive bud and slipped a finger inside her with a violent shudder of his own.

Tension and heat radiated from her in waves of building passion. She lifted her pelvis into his hand, driving his finger deeper even as she pushed at his shoulders again. "Go . . . go get the condoms," she panted raggedly. "Now."

Ian reached under his pillow and dangled one of the packets in front of her eyes, but then tapped it against her nose when he realized she couldn't see it. "Look what I remembered to bring, and I didn't even get an invitation to this party."

"What was that term again for *jackass*?" she rasped, snatching it out of his hand and tearing it open.

He snatched it back and rolled onto his side enough to slide out of his pajamas and sheath himself, then got to his knees between her legs and slowly lowered his chest until it was touching hers—making Jessie suck in her breath when his chest hair brushed her left beaded nipple. Her hands rose, but instead of trying to cover herself or push him away, she reached up and undid the band tied at the nape of his neck. She ran her fingers through his hair as she brought her hands down to his shoulders and locked her elbows, both her nipples brushing his chest when she took a deep breath—apparently readying herself for an invasion.

Ian dropped his forehead to hers. "I do believe I've forgotten some of the rules of engagement," he said quietly. "Could ye maybe help me out here, Jess?"

"H-how?" she asked, her finger flexing on his shoulders.

"Well, I thought maybe you could start by breathing and then maybe guide me inside you." He kissed the tip of her nose. "I'm fairly certain I can take over from there. Do ye want me, Jess?" he whispered against her lips. "Show me. Invite me in." He rested his forehead on hers again, every muscle in his body aching in protest of being restrained. "Preferably sooner rather than later, lass."

She unlocked her elbows and reached down between them, making Ian grit his teeth when her fingers brushed his scrotum and she . . .

"Did you just giggle?" he growled.

"Absolutely n—"

The rest of her blatant lie was lost in his groan when Jessie lifted her hips at the same time she guided him inside her. And as promised, Ian took over from there by moving her hand away and pressing forward. He felt her stretching to accommodate him, her fingers digging into his biceps as he slowly seated himself deeply and then went perfectly still. He started sweating as his muscles rippled with the need to move, his eyes trained on her face for a sign that he could.

"O-ohmigod, Ian," she said, her voice quivering with— God, he hoped that was pleasure making her voice shake. "Please *move*."

He eased his hips back, then pressed into her again, her moan as she arced up to meet him and her fingers digging into his shoulders completely shattering his noble intentions to be gentle. This was Jessie, he finally remembered; his sassy, courageous *gràineag* who sure as hell wasn't going to let him treat her like some fragile flower.

Ian increased his rhythm, feeling her building passion tighten around him in waves of pulsating heat. He gritted his teeth to hold back the tidal wave of pleasure threatening his control when Jessie suddenly began cresting without warning, and pressed his mouth over hers to capture her scream as every cell in his body responded to her plea to join her. He drove deeply into her, throwing back his head and going perfectly still again, allowing her contractions to pull him into her powerful release.

Time suspended as their physical bodies ceased to exist, and Ian could actually feel the pure energy of pleasure emanating from Jessie to mesh with his, the sensation seeming to fill the room with the blinding light of a thousand suns.

Ian looked down through a haze of light-headedness to see as clearly as if it were daylight that Jessie had pulled a pillow from beneath her and was holding it over her face to muffle her long, keening cry, and he marveled that she

actually had the wherewithal to even think about not wanting to alarm Toby, considering he didn't even have sense
enough right now to breathe.

The pillow lowered to her chest, Jessie's ragged pants
pressing it like an accordion between them as Ian very
carefully eased his body down onto hers so he could kiss
first one of her fiery hot cheeks and then the other, afraid
to kiss her lips because she obviously needed to gulp in
copious amounts of air, too.

What to say . . . what to say . . . Ian realized he hadn't
thought about the rules for *after* the engagement, but figured he'd better say something that would let him engage
her again. "Say something, Jess," he whispered against her
cheek, deciding to put the onus on her, because hey, he'd
done a damn fine job of keeping her distracted long enough
to actually do it.

"I . . . I . . . I think I actually saw stars."

He rested his forehead against hers with a chuckle. "Just
stars? Hell, I saw a thousand suns." Figuring she'd caught
her breath enough for a quick kiss, Ian touched his lips to
hers, but lifted his head the minute she moaned.

"Oh yes, move inside me like that again."

He stilled, then sighed, then chuckled, wondering why
he was surprised the little *gràineag* would be demanding
in bed. "Like this?" he whispered tightly, pressing into her
then retreating, then advancing again when he realized he
still could. And what small amount of blood was left in his
brain suddenly shot straight to his groin when she pulled
the pillow back over her face and crested again, and Ian
saw the light of damn near every sun in the universe sweeping toward them.

Chapter Sixteen

Jessie woke up to discover she couldn't move; partly because muscles she'd forgotten she even had—in some really interesting places—were a little sore, but mostly because Ian had her wrapped up in his arms as if he were afraid she might try to sneak out of bed and go sleep with Toby or something. Jessie slowly reached up to gently lift his arm away so she could indeed sneak out to slip on her bathrobe before he woke up, but stopped breathing altogether when his hand instinctively tightened.

Oh God, he was holding her left breast. It still had a nipple and she could have displayed some impressive cleavage if she hadn't had the scar on her collarbone, but a bottom piece of what used to be a full C cup had been hastily repaired to save her life at the time, leaving a large dimple that made her boob look like a half-eaten apple.

Please be asleep, she silently petitioned as she once again tried to lift Ian's hand, only to stop breathing again when his thumb brushed over her nipple. And then her heart sank when his lips nuzzled her shoulder and she realized he was awake.

"Good morning," he said, his voice raspy. "Did ye sleep well?"

"Um . . . uh-huh. Ian, could you . . . do you think—oh!" She gasped when he gently pressed her nipple between his fingers. "Ian, please!"

"Please what?" he asked, sliding the flat of his searing hot palm down her belly to cup her mound and pull her bottom into his definitely wide-awake groin. "The word's *gràdhadair*, Jess; please, *gràdhadair*, take me to that magical place again." He moved his fingers intimately against her and then patted her mound with a sigh. "Sorry, but I only brought three condoms to bed."

Jessie captured his hand when it started back toward her breast. "Please, I'm uncomfortable with you touching me . . . there."

"Where?" he asked, dragging her hand right along with his to her breast. Only instead of cupping it, he guided her to cup herself. "Can you feel what I feel when I touch you *there*? The warm silkiness of your skin and your response when I do this?" he whispered, pressing her fingers together on her nipple. "Do you know why men prefer to keep the lights on when we make love?"

"Yes, to see women's boobs. Men are visual."

"Well, we do like things that jiggle," he said with a soft chuckle, giving her hand over her breast a gentle squeeze. "But what we're really wanting is to see your reactions. A woman surrendering to pleasure goes straight to a man's groin; the noises she makes, the flare of her eyes, her face becoming flushed with passion, has more power to turn a man to stone than perky breasts or enticing bottoms or full lips. Women worry about the size and shape and firmness of things, where men are more concerned with whether or not we can get a woman to respond with wild abandon."

He rolled Jessie onto her back and propped his head on his hand, the light of dawn revealing the crinkled corners of his beautiful eyes. "Will ye let me see what I held all night, so I can show you how much I don't care if you're lopsided or uneven?" He took hold of her chin when she slid her gaze away. "I believe it's rather important that we settle this matter this morning, Jess."

But when she couldn't seem to move, much less say anything—lost in the realization that he was right and she was an idiot—his smile faltered and he shrugged. "That is, if you're still wanting us to be a couple." He rolled onto his back and stared up at the ceiling. "Maybe I disappointed you last night and you're a bit underwhelmed this morning. Or *over*whelmed, maybe? Was I too demanding a lover, Jess?"

Was he serious?

Or was this just a sneaky ploy to see her naked?

Well, it was a damned good one. Good God, she'd been so *wild with abandon* last night, she'd completely forgotten she even had a body—scarred or otherwise—what with being so busy feeling such unbelievable pleasure. And passion; lots of wild, steamy, please-don't-stop passion.

He lifted the covers and started to roll out of bed, and Jessie realized she was taking too long to answer. She grabbed his shoulder and pulled him onto his back; bringing the blanket with her, she rolled onto his chest and looked him right in the eye. "I'll show you my boobs if you'll agree to let Roger come to Christmas dinner."

He stilled in surprise. "You're bartering your *boobs* for that crazy old bastard?"

Jessie tried but failed to stifle her smile, and nodded. "And I'll also sneak into the resort and go skinning-dipping with you some night in exchange for your explaining how come my walking stick is shrinking."

He arched a brow. "Why don't you just ask your good pal Roger?"

Jessie lowered the blanket halfway down her breasts, then pulled it back up the moment his gaze lowered. "And I'll cook you breakfast like a good old-fashioned lass if you take whatever that is that's poking my belly and put it someplace . . . else."

Other than his eyes darkening slightly, he didn't react. "Or," he said quietly, "you could show me your boobs in exchange for my promising to love you forever. Would that be a good trade for ye, Jess?"

He actually flinched when she gave a squeal, and he jackknifed into a sitting position with a grunt of alarm when she scrambled up his body to kiss him. "Oh, Ian!" she cried, wrapping her arms around him so tightly that she nearly knocked herself out bumping their heads together.

"Jessie."

"I love you so much! I thought . . . I'd just die if . . . you didn't love me back," she continued between kisses to his mouth and forehead and cheeks and then his mouth again. "I think I started falling in love with you the moment you promised not to let me stumble on the dance floor. And then when—" The bedroom door started rattling something fierce, Toby's frantic growls only slightly louder than his clawing at the door. "Oh, Toby!" she cried, jumping off the bed and rushing to the door and opening it. "It's okay, Tobes, we—oooph!"

Ian swept Jessie back up onto the mattress when Toby charged in and made a lunge for the bed—specifically at Ian as he tucked her behind him and reared away just in the nick of time.

"Tobias Pringle," Jessie snapped, pointing over Ian's shoulder at him. "Get a grip, you big lug! We're *playing*. Eeeww, what's all that crud?" she asked, pulling the blanket up to her nose.

Ian snorted. "That would be grease and bone marrow," he said, leaning over to point toward the living room. "Go on, get out of here, big man." He blew out a sigh. "And I'll be along in a few minutes to give you another bath."

Jessie tried to grab Ian's shoulder but missed as he got out of bed. "Wait. I thought I'm supposed to show you my boobs in exchange for your loving me forever."

He stood facing her, utterly gloriously naked, his hair hanging loose to his shoulders and his eyes bright with amusement. "The deal's been struck, lass; I saw every beautiful inch of ye when you jumped up to open the door.

She dropped her gaze to his groin, gave a sigh, then fell back onto the pillow and pulled the blanket up over her head. "What do I get for loving you forever?" she muttered from under the blanket.

She felt the bed dip just before the blanket was pulled down and Jessie found herself staring into deep green eyes—not a crinkled corner in sight. "You get me," he said roughly. "And all that that entails." He placed his fingers over her lips when she tried to speak. "And tonight when I take you to the summit of TarStone, you may bring your staff and I'll see what I can do to cure what's ailing it." He straightened and walked to the door but stopped. "And Jess? Ye need to know that we'll either be leaving the mountain bound together for life, or you'll be coming down alone."

"What? Why? W-where are you going?"

He gave a humorless chuckle, gesturing toward the window. "I'll most likely run off with de Keage. Don't come to the resort today, as many of the campers have already left; just stay home and relax and maybe take a nap, as I'm afraid you're in for a long night tonight." His smile finally reached his eyes. "Just try not to burn down the house when ye cook my supper," he said over his shoulder as he left.

Jessie pulled the blankets back up over her head again, listening to Ian coaxing and then dragging Toby into the bathroom. She heard the door close and the shower come on, and smiled when she heard the tussle taking place in the tub and realized they were showering together when Toby's snarling protests turned to gargled coughs.

But then her smile disappeared. Ian was taking her up the mountain tonight and curing what ailed her walking stick? Couldn't he just *tell* her why the damn thing was losing its burls and getting skinnier? And what in hell had he meant when he said they either left the mountain bound together for life or she left alone? Was that supposed to be some sort of marriage proposal?

Jessie lowered the blanket with a gasp. Was Ian planning a romantic proposal up at the summit house tonight, but thought he better give her a little warning so she wouldn't be caught with . . . with her pants down, she thought with a smile?

But then she frowned. The man knew she'd been rushed into marriage once already, and he also knew how wonderfully that had worked out for her. So what was the all-fire hurry, anyway?

But he *had* said he loved her, and unlike with Eric, she actually believed him. And she absolutely, positively, irrevocably loved him—atavistic tendencies and all. And being engaged was very traditional, so they could set the wedding date for a year or eighteen months from now and get to know each other better during that time. After all, that's what engagements were for.

Thank God that persistent brochure had refused to be thrown away, even if she couldn't explain *how* it had kept reappearing. How else would she have realized her dream of making love again—three times in one night!

Oh yeah, she'd definitely gotten her miracle and then some.

Jessie pulled the blanket back over her head when she heard the bathroom door open, and Toby came scrambling into the bedroom giving little muttered growls, obviously trying to tattle on Ian to her. She rolled to the edge of the mattress to give him a commiserating pat, only to laugh at the sight of him wearing a fluffy pink towel.

Hearing the water running in the sink, Jessie leaned down to slide out her stool and patted a spot beside her. "Come on, Tobes," she whispered, holding back the blankets. "You can hide in here with me; I'll protect you from that big meany."

"I heard that," Ian called from the bathroom.

"Yeah, so, what are you going to do about it?" she called back, grabbing the towel as Toby scrambled up onto the bed. She held him away and set it on the sheet for him to lie on, then quickly covered them both up with the blanket.

Ian walked into the bedroom actually wearing a towel around his waist—also pink—and stopped to eye the lump beside her. "He's getting my side of the bed wet."

"I guess it sucks to be you." Jessie looked at the night-stand clock on her *former* side of the bed. "Aren't you late for work?"

He arched a brow. "Which begs the question, how come you're not out there making my morning coffee and packing my lunch and kissing me good-bye at the door?"

Jessie sighed. "I guess I haven't gotten the hang of being an old-fashioned lass."

He walked to the closet and got some clothes, and Jessie pulled the blanket up over her head again when she saw the towel drop and he started to dress. "Hey," she said. "Don't you have to go to Megan and her sisters' birthday party tonight? I still can't believe all seven of them were born on the same day."

A finger curled over the top of the blanket and lowered it to her chin. "We were both invited, but going up the mountain is more important." He tapped the tip of her exposed nose and walked over to grab his shirt off the chair with a chuckle. "Don't worry; we won't even be missed. Gù Brath on the winter solstice makes Camp Come-As-You-Are seem like church in comparison."

Jessie knew Gù Brath was the name of Greylen and Grace MacKeage's home, which sat back in the woods from the ski resort at the base of TarStone. She'd only seen the outside and had really been looking forward to seeing the inside, because the place was actually a castle. It was built of black stone someone had told her came from the mountain, it barely had any windows except in the addition on the back, and there was even a bridge leading up to the front doors over a gushing stream just like a moat.

"You're either going to have to burn Toby's old bed or take it outside and drown it in hot water before you put it in the washer," Ian said, stopping beside her as Jessie lowered the blanket. He shook his head. "Next time ye want to give him a treat, try a large rawhide he can gnaw on. There's enough grease covering his bed and the floor and the hearth to fry doughnuts."

Jessie snuggled into the pillow and closed her eyes on a sigh. "I think I'll take my nap first," she murmured, waving him away. "Could you be a dear and start the coffeepot on your way out? And could you—"

Ian leaned over and kissed her quite soundly, his hand sliding under the blanket to the juncture of her thighs, and Jessie's gasp of surprise turned into a moan. "Is there anything else I can do for you before I leave?" he whispered against her lips, even as his thumb caressed her intimately.

"I'm . . . ah . . . oh, that's good," she groaned, lifting her hips into his touch.

A growl came from the lump next to her as it started moving, and Ian pulled away with a laugh. "Sorry, *gràineag*, but there doesn't seem to be room in your bed for me at the moment." He headed out to the hall. "See if you both can't stay out of trouble today."

Jessie waited until she heard the front door close, then pushed back the covers and threw herself on Toby. "Oh, Tobias," she whispered, giving his damp head a kiss. "Miracles *must* be real, because we just got one."

Jessie had every intention of going back to sleep, but after ten minutes of sighing and smiling and fidgeting so much that Toby finally jumped down to lie on the floor, she decided she was too excited to go back to sleep. So she got up and spent the morning cleaning the mess Toby had made—promising herself to never, ever buy the big lug another bone—as she continued to sigh and smile while cleaning up the mess she'd made cooking dinner last night.

That is, when she wasn't frowning, wondering how she

could persuade Ian to stay while her parents visited over Christmas. But she finally gave up on that notion, realizing he was just too old-fashioned to sleep in her bed with her parents in the house unless he was married to her. Honest to God, she hadn't realized they still made men like Ian, much less an entire clan of men and women who acted as if they were living in medieval Scotland. Imagine boys growing up believing they *had* to take over the family business, and girls being constantly chaperoned. On the one hand it had to be stifling, but Jessie had to admit there was also something comforting about holding to tradition.

But was she prepared to become part of such a close-knit family if Ian proposed to her tonight? Jessie finished sliding the couch into position to face the Christmas tree and flopped onto it with a sigh as she looked down at her bare left ring finger and started smiling again. Oh yeah, she would say yes tonight when Ian got down on one knee in the summit house and asked for her hand in marriage, and next winter or the following spring she would finally have the grand wedding she and her mom had been planning since Jessie was a little girl.

Well, grand by Pine Creek standards, anyway, where instead of a beautiful stone cathedral in the heart of the city she would be walking down the aisle of a quaint New England white clapboard church. Ian's family would fill up two-thirds of the pews, outnumbering her few aunts and uncles and cousins ten to one. Heck, the wedding wouldn't even make a dent in the portfolio Jacob Pringle had been nursing along the last twenty-eight years for the sole purpose of paying for his only child's wedding.

Jessie wrapped her arm around Toby when he jumped up on the couch beside her. "Roger said I was going to have at least three children, Tobes," she whispered, placing a hand on her belly. "And so far his predictions have been right on the money, which means I really might have babies for Grammy and Grampy Pringle to spoil rotten. And you, you big lug," she said, giving him a kiss, "will get your own little herd of children to watch over.

Oh yeah, she would definitely be saying yes tonight.

Chapter Seventeen

THE TABLE WAS SET AND A STUFFED CHICKEN WAS IN THE oven, the house was spanking clean, all Ian's clothes were washed and hanging in the closet next to hers, and Jessie was feeling pretty old-fashioned proud of herself. She'd tossed Toby's bed in the trash and set the one from L.L.Bean beside the hearth, then watched him spend the entire afternoon scratching and mauling the thing to get the lumps in just the right places. She'd gone on to take a long relaxing bubble bath, dabbed perfume in all the right places, and used a curling iron *and* hot rollers until she was satisfied her hair perfectly framed her sultry eye-shadowed eyes and lightly made-up face. Because really, a girl had to look perfect when her miracle got down on one knee and asked her to marry him.

She'd also spent a good deal of time digging through some of the boxes she and Merissa hadn't gotten around to unpacking, looking for just the perfect items to fill the picnic basket she'd run out and bought at Dolan's Outfitter Store this morning. Well, it was actually an ice fishing backpack basket, but this was *Maine*, so Jessie had decided it would make a perfectly Maine-ish picnic basket. Because really, a girl needed to be flexible if she intended to accept a mountain man's marriage proposal.

She'd ended up rearranging the furniture again, making a place for Ian's large leather recliner next to her chair, planning to surprise him by asking Alec and Duncan to sneak away and move it for her tomorrow. Because honestly, there wasn't any reason for Ian to go back to his place when her parents came if they were *engaged*. Her mom and dad were pretty cool people, and the moment they realized how much she loved Ian and how happy he made her, they would welcome him into the family faster than that fancy snowmobile of his could go.

"Jessie MacKeage," she whispered, trying it out loud. She turned from closing the damper on the stove to sit on the hearth facing her perfectly arranged home. "What do you think, Tobias MacKeage?" she asked, glancing over at him. He stopped from trying to chew the tag off his bed and canted his head at her as if considering the prospect. "You get a name change, too, when Ian and I say 'I do.' You know what? There's no reason you can't be in the wedding ceremony. I'll even get you a boutonniere to put on your collar that matches Ian's."

Jessie heard the rumble of a large machine pulling into the driveway and stood up and went to the door to see Ian climbing out of one of the resort trail groomers. Well, at least he wasn't taking her up the mountain tonight on that ugly snowmobile of his, because she'd really been worried about carrying the picnic basket. But then she laughed, going to the oven to check on dinner. Of course Ian had brought the groomer because of Toby. It might be a *big* ugly snowmobile, but it certainly wouldn't have fit the three of them.

"Something smells good," he said, coming through the door and taking off his parka. He stopped in the act of pulling down the bib of his pants and sniffed, then smiled at her. "Roast chicken?"

"Stuffed," she said with a nod. "And baked potatoes and green beans."

He walked over with his ski bib hanging down to his waist and pulled her into his arms. "My, aren't we becoming domestic," he murmured just before giving her a warm, tender kiss that quickly turned heated. He leaned away with a sigh. "I suppose since you went to all the trouble, I'll have to sit down at the table like a civilized man and eat it instead of carrying you off to the bedroom first."

Jessie's heart quickened at the look in his eyes. "Um . . . dinner can wait."

He sighed again and dropped his arms away, then turned and walked to the pegs by the door and took off his boots and ski pants. "Nope, you made the effort to cook me supper, and . . ." He looked around the spanking-clean living room and kitchen and smiled at her. "And you even did it without burning down the house, so it's the least I can do."

Oh, two could play this game. Jessie spun around and grabbed her mitts, then bent over to open the oven door. "Yeah, I figured you might need a hearty dinner because I put the whole box of condoms in the nightstand when I was tidying up today."

She gave a squeak when his hands grasped her hips and he pulled her backside into his groin, only to gasp when he slid them up her ribs to cup her breasts when she straightened. "I believe you might want to keep some here in the kitchen, lass, if your eyes and hair are going to be done up like that when I get home," he whispered into her curls as he stroked his thumbs over both of her nipples.

Jessie shivered in response and wiggled her backside against the bulge in his jeans, only to laugh when his stomach gave a hungry growl.

He stepped away with another sigh and headed toward the hall. "Hey, big man, I see you have a new bed," he said, stopping to squat in front of Toby.

"He doesn't like it," Jessie said, fanning herself with the mitts before putting them on to pull the roaster out of the oven. "Apparently he had all the lumps in his old bed just where he wanted them, and he spent most of today trying to get his new bed to conform." She set the roaster on top of the stove and turned. "When are we going up the mountain, right after dinner or later in the evening?"

He roughed up Toby's head and stood up. "It's a two-hour ride in the snowcat to where I'm wanting to go, so we should leave by nine or no later than nine thirty so we can be in place by midnight." He started to leave but hesitated. "That is, if you're still willing to go."

"Oh, yes. I even put some things in a basket to bring with us," she said, waving at the basket sitting on the peninsula.

He stilled. "What did you pack?"

Not wanting to spoil whatever plans he'd made or what he might have set up at the summit house, Jessie batted her lashes. "It's a surprise." She waved him away. "Go on, go get cleaned up and we'll eat, and then we can . . ." She turned to the stove while shooting a coy smile over her shoulder. "Well, I'm sure we can find *something* to do until nine. Maybe crossword puzzles."

Only they didn't gravitate to the bedroom after dinner

like Jessie expected, nor did they do crossword puzzles, because Ian had gotten up from the table, given her a quick kiss on her lips—making her nearly fall out of her chair when she'd leaned in expecting him to pull her into his arms instead of straightening away—and left, saying he was going to walk down the road and check on his cabin.

And he hadn't even taken his own plate to the sink; just left the good little lass home alone to clean up the mess she'd made cooking him a wonderful dinner while he went out and did good old-fashioned man stuff. Yeah, well, forget getting down on one knee tonight; he was going to be kneeling on both before she said yes. When she finally heard him kicking snow off his boots on the porch and she looked at the clock and saw it was ten after nine, Jessie decided she just might make him sweat for at least twenty minutes before she said yes.

"Are you ready to go?" he asked, walking into the house like he owned the place and heading directly into the bedroom without taking off his boots. "I hope you put on long johns. And do you have a good warm scarf to wear?"

Jessie waltzed into the bedroom behind him and over to her bureau, pulled out the wool scarf Roger had given her, and slipped it around her neck, figuring they still had twenty minutes before they absolutely *had* to leave. "Is this one warm enough, do you think?" she asked in her best sultry purr.

He turned to her holding his rifle in his fist, his expression making her take a step back. "Did you pull the bolt out of this today, Jessie?" he asked quietly.

"No. I don't know the first thing about rifles; I wouldn't even dare touch it." She glanced at the gun then back up at him. "What's a bolt?"

"It's a long steel cylinder the size of a finger that slides in here," he said, turning the gun to point at the gaping hole in the middle. "It contains the firing pin that strikes the bullet that goes in here," he explained, pointing at the handle end of the barrel. He looked around the room at the bureau and nightstands and back at her, then tossed the apparently useless rifle on the bed and suddenly walked to the nightstand nearest the door. He opened the drawer and took out the small revolver, flipped open the cylinder, and held it with the barrel pointing toward the ceiling. And since the revolver was hers and she knew how it worked, Jessie could see it wasn't loaded. "Where are the bullets?" he asked. "Did you take them out?"

"No. I haven't even touched that gun since I put it in there when I moved in."

He tossed the handgun on the bed next to the rifle and stared at them in silence, and Jessie saw him suddenly stiffen. "I saw Dixon go into the house alone before he left," he said, turning to her. "Does he know you keep a gun in your nightstand?"

"Yes. Brad's the one who gave me that revolver," she said, gesturing at it, only to also stiffen. "Wait, what do you mean you *saw* Brad go in the house before he left?"

"Do ye honestly believe I was going to leave you alone with him?"

"You *spied* on me?"

He nodded. "I can be a real bastard like that sometimes."

"And exactly what were you planning to do if I *had* left with him?"

He shrugged. "Some things are best kept a mystery between a man and a woman." He walked over and pulled her into his arms. "Ye did give me a bit of a scare when ye headed out the road not five minutes behind him, though."

"Oh, Ian," she said, wrapping her arms around his waist to melt against him. "You really are old-fashioned, only scarier, because you *know better* than to coddle me."

"Aye, it's a fine line I'm having to walk between my father's world and mine."

She leaned back to look up at him, only to find him scowling over her head at the bed. "But it doesn't even make sense for you to think Brad would take the bolt out of your rifle and the bullets out of my gun," she told him. "Unless . . . Could he have been afraid that . . . Do you think he was worried you might hurt me or something?" She frowned. "Only it doesn't make sense that he'd unload my gun and not tell me, because then I'd be completely defenseless."

This time she felt more than saw Ian stiffen, his gaze snapping to the hallway. "Did you feed Toby his dry food last night?"

"Yeah, just like always. Why?"

He let her go and walked into the living room and over to Toby's dishes on the floor at the end of the peninsula. "There's still food in here. Did you fill it up again this morning?"

"No," she said, stopping beside him and looking down. "He must not have been hungry last night because I gave him a big bowl of beef and gravy and vegetables." She snorted. "And then didn't eat anything today because he had devoured that entire bone." She grabbed Ian's arm when he reached down to pick up the bowl. "Why are you asking about Toby's food?"

He straightened, holding both the food and water dishes. "Toby's just as lethal as your gun, Jessie," he said, dumping the water down the sink then going to the pantry. He slid out the thirty-pound bag of dry dog food, dumped what was in the bowl into the bag, then rolled the top closed and set it on the counter. "Don't feed him anything from this bag, okay?"

"Ian, what's going on?"

He took hold of her shoulders. "Honestly, I'm not sure. But if neither of us disarmed our guns, then who did? Who else has had access to this house in the last two days?"

"Roger?" she gasped. "But why would he take my bullets or your bolt?"

Ian looked momentarily surprised then shook his head, his grip on her shoulders tightening. "Not Roger, Jessie; Brad Dixon. He's the only one who's been in here alone. And he knew you kept a gun in your nightstand because he gave it to you, and my rifle was in plain sight." He gestured toward the bag on the counter. "And the only way he could deal with Toby would be to put something in his food that would at least make him sick enough not to pose a threat."

Jessie gathered Ian's shirt in her fists. "But why? Why would Brad do . . ." She jerked away and hugged herself, shaking her head. "You're implying he's deliberately intending to harm me, but *why*?" she repeated. She gestured angrily toward the bedroom. "You think Brad feels like some jilted lover or something? And that he's going to sneak in here in the middle of the night and . . . and what? Murder us in our bed?" She stepped up and grasped his sleeves. "Ian, *Eric* wouldn't have been capable of doing something that heinous, and Brad's far more civilized than he was."

"What did you and Dixon talk about on your walk yesterday morning?"

She gestured dismissively. "He tried to persuade me to go back to Atlanta with him, pointing out everything he had to offer me as well as the differences between the city and Pine Creek."

"I saw you get upset, and so did he. And I was close enough to hear him tell you to stop reliving it. Were the two of you talking about the night you were attacked?"

Jessie stepped away and rubbed her arms. "Yes. Brad wanted to know if I had remembered anything about what had happened, and he got upset when I told him that I was starting to remember bits and pieces."

"What sort of bits and pieces?" Ian asked quietly. "You told me Brad was there that night; were you telling him you remembered seeing him?"

"No, I said I'd found out just that day that Eric was having an affair, and that I remember hearing a woman's voice only I still don't know if she was in the house or I heard her on the phone. And I said that I remembered parts of the attack, like being carried from the bathroom into the bedroom *after* I heard gunshots." She looked up in surprise. "I told him I didn't think I had shot my attacker, but that someone else did."

"And what was Dixon's reaction to that?"

"I . . . I can't remember what he said, because that's when my cell phone started blaring and Roger sent me a text that said *Stop talking, missy.*" She stepped forward and wrapped her arms around Ian's waist, leaning into him, hoping his solidness would stop her trembling. "What's going on, Ian? What do you and Roger know that I don't?"

He held her head pressed to his chest. "I can't speak to what Roger might know, and I'm only taking a guess here, Jessie, but I believe Brad Dixon didn't tell the police everything that happened that night or at least not in the order it happened." He tilted her head back to look at him. "Has this been an ongoing conversation between the two of you these last four years, with Dixon repeatedly asking you what you remember?"

She nodded then pressed her face to his strongly beating heart, suddenly feeling cold despite her layers of wool and long johns. "That still implies Brad wants to hurt me or that he was . . ." She looked up. "Do you think he *knew* the robber?"

He clasped her face in his warm hands and kissed her forehead, then stepped back. "The only way we'll know for certain is to be standing on TarStone's summit at the exact time of the winter solstice," he said, going over and taking his parka off the peg. "Which means we need to leave now, so I can stop and get another rifle from home. Come on, Jess," he said, holding out her coat. "I believe it's time I introduce you to the magic."

IAN'S GUT TIGHTENED WHEN JESSIE BEGAN BACKING AWAY, her eyes a mixture of confusion and fear. "Jess," he growled when she turned and bolted for the bedroom, Toby scrambling after her. "Jessie!" he snapped, going after them and hoping like hell Toby remembered they were on the same side, only to find Jessie trying to hide behind the clothes in the closet. "Ah, Jess," he said softly, walking around the bed. "I didn't mean to scare you. There's no—" Ian staggered backward when she emerged holding a thick, burl-ridden staff nearly as tall as *he* was. "For the love of Christ, woman, don't point that at anything!" he snapped when she thrust it at him. "Where in hell did you get it?" he asked a bit more calmly when she paled.

"F-from Roger," she said, holding it away from herself. "He . . . he told me to give this to you when the time came." She took a step toward him. "And I think this is as good a time as ever. Here, take it."

Ian took another step back, shaking his head even as he

watched his hand reach toward it as if the accursed thing was magnetized. "Lean it against the mattress, Jess. I don't want ye holding it when I touch it."

"No, it's okay. It didn't spark when I touched it like mine did."

"Set it down and step back, Jessie. Now."

The fear and confusion came back in her eyes again as Ian watched Jessie lean the staff on the mattress and step back hugging herself, only to give a soft snort. "Roger said it was too powerful for a woman to handle," she whispered, her gaze going from the stick to him when he didn't move. "And he never actually *gave* it to me. I just found it in the back of my closet this morning when I was moving stuff to make room for your clothes." She grabbed Toby's collar to pull him back when he tried to sniff the stick. "So, are you going to take it or not? I don't know why, but I feel we should bring it with us . . . along with your rifle, too. Go on, take it. If it's meant for you, it'll only give a little shock; you know, like static electricity."

Once you own the power, there's no going back, Roger had told him. And Ian knew the moment he touched that staff, TarStone would own him as well. "Step back, Jess," he said, moving closer.

Ian waited until she pulled Toby all the way to the closet, then moved to put himself between them and the staff. He reached out to hold his fingers open around the smooth handgrip on the thick shaft, and felt the powerful hum of energy pulsing through the wood. Planting his feet against the assault he knew was coming, he took a deep breath and snapped his fist around it in an iron grip.

Only instead of feeling a shock of static electricity, the damn thing nearly knocked him off his feet when it exploded in a thunderous burst of energy, filling the bedroom with blinding light of every imaginable color. The sizzling bolts swirled around him in arcing snaps that shook the walls and rattled the windows as every cell in his body seemed to expand and start pulsing in rhythm with the swirling light.

Or rather, the light began pulsing to the rhythm of his beating heart.

He turned the staff and the light swirled in response, and Ian mentally commanded the energy to return to the wood, resting the tip of the staff on the floor as the maelstrom was sucked into the bark-covered burls like a vacuum cleaner and the bedroom went dark but for the soft light of the bedside lamp.

And Jessie and Toby were nowhere to be seen.

"Jessie? Where are ye, lass?" he asked, smiling when he saw the clothes on the hangers move. He walked over and pushed them apart, and looked down to find Toby and Jess sitting pressed up against the back corner. Jessie was hugging Toby so tightly it was a wonder the dog could breathe, both their eyes clamped shut. "It's okay, you two."

Jessie mutely looked up at him, then leaned over to look out past him, and then looked up at him again. "What was . . . What just happened?" she whispered, still hugging Toby—only to press even farther away when Ian held the staff for her to see.

"I was getting acquainted with the lovely present you just gave me." He arched a brow. "Can I ask what you had to barter Roger for it?"

She snorted. "From what just happened, I'd say my soul." She gave the staff a worried glance then looked up at him again, apparently not quite ready to come out of hiding. "Um, you do know that you don't have to *accept* a gift just because someone gives it to you, don't you? It . . . You won't hurt my feelings if you don't want the . . . the walking stick. There's still time for me to get you something else. Say, a nice cardigan sweater or slippers to match your robe."

He used the stick to lean on and reached a hand down to her with a laugh. "Too late; the gift's been given and accepted, and now it's time we go find out what this big gnarly boy can do."

"Do?" she squeaked, snatching her hand back. "It *does* stuff?" Her eyes narrowed. "Is it going to shrink like mine has?"

"Sorry," he said, reaching down to her again. "I'm afraid mine's only going to grow stronger." He caught her hand and pulled her to her feet, then had to catch her when she bumped into his staff and jumped away with another squeak. "It's not going to hurt you, Jess; it only responds to my touch." He pulled her into his arms and kissed her until he felt her relax against him. "Much the same way you do." He let her go to snag her hand. "There, that's done," he said, leading her around the bed. "Now it's time we got down to business. Come on, Toby, you're not going to want to miss this."

Ian led Jessie into the kitchen, leaned his staff against the counter, and started stuffing her into her coat—only to stop. "What did you just say?" he asked quietly.

"Nothing," she said, finishing dressing herself.

Ian captured her hands when she started buttoning her coat. "I believe you just mentioned something about a marriage proposal."

She became very interested in the zipper on his ski bib. "I might have been telling Toby that . . . not to . . ." She sighed and looked him right in the eyes. "You didn't spend the day setting up a romantic scene in the summit house, did you, where you were going to get down on one knee and . . . and ask me if I'd do the honor of . . . oh, for the love of God, come on!" she snapped, grabbing her perfectly smooth walking stick and heading outside—completely forgetting the basket she'd packed them.

Ian stood staring at the humming door she'd slammed shut and then scrubbed his hands up and down his face with a groan. He'd spent the day preparing to barter his very soul for Jessie's life, and she'd been floating around here picturing him asking her to marry him tonight? On his knees? Up at the summit house? No, at a *romantically staged* summit house. Considering he knew Eric Dixon had hustled her to the altar in less than five weeks, did Jessie expect him to hustle her into marriage in only three?

Ian gave his face one last scrub, wondering if he did propose what her answer might be after what she was about to witness. Sure as hell not yes, he thought with a snort, grabbing his staff and the food basket and heading out the door—making sure to leave it unlocked. He walked to the snowcat parked in the driveway just in time to find Jessie trying to help Toby get in. He nudged her out of the way and lifted the dog into the cubby behind the seats, then lifted Jessie over the track and set her inside, plopped the basket on her lap, and softly closed the door on her scowl. But her scowl quickly turned to panic when he opened his door and wedged his staff next to her walking stick between them before he got in.

After stopping at his cabin to get another rifle, the ride up the mountain was made in silence, even Toby seeming to know something was afoot tonight. Either that or the dog had decided not to argue with him anymore since seeing him handling a thunderstorm in the bedroom.

It was just nearing midnight when Ian stopped next to TarStone's faded old snowcat and shut off the engine. But instead of opening his door, he stared out the windshield at the lone figure standing on an outcropping of ledge at the very peak, dressed in a dark billowing robe and leaning on a tall, gnarly staff twice as thick as his and riddled with three times more burls. Ian turned just enough to see Jessie out of the corner of his eye, and found her also staring at Roger, her hands clasping her coat at her throat and stark terror shining in her starlit eyes.

He reached over and pulled her hands down and held them in one of his, rubbing a thumb over her knuckles. "There's nothing to be afraid of, Jess. Do you remember the second thing I told you to remember about the magic?"

"Th-that it will keep knocking me on my butt until I . . . I believe."

"Well, after tonight your butt should be safe," he said with a soft chuckle, giving her hands a squeeze. "Do you remember the first rule?"

"No."

He gave her another squeeze and chuckled again. "You don't try to explain the magic; you simply accept it. And lastly, once you do, anything is possible." He lifted her hands to his mouth and kissed the back of her glove. "Including miracles."

He saw her pull in a deep, shuddering breath before she finally looked at him. "I got my miracle last night, but I still don't know what miracle I'm supposed to give you."

He gave her hand one more kiss, then opened his door and got out and turned to face her. "I'll give you until Christmas day to figure out what it is. Come on," he said, reaching back to help Toby down over the track. "Let's go see what's brought our good pal Roger out on this cold winter night."

He took out his staff and walked around the snowcat to

help Jessie wade through the knee-deep snow up to the windswept ledge, then helped to steady her when Roger turned toward them. Oh yeah, the old bastard was dressed in full regalia, right up to his pointy velvet hat.

"Welcome home, Jess," Roger said, his eyes seemingly lit from within. "And Tobias," he added with a slight bow to the dog. "Aren't you being a brave lad following your lady up here without question? Ian," he said with a regal nod, his eyes flaring when Ian pulled his own staff from behind his back and set the tip of it on the ledge with a soft thump. "You've decided," Roger whispered, his thick white beard bristling with his grin. "I thought I saw fireworks coming from Frog Point earlier."

Roger slid his gaze to Jessie. "Ah, lass, ye needn't look so frightened. Ye have two mighty warriors flanking your sides, each prepared to lay down his life to protect you." He threw back his shoulders on a deep breath. "But I'm bound by my oath to let you know that ye have a choice, Jess, to not be here tonight."

"No, she doesn't," Ian growled before she could answer. "She stays until I get what I came here for."

"That's not how it works, MacKeage. We all have free will, and ye can't force her to do anything she's not wanting to do."

"I can if it's for her own good," Ian drawled, stifling a smile when Jessie gasped hard enough to nearly topple off the ledge, then breaking into a full grin when she stepped toward Roger.

"Exactly what am I supposed to be choosing?" she asked.

"Whether or not you wish to believe in the magic," Roger told her.

Jessie snorted. "I'm pretty sure I already do." She swept

her sad-looking walking stick in an arc. "I'm standing on the top of a mountain—of my own free will, I want to point out—with a man who looks like Santa Claus only dresses like Merlin, and another man who nearly blew up my beautiful home two hours ago with nothing more than a piece of wood." She held up her stick, shaking it at Roger. "And the more I use this, the smaller it becomes."

Roger blew out a heavy sigh. "Ye haven't had it two weeks and you've spent nearly all that wonderful energy that had to travel all the way from the sun and moon and stars. Do you have any idea how long it took that power to get here?"

She waved the stick in the air, pointing it at the stars. "I'm pretty sure there's more where it came from." She thrust it at him. "So could you please plug this in somewhere and recharge it for me, because I still need to create one more miracle."

"MacKeage," Roger snapped. "Ye need to control your woman."

"I'm not his yet," Jessie snapped back before Ian could answer. "He hasn't gotten down on his knees and proposed to me."

Roger looked incredulous. "For the love of God, Jessie, the man's been on his knees since the day he laid eyes on you."

Apparently deciding she wasn't getting anywhere with Roger, Jessie turned to Ian. "Will you please tell me why we came up here?"

"To save your life," he told her, "and to end your four-year-long nightmare."

"It's already ended, Ian." She inched toward him. "It stopped last night in bed," she whispered. "You vanquished my last ghost."

"Nay, it's not quite over, I'm afraid," Roger said, making her turn to him. "And it won't be until justice is served." He gestured at Ian. "Ian brought you up here so he can see for himself what really happened that night. But in order to do that, he's going to need you to be courageous enough to return there with him."

She backed up until she bumped into Ian's chest, and he wrapped his arms around her. "Can ye do that, Jess?" he asked against her ear, tightening his embrace against her trembling. "You'll be perfectly safe because I'll be right there with you."

"But why?" she softly cried, twisting to look up at him. "Why do we have to dredge up the past? It's done. Over. It can't be changed." She gasped. "Can it?"

"No, the past can't be changed," he told her, driving his staff into the snow so he could turn her to face him. "But it didn't happen the way Dixon says it did. He's hiding something, and has been living in fear these last four years that you will remember. That's probably a good part of the reason he's stayed close to you."

"But how can you possibly know that?"

"Because I know men, Jessie; I know how our minds work. And if Dixon was even slightly interested in you as a woman, he would have done something about it long before now." He brushed a lock of hair off her face and palmed her cheek. "I'm sorry, but I have a feeling Brad Dixon was behind the attack that killed his brother and nearly killed you, and I suspect his wife's death not two months later is connected."

"Tracy? You . . . you think it wasn't a boating accident?"

He shrugged. "Only Dixon knows for sure. But tonight we at least have the chance to find out if he was involved in *your* tragedy."

"H-how?" she asked, glancing over her shoulder at Roger.

Ian gave her a squeeze to make her look at him. "By stepping into the light you saw in your bedroom earlier with me, and letting me . . . into your mind."

She leaned back as far as his embrace would let her. "You can do that?"

He smiled. "Apparently."

Her eyes narrowed. "Have you been able to do that all along?"

"No." He glanced over her head at Roger, then back to her. "I only received the gift tonight, when you gave me the staff."

"Did you know what grasping that stick—that staff meant?"

"Not completely. I only learned the full scope of its power when I connected with it." He kissed her forehead on a sigh. "Can we finish this discussion after we deal with Dixon? I have a suspicion he's on his way to your home right now, and I prefer to know the full extent of his wickedness before I confront him."

Her hands dug into his jacket. "You can't confront him! We'll go to Jack Stone together and tell him what we know, and he can deal with Brad." Ian wasn't sure but he thought she tried to shake some sense into him. "Do you hear me? You're not Iron Man, and I'm not going to let you confront him."

He kissed her forehead again, then looked past her and nodded to Roger, tightening his embrace when Roger walked off tapping his leg as he called to Toby.

"No!" Jessie cried, trying to get free. "Toby, stay." She glared up at Ian as Toby obediently waded through the snow after Roger. "Where's he taking him?"

"They're just going to the snowcat, and Roger will sit with him until we're done." He took hold of her shoulder and bent to eye level. "Toby will sense your terror from that night, Jessie, and not be able to help you. Can ye do this, lass? Can you enter the maelstrom with me and relive the terror?"

"And *then* will it be over forever?"

He nodded, giving her a smile. "And I'm willing to bet my snowmobile that you won't ever have another flashback. Think back, Jessie, to the ones you've had here, and when you had them in Atlanta; do you know what might have precipitated them?"

"No," she said, shaking her head. "The doctors and psychiatrists tried everything but they couldn't find any common factor. I would just suddenly be back in the bathroom hearing that guy killing Eric and then ramming the bathroom door."

"The two you had here in Pine Creek; what were you doing just before them?"

"I . . . I was . . ." She smiled. "I was dancing with a complete stranger just before the first one." She sobered. "And I was walking out to check the mail the second time. I'd just gotten two texts from Merissa saying Brad had stopped into the hospital to ask her for my address, and then Brad called and said he was coming to visit so he could see for himself that I was okay."

"Didn't you get a text from Brad that night in the bar?"

"Well, yeah, I did."

"And you were fine up until then, but after the text I could see the tension building in you." He let go of her shoulders and took hold of her hand, pulled his staff out of the snow, and led her up the outcropping to where Roger had been standing. "It's a moot point, Jess," he said, stopping and turning so they were facing each other. "We'll know everything we need to know in a few minutes."

He stepped back and looked down, his gaze searching the ground until he found a small crack in the granite. "Okay, come here and wrap your arms around my waist," he said, waving her over and lifting his free arm to tuck her up against his side. "Now, I'm going to drive this staff into TarStone, and blinding energy is going to swirl up from deep inside the mountain and come screaming out through all the burls, okay? It's going to snap and howl and sizzle with an unbelievable force far worse than it did at home, but it's not going to hurt you. Understand? I'll be right here beside you the entire time." He kissed the top of her head when he felt her shivering against him. "I won't let anything happen to you, little *gràineag*, but I'm afraid I can't stop you from going through the terror again."

"Wait," she said when he lifted the staff to drive it into the crack. "I need to know what you meant when you said that I might be leaving this mountain alone. I'll be safe, but will *you*?"

"Aye, Jess. I'll walk out of the maelstrom with you. The true question is—and always has been—can you live with the knowledge of who I am."

She tilted her head back to see him. "W-who are you?"

"TarStone," he said, driving the staff into the top of the mountain.

Chapter Eighteen

IT HAD BEEN A HELL OF A LOT MORE POWERFUL THAN A maelstrom, which Jessie always thought meant a really scary and confusing storm, like a tornado or something. But there hadn't been one damned confusing thing about what she'd just experienced, because everything, right down to the last detail, had been frighteningly clear and in vivid Technicolor. Hell, she could still *smell* the blood, which is probably why it was taking every ounce of willpower she possessed not to throw up again.

She had dropped to her knees the moment the terror had ended and the light had disappeared, and hurled until she'd thought she was going to turn inside out. Ian had held her trembling shoulders while she'd purged herself of the terror, even if she still couldn't believe what she'd learned.

"At least we know Brad isn't totally evil," she whispered to Ian as he sat staring out the windshield of the softly idling snowcat with the heaters running full blast. "He . . .

he tried to stop the attack when he found out I hadn't gone on my business trip and Tracy wasn't with Eric like he thought. He . . . he saved my life."

Ian looked over at her, incredulous. "The bastard hired a man to kill his wife and brother, Jessie, because they were having an affair and Eric was draining their business dry. And then he finished the job by hiring someone to kill Tracy in Nassau two months later and make it look like a boating accident." He reached over and covered her trembling hands. "And now he has to kill you, too, because he knows you're starting to remember."

"If killing is so easy for him, then why hasn't he just killed me before now?"

"For the same reason he rushed over trying to stop the attack that night." Ian snorted. "In his sick, convoluted mind, Brad Dixon has always seen you as young, naive, innocent Jessie Pringle. You heard him yourself just now; he thought he was rescuing you by killing Eric while also ridding himself of an unfaithful wife and troublesome brother." He gave her hands a squeeze. "At least you know you didn't kill anyone. Brad took the gun out of the night-stand and interrupted the man he'd hired attacking you in the bathroom. The guy walked into the bedroom and Brad shot him, then *Brad* carried you into the bedroom, put the gun in your hands, and put three more bullets into his head so there'd also be gunpowder residue on you. And he told the police he thought there was some art missing to make them think it was a botched robbery attempt."

"I'm sorry, Jess," he said when she sucked in a shuddering breath. "Not only for what you went through four years ago, but for making you go through it again tonight. But I needed to know if my suspicions were right in order to set a trap for Dixon." He lifted her hands to his mouth.

"And I believe it was important for you to know the truth also. You've thought you were fighting the intruder in your flashbacks, but all this time you were fighting Brad."

"Can . . . can we go home now?"

"I'm sorry, no. Not until Dixon's in custody." He gave her hands one last kiss, then gently placed them back in her lap, gave Toby's head lying on her shoulder a pat, then touched the throttle but didn't push it. "I would have preferred to take you to Gù Brath where I know you'd be safe, but considering the party's still going on there, I've decided you'd be more comfortable in that big comfy chair at my place."

Jessie eyed him suspiciously. "Are you going to be there with me?"

He finally engaged the throttle and started down the mountain. "Not until Dixon is in custody," he repeated.

She grabbed his arm. "You expect me to sit in that chair like a good little lass while you go set a trap for Brad?"

Ian gave a humorless laugh. "Not unless I expect hell to freeze over."

"Damn right," she growled. "So let's go tell Jack what we know and let *him* wait at my house for Brad to show up."

Ian scowled over at her. "Exactly what are you going to tell him? That he needs to arrest Dixon because you had a vision?"

"I was there four years ago. I'm an eyewitness who just suddenly remembered everything. That's enough. Wait— Jack's family. Does he know about the magic?"

"Stone? Hell, the man's a *shaman*. Although he still refuses to admit it," Ian muttered. The dash lights allowed Jessie to see him shake his head. "It's better to catch Dixon breaking into your home with the intention of murdering you." He snorted. "I mean *us*. Don't worry, Jess," he said, patting her leg as he guided the surprisingly nimble machine down a path apparently only he could see. "I won't be alone. This afternoon I quietly told Jack and Duncan and Alec and Robbie what I suspected, and the four of them had your home surrounded before we even left there this evening. I'll drop you off at my place and go tell them what we've learned, and the five of us will be waiting for Dixon to show up."

"What if he doesn't come tonight?"

"Then we'll be there around the clock until he does." His hand resting on her leg gently tightened. "But it'll be tonight. There's been just enough time for him to establish an alibi somewhere else, and for the poison to work on Toby."

"Do you really think Brad tried to poison Toby?" Jessie asked, reaching up and tickling Toby's chin, which was still resting on her shoulder as the dog leaned against the back of her seat to steady himself.

"Dixon knows he wouldn't even make it onto the property without Toby knowing," Ian said, also reaching up and ruffling Toby's head with a chuckle. "And I'm certain the big man would love to sink his teeth into Dixon. There's a good chance Toby felt your unconscious fear of Brad and that's why he's never liked him." He looked over at her. "That's probably also why you don't like being carried." He smiled. "Except by me."

Jessie suddenly gasped. "Oh, my stick! I forgot it up on the summit."

"I'm afraid I couldn't cure what ailed it, Jess," Ian said sadly. He patted her leg again. "Ye might not need it anymore, but if you do, I'll cut you a new stick."

"But I want that one, because it . . . it did stuff."

"Did you nap today?" he asked when she suddenly yawned, apparently not wanting to discuss her getting a new magic wand.

"I tried to nap," she said, blowing out a tired sigh that

she didn't think had anything to do with the fact that it was nearly two in the morning. Honest to God, maelstroms were draining. "But I was too busy planning a nice September wedding."

Oh God, she hadn't really just said that, had she?

But she must have, because Ian nearly ran the snowcat into a tree.

"Yes, well, I think I'll take a nap *now*," she muttered, wrapping her MacKeage scarf around her cheeks just in case the dash lights were bright enough for him to see her blush. "Wake me up when we get to your place." She opened one eye to look at him. "How come you aren't falling-down tired? You were in the maelstrom, too."

He smiled over at her. "Sorry; it only makes me stronger."

"Wonderful," she muttered, closing her eyes again. She suddenly snapped them open and sat up. "Wait a minute. If Roger is some badass . . . what, wizard? If he's some powerful wizard," she continued when Ian merely shrugged, "then why didn't he just take his own fancy staff and zap Brad to smithereens or something? Why make us go through all this maelstrom malarkey?" she said, waving at nothing. "I mean, really, he kept taking that dumb TarStone brochure out of the trash can every time I threw it away, he seems to know what we're doing and saying even when he's not around, and he's using a cell phone that doesn't even have *service*. Why can't he just turn Brad into a slug or a cockroach or a . . . a . . ."

"A toad?" Ian offered with a chuckle. "Because he can't actually *do* anything to anyone, Jess. Roger can only make suggestions and give people nudges in the right direction. Now go to sleep. I'll wake you when the time comes."

Jessie slumped against Ian's shoulder with a sigh,

feeling more drugged than tired, like she'd taken two pain meds at once or was coming down off an adrenaline high or something. When she finally did open her eyes again, it was to find herself being swallowed up by Ian's large leather recliner in his cabin, all alone except for Toby, who was lying beside her in the chair, sound asleep.

Jessie became frantic when she realized there was bright light shining through the windows, and judging by its strength, she figured it was late morning. She woke Toby and pushed at him to get down, then closed the footrest and rushed to the door with Toby sleepily padding behind her. But when she threw it open, they were confronted by a wall of snow. She reached out and touched it, only to find it was solid white ice, thick enough that she couldn't see through it but apparently thin enough to transfer sunlight. She ran to each of the windows and found the same thing, then slowly backed to the center of the cabin, undecided if she was angry at Ian for trapping her like a disobedient child, or disconcerted by the fact that he *could*.

She walked over and started rummaging through his pile of sporting equipment looking for something to hack away at the ice with, and found what looked like an actual ice axe that climbers use. "Okay, Tobes," she said, giving it a few test swings. "I'll have us out of here in no time." She walked over and stood in the open door and looked for any cracks or weaknesses in the ice. "And you have my permission to lift your leg on Ian's snowmobile anytime you feel the urge," she said, drawing her arm back and swinging at a spot over her head, putting all her weight into the blow.

Only just as the sharp pick was about to connect, the wall of ice disappeared and Jessie drove the axe into the pack basket Ian was holding as she stumbled forward.

"Sweet Christ!" he shouted, dropping the basket to catch her when she fell to her knees. "What in hell are you doing?" he growled, standing her back on her feet.

Jessie ran shaky fingers through her hair. "I was trying to break off a chunk of ice to put in a glass of water," she growled right back at him, spinning on her heel and walking back into the cabin.

He picked up the axe-skewered basket and walked in behind her just as Toby trotted outside and lifted his leg on the groomer parked in the driveway. "Did you sleep well?" Ian asked, setting the basket on the counter.

"Wonderful. Just peachy. I'm so rested, I feel like hiking a mountain."

She heard him sigh clear over to the woodstove she was standing in front of. "Jessie, I couldn't be worrying about you while we dealt with Dixon."

She turned to him. "And?" she whispered.

"He'll be transported to the county jail where he'll be staying until he's charged with arson and attempted murder here and then extradited to Georgia." He shot her an uncivilized grin. "Just as soon as the hospital is done putting a cast on his broken arm and suturing a few . . . cuts."

Jessie hugged herself. "Brad was . . . He really intended to kill us?"

Ian walked over and pulled her into his arms and started rubbing her back. "Oh yes, he was coming after both of us. While we were up the mountain, Jack, Alec, Robbie, and Duncan stood guard the entire length of the road. They spotted Dixon around four this morning, and we all waited until he actually got a small fire started on your porch by short-circuiting the Christmas light wires on the cultured tree—after, that is, he wedged the back sliding door so it wouldn't open, then doused all four sides of your house with gasoline."

Jessie closed her eyes against Ian's shirt. "He . . . he must have tried to poison Toby and thought he was at the vet." She leaned back to look up. "So it's over?"

"For now. You're going to have to be a witness at his trials; at least the one he'll have in Atlanta." He stopped rubbing her back and gave her a gentle squeeze. "But I'll be right beside you the entire time. And so will Toby." He smiled down at her. "Are you hungry? We might as well eat the snack you packed for us to take up the mountain." He let her go and walked to the counter. "Assuming it's not skewered to death."

Jessie rushed past him and stood blocking the basket. "Um . . . I'm not really that hungry right now. Let's just go home and I'll make us something to eat later."

He arched a brow as he reached around her and snatched the basket off the counter, lifting it high over her head when she made a grab for it. "You're really going to have to do something about controlling that little twitch at the corner of your mouth, Jess, because now I'm curious about what you packed."

He set the basket on the counter, crowding her out of the way as he pried the axe out then reached in and pulled out a thick roll of fluffy towels she'd wrapped tape around. He peeled back the tape and then the towels to reveal a pair of fine crystal champagne flutes, staring down at them in a silence so thick that Jessie would swear she could hear the gears turning in his brain. He finally laid the flutes on the towels, then reached in the pack again and pulled out a magnum of champagne.

Well, dammit, she'd figured he would have gotten a bottle of wine, but you need champagne to properly celebrate a marriage proposal.

He set the bottle on the counter and reached in and

pulled out a bag of rawhide chews, his gaze going from them to her as he arched a brow. Feeling every vein in her face flushing with heat, Jessie watched him set the rawhide on the counter and reach into the pack basket again, this time his hand emerging with the box of condoms.

He set them on the counter with a sigh, then looked inside the basket and sighed again when he saw what she knew were a half dozen votive candles in crystal holders carefully placed in the bottom. He closed his eyes, not moving so much as a muscle.

"You thought I was taking you up the mountain to propose," he said quietly, still not moving, still not opening his eyes. "After our knowing each other only three weeks."

"Y-you said you loved me," she whispered, "and mentioned something about us being bound together for life when we came back down. From a woman's perspective, that usually means . . . that sounds like . . ." Jessie sucked in a shuddering breath and walked out the still open door.

Ian caught up with her just as she was walking past the snowcat and pulled her to a stop and turned her to face him. "Too much has been happening too quickly in your life right now, Jessie. I'm not about to rush you into marriage before you've even managed to catch your breath."

"I understand," she said, trying to pull away.

His grip on her shoulders tightened. "No, you don't. You've been here just over three weeks and you've already been introduced to something most people would need an entire lifetime to digest. You're overwhelmed by the magic right now, and you're looking for something solid to hold on to, and you think that's me."

"I'm not a naive twenty-four-year-old anymore, Ian. Nearly getting killed and losing a baby and having to learn to walk again is a hell of a lot more of a maelstrom than your fancy light display up on the mountain. It took me four years to know who I am, and a couple of nudges from a persistent old goat to make me realize what I want from life." She jerked away and started walking out the driveway again. "And at the moment that life is waiting for me half a mile down the road," she said softly without looking back.

Not that she could see ahead, either, she was crying so hard.

Chapter Nineteen

JESSIE SAT ON HER COUCH, STARING AT HER BEAUTIFUL little fir tree as the first rays of Christmas morning sunlight touched it, trying to decide who was more depressed, she or her dog. Even though he'd spent the last four nights in Ian's monstrous bed with her, Toby had also spent the last four days lying on the rug in front of the woodstove instead of his new bed, pushing his food around in his dish instead of eating it, not even interested in playing find-the-squeaky-toy with her. About the only time Jessie saw him perk up was when he heard an engine and he'd run to the window to see a snowmobile go by on the frozen lake, but then he'd go back and flop down in front of the stove when the machine would continue around the point.

But truth be told, Jessie also perked up whenever she heard an engine, only to flop down on the couch when she realized it wasn't Ian.

She'd thought maybe part of Toby's depression was that

he wasn't feeling all that useful anymore, since she no longer needed her cane and hadn't had a flashback in over a week. Jessie had gone so far as to pretend she felt one coming on, told him to find a safe place, and curled up in a ball in her closet hoping to pull the poor dog out of his funk. Only Toby had stood in the bedroom staring at her, his expression asking if she was insane. Which Jessie had figured she was, because she'd hidden her face in her hands and burst into tears. Toby had come in the closet and sat down beside her, tucked his big warm head on her shoulder in a doggy hug, and she'd swear he had shed a few tears himself.

What in hell was the matter with Ian? For crying out loud, the man had saved her life and then simply let her walk out of his. Although to be fair, he was probably working day and night because TarStone was in full operation, as she could barely get through town or any of the stores without bumping into a group of skiers.

But still, he could at least have called.

She hadn't heard from Roger, either, since that night on the mountain. And really, considering her four-year nightmare, the ending had been rather anticlimactic. Jack Stone had come to see her later that afternoon, and explained a bit more about how they'd caught Brad red-handed lighting her porch on fire. It would be up to the courts to decide which state got first dibs on prosecuting Brad, Jack had told her, Maine or Georgia. But, he'd gone on to assure her, she was perfectly safe now.

Depressed as hell, but perfectly safe.

Jessie wiped her eyes to make sure she didn't have any stray tears when she heard her parents stirring upstairs. They'd arrived yesterday afternoon and instantly fallen in love with her new home; her dad quite proud of her for driving a hard bargain on the price, and her mom utterly mesmerized by the flocks of colorful birds constantly fluttering around her large bird feeder on the deck.

The bird feeder hadn't been there yesterday morning when she'd driven into town to get some last-minute gifts to stuff in the five stockings she had hanging on the mantle behind the stove. She had a sixth stocking filled with male necessities—including a box of condoms stuffed in the toe—hidden in the bottom drawer of her bureau, but she was waiting to see if she should bring it out.

It wasn't looking good so far.

"Good Lord, the crows are better alarm clocks than roosters," Maureen Pringle said as she came down the stairs. She stopped at the bottom and smiled at the little fir tree, then slid her smile to Jessie. "Merry Christmas, baby."

"Merry Christmas, Mom. Did you sleep well?"

Maureen headed into the kitchen with a laugh. "I can't even remember my head hitting the pillow," she said, opening cupboard doors until she found the mugs. "I thought I was going to have trouble getting to sleep because it's so quiet here, but I guess all this wonderful fresh air—and all those glasses of wine—took care of any problem I might have had." She came back into the living room carrying a mug of coffee, sat down on the couch, and patted Jessie's knee. "I've never seen you looking healthier, Jess." She waved her mug toward the window. "And Dad and I have to admit that we were wrong; moving here appears to be the smartest thing you've ever done." She shifted to tuck her foot under her body to face Jessie, her I'm-your-mother-so-don't-even-try-to-lie-to-me look making an appearance. "So considering this is the first time in four years I've seen you so . . . alive, I think you'd better explain the sadness that comes into your eyes when you think no one is looking," she said gently, touching Jessie's arm. "What's the matter, baby?"

Jessie pulled in a deep breath and looked out the window at the birds already flocking to the feeder. "I've fallen in love with Ian."

"In four weeks?" Maureen asked in obvious alarm. Her hand on Jessie's arm tightened. "Are you sure, Jess? Is it possible that it's only . . . infatuation?"

"Oh, it's definitely love."

"Then why the sadness?"

Jessie finally looked at her. "Because even though he said he loved me, I haven't seen Ian since he saved my life four days ago," she quietly explained, already having told her parents about Brad and what had really happened back in Atlanta as well as three days before they'd arrived— hence the many glasses of wine she and her mother had consumed and the goodly amount of bourbon her father had downed.

Maureen glanced toward the hallway, then looked back at Jessie and smiled. "The man left his bed, so I assume he's planning to see you sometime in the near future. Say, once your parents are no longer sleeping upstairs?"

"You weren't here for the last three days," Jessie pointed out. "And he hasn't called or texted me, not once." She waved toward the deck. "He waited until I went into town yesterday to sneak over and put up that bird feeder."

"Maybe he's a little panicked. Men get funny like that when they suddenly realize they've fallen in love. Hell," Maureen said with a laugh, lifting her mug toward the ceiling, "I didn't see your father for almost a month after he declared his undying love for me. He claimed he had a pressing deadline for a museum he was head architect on, which kept him so busy, apparently, that he couldn't even pick up the phone and call." She squeezed Jessie's arm again. "It appears as though love takes men by surprise, baby, and they go a little crazy when they suddenly discover they can't breathe properly unless they're drawing in the scent of the woman they love."

"Yeah, well, I hope Ian's passed out cold on his mountain from lack of air."

"Oh dear, you've got it bad," Maureen chuckled, lifting her mug to her lips just as Jacob Pringle came down the stairs.

He stopped beside the tree and smiled at them. "Now there's a sight to greet a man first thing Christmas morning: the two women he loves cuddled together on a couch, looking positively radiant." But then his smile disappeared and he rubbed his forehead. "Do you have any aspirin, Jess? I seem to have a bit of a headache this morning. Apparently my system's not used to all this fresh air."

Jessie got up with a snort. "Your system's not used to your downing a pint of bourbon in one evening.

"Are we going to meet the man who owns that bed today?" he asked, following her into the bathroom.

"I . . . I don't think so," she said, taking the bottle of aspirin out of the medicine cabinet. "Ian's pretty tied up at the resort. I imagine this is one of their busiest weeks."

"A man's never too busy to meet the parents of the woman he's sleeping with." He touched her arm. "You know I've always urged you to make your own decisions, but you've been here only four weeks and already you're living with the man." He touched her fleece over the scar on her collarbone and smiled sadly. "I'm just scared, Jessie, as a father who nearly lost his daughter when she was swept off her feet by a man she barely knew."

"I'm not twenty-four anymore, Dad, and believe me,

I've aged twenty years since then. Ian MacKeage is as solid as the mountain he works on and more honest and noble than any man I know." She smiled, patting his chest. "Besides you, of course." But then she sobered. "I love him so much, it hurts to breathe when he's not around."

Jacob took the aspirin out of her hand and leaned in to kiss her forehead. "Then stop looking so sad when you think no one is looking. The man will get his priorities in order soon. And you know why?"

"Why?"

"Because only a complete idiot would risk losing the smartest, prettiest, spunkiest woman I know. Besides your mother, of course," he said with a laugh, heading out into the kitchen, only to stop and squat down beside Toby in front of the woodstove. He lifted the dog's head by his chin. "And you, you big lug; don't tell me you're also smitten with this MacKeage fellow."

Jessie laughed, stopping beside them. "Toby wasn't won over all that easily, especially when he realized he had to forfeit his spot in my . . . bed," she finished lamely, feeling her cheeks heat to blistering red. She made a beeline for the kitchen. "I did *not* just say that," she said with a laugh.

"Good," her dad said as he stood up, "because then I'd have to go buy a shotgun and hunt the man down to make an honest woman of my daughter."

Jessie buried her face in the fridge, partly to cool her blush but mostly to hide her smile. If only her dad knew how real that threat would be coming from a MacKeage male if one of their women were involved, he certainly wouldn't be laughing.

Her mom came over and stood next to her looking in the fridge. "So, what's for dinner?" she asked. "And what do you want me to do? Should I peel the potatoes?"

Jessie pulled the crisper drawer out of the fridge and set it on the counter. "No, just wash the potatoes and let them dry, and then I'll oil and season them and put them in the oven an hour before we eat. But you can peel the carrots while I prepare the roast," she said, lifting the ten-pound hunk of beef she'd driven to Greenville to buy when it looked as if nobody was donating a venison roast.

Maureen stopped taking potatoes out of the crisper drawer and turned to her. "When did you learn to cook?"

"I've been a closet chef for over three years now." And the only reason she'd burnt the first roast she'd fed to the crows was because it had been the first time she'd cooked in an electric oven. Why in hell were the burners propane and the oven electric? "But don't tell anyone, okay?" she whispered through her smile. "Because then people will stop feeding me and expect me to feed them."

After finding a travel mug for his coffee, Jessie's dad took Toby for a walk, saying he wanted to check out the neighborhood, and she and her mom threw together a light breakfast for them to graze on while they finished putting dinner together. She was cooking enough to feed an army, and even though there might only be just the three of them, Jessie had her mom set two extra places at the table.

She'd walked out to the mailbox every day for the last four days, often stopping when she reached the spot where Roger had been set up selling his wares, and even called out his name. But he never came, despite her doing as he'd instructed by walking there with the intention of seeing him. Roger had also stopped texting her, and the couple of texts she had sent to her old phone number hadn't been replied to.

Apparently the old goat had also walked out of her life, now that he'd gotten what he wanted—which Jessie had decided was for Ian to accept the magic. The problem with that, however, was that she didn't think Ian had *wanted* to accept it, and she was beginning to believe the only reason he had accepted it was to save her from Brad. But now that she was safe, Ian was stuck with the magic and likely avoiding her because she had completely ruined his life.

By noon Jessie was just taking the roast out of the oven to let the meat rest before she carved it when she heard the distinct rumble of a trail groomer coming down the road.

"Oh my," Maureen said, looking out the door window. "Jessica, did you move to Maine or the North Pole?"

Jessie stood on her tiptoes to see out the sink window, and smiled through her disappointment when she saw the faded old groomer stop right in the middle of her front lawn. "I wasn't kidding when I told you to set a place at the table for Santa Claus," she said, laughing at her mother gaping out the window in the door.

Maureen scampered back to let Roger come inside, then scampered back even farther when he turned and carefully set the large wool sack he had slung over his shoulder down on the floor. "Merry Christmas!" he barked out to the house in general, even as his gaze landed on Maureen. He swiped his fur-lined hat off his head, ran his fingers through his wild mane of hair—further mussing it up—then smoothed down his beard bristling with his grin as he strode directly up to her.

"If'n I had to guess, I'd be thinking you're our Jess's mama, Maureen," he said, only instead of taking the hand her mom was tentatively extending to him, Roger used it to pull Maureen into his arms with a laugh. "'Cause I swear only a woman as handsome as yourself could create such a beautiful daughter. Yes, well, good to meet ye, Missus

Pringle," he said gruffly, stepping away when he spotted Jessie's father approaching somewhat aggressively. He extended his hand. "Roger AuClair de Keage, a good friend of your daughter's."

"Jacob Pringle," her dad said, shaking Roger's hand. "Maureen's *husband*."

"I guessed as much," Roger said with a nod, turning to Jessie and opening his arms, his eyes twinkling with mischief. "You figured out how to cook up a fine venison roast yet?" he asked as she walked into his embrace.

"I'm afraid you're going to have to settle for beef, as I forgot to go out and shoot me a deer this morning."

He gave a snort as he squeezed her so tight she squeaked, then walked over to his bag and carried it to the tree. "Now ain't this a fine-looking fir, if I do say so myself," he said as he started pulling neatly wrapped packages out of the bag and carefully arranging them under the tree with the others. "Tell me, Jess," he said when she walked over to stand beside her still-gaping mother and scowling father to watch right along with them. "Where exactly did ye get the poor little bugger?" He stopped and arched a brow at her. "I don't recall Michael MacBain selling any uncultured trees. He expand'n his business?"

She was saved from answering when Toby trotted over to the tree, looking perkier than he had in days, and started nosing one of the packages.

"You let that alone, big fella," Roger growled as he pushed Toby away. "I swear, you're more impatient than a five-year-old on Christmas morning," he said, laughing at his own joke. He grabbed Toby's snout when the dog tried to reach the package again. "I'm gonna take your gift back if'n you don't quit worrying it to death. Now you go over to that fancy bed of yours and wait until after dinner like the rest of us gotta."

"There'd better not be a bone in there," Jessie said, remembering the mess he'd made with the last bone as Toby walked back to his bed with his head hanging.

"You're just gonna have to wait and see like everyone else, missy," Roger chortled as he continued pulling packages out of the bag to set them under the tree.

Each gift was crisply wrapped in the same paper, a deep blue covered with gold suns and moons and stars that were so shiny, Jessie would swear they were real gold leaf, and each of the variously sized packages was tied with what appeared to be spun silver ribbon.

"Well, then," she said, heading to the kitchen. "I guess we'd better eat so we can get to the gifts."

Her mom rushed in behind her, and with her back to the living room she nudged Jessie's hip. "Who is he?" she whispered, glancing over her shoulder then giving Jessie a glare that was more amused than threatening. "And don't you dare say Santa Claus."

"He's an old relative of Ian's, actually." Jessie waved toward the windows. "Ian told me he lives on some mountain on the other side of the lake, and that he likes to keep to himself for the most part." She touched her mother's arm. "Just to warn you, though; you're liable to get something . . . well, funky from him for Christmas, okay? Roger's into bartering wares, so whatever it is will probably be used."

"He brought gifts for Jacob and me?" Maureen squeaked, clutching her throat. "But Jessie, we don't have anything to give him in exchange. We didn't know you were having anyone else over for Christmas dinner."

Jessie patted her mom's arm. "Don't worry, I filled a stocking for Roger and put all our names on the gift I bought him in case he showed up." She leaned closer. "But don't be surprised if he tries bartering with you, okay? Oh, and he might want to have a word with you about not teaching me to cook," she added with a smile when her mom went from worried to indignant. She shrugged. "Roger's a bit old-fashioned, so don't take it personally."

"But I *tried* to teach you to cook," Maureen said, apparently taking it personally. "But you were too busy being a social butterfly." She waved at the roast sitting in the large cast-iron pot on the stove. "And you obviously can cook, so what's his gripe?"

"That's just it: Roger loves to gripe," Jessie drawled, turning to grab her oven mitts. "Oh, and don't be surprised when he hauls out a bottle of Scotch after dinner and pours you a glass," she said, laughing when her mother went back to looking worried. "Apparently everyone in his family thinks Scotch is good for whatever ails a person."

She walked to the peninsula to tell the men to take a seat so she could serve dinner, only to find Roger had lined up four of the wine glasses on the edge of the table and was pouring Scotch into them. "Too late," she told her mother, turning with a lopsided smile. "I guess we're having Scotch as an appetizer."

"Or an appetite killer," Maureen muttered, carrying the sliced homemade bread Jessie had bought at the bakery to the table.

"You men might as well take your seats," Jessie said across the peninsula, "because dinner is served."

"Let's say we wait a little while before we eat," her dad said, carrying his glass of Scotch over to her chair next to the woodstove, but at the last minute gesturing for Roger to sit in it. He looked at Jessie. "There's still one more place set at the table, so that must mean everyone's not here yet."

"I . . . I don't think he's coming."

"Oh, I don't think it would hurt if we waited a few more minutes."

Jessie caught her breath at the look in his eyes. "Oh, Daddy, what did you do?"

Jacob used his glass to gesture at Toby. "Well, when we got about three-quarters of a mile from the house on our walk, the big lug suddenly started dragging me down someone's driveway, and wouldn't stop no matter how much I tugged on his leash or pleaded with him. And Toby walked right up to an old cabin and started scratching on its door."

"But nobody was home, right? *Right?*"

Jessie's heart sank when she saw her dad's eyes start to crinkle. "Well, the door opened and this tall, handsome, athletic man took one look at me and paled. But he invited us inside, and after making quite a fuss over Toby, he offered me a glass of Scotch." He smiled, holding the glass toward Roger. "Which I must say I'm coming to like quite a bit more than bourbon."

"You went inside and had a drink with Ian?" Jessie squeaked, holding the mitts to her mouth. "Why?"

"Well, for one thing, so I could thank him for saving your life four days ago. And then we just had ourselves a friendly little chat." He glanced toward the door then back at her and shrugged. "Dinner will keep a few more minutes, won't it, baby?"

"Oh, Daddy, what did you do?" she repeated. "What did you say to Ian?"

He looked down, swirling the Scotch in his glass.

"Jacob," her mother growled, "answer your daughter. What in hell did you do?"

He finally looked at Jessie again, and the naked love in his deep hazel eyes made her chest start pounding. "You might be a grown woman, Jessica, but I will always be your father," he said quietly. "And a father's conversation with the man his daughter has fallen in love with is best kept between them," he added, giving his wife a speaking glance, then looking back at Jessie and smiling sheepishly. "It's Christmas, Jess; give the guy another ten minutes."

She mutely turned away, going back to the stove as she took in slow, gulping breaths, undecided which frightened her more; that Ian wouldn't show up or what to say to him if he did. She really hadn't wanted an audience around when she threw herself against his big, solid chest and apologized for being an idiot for thinking he might want to marry her without even knowing her a full month.

"Your father acts so old-fashioned sometimes," her mom whispered, hugging Jessie from behind, "that I swear he's reincarnated from the eighteenth century." She turned Jessie around and brushed her hair back. "You'll work things out with Ian, Jess, in your own time and on your own terms, not your father's or anyone else's."

"But what am I supposed to do if he does show up today?" she whispered back, leaning her forehead on her mom's shoulder with a heavy sigh. "I was such an idiot for jumping to the conclusion that just because he said he loved me, he was going to propose two minutes later."

Maureen set her away in order to smile into her eyes. "Love turns us all into idiots at one time or another, and sometimes it turns us into forces to be reckoned with. I'm sorry, baby," she said, giving Jessie's shoulders a squeeze, "but I'm afraid this isn't the last time you're going to embarrass yourself, so try to remember that when Ian acts a little crazy sometimes, too, okay?" She snorted softly. "Trust me; your father and I had so many moments of idiocy in the first two years of our marriage that it's a wonder you were born." She laughed. "That's why it's called falling *madly* in love."

Jessie gave her a hug, squeezing her tightly. "I love you, Mom. You always seem to know just the right thing to say."

"I love you, too, baby. And I promise, you and Ian will be okay. And you know why? Because your father certainly wouldn't be waiting dinner on a man he didn't approve of."

"It's awful quiet in here," Roger said, walking into the kitchen carrying two wineglasses filled three-quarters full with Scotch. "And that's got me worrying that ye ruined Christmas dinner and are trying to figure out how to tell us."

Maureen took the glass he held out to her and Jessie took hers and then walked over to the stove and lifted the lid on the roast. "Does that look ruined to you?" she asked, smiling when he peered down inside the pot he'd left on her porch.

Roger reared up and then bent down to open the oven door and peer inside. He straightened to give Jessie a glare. "You think fun'n an old man by making him believe ye can't cook might be entertaining, missy?"

"You think assuming I can't cook just because I *don't* might be entertaining, you old goat?"

"Jessica," her mother said on a gasp, "that's rude."

"Aye, I was thinking that, too," Roger said, turning to her. "Ye know, Maureen, I'm willing to admit I intended to give you a good scolding—after dinner, of course—but seeing your daughter comes by her sassiness honestly," he said, his beard bristling with his grin, "I'm thinking maybe

I should be singing ye praises instead for raising up such a spunky lass as our little missy here. Go on now, have yourself a good taste of that fine Scotch I brought. You, too, Jess," he said, turning to her and giving a wink. "It's guaranteed to cure what I do believe might be ailing you at the moment."

Jessie raised her glass in salute to her mom, and they both took a sip only to both immediately start coughing. But to Jessie's surprise, her mother caught her breath and immediately took another, much longer sip.

"I daresay that's the finest Scotch I've ever tasted," Maureen said on a winded whisper, wiping her mouth with the back of her hand. She took another gulp then nodded demurely to an obviously stunned Roger and turned and headed into the living room. "Jacob, you must find out from Roger what brand this is. Isn't it wonderful?"

Realizing she rather liked the smooth burn that sent heat spreading throughout her, Jessie took another sip, only to end up gulping in a mouthful when she heard footsteps on the porch followed by a knock on the door. Roger patted her on the back, his laughter drowning out her sputtering gasps as she tried to catch her breath.

"Good enough, then; it looks like we're finally going to get to eat," he said, walking away. Only instead of going to the door, he waved at it on his way to the dining table. "You gonna answer that, Jess, or make the man stand outside the whole time we eat?"

Apparently Toby was the only one with enough manners to answer the door, except that he couldn't actually open it. Jessie looked at her father, but he merely arched a brow as her mother just gave her a smile and took another sip of her drink.

Okay, she would answer the door. Yeah, she could do

this. She'd just pretend that Ian was merely another guest, just like Roger. Yup, someone her dad had invited. Not someone who made her heart pound and her belly flip-flop and her insides clench. She could *do this*.

Jessie walked over and, using her knee to push Toby out of the way, she opened the door with the biggest, brightest smile in her arsenal, only to have it falter when she saw Ian MacKeage's head sitting on top of a dress shirt and tie and suit jacket, her gaze falling down to his slacks and leather dress shoes before snapping back up to his face.

She opened her mouth with every intention of saying hello like a civilized hostess, only to gasp when she was lifted off her feet and pulled outside, a vague sense of the door shutting as she was swept sideways and pressed up against the house. But even before her head could stop spinning, his mouth captured her second gasp and started kissing her senseless.

This was Ian, right? Her mountain man? The guy who hadn't called or texted or come to see her in four days? This wasn't a twin brother, was it, who wore dress clothes like a born businessman? Did twins *taste* alike?

A tie; was he really wearing a *tie*?

"Don't ever walk away from me again," he growled, resting his forehead on hers.

"You're *scolding* me?" she said into his deep green eyes burning into hers.

"We agreed there would never be anything you could do or say to embarrass yourself with me."

"You're honestly scolding me?" She shoved at his chest but couldn't budge him. "You don't come by or call for four days, and *you're* scolding *me*?"

He captured her righteous anger in his mouth again and

slid his hands up under her sweater to cup her breasts, brushing his thumbs over her nipples even as he spread her legs to press one of his thighs intimately against her. Jessie found her head swimming again, only this time at the memory of the unimaginable passion she'd found in his arms in bed, both of them naked as he'd taken her out to the sun and moon and stars and back time after time after time.

"Oh God, I'm sorry," she cried the moment he stopped kissing her to lean his forehead on hers again, except this time he was breathing as heavily as she was.

"No, you're not," he rasped, his hands now spanning her ribs to hold her upright on his thigh because her legs had turned to jelly. "I'm not looking for an apology, Jess; I'm looking for your promise to never walk away from me again."

"You didn't call."

"*You* walked away."

She hid her face in his chest. "I thought you were mad at me for ruining your life."

"I am. Because you did. *When you walked away.*"

"I'm *sorry.*"

"I told ye I don't—hey! Did you just wipe your nose on my tie?" he growled, rearing back and pulling the tie out of her hands.

"No. No, I'm pretty sure that damp spot is snow or something," she said, pulling it out of his hand and smoothing it down over his chest to cover a dark spot on his shirt.

He sighed hard enough to move her hair, slid his hand out from under her sweater, and gently pulled the hem of it down over her waist. Then he slowly eased his thigh from between her legs, his hands hovering in case she collapsed—which was a real possibility. And then he reached up and palmed her face and kissed her softly on the lips as he brushed his thumbs over her damp cheeks.

"I love you," he whispered against her mouth. "Forever."

He had to use his thumbs like windshield wipers again because her eyes started really leaking at his declaration. "I love you so much," she whispered against his lips. "And I promise I won't ever walk away again." She tilted her head back to grin up at him. "Well, not from embarrassment. I might walk away pissed, but only so I don't do something foolish like thump that big hard head of yours with your walking . . . staff."

He slowly shook his big hard head, his eyes not quite managing to crinkle at the corners. "It's a moot point anyway, as I decided on my way here that I'm not *letting* you walk away from me again." Finally, he smiled; except it wasn't a very nice smile as he used his body to press her up against the house again. "You think you can handle dealing with a real mountain man, Jess, and all that that entails?" he asked quietly.

She gave him an equally not-nice smile. "I'm pretty sure I've already proven that I can. Maybe the question is, can you handle dealing with a modern city girl?"

She nearly fell when he suddenly stepped away just one second before the door opened. "Are we eating today or not, people?" Roger asked. "'Cause Toby here is having a fit trying to get at his present, and I'm worrying the potatoes are going to be so dry, they're gonna taste like moose pellets if'n they ain't out of that oven in two minutes."

"God forbid a man should put on oven mitts and rescue them," Jessie muttered, smoothing down her sweater and then brushing her cheeks with her sleeves as she headed for the door on rubbery legs. But she suddenly stopped and turned to Ian, pressing her hand to his chest to make him stop.

"What did my father say to you this morning?" she asked in a whisper.

"Some things are best left between men, lass."

She rose up on her toes to better glare at him. "You are such an atavist."

Ian's eyes nearly crinkled shut, and he turned her around and gave her backside a rather boisterous nudge to get her moving. "Yeah, I can be a real bastard like that sometimes."

Dinner turned into quite a lively affair, partly because Roger was in full crazy-old-hermit mode, and partly because the five of them had to keep taking turns jumping up from the table to shoo Toby away from the presents until Ian finally took the big lug's face in his hands and did his way-with-animals thing. Toby stayed sitting in front of the woodstove after that, but he was on full alert, his eyes trained on one specific present.

Jessie just knew it had to be a fat, greasy bone.

They cleared the table—Ian and her dad actually helping—while Roger went over and sat down on the floor by the tree while urging them to hurry up. Jessie just put the perishable food away, then shooed everyone out of the kitchen, saying everything else would still be there after they all opened their presents.

She ran into the bedroom and took Ian's stocking out of the bottom drawer, ran into the living room and hung it on the sixth nail she'd put up when she'd hung the other five, and took her place on the couch between her mom and dad when Ian waved her over to them as he sat down in her chair.

"Okay, then," Roger said, carefully picking up Toby's gift and holding it on his lap. "You can come over now, big fella, and see what Santa had me bring ye."

Toby bounded over like a pup being called to dinner, nearly knocking Roger over when he skidded into him and tried to clamp his teeth on the box. Jessie sat up with a gasp that was echoed by her mother when the box suddenly made a noise.

"Ohmigod," Jessie whispered just as Roger pulled off the lid and reached in to pull out a kitten. "Oh. My. God."

Roger sat the kitten in front of Toby, and the dog immediately lay down and went perfectly motionless. The kitten immediately reared up on its haunches, slapped its little claws into Toby's snout, and started licking his mouth.

"Oh. My. God," Jessie whispered again, her hand clutching her throat. "Roger, you gave Toby a . . . a *kitten* for Christmas?"

"Nay, I didn't; Santa did. I'm just delivering the little bugger for him."

"But what am I supposed to do with a kitten? Service dogs can't have *pets*." She gestured weakly at Toby, who was now returning the favor and licking the kitten's head to a slick-backed wetness. "I don't think he's supposed to have anything to distract him from his job."

"What job?" Roger asked. "He ain't got to be worrying over you no more, so Santa figured the big fella needed something to keep him busy."

Jessie looked at Ian for help, but when he only shrugged, she looked back at Toby and sighed at the sight of the kitten trying to crawl up his back.

"This one be for you, Maureen," Roger said, holding out a small gift the size of his fist. "I'm thinking it might be just what you're needing."

Jessie jumped up and got the gift and brought it back to her mom.

"That was very sweet of you to bring something just for me," Maureen said, holding the box on her knees as if she was afraid it might also be an animal—although the package was small enough it had to be a mouse, Jessie was afraid.

"Go on, missus; open it."

Maureen carefully pulled the bow free and undid the wrapping, then smiled in relief at the small wooden box inside. "Oh, this is a beautiful trinket box, Roger. What's the wood it's made of?"

"I'm sure your husband recognized the bird's-eye maple," Roger said, "him being a fine architect. But the box ain't really the gift. Look inside."

Her mom lifted off the lid and gasped softly. "Oh my," she said, reaching inside and pulling out what looked like a wooden pendant with a finely spun gold chain trailing after it. "Oh, this is beautiful," she whispered, holding it at eye level then leaning over Jessie to show her husband. "Jacob, do you recognize the wood? I've never seen anything like it. It looks like some sort of knot; you know, what do they call them? Burls?"

"I've never seen one like that, though," Jacob said, taking the necklace in order to study it as Jessie leaned into him to also see it better. "It's amazing. It looks like a burl, but the center's been carved out and there's a . . ." He squinted. "What is that?" he asked, looking at Roger.

"The burl would be cherry and that stone inside is moonstone," Roger said, sliding his smile to Jessie. "Moonstone would be a powerful rock for women, Maureen," he said as he then slid his smile to her mother. "I'm thinking ye might find yourself feeling mighty fine when you're wearing it."

"Well, I'm certain I will, Roger, because it's simply so beautiful," she said, reaching across Jessie to take it away from her husband. "Can you clasp this on for me, Jess?" she asked, handing it to her and turning away.

Jessie opened the clasp and carefully slung the chain around her mom's neck, her fingers faltering when her mother suddenly gasped.

"Oh, I think it just gave me a little shock," Maureen said with a laugh, holding her hand over the pendant. "Is it on, Jess?"

Jessie tore her alarmed gaze away from Ian and clasped it on, then jumped up from the couch as her mother looked down at her gift, and walked over to Roger. With her back to everyone, Jessie bent down to glare at him, only to have him shove another gift at her.

"This one would be for your da, lass. Take it to him for me, would ye?"

Honestly, she didn't know if she dared. What in hell was Roger doing giving her parents magical gifts? The box she handed to her father felt empty it weighed so little, and being a man, Jacob didn't bother being as careful as he unwrapped it, but he did stop to admire the beautiful birch-bark box.

He lifted the lid and then stared down inside it, frowning, only to flinch when he picked up the rectangular smooth piece of wood the size and shape of a credit card. "You're going to have to get a humidifier for the house, Jess, because I just got a shock, too, from the dry air. Is this a . . . money clip?" he asked, looking at Roger.

"That it is," Roger said with a nod. "And don't you go worrying none that it's too delicate to carry a goodly amount of dollars, 'cause it be sturdier than it looks. A lot like your daughter," he said, his eyes squinted with laughter. "You carry that on ye, Jacob, and you'll find that when you're needing some money it'll be right there wait'n on you. Now here, Jessie, this one be for Ian," he said, handing her another small package.

"How come I get mine last?" she asked, trying to see around him to beneath the tree, then eyeing him suspiciously. Because honestly, she'd been hoping he'd brought her another walking stick, since she'd left hers on the mountain.

"You'll be getting exactly what you be needing when you're needing it, missy. Now go on, give that one to your man there."

Jessie had to walk around Toby and the kitten, which was now curled up between Toby's paws, its little head resting on one of his legs, sleeping the sleep of the innocent—apparently unaware that it could have become dinner as easily as it had become a friend. "Um . . . Roger?" she asked as she handed Ian his present and walked back to stare down at Toby. "Is that a boy kitten or a girl kitten?"

"Well, I guess Santa figured that if Toby was used to worrying over a female, he should probably have a girl kitten for a pet, wouldn't you say? Here, this one is for you, missy. Now go sit down and open it while I open mine from you."

She turned back to him with a smile. "What makes you so certain I got you a Christmas present? Since I haven't heard from you in almost a week, I might have decided you probably weren't coming today."

He reached under the tree and picked up his gift without even reading the label, smiling smugly up at her as he started tearing the paper away. Jessie sat down between her mom and dad and set the big heavy gift Roger had handed her on her knees. She slowly undid the bow, then

ran her fingers over the beautiful paper, thinking that it
really looked like gold leaf.

"It sure seems real, doesn't it, Jess?" her father said,
leaning in to whisper. "And if I didn't know better, I'd
swear the ribbon is sterling silver." He shook his head. "But
that's just a bit much. Who did you say Roger is again?"

"He's related to Ian somehow," she whispered back,
finally slipping her finger under a corner of the wrapping—
not a piece of tape in sight—and slowly folding back the
paper to reveal a thick, leather-bound tome. She opened it
to find page after page of handwritten recipes for every
conceivable food ever cooked.

"That would be a collection handed down through
the generations, lass," Roger said, looking up from the
unwrapped but unopened gift she'd bought him. "Dating
back to the very first MacKeage wife. If something's not
in there, it probably shouldn't be eaten," he added with a
smile—the real Roger de Keage briefly emerging then
disappearing right before her eyes as the bartering old
hermit held up his gift and frowned. "Mind telling me what
in tarnation this thing be?"

"It's one of them new-fangled iPads," she said, mimick-
ing his burr. She waved toward the window. "It has Wi-Fi
and 3G, so you can use it near any one of those blasted
towers for sending e-mails and surfing the web."

His eyes danced with merriment. "Oh, I'll be liking
this, then," he said, tearing into the box.

Jessie looked down at her MacKeage book of recipes
and, keeping her head lowered to hide her blush, she
glanced over at Ian, only to find him staring down at the
opened small box in his hands; the gaze he finally lifted
to her was so profoundly serious that she instantly paled.

"Okay, then," Roger said with a grunt as he got to his feet. "Ye wanting me to pass out all these other gifts, or might you Pringles be want'n to have yourselves some private family time?" he asked, even as he bent over and pulled out the gift Jessie had wrapped for Ian over a week ago. "Ye might wanna be giving this one to your man, though, before we leave."

Jessie shoved her cookbook onto her mom's lap and jumped to her feet. "No! I mean, that's okay, Roger," she said, taking the heavy package from him and setting it back on the floor, then using her foot to push it behind the tree. "I'll give it to him later."

"Ian, what did Roger give you?" her mom asked. "You're being awfully quiet."

Ian smiled at Maureen, not that it came anywhere near his eyes, then looked at Roger for an awkwardly long time. He finally turned his gaze on Jessie and slowly stood up.

Everyone and everything in the room receded until only Ian remained as he walked to her, his winter spruce eyes making Jessie's insides suddenly clench as his power radiated ahead of him in waves of . . . oh God, he was getting down on his knees in front of her.

He reached out and captured her hand when she tried to step away, then lifted the box he was holding for her to see the two . . . honest to God, those looked like two matching wedding rings in his and her sizes, only they appeared to be made of some sort of black stone instead of metal, with tiny flecks that glittered like starlight.

Jessie's legs went from rubber to jelly, and Ian had to catch her when she fell to her knees.

He lifted her chin to make her look at him. "Will ye do me the honor of being my wife, Miss Pringle?" he asked quietly. His eyes got the faintest crinkles at the corners. "With your father's permission, of course."

She leaned closer. "Oh, Ian, I want to, but I . . . I can't," she whispered so only he could hear. "Not until I give you a miracle, only I don't know what it is. I thought it was getting you back in school so you can be a wildlife biologist, and that's why I wrapped up a bunch of college catalogs," she said, gesturing weakly at the tree behind her. "But now I don't think that's it, because . . ." She leaned closer again. "Because I think you're exactly where you're supposed to be, on . . . on your mountain."

"Ah, Jess," he said quietly, brushing a finger across her cheek. "You gave me two miracles, lass; one when you gave yourself to me, and then when you gave me TarStone." He leaned in until his nose touched hers. "Say yes, Jessie, and then say thank you."

"But those rings are from Roger, not yo—"

Still keeping their noses touching, he placed his palm over her mouth as he softly chuckled. "You willing to go with a nudge, or are ye waiting for him to *knock* some sense into us? It's going to happen, so why waste time *waiting* for it to happen?" He straightened away and held the box up between them again. "Will you marry me, Jessie Pringle, so I can start breathing properly again?"

"I . . . oh . . . yes!" she cried, throwing herself into his arms. "Yes! Yes! Yes!"

"There now, that's done," Roger suddenly barked, clapping his hands together. "So come on, people, we got us a wedding to throw together. Ian, you call your mama and papa and tell them to spread the word that we need everyone up at the summit house by sunset if'n they're wanting to witness the nuptials. Oh, and have Greylen and Callum get them tourists off the top of the mountain by then, so we got the place to ourselves. This here marriage is a solemn matter, not some spectator sport."

"Today?" Jessie squeaked, scrambling to her feet even as her mom jumped up off the couch with a gasp of horror. "You think we're getting married in *three hours*?"

Roger puffed up his chest and smoothed down his shirt. "I am a duly ordained justice of the peace, you know."

"In *Maine*?" Jessie whispered tightly as she stepped closer. "In what *century* were you ordained?" she asked, narrowing her eyes at him.

He narrowed his eyes right back at her and stepped away to point a threatening finger. "I'll have you know I married Camry and Luke to each other just two years ago; if ye don't believe me, then go to the county courthouse and see if you don't find their marriage certificate duly notarized and recorded."

"But I'm supposed to have a grand wedding in a beautiful white clapboard church, and be wearing a pretty gown and have bridesmaids and flowers and a live band and dancing." She gasped. "And Merissa—I can't get married without Mer!"

"Ye got three hours to get her here, then," Roger snapped. But then he sighed, shaking his head. "What is it with you women, anyway? They ain't built a finer church than a mountain, and you'll have an entire forest of trees for flowers and a sky full of stars for decorations. And the only music you'd be need'n is the joyful sound of family wishing ye well." He looked at Ian and sighed again. "I'm sorry, big fella," he said with a shrug. "I thought she was perfect for you."

Ian scrambled to his feet and pulled Jessie to a stop when she started toward Roger with her hands balled into fists. "She's close enough to perfect," he said with a laugh, hugging her in restraint. "And she's a quick learner. So I guess she'll have to do for the next seventy years," he muttered.

"Well, okay then," Roger barked, clapping his hands together again as he started for the door. "It looks like I'll see ye all up at the summit house in two hours and forty-five minutes." He stopped and looked back. "And just so ye know, I don't perform weddings for free, so ye better be bring'n something to barter that I might be needing," he said as he disappeared, the door closing on his laughter in stark contrast to the stunned silence of the house.

"Ohmigod, where's the kitten?" Jessie said, clutching her throat as she looked down to find Toby lying next to the tree, only to sigh in relief when he lifted his head to reveal the kitten curled up against his chest, sound asleep. She looked at her mother, clutching her throat again at a new horror. "What am I going to wear?"

Ian placed his hands on her shoulders and pulled her back against his chest again. "If you have a white blouse and maybe some black leggings, I have a MacKeage plaid at my place you can wear. It's not a fancy wedding dress, but it is . . . traditional."

Jessie sighed at the amusement in his voice.

"It's not about the ceremony, Jessica," Maureen said, walking up to them. "It's about the man you marry." She pulled on Ian's sleeve to make him lean down and gave him a kiss on the cheek. "Thank you for making our daughter so happy. There was a time her father and I thought she might never know real happiness again. And thank you, too, for saving her life."

"I assure you, it was my pleasure," Ian said, turning both himself and Jessie when her dad walked up and held out his hand.

"Congratulations, son, for making a wise choice," Jacob said gruffly as Ian shook his hand. "Because Jessie is more like her mother than either of them cares to admit, so I can assure *you* that at least the next thirty-two years won't be boring." He looked over at his wife with a tender smile. "And after that . . . well, I imagine they'll only get better with age, like a really fine Scotch."

Epilogue

APPARENTLY THE MACKEAGES AND MACBAINS AND Gregors didn't find anything strange about suddenly being asked to pack up their Christmas dinners and bring them to the top of TarStone Mountain to celebrate a fellow clansman's wedding. The actual ceremony took place out on the deck of the summit house in the light of the setting sun, the air surprisingly balmy for a mountaintop on the twenty-fifth of December, and Jessie decided she couldn't have had a grander wedding if she'd spent another twenty-nine years planning it with her mom—who she'd had stand in as her matron of honor.

Toby had been the ring bearer, although his attention had been torn between his role of helping Jessie get married and worrying over the kitten sleeping tucked inside Ian's plaid. The love-struck dog had refused to leave the house if the kitten wasn't coming with them.

Besides wearing an ancient plaid instead of a kilt, Ian

also had an actual *sword* slung on his back that Jessie had seen his father place there. It looked positively ancient and definitely more functional than ceremonial. Jessie had thought Duncan or Alec or even Morgan would stand up for Ian, but apparently Greylen was also known as *Laird* MacKeage, and he had stood in as best man.

The remains of the birthday party decorations had been brought from Gù Brath to the summit house, and Jessie didn't at all mind that several of the slightly deflated balloons said Happy Birthday; after all, today was a rebirth for her, wasn't it?

Jessie sat on a bench out on the deck in the gently crisp air under the moon and stars, taking a breather from the festivities inside—that Ian had been right to warn her made Camp Come-As-You-Are seem like church in comparison—and fingered the warm stone band on her left ring finger. It was made of the same black stone that ran in fissures throughout TarStone, Ian had told her when he'd pulled her into a closet after the ceremony to kiss her senseless, his eyes the deep green of winter spruce. The same stone, he'd said, that also ran through his veins like blood.

Her husband wasn't telling anyone about his newly realized ability to manipulate the magic, apparently, but Jessie had caught many of his clansmen suspiciously eyeing the tall, perfectly smooth, seemingly innocuous walking stick Ian had held between them and asked Jessie to also grip as they'd said their vows—which had been completely in Gaelic, much to her mom and dad's delight.

Everyone but her parents had also been eyeing Roger suspiciously—though also reverently. And Roger . . . well, he'd reverted to full crazy-old-hermit mode within seconds of blessing their marriage. Jessie wasn't sure, but she thought he'd bartered himself a few more wares off his clansmen, intending to in turn barter them off on the next unsuspecting target he thought might *be need'n* a nudge or two.

And speaking of the devil, Roger's cackling laughter preceded him through the doors when he came strolling out onto the deck with Ian—who was obviously looking for his missing bride, as his scowl turned to a relieved smile when he spotted her.

"You know," Jessie said, standing up and walking into his embrace, "I hope these late nights on top of your mountain aren't going to become a habit." She leaned into him with a yawn. "Have either of you seen Toby?" She shot Roger a glare. "I hope you know you completely ruined a very expensive, highly trained service dog. He's supposed to be worrying over *me*, not some silly little kitten."

Ian gave her a squeeze. "I'm your very expensive, highly trained protector now, *gràineag*," he said with a chuckle.

"Toby will be there for ye when you need him," Roger assured her. "He's just smitten with his new pet at the moment." He suddenly clapped his hands and rubbed them together, then thrust one toward Ian. "Well, I do believe I must be going now, so I'll take what's coming to me in exchange for having married you up proper, MacKeage."

"And that would be?" Ian asked, arching a brow.

Roger waggled the fingers on his outstretched hand. "I believe that would be the keys to that pretty new snowcat you brung up the mountain five nights ago."

Ian snorted. "Not likely, old man," he said, even as he reached into a pouch dangling from the belt holding his plaid. He slapped a set of keys into Roger's hand with a sigh. "But you can have my pickup, which should make it easier to lug home all your new *wares*."

Roger stared down at his hand, looking as if he'd just been given the keys to a mortuary, his eyes narrowing when he lifted them to Ian. "Ye might want to think about staying on my good side, big fella," he said softly, curling the keys into his fist so he could point a finger at Jessie even as he continued looking at Ian, "if'n ye don't want me giving her another, slightly more powerful walking stick."

Jessie's eyes widened when Ian reached into the pouch again and pulled something out, and traded it for the keys in Roger's once again open palm. "You ruined a perfectly good groomer in only two years; I'm not letting you have another one, especially at the height of our season. You take my snowmobile or you *walk* away."

Jessie frowned. Ian was giving up his snowmobile just so she wouldn't get a more powerful staff? "Hey, wait," she said, snatching the funny-looking key out of Roger's hand before he could close his fingers around it. She shoved the key at Ian. "I want a new walking stick."

"I told you I would cut you a new one."

"No, I want one that will do stuff. Powerful stuff." She smiled at Roger. "I'll give you the keys to my Volvo if you give me a big gnarly stick like Ian's."

The old hermit actually stepped back, shaking his head. "I told ye, that kind of power in the hands of a woman is . . . is . . ." He shot Ian a threatening glare and turned and strode into the summit house, muttering something about women today wanting to wear britches like they were men.

Ian turned Jessie into his embrace with a chuckle. "Well, wife, I do believe that just put the fear of God into him." He kissed her lips—which were pouting because she still didn't have a stick. "Hopefully we won't be seeing him for another year or two." He smiled. "Are ye ready to go home?"

She arched a brow. "You expect me to spend my wedding night with my parents sleeping upstairs?"

He shook his head, the light of a thousand suns shining in his eyes. "Dad gave them one of the resort cabins for the rest of their visit."

Jessie's heart quickened. "Then I guess I'm ready to go home," she said, stretching to meet his descending mouth, only to feel him suddenly stiffen just as she heard the distinct rumble of a trail groomer engine purr to life. "Looks like you're still not getting your old groomer back," she said with a laugh.

"Old, my ass," Ian growled, breaking away and running to the railing. "That's our newest groomer!"

Jessie ran to the rail and wrapped her arms around his waist, leaning into him when his arm came around her with a resigned sigh. "We can text him tomorrow and tell him he forgot his iPad at the house, and when he comes to get it, I'll keep him busy while you sneak out and disable the groomer."

Ian looked down at her. "I don't know why Roger thinks you're only dangerous if you have a stick," he muttered, giving her a squeeze, "because I happen to think you're powerfully scary all on your own."

Jessie stepped in front of him and reached up, twining her fingers through his loose hair to pull his mouth down to hers. "Damn right. So let's go home, husband, because I have at least three more little miracles I want to start creating, but I'm pretty sure I'm going to need your help."

Keep reading for a sneak peek at
the next magical romance from
Janet Chapman,

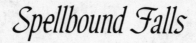

APPARENTLY MARK BRIAR WASN'T USED TO ANYONE TELL-
ing him no, be it the girlfriend who'd just sent him a Dear
John letter or some lonely widow to whom he was magnanimously offering sexual favors. Not only did Mark keep
trying to point out what Olivia would be missing if she
didn't come to the bunkhouse tonight; it appeared that her
repeatedly gentle but firm refusals were making him angry.

Well, that and the Dear John letter he'd crumpled into a
ball and thrown at her feet after reading her the more interesting parts. Added to that, his driving had gone from reckless
to downright scary. If she'd taken ten minutes to pull the rear
seat out of her van, she'd be in only half the mess she was in
now; she might still be dealing with an angry young man but
at least the pine trees wouldn't be speeding by in a blur.

"Look, Mark," Olivia said calmly. "It's not that I'm not
flattered by your offer, but I have a very firm rule about
fraternizing with my employees."

"Employ*ee*. You only have one right now. So it's not like anyone can complain the boss is playing favorites or anything." His eyes narrowed menacingly. "What about the campers?" He snorted. "Or is that how you fill up your single father sessions?"

Olivia counted to ten to keep from smacking the belligerent snot. "Ohmigod!" she shouted, pointing out the windshield. "Quick, pull off the road!"

Mark hit the brakes then veered into a small gravel pit before bringing the truck to a stop and shutting off the engine. "What did you see?"

Olivia immediately undid her seatbelt and got out. "A moose just crossed the road in front of us," she said, pointing towards the trees when he also got out. "And hitting an animal that size would total your truck."

"I didn't see anything. You just made that up," he said, storming around the front of the truck. "What in hell is it with you women, anyway? You think you can just dump me like yesterday's trash to go after some rich guy just because he's got a career and drives a Porsche?"

"Hey, wait a minute." Olivia started walking backward. "I'm not your girlfriend; I'm your *boss*."

"Not anymore, you're not, because I quit."

Well, that took care of that little problem. Now she just had to deal with being in the middle of nowhere with this idiot. "Wait," she said, holding up her hand to stop him. "You have to give me time to consider your offer," she said, matching him step for step when he didn't stop. "It's just that you caught me off guard earlier."

He finally stopped and looked around the small gravel pit, his eyes growing suspicious again. "So what say we get a little practice in right now?"

Okay, maybe running would be wiser. Olivia bolted for

the woods, figuring Mark would probably catch her in an open footrace down the road. Besides, maybe she could find a stick and beat some sense into the idiot. Only she shouted in surprise when he grabbed her shoulder, and yelped in pain when she stumbled to her knees and he landed on top of her.

For the love of God, this couldn't be happening. He was just a kid!

Olivia tried shoving him away; his fingers bit into her arms as he rolled her over, and she cried out again when his mouth slammed against hers. Okay, it was time to panic; they were in the middle of nowhere, she couldn't seem to get control of the situation, and the idiot was flat-out attacking her! Olivia kicked at his legs and squirmed to push him off as she twisted away from his punishing mouth. "Mark! Stop this!" she cried. "You need to stop!"

"What in hell kind of camp doesn't have girls?"

Olivia stopped struggling. Talking was good. If she could keep him talking then maybe he'd calm down. "Th-there will be girls your age in town once college lets out," she said, panting raggedly as his weight crushed her into the gravel.

"That's over two months away!"

Olivia shouted in outrage as she turned away from his descending mouth, and put all her strength into bucking him off even as she drove her fist into his ribs. He reared up, his own shout ending on a strangled yelp as his weight suddenly lifted off her. Olivia rolled away then stumbled to her feet, scrambling around Mark's truck—only to run straight into another vehicle. She stumbled back to her feet just as she heard Mark shout again, and started running toward him when she saw a stranger drive his fist into Mark's stomach. The boy hadn't even doubled over when the man's fist slammed into his jaw, tossing him into the air to land on the ground on his back, out cold.

"No!" Olivia cried, grabbing the stranger's arm to stop him from going after Mark again. "Don't hurt him any more!"

The man shrugged her off and turned toward her, the dangerous look in his sharp green eyes making her take a step back. "Forgive me," he said gutturally. "I was under the impression the bastard was attacking you." He gestured toward Mark even as he gave a slight bow. "I will leave you to your little game, then," he said, turning away and striding to his truck.

Olivia ran after him. "No, don't leave! He *was* attacking me."

He stopped so suddenly she bumped into him and would have fallen if he hadn't grabbed her shoulders. And that's when Olivia's knees buckled, the magnitude of what had nearly happened turning her into a quivering blob of jelly.

Her rescuer swept her off her feet before she reached the ground. He carried her to a small mound of dirt at the entrance to the gravel pit and set her down, then shrugged out of his jacket and settled it over her trembling shoulders. But when he crouched down in front of her and started to reach toward her throbbing cheek, Olivia buried her face in her hands and burst into sobs.

"It's okay. You're safe now."

"I can't believe he a-attacked me. He . . . he's just a kid." She straightened to pull his jacket tightly around her as she took gulping breaths. "Oh God, I can't breathe!"

He cupped her jaw in his broad hand, his penetrating gaze inspecting her face before coming to rest on her eyes. "You have my word; the bastard won't ever hurt you again. Henry, come here," her rescuer called over his shoulder.

The rear passenger door of the pearl white SUV opened and a young boy got out. Olivia immediately tried to stand up, not wanting the child to see her like this, but the gentleman set his large hand on her shoulder. "Come here, son. This lady has just had a fright, Henry, and she needs comforting," he said, gesturing at Olivia. "Sit here and hold Miss . . . what's your name?" he asked, giving her a gentle smile.

She didn't know if it was his smile that did it, or the fact that she needed to pull herself together for the sake of the child, but Olivia took a shuddering breath and released her death-grip on his jacket. "Olivia Baldwin," she told the boy—only to gasp. "You're Henry! And Mr. Oceanus," she cried, looking at the man. "You're arriving today!" She hid her face in her hands again, utterly humiliated. "Ohmigod, this is terrible. You shouldn't see me like this." But when a small arm settled over her shoulders, the young hand at the end of that arm gently patting her, Olivia quietly started sobbing again.

That is until she realized Mr. Oceanus was no longer crouched in front of her. Olivia shot out from under Henry's comforting arm. "No, you can't hurt him!" she shouted, rounding the vehicles in time to see Mr. Oceanus hauling Mark to his feet.

"He's just a dumb kid."

"Go sit in my truck, Olivia. I merely intend to have a little discussion with him."

"Not in front of your son, you're not," she said, grabbing his arm. "What are you teaching Henry by beating up a defenseless kid? He saw you rescuing me, but it's equally important that he also see sees you acting civilized to my assailant."

"I would hope I'm teaching the boy that he has a duty to rescue a woman who's being attacked."

"But you did that already," she said, keeping her voice low so Henry wouldn't hear them. Good Lord, Trace Huntsman hadn't been kidding when he'd told Olivia that his friend didn't have a clue about how to deal with his newly discovered son. "Look, Mr. Oceanus, this—"

"I prefer you call me Mac. And if by acting civilized in front of my son you are suggesting I do nothing, then I suggest you and Henry go for a little walk. You have my word; I will wait until you're out of sight to have my little discussion."

He couldn't possibly be serious. "Please let him go, Mac," Olivia pleaded, her shoulders slumping as she pulled his jacket tightly around her. "I-I just want to meet my daughter's bus at the turnoff and go home before I fall down."

The sudden concern in his eyes disappeared the moment he looked back at Mark. "If I catch you within fifty miles of Spellbound Falls after sunset today, I will kill you. Understand?" he said ever so softly, his hand tightening around Mark's throat until the red-faced boy nodded. Mac released him so suddenly that Mark fell to the ground, and Olivia didn't even have time to gasp before her rescuer lifted her into his arms.

"Henry, open the front door of our truck," he said, striding to the SUV and setting her inside. He reached into his pants pocket and pulled out a handkerchief. "Your lip is bleeding," he said, handing it to her. "Where is the turnoff you spoke of? You said you wish to meet your daughter."

She took the handkerchief and shakily dabbed at her mouth. "It . . . it's another couple of miles up the road."

He nodded and closed the door, then opened the door behind her. "Get in and buckle up, son," he said, closing the door once Henry climbed in.

But instead of walking around to the driver's side, Mac

strode back around Mark's truck. Olivia started to go after him, but the door wouldn't open even after she pushed all the buttons on the handle. She was just about to start pounding on the buttons when a small, unbelievably firm hand clasped her shoulder.

"Father will be civilized," Henry said, giving her a nod when she turned to him. "I believe he's just making sure the bastard understood his instructions."

"You *heard* what we were saying?"

"I have very good hearing." He patted her shoulder. "You can get over your fright now, Olivia; Father won't let that bastard hurt you again."

She twisted around in her seat. "Henry, you can't keep calling him a bastard; it's a very bad word."

His eyes—as deeply green as those of the man who'd sired him—hardened in an almost mirror image of his father's. "Is it not appropriate to use a bad word when referring to a bad person?"

Good Lord, he even talked like his father!

But Trace Huntsman, a military buddy of Olivia's late husband who lived several hours away down on the coast, had told her that Henry had come to live with Mac only a few months ago, after the child's mother had died. And that up until then the two had never met, as Mac hadn't even known Henry existed.

"How come you call him *Father* instead of *Dad?*" Olivia asked.

Henry's tiny brows knitted into a frown. "Because that's what he is. He calls me Son and I call him Father." His frown deepened even as his face reddened. "And please forgive me, for I believe I'm supposed to call you Madam, not Olivia. My mama would be quite upset with me if she knew I was calling a lady by her Christian name."

Olivia smiled warmly. "And what's your mama's name?"

"Cordelia. But when father speaks of her, he calls her Delia. My last name used to be Penhope, but now it's Oceanus." He went back to frowning again. "Only Father is also thinking of changing my first name. I suggested we might change it to Jack or even Jake, only he said those names aren't noble enough."

"But what's wrong with Henry?"

The boy shrugged. "Father says Henry is too English."

"It's too—" Olivia turned at the sound of a truck door slamming, and saw Mark push down the locks before blindly fumbling with the ignition as he watched Mac through the windshield—who was standing a few paces away, his arms folded over his chest, staring back at him. The pickup started and the tires spun on the loose gravel as Mark sped onto the road without even checking for oncoming traffic.

"See; I told you Father would be civilized," Henry said, giving her shoulder one last pat before he hopped in his seat and fastened his seatbelt. "He didn't kill the bastard even if he did deserve to die."

DESPITE ONLY MEETING MAC AND HENRY LESS THAN thirty minutes ago, Olivia had a feeling they were going to be a tad more of a bother than merely setting two more places at the table. For as precocious and direct as Henry was, his father was even scarier. Maximilian Oceanus was an undeniably large, imposing figure; the sort of man who not only would stand out in a crowd but would likely command it. He had to be at least six foot four, his shoulders filled a good deal of the front seat of his full-sized SUV, and he had picked her up—twice—as effortlessly as if he'd been handling a child. But it was when he looked directly at her with those intense green eyes of his that Olivia felt her world tilt off center. Kind of like when a person stood in a receding wave on a flat sandy beach, and had the illusion of being sucked out to sea even while standing perfectly still.

She should have never let Eileen talk her into breaking her rule of no private parenting sessions. She should have at least recognized what she was getting herself into when Mac had summarily dismissed her repeatedly gentle but firm refusals to let him come to Inglenook three weeks early—much the same way Mark had dismissed them this afternoon. Only where Mark had attacked her, Mac had gotten his way using good old-fashioned bribery.

She was still shaking uncontrollably and fighting back tears, which is why she'd jumped out of the truck the moment they reached the turnoff, before she humiliated herself again. Only Henry had shot out of the truck right behind her. At first it was obvious he'd felt duty-bound to continue comforting her, but once Olivia had assured him she was feeling much better, the boy had taken off to explore the nearby woods instead.

That is, after he'd dutifully run back and asked his father's permission.

Mac had also gotten out of the truck but had merely leaned against the front fender, his feet crossed at the ankles and his arms folded on his chest, apparently content to let his son deal with the welling tears he'd seen in her eyes. She was still wearing his leather jacket, and should probably give it back since he was standing in the cool March breeze in only his shirt, but the warm security of its weight surrounding her simply felt too wonderful to relinquish.

She buried her hands in its roomy pockets with a heavy sigh. Now what was she supposed to do? Without Mark, there was no way she could get Inglenook fully functional in three weeks. Olivia started slowly walking back toward the main road, but picked up her pace when she realized she couldn't see Henry anywhere. "Henry?" she called out, scanning the woods on both sides of the road. "Henry, where did you go?"

"He's fine, Olivia," Mac said, straightening away from the fender. "He climbed down to the brook and is throwing rocks."

"There are some deep pools in that brook," she said, trying to pierce the dense woods. "And there's still snow in places. He could slip and fall in, or wander off and get lost. Little boys have a tendency to follow anything that catches their interest without realizing how far they're going."

"He may get wet but he won't drown," Mac said. He pointed downstream of the bridge that sat a hundred yards up from the entrance of the turnoff. "And I will call him back if he wanders too far. Is it not my son's job to explore the world around him, and my job merely to keep him safe while he does?" He frowned. "At least that's what I've surmised from the books I've been reading."

Olivia couldn't help but smile. "You've been reading books on parenting?"

Instead of returning her smile, his frown deepened. "At least a dozen; only I've discovered a good many of them contradict each other, and one or two had some rather disturbing notions about discipline."

"Parenting is more of a hands-on, trial-by-fire sort of thing, Mr. Oceanus. And though several people have tried, no one's been able to write a definitive book on child-rearing because humans are not one-size-fits-all."

Good Lord; there she went sounding like Eileen again.

He finally found a smile. "So I have your permission to ignore everything those books said, Mrs. Baldwin?"

Oh yeah, his eyes definitely turned a deep vivid green when he was amused. "Actually, you have my permission to throw them away. And please, call me Olivia."

Up went one of his brows. "Forgive me; you led me to believe we were no longer on a first name basis."

"My mistake . . . Mac." She arched a brow right back at him. "Do you know where your son is right now?"

"Just downstream, crossing the brook on a fallen log."

Olivia turned, trying to locate Henry. "Where? I don't see him."

"Then I guess it's a good thing I have very good eyesight as well as exceptional hearing. He's just reached the end of his courage and is heading back toward us."

"Speaking of good hearing, apparently your son has inherited yours. You're going to have to watch what you say around him, Mac. He kept calling Mark a bastard."

"Is that not the appropriate term?"

"Not for a six-year-old boy, it's not." When she saw the sparkle leave his eyes, Olivia wondered if she'd ever learn to read this man. "I don't think you understand what Henry's doing. When Trace first called me, he said that in the course of only a few months your son's mother died and he came to live with you, even though the two of you had never met. Is that correct?"

Mac silently nodded.

"Well, coming to live with a complete stranger after suffering such a loss has been far more traumatic for Henry than for you," she said softly. "And from what I've seen in the last half hour, your son is trying very hard to be what he thinks you want him to be. Henry's like a sponge, soaking you up; emulating your mannerisms, your language, and how you treat people." She smiled, gesturing at the road she'd been pacing. "Heck, he even walks like you."

"Excuse me?"

Still unable to read his expression, Olivia widened her smile. "You have a rather direct stride, Mac. You want to see what it looks like sometime, just watch Henry."

"Are you saying I should discourage him from emulating me?"

"No. That's a good thing. It means Henry is looking to you as a role model." She shoved her hands in the jacket pockets again. "You really should be talking to my mother-in-law about this; Eileen's the expert. I'm just trying to point out that when you call someone a bastard, even if he is one, Henry's going to call him one, too. And if you beat up that bastard, even if he deserves it, Henry's going to beat up any kid his young mind believes might deserve it. So I'm only suggesting that you be aware of what you say and do in front of him. All children are highly impressionable, but Henry's even more so, because not only is he trying to figure out exactly where he fits in your life, he's desperately trying to find his place in your heart."

Mac unfolded his arms to shove his hands in his pants pockets, and turned to face the woods. "I have no business being anyone's role model, especially not an impressionable young child's." He glanced over his shoulder at her, then back toward the brook. "I am the worst son a man could have, and there's a very good chance I will be an even worse father."

"You already are a wonderful father, Mac."

"How can you possibly say that?" he asked without looking at her. "You know nothing about me."

"I know how completely focused you are on Henry. And

your insisting on coming to Inglenook early and then staying through the entire summer certainly proves how determined you are." She started walking toward the main road
when she heard the school bus approaching, but stopped
and turned with a smile. "Parenting's not about you versus
Henry, Mac; it's about you and Henry versus the world."

FOR THE FIRST TIME IN NEARLY THREE MONTHS—SINCE A
mysterious, overly intelligent, pint-sized person had come
to live with him—Mac felt a glimmer of hope that he might
actually survive this. He hadn't even made it to Inglenook
yet and already he was seeing his son in a whole new light;
the most surprising revelation being that Henry was soaking up everything he said and did like a sponge. Which,
now that he thought about it, was frighteningly true; within
days of their tumultuous meeting, Henry had started mim-
icking him to the point that Mac realized he could be looking in a thirty-year-old mirror from when *he* was six. But
maybe the most insightful—and reassuring—thing Olivia
had said was that he and Henry were on this journey
together.

And that simple notion intrigued him as much as the
woman who'd said it.

Which could be a problem. He was here to learn how to
become a good father, and he really didn't need the distraction of finding himself attracted to the teacher; no matter
how beautiful she might be, or how warm and inviting
her smile was, or how compassionate she was—to a fault.
Damnation, he'd hadn't known which had angered him
more: that she would have been raped if he hadn't happened
along, or that she had in turn protected the bastard.

"It's a good thing we were driving by when the lady

was being attacked, wasn't it, Father?" Henry said. "It's too bad she wouldn't allow you to kill the bastard, though, because I think he deserved it. Your letting him go might lead him to believe he can attack another woman and get away with it again."

Mac looked down to find his son standing beside him, the child's arms crossed over his chest and his feet planted to relax back on his hips as he watched Olivia walk across the main road in front of the stopped school bus. Sweet Prometheus, how could the boy possibly know his very thoughts?

Mac unfolded his arms and shoved his hands in his pockets. "Apparently 'bastard' is an inappropriate term for a six-year-old to use, Son. So maybe you should cease saying it until you're older."

"How much older?" Henry asked, also shoving his hands in his trouser pockets as he frowned up at Mac. "Can I say it when I'm ten? Or fifteen? Or do I have to wait until I'm your age?"

The boy always took everything so literally! "Maybe that's a question you should ask Olivia."

"And do I call her Olivia when I ask, or Madam?"

Mac dropped his head in defeat. "You might wish to ask her that, too. And, Henry, don't mention to her daughter what happened today," he said when he saw Olivia walking back across the road holding the hand of a girl who appeared to be a year or two older than Henry. "Olivia might not want her to know for fear of worrying her. Now go put your things behind your seat to make a place for her to sit," he instructed, looking toward the main road as Henry ran to the truck.

The two women could have been twins but for their ages; the younger Baldwin had wavy brown hair that fell over her shoulders to frame an angelic face, an effortless smile, and an energized beauty that seemed to swirl around her like liquid sunshine—exactly like her mother. The young girl even took on Olivia's same expression of concern when she spotted her mother's swollen lip and puffy eyes. She then tugged on the unfamiliar jacket her mother was wearing over her own. Mac watched Olivia glance guiltily toward him as she started unzipping it, but her daughter stopped her by grabbing her hand and pushing up the sleeve, exposing a bruise on Olivia's wrist that had darkened enough for Mac to see from where he was standing.

"Sophie looks just like her mother," Henry said, having come back from his chore to once again stand with his hands in his trouser pockets.

"Sophie?" Mac repeated.

"Didn't you hear Olivia tell me her daughter's name is Sophie, and that she's eight years old and in the second grade?" Henry glanced up at him then looked back at the women. "I don't think I would have let the bast—that man drive away if I had caught him hurting Sophie." He suddenly grinned menacingly. "I would have at least sent him home carrying his stones in his pocket."

Mac broke out in a sweat. Henry wasn't merely walking and talking like him; his son even *thought* like he did!

How could he have forgotten that people became who they lived with?

Especially impressionable young children.

There were a lot of things he'd forgotten, apparently, about the inherent nature of man; which, considering his line of work, could be hazardous. But indulging in the more pleasurable aspects of human desires for the greater part of his adult life, Mac realized he had obviously

Janet Chapman

dismissed as unimportant many of the more mundane laws governing the universe.

Nothing like having a son to put everything into perspective.

Yes, for as much as he hadn't wanted to travel even this short a distance from the ocean, bringing Henry to Inglenook just might prove to be one of the wisest decisions he'd made in several centuries.